Award-winning author **Jennifer Faye** pens fun, heart-warming, contemporary romances with rugged cowboys, sexy billionaires and enchanting royalty. Internationally published, with books translated into nine languages, she is a two-time winner of the RT Book Reviews Reviewers' Choice Award. She has also won the *CataRomance* Reviewers' Choice Award, been named a TOP PICK author, and been nominated for numerous other awards.

Brenda Harlen is a former attorney who once had the privilege of appearing before the Supreme Court of Canada. The practice of law taught her a lot about the world and reinforced her determination to become a writer—because in fiction, she could promise a happy ending! Now she is an award-winning, RITA® Award–nominated national bestselling author of more than thirty titles for Mills & Boon. You can keep up-to-date with Brenda on Facebook and Twitter or through her website, www.brendaharlen.com.

Discover more at millsandboon.co.uk

BEAUTY AND HER BOSS

JENNIFER FAYE

THE SHERIFF'S NINE-MONTH SURPRISE

BRENDA HARLEN

MILLS & BOON

First Published in Great Britain 2018
by Mills & Boon, an imprint of HarperCollinsPublishers,
1 London Bridge Street, London, SE1 9GF

Beauty and Her Boss © 2018 Jennifer F. Stroka
The Sheriff's Nine-Month Surprise © 2018 Brenda Harlen

ISBN: 978-0-263-26477-7

38-0318

MIX
Paper from
responsible sources
FSC™ C007454

This book is produced from independently certified FSC™
paper to ensure responsible forest management.

For more information visit: www.harpercollins.co.uk/green

Printed and bound in Spain
by CPI, Barcelona

BEAUTY AND
HER BOSS

JENNIFER FAYE

PROLOGUE

"THIS CAN'T BE HAPPENING."

Gabrielle Dupré frowned as she perched on the edge of a hard, black plastic chair. The room was small with gray walls. Outside the little room, there was the buzz of voices and phones ringing. But inside the room, a tense silence hung in the air like a dense fog. This was a place she'd never been in her life—a police station. How had things spiraled so far out of control? Her head pounded and her stomach churned.

After being here for more than two hours, the situation wasn't looking good. Not good at all. She'd just played her final card and she'd been praying ever since that it would pay off.

"Don't worry, daughter." Her father stared at her from across a black nondescript table. "Everything will be all right."

"All right?" She struggled not to shout in frustration. "Things are so far from all right." With each word, her voice crept up in volume. Realizing that losing her cool right now would not help their cause, she paused and swallowed hard. "Father, do you know how much trouble you're in?"

"Gaby, don't you understand? If I got word out about that monster, then it was worth it." His voice was filled with conviction. "Sometimes a man has to do what he has to do."

"And sometimes he needs to think before he acts," she said in a heated whisper. Anger pulsed through her veins, but it wasn't her father that she was upset with—it was herself.

Her father reached out and patted her hand. "You'll see. This will all work out."

She blamed herself for not being there to reason with her father. And to stop him from acting rashly. For the past six months, she'd been working two jobs to pay their outstanding bills but she was still losing financial ground. Things were so bad she was considering taking on a third job. With her father's health declining and him now in a wheelchair, it was up to her to make ends meet.

And through it all, she'd made sure to be there for her father every single day. He had been grieving ever since her aunt's deadly car accident almost four months ago. And it didn't help that the police had failed to release the truth about the accident. Although, that didn't stop the gossip sites from pointing fingers, including the magazine she'd recently started doing an admin job for, *QTR*. By way of some unnamed source, they were accusing an award-winning movie star, Deacon Santoro, of being at fault.

Gaby was still trying to figure out the how and why of her father's actions. "So you've been sneaking off to Deacon Santoro's estate all week?"

His gaze narrowed. "I wasn't sneaking. I didn't want to bother you so I took the bus."

She shook her head in disbelief. "I thought you had a girlfriend that you weren't ready to tell me about. If I'd have known what you were up to, I would have stopped you."

With her father's elbows resting on the table, he leaned toward her. His bloodshot eyes pleaded with her. "Don't you want the truth?"

"Of course I do. How could you question that? I loved her, too. She was like a second mother to me. But there are better ways to get to the truth. You shouldn't have staged a loud, disruptive protest in front of the man's house and accosted his staff."

Her father expelled a heavy sigh as he leaned back in his wheelchair. "Nothing else has worked. I've made phone call after phone call to the authorities. All I get is the runaround. They keep saying the accident report will be released as soon as the investigation has been completed."

Gaby couldn't believe what she was about to say, but someone had to reason with her father. With her mother and now her aunt gone, the responsibility landed squarely on Gabrielle's straining shoulders.

"Do you even realize how much power Mr. Santoro wields?"

Her father's bushy, gray eyebrows drew together. "Why do you think I went there? The police aren't helping us get the truth because he bought them off."

Gaby shushed her father. "Don't say those things."

"So I thought the media might help. After all, they'd do anything for a big headline."

"You certainly got their attention." Sadly, she didn't think this tactic was going to work, but she sure hoped she was wrong because the not knowing was eating at her, too. "There were so many reporters standing outside the police station that I had to be escorted through the back entrance."

Her father's tired face, with its two days' worth of

stubble, lifted into a satisfied smile. "It's working. You'll see."

Her father had a bad habit of acting first and thinking later. And she was left with the task of cleaning up his messes. But this was his first and, if she had any say in it, his last arrest. "And is it worth you going to jail or paying a stiff fine that will financially wipe us out?"

Before her father could answer, the door swung open. A tall police officer with salt-and-pepper hair stepped just inside the room. "We've contacted the complainant."

"And…" Gaby knew this was the time for restraint but there was so much on the line.

The officer shook his head. "He refused to meet with you."

That was not what she'd wanted to hear. She was hoping to plead with the man and hopefully get him to drop the charges. Her father was not physically well and punishing him would not help anyone, least of all Deacon Santoro. "Surely there has to be some way I can speak with him."

The officer cleared his throat. "I was about to tell you that he's on the phone. You may speak with him at my desk."

That was all the invitation she needed. In a heartbeat, she was on her feet and rushing out the door. She didn't so much as pause to assure her father that she'd straighten out this mess—because in all honesty, she wasn't sure she could fix things this time. But she was willing to do anything to protect her father—even from his own misguided sense of justice.

The police officer led her to his desk, where he handed over the receiver. Before she got a word out, the officer was called away to help with an unruly arrestee, who appeared intoxicated and quite belligerent.

Turning her back to the scene, Gaby said, "Hello."

"I am not dropping the charges." Deacon Santoro didn't even so much as utter a greeting, friendly or otherwise.

And yet his voice caught her attention. It was deep and rich, like a fine bourbon. She didn't need to verify who she was speaking to. After watching each and every one of his movies countless times, she would recognize Deacon's voice anywhere.

"I would really appreciate if we could talk this out."

"I've done all of the talking that I intend to do." His sexy voice was short and clipped. "Now, I've spoken to you. That is all I agreed to. I must go—"

"Wait!"

"This is a waste of time. Your father is guilty. He will have to take it up with the judge."

With each syllable the man spoke, her body betrayed her by being drawn in by the deep timbre of his voice. Logic dictated that he was the absolute last person she should be fantasizing about, but there was another more primal part of her that wanted to hear his voice again.

Gaby gave herself a swift mental jerk. She had to stay on point. Her father's future was depending on her getting this right.

"But he didn't do anything serious—"

"I'd call stalking a serious charge."

"Stalking?" This was the first she'd heard of this allegation. She couldn't help but wonder what else her father had failed to tell her.

"Yes. He's been making harassing phone calls, skulking outside my residence with binoculars and hounding my entire staff."

"I'm sorry. He hasn't been himself lately. He wouldn't hurt a soul. If you knew him—"

"I don't. And I don't plan to. None of this is my problem."

Mr. Santoro was right on that point, but would it hurt him to be a little generous? Perhaps she needed to explain the situation better. "My father, he isn't young. And his health is failing."

"Again, not my problem."

This man wasn't going to give an inch. His stirring voice ceased to affect her as she went into protective mode. "Listen, Mr. Santoro, I am sorry for the trouble my father has caused you, but pressing charges against him won't fix anything. Surely there has to be another way to work this out."

"Your father should have thought of all of this before he decided to cause trouble for me."

Why did this man have to act as though he was the innocent party here? If it weren't for his actions on that fateful night, her father wouldn't have bothered him. Angry accusations bubbled up within her and hovered at the back of her throat. It would be so easy to lose her cool—to tell this man exactly what she thought of him, which wasn't much.

What good would that do her? Yes, it'd temporarily make her feel better.

But in the long term, would it do anything to help her father? Definitely not.

Gaby's jaw muscles clenched. Her back teeth ground together.

"If that's all, I must go."

"It's not all." He wasn't getting off that easy. "My father was doing what he thought was best for my aunt."

"What does your aunt have to do with this? Or was she one of those misguided people that he coerced into shouting lies and throwing garbage onto my property?"

Gaby wasn't going to let this man go on about her father and aunt. Did he really not know who her father was? "My aunt wasn't outside your house. She—she died in the car accident."

There was a swift intake of breath as though at last he understood the gravity of the situation. A long silence ensued. Was it possible she'd finally gotten through to him?

Still, she didn't breathe easy—not yet. In just the short period of time that she'd spoken with this man, she'd learned that he didn't change his mind easily. And yet, she couldn't give up.

Every muscle in his body tensed.

Deacon Santoro didn't utter a word as he processed this new piece of information. How was this the first he'd heard of the woman in the accident having a family?

He searched his impaired memory for an answer. And then he latched on to the vital information. The police had said the woman had no family—no living parents, no ex-spouses and no children. Just a surviving brother. Deacon had never thought to ask about nieces and nephews.

Deacon swallowed hard. "You're her niece?"

"Yes. My name's Gaby."

"As in Gabrielle?"

"Yes. My aunt was the only one who called me Gabrielle."

Take care of Gabrielle.

Those words haunted him each night in his short and troubled sleep. Until now, he'd never understood what they meant. He didn't know anyone named Gabrielle. But suddenly a jagged piece of a memory from the accident came back to him. It wasn't an image but rather a voice. The woman from the accident had told him to take care of her niece.

And it was his chance to make sure the woman's final words were fulfilled. The need to help Gabrielle was overwhelming. But how? He needed time to absorb this revelation—to form a viable plan.

Deacon cleared his throat. "I didn't know she was your aunt. No one told me."

"Now you can understand my father's actions. He's grieving for his younger sister. He isn't thinking clearly."

"But that still doesn't make up for what he's cost me." Thanks to her father, another in a string of employees had quit. And thanks to the negative publicity, associates were shying away from doing business with him.

"I will do whatever I can to make this right."

He applauded her for trying to clean up a mess that wasn't hers. "How much are you talking about?"

"You want money?" Her voice took on a note of distress.

No. He had enough of his own, but he didn't want this conversation to end—not until he knew a bit more about this woman. "You did offer to make things right and I lost a lot of money when two promising business ventures fell through thanks to your father's actions."

"I—I don't have any money. Please believe me. I work two jobs to keep us afloat."

"Us?" The word rolled off his tongue before he could stop it. Suddenly he pictured this woman with a husband and children—her own support system.

"Yes. Me and my father."

At this point, Deacon should just hang up, but he couldn't do it. The father may have stepped over the line, but the daughter hadn't. And those words kept haunting him—*take care of Gabrielle.*

"What do you have in mind?" he asked.

"I could go outside and talk to the media. I could explain my father's actions—"

"Don't. The less said the better." All the while, he was considering how best to help this woman, who obviously had too much on her plate.

"So if my father and I agree not to say another word, you will see that the charges are dropped?"

"No. Not only has my name been slandered in the news, but my assistant was coming back from lunch when your father's protest was at its height. She was verbally assaulted and had things thrown at her. She has quit. And the temp agency doesn't want to send anyone else."

"Oh." Gabrielle paused. "I don't know what you want me to do to make this right."

"You don't need to do anything. You did not cause this mess." Something told him this wasn't Gabrielle's first time cleaning up after her father. Perhaps taking care of Gabrielle meant freeing her from being constantly at her father's beck and call. "Your father must face up to what he's done."

"But he's in no physical condition to go through the legal process—"

"This isn't your first time fixing things for your father, is it?"

"No." She quickly added, "But he needs me."

"Your father, can he cook for himself?"

"Yes, but—"

"Do his own laundry and shopping?"

"Yes, but—"

"You do most everything for him, don't you?"

"Of course I do. I'm his daughter. Now tell me what I can do to remedy things."

In that moment, Deacon knew what needed to be done.

Without giving himself a chance to back out, he said, "There is one thing and it's nonnegotiable."

"Name it."

"Come work for me."

CHAPTER ONE

Two days later...

WHAT EXACTLY HAD she agreed to?

Gabrielle Dupré's heart beat faster as she turned into the gated drive of the Santoro estate. Her gaze shifted to the clock on the dash. The drive from Bakersfield had taken more than four hours. She definitely wouldn't want to deal with that long commute each day. Thankfully Newton, an old friend from the neighborhood, had recently moved back to town and was renting a room from her father and had agreed to keep an eye on him while she worked here at the estate. Newton had changed since she'd last seen him, but he was happy to be there for her father, and they seemed to get on.

Deacon had offered her more money to work here than both of her jobs combined. It also included free room and board. Under different circumstances, she'd be excited about the opportunity. But with her father convinced that Mr. Santoro was the reason her aunt had died, being here felt uncomfortable to say the least.

She swallowed hard and reached out the driver's side window, pressing a finger to a button on the intercom. She waited for someone to speak to her. However, without a word the gate swept open. She had to admit she was curious to see what awaited her on the other side of the wall. She'd done an internet search, but it hadn't turned up any pictures of the estate.

Gabrielle eased her father's vintage red convertible onto the overgrown grounds. It certainly wasn't the grand estate that she'd been anticipating. Perhaps at one time this place might have been beautiful, but now it was woefully neglected. The grass appeared not to have been cut in ages. The bushes were overgrown and gangly. The flower gardens were overrun with weeds that were strangling out the few remaining flowers.

The internet sites said that Deacon Santoro had become a recluse since he'd been involved in the deadly accident. Apparently for once, the paparazzi hadn't been totally wrong. There was definitely something amiss on this estate.

The Malibu beach house was a stunning piece of mid-century architecture. Gabrielle slowed the car to a stop to have a better look around. Feeling as though someone was staring at her, she glanced up at the massive white mansion. There was no one standing in any of the windows. But there was a window on the top floor where the sheers moved. Cold fingertips inched down her spine.

Stop it. You're just being melodramatic. It's not like this is a haunted mansion.

No matter what she told herself, she couldn't shake her uneasiness. If it wasn't for her father, she'd turn around and leave. But a deal was a deal.

When she'd handed in her immediate resignation at the library, they'd refused to accept it. The staff was small and they were all close, like a family. So, she was on sabbatical leave until her deal with Deacon was concluded. She was so grateful to have a job to return to. It was one less thing she had to worry about.

However, when she'd resigned at the tabloid, she'd made the mistake of letting Deacon Santoro's name cross her lips. That spiked everyone's interest. She'd been passed up the chain of management until she'd been sitting across from the managing editor. And when the whole sordid truth came tumbling out, the editor had assured her that she didn't need to quit. In fact, they'd increased her pay.

The editor was putting Gaby on an assignment. The money was most welcome as her father's mounting medical expense were beyond her means. She had been shocked until it became clear that they wanted her to feed them every bit of dirt she could dig up on Deacon Santoro. She'd initially refused. Finding out the truth about her aunt's death was one thing. Digging up information about his private life just for sensational headlines was something else.

In the end, they'd all agreed that she would remain on the payroll and submit a daily report with information regarding the deadly accident. After all, if the legal system wouldn't do anything about it, someone had to seek justice in whatever way possible. And so Gaby had come here not only to protect her father, but also to uncover the truth about the accident and to expose Deacon's actions to the world.

At the time, the plan had seemed so easy. She'd play along as his assistant and befriend the man, which from the looks of the desolate place wouldn't be hard. Then she'd get him to open up about the accident. She would prove that he was responsible for her aunt's death. At last the world would know the truth, just like her father had wanted for so long. And then she could return to her life—a life that was temporarily on pause.

Gabrielle wheeled the car into a parking spot next to

a late model gray sedan. She'd arrived early this morning as she'd wanted to make a good impression on Mr. Santoro. She didn't want to give him any reason to go back on his agreement to drop the charges against her father, and that included keeping her connection with *QTR* magazine hush-hush.

She climbed out of the car and lifted her head to the blue sky. There was a gusty breeze. The forecasters said there was a storm brewing over the Pacific, although it hadn't reached them yet. But there was an ominous tension in the air.

She turned to head inside, but she wasn't sure where to go. There was yet another fence surrounding the building. There were numerous gates but no signs indicating where each led.

A movement in the corner of her eye caught her attention. Her gaze strayed across the outline of a figure in the distance.

"Excuse me," Gabrielle called out as she rushed forward.

The man's back was to her.

She called out again.

The man straightened from where he was bent over a rosebush. He was wearing jeans, a black long-sleeved shirt and a ball cap. He didn't turn around. Did he hear her?

"Hey, could you tell me where to go?" Not about to continue screaming across the grounds, she started down to a set of stained concrete steps leading to the garden.

By the time she reached the bottom step, the man was gone. Perhaps he hadn't heard her. He could still be around here somewhere. She started walking around in hopes of spotting him again. However, he was nowhere to be found. How was that possible? He was just here a second ago. She turned around in a circle. Where had he gone so quickly?

She sighed and was about to walk away when she paused to take in her surroundings. She stood on the edge of an expansive rose garden with a winding footpath. Unlike the rest of the overgrown yard, this section was neat and tidy. She found this shocking. What made this garden so special? It was just one more question that she had for Mr. Santoro.

Gaby headed back up the steps to the parking area. If worse came to worse, she would try all the gates and open all of the doors she encountered until she found where she belonged. You really would think Mr. Santoro would greet her or at the very least call her.

Time was getting away from her. If she didn't hurry, she was going to start off this arrangement by being late. Talk about making a bad situation worse. She picked up her pace.

At the top of the steps, she glanced around. On both sides of the parking area were doors. There was the large main house and there were six garage doors with what appeared to be a guesthouse atop them. Would he have put the office in the guesthouse?

Her gaze moved back and forth between the two structures as she tried to make up her mind. Just as she decided to try the main house, a gate swung open. At last, Mr. Santoro had come to greet her.

She rushed toward the door, but she came to a halt when an older woman with white hair and a round, rosy face came hurrying out. The woman was muttering something under her breath and shaking her head, but Gaby wasn't able to make out what she was saying.

When the woman's gaze met hers, a smile softened the woman's face. She had kind eyes and a warm smile.

"Ah…hello, dearie. You must be Mr. Santoro's new assistant."

Gaby smiled back at the woman. "I am. My name's Gaby Dupré."

"Welcome Ms. Dupré. And you can call me Mrs. Kupps. Mr. Santoro, he likes formality."

"I'm pleased to meet you, Mrs. Kupps." Gaby held out her hand to the woman. "But please feel free to call me Gaby."

The woman giggled and placed her hand in Gaby's for a brief shake. "I'm pleased to meet you, too," she whispered, "Gaby."

"Will you be showing me what I need to do?"

The woman shook her head. "Not me, dearie. I wouldn't have a clue. I'm the housekeeper and cook."

Gaby was disappointed. Working with Mrs. Kupps would have certainly made her workday interesting. "Do you know who will be showing me what I need to do?"

"I assume that would be Mr. Santoro."

"Oh, will he be out soon?"

The woman clucked her tongue. "Mr. Santoro does not get out much these days."

"Not even on his own estate?"

The woman shook her head as a serious look came over her face. "He prefers to stay in his suite of rooms."

This arrangement was getting stranger by the minute. "But how will I be able to work with him?"

"He will phone you."

And then Mrs. Kupps pointed out the way to the office. Gaby made it there with ease. Once inside, she glanced around the office, taking in the white walls and two desks that faced each other from across the room. They were both sparsely set up, but the one to her left looked a bit haphazard, as though the person had been in a rush to get out the door.

The room was adorned with beach decorations and a couple of prints of the ocean. It was pretty, but there was nothing of the man that owned this spacious estate. There were no movie posters, no snapshots of Mr. Santoro with costars and no awards. It was though he'd purposely removed himself from the room. But why?

Gaby moved to one of the desks and placed her purse as well as her pink-and-white tote on the desk chair. Her gaze scanned the desk as she searched for any instructions of what was expected of her or a number that she was supposed to call upon arrival.

Then the phone rang.

He should have never agreed to bring Gabrielle here.

The decision had been made in haste.

And it was a mistake.

Deacon paced back and forth in his private study. This woman with the honeyed voice was dangerous, as she was poised to be a distraction from the stark reality of his situation. She would make him think about all of the damage that had been done. If only he could remember the accident—remember if he was at fault.

He would need to be on constant guard around her. With her being the niece of the woman who had died in his arms, she would be out to finish what her father started—destroying him.

And then he'd almost been caught by Gabrielle while he was in the rose garden.

It was his oasis. His chance to feel like a normal person, not a man hunted and hounded for the truth—something he didn't possess. How exactly had she missed the sign that explicitly said Do Not Enter?

Luckily he'd had enough time to make a clean escape. But as her sweet voice called out to him, he'd hesitated. An overwhelming urge came over him to capture a glimpse of the face that went with such a melodious voice.

In the shadows, he paused and turned back. He'd been awestruck. He didn't know how long he'd stood there in the shadows watching her move about the garden searching for him. Her long hair had bounced around her slim shoulders. Her face—it was captivating. It wasn't the type of beauty that was created with powder and makeup. No. Hers was a natural, undeniable beauty.

Her creamy complexion was flawless. He was too far away to catch the color of her eyes. He imagined they would be blue. His gaze strayed down past her pert nose and paused on her lush, rosy lips. Oh, she was definitely going to be a big distraction.

He jerked his meandering thoughts to an immediate halt. What was done, was done, as his mother would say. Now he had to deal with the consequences.

Deacon Santoro gripped the phone in his good hand and pressed the number for the office. He lifted the receiver to his ear. Two rings later, Gabrielle answered. The tone of her voice was a sweet blend of vanilla and caramel with a touch of honey.

He did not have time to get caught up in such nonsense.

Focus.

Deacon resumed pacing. "I see you decided to abide by our agreement."

"I don't see how I had any choice?"

"Everybody has choices—"

"Not in this case."

"And you were able to find someone to check in on

your father?" He didn't know why he'd asked except that when he'd first made this proposal, Gabrielle had been quite hesitant to leave her father.

"I have a friend staying with him. Newton just moved back to the area and my father had a spare room. It seemed like a good idea at the time."

"I take it you've since changed your mind about this Newton."

Gabrielle hesitated. "Let's just say I've gotten to know him better and he's not the same as I remembered."

"I see." Deacon's curiosity spiked, but he forced himself to drop the Newton subject. "At least you won't have to worry about your father."

Deacon was impressed by her allegiance to her father, but that wouldn't be enough to sway him to concede. Her father had cost him more than just bad press, a mess in his yard and upset employees—her father had stirred up the paparazzi. Once again, there were news reports on television and the internet. His phone—with its private number—was now receiving calls from journalists wanting "the truth."

The little sleep he did get was once again riddled with nightmares—fiery, jagged dreams. But when he woke up, the images blurred and the memories receded to the back of his mind. With each dream, he hoped he'd be able to latch on to the elusive truth of what happened on that deadly night. But try as he might, his memory had holes the size of craters and images blurred as if in a dense fog.

The doctors had warned him that the memories might never come back to him. That was not the answer he'd wanted to hear. He needed the truth—even if it meant he was responsible for taking another person's life. Trying to live with the unknown was a torture that had him knotted up inside.

"If you would just tell me where to meet you, we can sit down and go over what is expected of me." Gabrielle's voice cut through his thoughts.

"That won't be necessary."

"Of course it is."

He could hear the confusion in her voice. She wasn't the first assistant that had been uncomfortable with his distant style of management, but it was the way it had to be. He didn't need anyone eyeing him with pity. He didn't deserve anyone feeling sorry for him. It was best for him to keep to the shadows. The accident had left permanent scars on him both inside and out. His career as an actor was over. And he was now struggling to find a new position for himself in the background of Hollywood.

He cleared his throat. "All of your instructions are on your computer. The password is capital B-e-a-c-h."

"Will you be stopping by the office later?"

"No."

"I don't understand—"

"We will conduct our business via the phone or preferably by email."

"But what if I have papers for you to sign? Or mail. I'm assuming that I'll be receiving your business correspondence."

"You will. And if you check next to the interior door, there is a mail slot. Drop whatever correspondence needs my attention in there and I'll get to it."

"But that doesn't seem very efficient. I don't mind bringing it to you—"

"No!" His voice vibrated with emotion. He clenched his jaw and swallowed hard. He didn't want to have to explain himself. After all, he was the boss. In a calmer voice, he said, "This is the arrangement. If you don't like it, you are free to leave. Our deal will be null and void."

"And my father?"

"He will face the judge and pay for the trouble he caused."

"No. I can do this." Her words were right, but her voice lacked conviction.

In all honesty, if she quit, he didn't know what he'd do for help. The temp agencies had blacklisted him after he'd gone through a dozen temps in the past couple of months. But he'd make do, one way or the other. He always had in the past. "You're sure?"

"I am."

"Then I will let you review the document that I've emailed you. It should explain everything including the fact that I work late into the night, but I don't expect you to. However, I will have work waiting for you each morning." When sleep evaded him, he found it best to keep his mind busy. It kept the frustration and worries of the unknown at bay.

"Does anyone else work in the office?" she asked.

"No."

She didn't immediately respond.

He hadn't considered that she wouldn't like working alone. It had been one of his requirements through the temp agencies, but Gabrielle hadn't given him time to get in to specifics when they'd spoken on the phone. Maybe this was his way out—even if the voice inside his head kept saying that he needed to watch out for her.

He cleared his throat. "If working alone is going to be a problem, we could end this now."

The silence on her end continued. He really wished he could look into her eyes. For the first time, he found communicating via the phone frustrating.

"No. It won't be a problem." Her voice sounded confident. "But I have a stipulation of my own."

"And that would be?"

"I need to speak with my father at least once a day—"

"That's fine."

"Would you reconsider letting me visit him? He will miss me."

This separation was to punish her father—not her. He'd cost Deacon and now the man had to pay a price—even if it wasn't dictated by a judge. Her father would learn not to take Gabrielle for granted.

"He should have thought of that before he allowed you to pay the price for his actions. Our arrangement will hold. You will stay here and work for three months."

Deacon knew what it was like to be alone. Both of his parents had passed on and he had no siblings. Other than Mrs. Kupps, the housekeeper, he was alone in this big rambling estate—except now Gabrielle was here. And somehow her mere presence seemed to make this place a little more appealing and less like a prison.

"My father didn't make me do anything. I volunteered." Her indignation came through loud and clear.

"Now that everything is settled, I'll let you get to work." Deacon disconnected the call.

Something told him this was going to be a very, very long three months. But it definitely wouldn't be boring.

CHAPTER TWO

THIS DEFINITELY WASN'T her best first day on the job.

In fact, it ranked right up there as one of the worst.

And the day wasn't over yet.

A loud crack of thunder shook the windows at the same time as lightning lit up the sky around the guesthouse. Gabrielle rushed to close the French doors. Somehow the weather seemed rather fitting.

She had one more piece of business before she curled up with a book and escaped from reality. She had to file her first report with *QTR*.

Gaby sat down at the granite kitchen bar and opened her laptop. She stared at a blank screen with the cursor blinking at her...mocking her. What would she say? She didn't even know what format to use. Did they expect her to tell a story or stick to bullet points?

Sure, she'd earned a bachelor's degree in journalism, but with a downturn in the economy, she hadn't been able to land a position in publishing, so she'd returned to school. She'd gone on to get a second degree in library science. Books had always been her first love.

And as much as she loved words, right now they wouldn't come to her. She typed a couple of words, but they didn't sound right. She deleted them.

This is ridiculous. It's not an article for the public to

read. It doesn't have to be perfect. It just needs to be the facts. So start writing.

The man has closed himself completely off from others. Is it the result of guilt? Or something else?

As she pressed Enter to begin the next point, the land-line rang. That was odd. She hadn't given anyone that phone number. Her father had her cell phone number.

She picked up the phone. "Hello."

"Did you find everything you need?" Not a greeting. Just straight to the point.

"Yes, I did."

"I wasn't sure what you like to eat, so I had Mrs. Kupps prepare you a plate of pasta, a tossed salad and some fresh baked bread. You will find it in your kitchen."

Outside the storm raged on with thunder and howling wind. Gaby did her best to ignore it. "Thank you." Had he called purely out of courtesy? Or was this his way of checking up on her? Perhaps this was her opportunity to flush him out of the shadows. "Will you be joining me?"

"No." His voice was firm and without hesitation. He was certainly a stubborn man. "In the future, you can let Mrs. Kupps know what you eat and don't eat, so that she can plan the menu appropriately."

"I—I can do that." She hesitated. "The guesthouse is nice." There was some sort of grunt on his end of the phone. She wasn't sure what it was supposed to mean, so she ignored it. "What time would you like to get started in the morning?"

"I start before the sun is up. You can start by eight. Will that be a problem?"

"No. Not at all." She was used to opening the library

at eight each morning. "I have a few things that I'd like to go over with you. Shall we meet in my office?"

"I thought you understood that this arrangement is to be by phone or email. I don't do one-on-one meetings—"

"But—"

"There are no exceptions. Good night."

And with that terse conclusion, he'd hung up on her. She stared at the phone. She could not believe that this man was so stubborn. Working for him was going to be difficult, but trying to get information about the accident from him was going to be downright impossible—unless she could get past this wall between them. And she hadn't come this far to give up.

Gaby hung up the phone and turned her attention back to the report for *QTR*. She'd lost her concentration after speaking with Deacon. She was back to staring at the blinking cursor and wondering what she should write.

QTR had assured her that before anything was published, they would get her approval. She wouldn't have agreed to the arrangement otherwise. After all, she didn't want them getting the facts wrong.

Although at this point, there wouldn't be much to write about the elusive Mr. Santoro. Giving herself the freedom to write about anything she'd learned so far, she resumed typing.

His estate in in disarray with overgrown vegetation. Was it always this way?

He's run off multiple assistants. What has happened? Has he fired them? If so, for what?

Locked door between the office and the rest of the house. What is he hiding?

The man lacks social niceties. Has he always been this way? Or is this a new thing?

It certainly wasn't a stellar first report. Would they be upset that it contained more questions than answers? Or would they appreciate her train of thought and look forward to the answers?

Accepting that it was the best she could do now, she proofread the email. Gabrielle pressed Send and closed her personal laptop.

She moved to the French doors and stared at the sky—the storm had now moved away. She opened the doors, enjoying the fresh scent of rain in the air. In the distance, the lightning provided a beautiful show. Was Mr. Santoro staring at the sky, too? She instinctively glanced in the direction of the main house, but she couldn't see it as it sat farther back than the guesthouse.

Still, she couldn't stop thinking about her mysterious boss. There had to be a way to break through the man's wall. She would find it, one way or the other.

CHAPTER THREE

TWO DAYS...

Forty-eight hours...

Two thousand, eight hundred and eighty minutes...

One hundred seventy-two thousand and eight hundred seconds...

No matter how Gaby stated it, that was how long she'd been at the Santoro estate and how long she'd gone without laying eyes on her new boss. It was weird. Beyond weird. What would that be? Bizarre?

Gaby sighed. Whatever you called it, she wasn't comfortable with this arrangement. Not that her accommodations weren't comfortable. In fact, they were quite luxurious. And unlike the estate's grounds, the guest suite was immaculate, thanks to Mr. Santoro's housekeeper, Mrs. Kupps. The woman had even written her a note, welcoming her.

Gaby glanced at her bedside table and realized that she'd slept in. She only had five minutes until she was due at the office. She had to get a move on. She slipped on a plain black skirt to go with a gray cap-sleeve blouse. There was a jacket that went with the outfit, but she rejected it. It was a warm day and she was more comfortable without the jacket. After all, it wasn't as if she had any business meetings. When Mr. Santoro said that he would limit their interactions to strictly email with the rare phone call, he hadn't been exaggerating.

She stepped in front of the full-length mirror and slipped on her black stilettos. With her height of only five foot two, the extra inches added to her confidence.

A knock sounded at the door, startling Gaby. She knew who it was without even opening the door. It would be Mrs. Kupps trying to lure her into eating breakfast. Gaby already explained that she didn't eat much in the mornings. In all honesty, she loved breakfast but never had time for it. She'd grown used to her liquid diet of coffee, with sugar and milk. It was easy to grab when she was on the run. Upon learning this, Mrs. Kupps had clucked her tongue and told her that she would end up with an ulcer if she didn't take better care of herself.

Gaby rushed to the door. "Good morning."

Mrs. Kupps stood there with a bright smile, a tray full of food and a carafe of coffee. "Good morning to you, too. I just brought you a little something to eat." Mrs. Kupps rushed past her and entered the small kitchen, placing the tray on the bar area. "I know you're in a hurry, but I'm determined to find something you can eat quickly."

"Mrs. Kupps, you don't have to do that." And then, because she really didn't want to hurt the woman's feelings, she added, "But it is really sweet of you. And the food looks amazing."

Mrs. Kupps beamed. "Oh, it's nothing, dearie. I enjoy having someone around here to spoil. Lord knows Mr. Santoro doesn't let anyone fuss over him since the accident. He's like a big old bear with a thorn in his paw."

"So he wasn't always so standoffish?"

Mrs. Kupps began setting out the food. "Goodness, no. He was always gracious and friendly. Perhaps he was a bit wrapped up in his acting career, but that's to be expected with his huge success. But now, he lurks about all alone in that big mansion. He doesn't see guests and rarely takes phone calls. I cook all his favorites, but his appetite isn't what it used to be. I'm really worried about him."

"Do you know what's wrong with him?" Gaby couldn't help but wonder if the guilt over the accident was gnawing at him.

Mrs. Kupps shrugged. "I don't know. And I really shouldn't have said anything. I just don't want you to leave. We need someone young and spirited around here. Lord knows, we've gone through assistant after assistant. He's even tried to run me off but it's not going to happen." The woman smiled at her. "You're a breath of fresh air. I have a good feeling about you."

Mrs. Kupps checked that everything was as it should be and then made a quick exit. It wasn't until the door shut that Gaby thought of a question for the very kind woman. Why did she stay here? Mr. Santoro was not the easiest person to work for. In fact, he was demanding and expected nothing but perfection with everything that Gaby did. And when she messed up, there was a terse note telling her to fix said error. And he didn't spare the exclamation points.

Still, she had agreed to this arrangement to save her father—a father who was now more eager to know what dirt she had dug up on her boss than worrying about how she was making out in such strained circumstances. It was all he'd wanted to talk about on the phone. His full attention was on making Mr. Santoro pay for the accident.

Gaby's gaze scanned over the croissant and steaming coffee. There was also a dish of strawberries. Okay. So maybe she had enough time to enjoy a few bites. Her stomach rumbled its approval. Perhaps some nourishment would help her deal with the stress of the day.

She couldn't help but wonder if this would be the day that Mr. Santoro revealed himself to her. He couldn't hide from her forever.

Deacon awoke with a jerk. His gaze sought out the clock above the door. He'd slept for more than two hours without waking. That was a new record for him, but it had come at a cost. He'd had another nightmare and, even worse, he was late.

It'd been another night spent in his office. He preferred it to staring into the dark waiting for sleep to claim him. Because with the sleep came the nightmares.

A couple of months after the accident, his nightmares had started to subside. But then Gabrielle's father had staged his protest with a megaphone, and he'd shouted horrible accusations. It was then that the nightmares had resumed. Sometimes Deacon remembered bits and pieces. There were brutal images of fire, blood and carnage. He had to wonder how much was real and how much had been a figment of his imagination.

Other times, he was left with a blank memory but a deep, dark feeling that dogged him throughout the day. It'd gotten so bad that he dreaded falling asleep. That's when his insomnia had set in with a vengeance. After spending one sleepless night after the next, he'd given up sleeping in his bed. In fact, he'd given up on sleep and only dozed when utter exhaustion claimed him.

It'd helped to keep his mind busy. And so he'd become a workaholic. Knowing the movie industry inside and out, he was working on starting his own production business. But being the man behind the curtain meant he had to find people he could rely on to do the legwork for him. That was proving to be a challenging task.

He'd just sat down to read over the lengthy letter that

Gabrielle had typed up for him. It had been late in the night or early in the morning, depending on how you looked at it. He'd made it to the last page when his eyes just wouldn't focus anymore. Blinking hadn't helped. Rubbing them hadn't made a difference. And so he'd closed them just for a moment.

He jumped to his feet and gathered up the papers that he'd reviewed. If he didn't get these on Gabrielle's desk before she arrived, it would have to wait until lunchtime. Because the mail drop in the wall only went one way. There was no way for him to deliver any documents anonymously for his assistant. He would have to see about rectifying that, but for now, he had to beat Gabrielle to the office.

He strode toward the door. When he reached out his hand for the doorknob, he couldn't help but notice the webbed scars on the back of his hand. They were a constant reminder of the horror he might have caused that impacted so many lives—especially Gabrielle's.

It was no secret that he'd liked his cars fast and he'd driven them like he was on a racetrack. He couldn't remember the details of that fateful night, but it wouldn't surprise him if he'd been speeding. If only the police would just release their findings. Gabrielle's father wasn't the only one anxious for that report.

His attorney had told him there were a number of complications. There had been an intense fire that destroyed evidence followed by a torrential downpour. Deacon didn't care about any of it. He just needed to know—was he responsible for taking a life?

Deacon moved through the darkened hallway, past the dust-covered statues and the cobwebs lurking in the corners. He didn't care. It wasn't like there was anyone in the house but him. Not even Mrs. Kupps was allowed in this part of the house. She kept to the kitchen and the office suite.

He descended the stairs in rushed steps. When he reached the locked door that led to the office area, he paused. There was no light visible from under the door and no sounds coming from within. He hated sneaking around his own home, but he didn't have any other choice. He didn't want to startle her with his appearance.

He recalled what had happened when his friends, or rather the people he'd considered friends, had visited him in the hospital right after his accident. They were unable to hide their repulsion at seeing the scars on his face, neck and arms. And then he'd held up a mirror to see for himself. The damage was horrific. After numerous rounds of plastic surgery, his plastic surgeon insisted the swelling and red angry scars would fade. Deacon didn't believe him. He'd already witnessed the devastating damage that had been done. It was so bad that he'd removed all the mirrors in the house as well as any reminders of how he used to look.

Deacon banished the troublesome thoughts. What was done, was done. He moved into the office and placed the stack of papers on Gabrielle's desk. That would definitely keep her busy today and probably some of tomorrow.

He noticed that her desk was tidy. However, there were no pictures or anything to tell him a little about her. It was though she wasn't planning to be here one minute longer than necessary to repay her father's debt. Not that Deacon could blame her—no one wanted to be here, including him. But he couldn't go out in the world—not until the accident was resolved and answers were provided.

Without tarrying too long, he turned to leave. He was almost to the door when he heard a key scrape in the lock. For a moment, he wondered what it would be like to linger in the office and have a face-to-face conversation with Gabrielle. In that moment, he realized how much he missed human contact. Maybe if he were to stay—maybe it would be different this time. Maybe she wouldn't look at him like he was a monster—a monster that killed her aunt.

He gave himself a mental shake. It was just a bunch of wishful thinking. He moved with lightning speed to the other door. He grasped the doorknob and, without slowing down, he gave it a yank, slipped into the outer hallway and kept moving. He needed distance from the woman who made him think about how one night—one moment—had ruined things for so many people.

CHAPTER FOUR

DIDN'T THIS MAN SLEEP?

It was almost lunchtime and Gaby hadn't even scratched the surface of all the tasks her boss had left for her. It didn't help that the phone rang constantly. Most calls were from reporters wanting to speak with Deacon. She had been left strict instructions to tell them "no comment" and hang up. With business associates, she was left with explaining that Deacon didn't take phone calls. When she explained that they would have to deal with her, it didn't go over well. Still, Gaby persisted. She had a job to do.

With a sigh, Gaby pressed Send on an email requesting the script for a film that Deacon was considering backing. But from what she could gather from prior correspondence and the files in the office, he had requested a lot of screenplays, but had yet to back one. She wanted to ask him how he decided which would be worth his money and which wouldn't.

Gaby got up to place the mail in the allotted slot for Mr. Santoro. When she approached the mail slot, she noticed the connecting door was slightly ajar. She slipped the papers into the slot and then turned back to the door. It beckoned to her.

What would it hurt to go see what was on the other side?

She knew if Mr. Santoro caught her, he would not be happy. In fact, it could very well blow up their whole deal. But if she didn't take a chance now, would she ever find out what he was hiding?

And to be fair, she was never told that she couldn't enter the house—only that mail was to go in the slot and communication would be phone or email. She had a hard time believing that he was as bad off as Mrs. Kupps had let on. This place wasn't exactly a dungeon by any means. He probably was just avoiding all the unanswered questions about the accident. And it was high time he stopped hiding from the truth and faced up to what had happened.

With a renewed determination, Gaby placed her hand on the doorknob and pulled the door open. It moved easily and soundlessly. There were no lights on in the hallway, but a window toward the back of the house let in some sunshine, lighting her way.

She didn't know what she expected when she crossed the threshold—an enraged Deacon Santoro, or a dark, dank house?—but she found neither. The house was done up in mainly white walls and marble floors. What she did notice was all of the empty spaces on the walls. There were mounted lights as though to illuminate a work of art or a framed photo, but there was nothing below any of the lights, as though even the hangings had been removed. *How odd.* The oddity was beginning to become a theme where Mr. Santoro was concerned.

The first set of doors she came to had frosted-glass inserts. One door stood ajar. She peered inside, wondering if at last she'd come face-to-face with Deacon Santoro, the larger-than-life legend. But the room appeared to be empty—except for all of the books lining the bookshelves.

Her eyes widened as she took in what must be thousands of titles. She stepped farther into the room, finding the bookcases rose up at least two stories. Like a bee to honey, she was drawn to the remarkable library. There was a ladder that glided along a set of rails to reach the top shelves. And a spiral staircase for the second floor of shelves with yet another ladder. It was truly remarkable.

She didn't know whether she had walked onto the set of *My Fair Lady* or the library of *Beauty and the Beast*. She'd never seen anything so magnificent. She moved to the closest bookshelf and found an entire row of leather-bound classics. It was then that she noticed the thick layer of dust and the sunshine illuminating a spiderweb in the corner. Who would neglect such a marvelous place?

Gaby ignored the dust and lifted a volume from the shelf. She opened the cover to find that it was a first edition—a *signed* first edition. It was probably priceless or at least worth more than she could ever pay.

And then she realized that if it was so valuable, she shouldn't be holding it in her bare hands. When she reached out to return it to the shelf, she heard footsteps behind her. She paused, not sure what to do. She moved the book behind her back. The time had come to face Mr. Santoro and suddenly she was assailed with nerves. It probably wouldn't help her case to be found hiding a collector's item. Her hand trembled and she almost dropped the book, but with determination, she gently placed it back on the shelf.

She leveled her shoulders, preparing for a hostile confrontation, and turned. The man had just entered the library and caught sight of her at the same time she had spotted him. He wore jeans and a long-sleeved shirt, which struck her as odd considering it was warm outside. And then she realized he was the man she spotted the first day that she'd arrived. He was the mysterious man from the rose garden.

"Who—who are you?" She didn't take her eyes off him.

His dark eyes narrowed. "I'm the one who should be asking questions here."

The voice, it was familiar. Was it possible that this was Deacon Santoro? She peered closely at him, trying to make up her mind. She supposed that it could be him. But it was his hair that surprised her. It was a longer style, if you could call it a style. The dark strands brushed down over his collar and hung down in his face.

She'd never seen him wear his hair that long in any of the movies he'd played in and yes, she'd seen them all. At one point, she'd have been proud of that fact, but after the accident, she'd wondered what she'd ever seen in the man.

When her gaze returned to his face, she had to tilt her chin upward. He was tall, well north of six feet.

And by the downturn of his mouth, he was not happy to find her in here. Her heart picked up its pace. She should turn away, but she couldn't. She needed to size up the man—all of him. She swallowed hard and jerked her gaze from his mouth. She really had to get a grip on herself. After all, he was the enemy, not some sexy movie star... Okay maybe he was that, too.

Ugh! This is getting complicated.

Her gaze took in the full, thick beard. It covered a large portion of his face. Between the beard and his longer hair, his face was hidden from view, for the most part. Except for his eyes. Those dark mysterious eyes stared directly at her, but they didn't give away a thing.

"What are you doing here?" His voice was deep and vibrated with agitation.

"I was looking for you." She refused to let on that his presence unnerved her. She clasped her hands together

to keep from fidgeting. "I thought it was time we met."
She stepped forward and held out her hand. "Hello, Mr.
Santoro."

His eyebrows drew together and he frowned as he
gazed at her hand, but he made no move to shake it. "I
told you I don't do face-to-face meetings. And you may
call me Deacon."

Gaby recalled what Mrs. Kupps had said about him
preferring formality and was surprised he'd suggest she
call him by his given name. Perhaps he wasn't as stuck
in his ways as she'd originally thought.

"And I don't like to be kept isolated." Ignoring the
quiver of her stomach, Gaby withdrew her hand. "If I
am going to work with a person, they need to have the
decency to meet with me—to talk one-on-one with me."

"You've seen me. Now go!"

She crossed her arms, refusing to budge. It was time
someone called him out on his ridiculous behavior. "Does
everyone jump when you growl?"

"I don't growl."

She arched a disbelieving eyebrow at him.

"I don't." He averted his gaze.

"You might want to be a little nicer to the people who
work for you." And then she decided that pushing him too
far would not help her cause, and said, "I have a request
that just came in today for you to make an appearance
at the upcoming awards show to present an award—"

"No."

"No? As in you don't want to attend? Or no, as in you
won't be a presenter?"

"No, as in I'm not leaving this house. And no, I'm not
presenting any awards. Have you looked at me? No one
would want me in front of a camera."

The fact that he'd dismissed the idea so quickly surprised her. For some reason, she thought he would enjoy being in the spotlight. Isn't that what all movie stars craved?

Deciding it might be best to change the subject, she said, "You have an amazing library."

At first, he didn't say a word. She could feel his gaze following her as she made her way around the room, impressed that the books were placed in the Library of Congress classification system. Was it possible Mr. Santoro... erm, Deacon loved books as much as her?

"I see you have your books cataloged." She turned back to him. "Do you also have a digital catalog?"

He nodded. "The computer that houses the database is over there."

She followed the line of his finger to a small wooden desk next to the door she'd entered. "This place is amazing. I've never known anyone with such an elaborate private library."

His dark eyebrows rose behind his shaggy hair. "You like books?"

"I love them. I'm a librarian and..." Realizing that she was about to reveal that she was an aspiring journalist would only make him more wary of her.

"And what?"

"I was going to say that I read every chance I get." She turned back to him. "I take it you read, too."

He shrugged. "I used to. These days my reading is all work-related."

"That's a shame, because books are the key to the imagination. You can travel the world between the pages of a book. Or visit another time period. Anything is possible in a book."

"What is your favorite genre?"

"I have two—suspense and romance. And cozy mys-

teries. And some biographies." She couldn't help but
laugh at herself. "I have a lot of favorites. It depends on
my mood." Perhaps this conversation was her chance to
get past his gruff exterior. "How about you?"

"Mysteries and thrillers." He turned toward the door
but paused. Over his shoulder, he said, "You—you may
make use of the library while you are here." Then his
voice dropped to the gravelly tone. "But do not wander
anywhere else. The rest of the house is off-limits."

He certainly growled a lot, but she was beginning to
think that his growl was much worse than his bite. So
far, so good. Now if she could just get him to open up to
her, perhaps she could find the answers to the questions
that were torturing her father.

But before she could say another word, Deacon strode
out the door.

Why had he gone and done that?

Later that afternoon, Deacon strode back and forth
in his office. He never gave anyone access to the house.
Even Mrs. Kupps, who had been with him for years, had
restricted access. Now, his house was being overrun by
women and he didn't like it.

He'd rather be left alone with his thoughts. His repeated attempts to uncover the truth had been unproduc-
tive. He kept coming back to one question: had he been
responsible for Gabrielle's aunt's death?

As long as Gabrielle stayed in the library and the office, he could deal with her unwelcome presence. If he
wanted a book to distract him from reality, he would
make his visits late at night, when he was certain that
Gabrielle would be asleep.

The thought of having that beauty staying on the estate gave him a funny sensation in his chest. It wasn't a

bad feeling. Instead, it was warm and comforting. Dare he admit it? The sensation was akin to happiness.

It was wrong for him to be excited about Gabrielle's presence. He didn't deserve to be happy. But there was something special about her and it went beyond her beauty. She was daring and fun. He admired the way she stood up to him. He could only imagine that she was just as fiery in bed.

In that moment, his imagination took over. The most alluring images of his assistant came to mind. He envisioned Gabrielle with her long coppery hair splayed over the pillow while a mischievous grin played on her lips. With a crooked finger, she beckoned him to join her.

Eagerness pulsed through his veins as he shifted his stance. He'd been alone so long and she was an absolute knockout. He imagined that she could see past his scars and—

Knock. Knock.

Immediately his lips pulled down into a distinct frown. Who was disturbing his most delicious daydream? Wait. Who was in his private area?

Deacon spun around. Heated words hovered at the back of his mouth. And then his gaze landed on Gabrielle. A smile lifted her glossy red lips. Her eyes were lit up like they had been in his fantasy. He blinked and then peered into her eyes once more. Instead of desire, there was uncertainty.

"What are you doing here?" His words came out much gruffer than he'd planned.

"I—I have some correspondence for you to approve, and I have an idea I want to run by you."

"And for that you marched up here to my private office? You couldn't have emailed me?"

Her lips lowered into a firm line just as her fine eyebrows drew together. "I didn't think you were serious about resuming that ridiculous nonsense of emailing each other. I thought now that you've granted me access to your home, we could start working together like two professionals instead of being pen pals."

His prior assistants never would have been so bold. His respect for Gabrielle grew. And that observation caught him off guard. If he wasn't careful, her tenacity would lead them into trouble. However, she certainly did liven up his otherwise boring existence. Maybe he could risk having his life jostled just a bit.

"Well, you're here now, so out with it. What's your idea?" He had to admit that he was curious.

"I've been thinking over your concern about your public image. And I know that my father didn't help with that. But I've thought of something that might help—"

"Help?" He was utterly confused. "You want to help me?" When she nodded, he asked, "Why?" He was certain there had to be some sort of catch. There was no way she would want to help the person that was involved in an accident that killed her aunt. No one had that good of a heart.

Gabrielle lifted her chin. "During our first phone conversation, you appeared to be upset with the negative publicity, and I've thought of a way to negate some of it."

Some people may call him a pessimist, but the possibility of countering the bad publicity was definitely too good to be true. There was a catch and he intended to find it. "And what's in it for you?"

Her eyes widened. "Why does there have to be more?"

"Because you aren't here out of choice. There is absolutely no reason for you to help me. So out with it. What do you stand to gain?"

She sighed. "Fine. There is something—"

"I knew it." He felt vindicated in knowing that behind that beautiful face was someone with an agenda. "Well, by all means, don't keep me in suspense. What do you want in exchange?"

She frowned at him. "Why do you have to make it sound so nefarious?"

"And why are you avoiding the answer?"

"If my idea works, I was hoping you'd see fit to shorten my time here."

He smiled. "I was right. There is a catch."

"I just think we can help each other is all. Would you consider sponsoring a fundraiser?"

A fundraiser? He had to admit he hadn't seen that coming. "I am the last person who should be asking people for money."

Gabrielle shrugged. "I don't agree. People know who you are. You're up for a couple of awards for your latest movie release. And you have another movie about to be released. I think you'd be surprised by the public's support."

Deacon shook his head. "It's not going to happen."

"Consider it your way to put some good back in the world."

"You mean my penance."

She shrugged and glanced away. "I suppose you could put it that way."

There was no penance big enough, generous enough or selfless enough to undo his actions. "No."

"Because you don't want to do something good?"

Why did she have to keep pushing the subject? He had to say something—anything—to get her to let go of this idea. And then he thought of something that might strike a chord with her. "Have you looked at me?"

"Yes, I have." Her gaze was unwavering.

"Then you know that I have no business being seen in public."

Her gaze narrowed. "I think you're trying to take the easy way out."

"Easy?" His hands clenched. "There is nothing easy about any of this. You of all people should know that."

"You're right. I'm sorry. That didn't come out the way I meant."

He wanted to know what she had meant but he decided the subject was best left alone. "I need to get back to work."

"I think with a haircut and a shave that you'd look…" She stepped closer to him. At last, she uttered softly, "Handsome."

Too bad he didn't believe her. There wasn't a stylish enough haircut to distract people from his scars. And a shave would just make those imperfections obvious. He shook his head. "It isn't going to happen."

"What isn't? The haircut or the shave? Or the fundraiser?"

"All of them." Why couldn't she just leave him alone? It would be better that way.

She crossed her arms and jutted out her chin. "I can do this. And you can participate as much or as little as you want."

"What do you know about fundraisers?"

"Enough. I've organized one for my library each of the past five years."

"A library fundraiser?"

She nodded. "Funds are being withheld from libraries across the country. Lots of them are closing. In order to keep doors open, libraries have become creative in raising money. So many people need and use the resources made available by the library, but the government is of less and less help at keeping the lights on. It's a real struggle."

"I didn't know." It'd been a very long time since he was in a public library. "My mother used to take me to the library when I was very young. I remember they had reading time where all the kids sat around in a circle and they read a story to us. I think that's when I got the acting bug. I'd listen to the librarian use different voices for the various characters and it struck a chord in me."

Gabrielle's smile returned and lit up the room. "As a librarian, that's the best thing I could hear. I love when we are able to make a difference in someone's life, big or small."

"So, what you're saying is that you'd like me to do a fundraiser for your library."

She shook her head. "Not at all. The library is what is close to my heart. You need to find what's closest to yours."

He took a second to think of what charity he'd most like to help and the answer immediately came to him.

"You've thought of something. What is it?" She stared at him expectantly.

"Breast-cancer research. *If* I were going to have a fundraiser, that's what I would want it to be for."

"Why?" she asked, curiosity ringing from her gaze.

He shook his head. He wasn't going to get in to this. Not with her. Not with anyone. It was too painful and still too fresh in his mind.

After a few moments, Gabrielle asked, "Will you at least consider the idea?"

It would be more efficient and less hassle to just write a hefty check, which he did every year in memory of his mother. But Gabrielle seemed to have her heart set on this. Perhaps if he didn't readily dismiss the idea, with time she'd forget about it.

"I'll think about it." When a smile reappeared on her face, he said, "But don't get your hopes up."

She attempted to subdue her smile, but there was still a remnant of it lighting up her eyes as she placed some papers on his desk. Those eyes were captivating. They were gray, or was it green? Honestly, they seemed to change color. And they had gold specks in them. They were simply stunning, just like Gabrielle.

And then as he realized he was staring, Deacon turned away. "I'll get these back to you by morning."

He gazed out the window at the cloudless sky until he heard the clicking of her heels as she walked away. It was then he realized he'd forgotten to tell her something.

He turned around but she was out of sight. He was going to tell her not to enter this part of the house again—that it was out of bounds. But something told him she would have just ignored him anyway.

CHAPTER FIVE

THE NEXT MORNING Deacon couldn't concentrate.

He should be working, if he was ever to get his fledgling company firmly ensconced in the movie business. He'd made a lot of inroads so far. The legal documents were all signed and filed with the appropriate agencies. Financial business accounts were opened. Sunsprite Productions was at last ready to do business.

In front of him sat a stack of proposed movie scripts to read. However, every time he sat down, his mind would venture back to Gabrielle. Why had he agreed to keep the door unlocked? To give her access to his space?

He'd avoided the library like the plague and, so far, she hadn't returned to his office. The way she'd looked at him—well, it was different than others. She hadn't shuddered. And she hadn't turned away. If anything, she'd been curious. In fact, she'd even stepped closer to him. What was he to make of that?

No one who'd come to see him in the hospital, people who were supposed to be his friends, had been able to look him in the eye. Most had hovered at the doorway, unwilling to come any closer. But not Gabrielle. She was different. And his curiosity about her kept mounting.

He had to wonder why her aunt had found it necessary to use her last breath to tell him to take care of her niece. He had to be missing something. Gabrielle Dupré was quite capable of taking care of herself.

She hit things straight on and treaded where others feared to go. And she was smart, as she'd demonstrated by coming up with that idea to improve his public image—though he doubted it would work. He needed to tell Gabrielle that he wasn't going to take her up on the offer; he just hadn't gotten around to telling her yet. It wasn't like he had to worry about letting her down. Gabrielle was no damsel in distress. She was sharp and would always land on her feet. Deacon wondered if her father knew how lucky he was to have her by his side.

He halted his train of thought. Listing all of her positive qualities was doing him no favors. No matter how much she intrigued him, nothing could ever come of it.

Because there was a look in her eyes, one that was undeniable. She looked at him with anger. She blamed him for her aunt's death. And for all he knew, she might be right.

Feeling the walls closing in around him, Deacon made his way down to the rose garden. It was the one place where he found some solace. With the gentle scent of the roses that reminded him of his mother and the sea breeze that conjured up memories of sailing, his muscles relaxed. It was here that the pulsing pain in his temples eased.

He moved about the garden. His doctor and physical therapist had told him to make sure to get plenty of movement as that would help heal the injury to his leg caused by the crash. He wasn't about to venture outside the estate gates. He knew the press would soon catch up to him. And then the probing questions would begin.

And so he spent time here in the spacious rose garden. He hadn't spared any expense creating this retreat. The garden ran almost to the edge of the cliff overlooking the ocean. Wanting a wide-open feel, he'd declined building a wall around the garden. He used to think that this garden was a little piece of heaven on earth.

Deacon took a deep breath, enjoying the fresh air. Out here he could momentarily forget the guilt that dogged him. Out here, he could pretend there wasn't the most amazing yet unobtainable woman working for him. For just a few precious moments, his problems didn't feel so overwhelming.

He followed the meandering brick path to the far edge of the garden. He paused to prune a dying purple rose from a newly planted bush. He'd surprised himself by finding that he didn't mind gardening. In fact, he found the whole process relaxing. Who'd have ever guessed that?

A glint of bright light caught his eye. He glanced around, finding an idle speedboat bobbing in the swells not far off the shoreline. The light must have been a reflection. It wasn't unusual for the water to be filled with boats on these beautiful sunny days. And today, with the brilliant sunrise, it wasn't surprising that people were out enjoying the warm air and the colorful sky.

He didn't give the boat any further attention as he turned back to his task. He continued to trim the dead blooms from the bush when a movement out of the corner of his eye caught his attention. Was it animal? Or human?

Deacon swung around. He didn't see anything. Perhaps it was just his exhaustion catching up to him. With a shake of his head, he returned to his task.

"Good morning."

The sound of Gabrielle's voice startled him. He turned with a jerk. "You shouldn't be here." Did she have to invade every part of his life? Frustration churned within him. "Go!"

Her eyes widened. "I... I'm sorry."

She stepped back. Her foot must have struck the edge of a brick because the next thing he knew, her arms were flailing about and then she was falling. He started toward her, but he was too far away to catch her. And down she went. Straight into a rosebush.

Deacon immediately regretted his harsh words. He didn't mean to scare her. He inwardly groaned as he rushed over to her.

The first thing he spotted was blood. Little droplets of blood dotting her arms and legs from the thorny vines. And it was all his fault. Since when had he become such a growling old bear—so much like the father that he swore he would never turn into. And yet it had happened...

Take care of Gabrielle. There it was again. Her aunt's last dying wish. He was certainly doing a dismal job of it.

As he drew near her, he watched as Gabrielle struggled to sit up. Her movements only succeeded in making the situation worse and a pained moan crossed her lips.

"Don't move," he said, coming to a stop next to her.

This was one of the rosebushes he hadn't gotten to. The limbs were long and unruly. He pulled the shears from his back pocket and hastily cut the bush. He worked diligently to free her.

And then he had her in his arms. Her eyes glistened with unshed tears. She sniffled but she refused to give in to the pain. Her strength impressed Deacon. He was used to women who lashed out or gave in to the tears. Gabrielle was stoic—or perhaps stubborn fit her better.

He started toward the house with her in his arms.

"I can walk," she insisted.

"I've got you."

"Put me down." There was steely strength in her voice and the unshed tears were now gone.

He hesitated, not wanting to put her down. To his detriment, he liked holding her close. She was light and curvy.

And she smelled like strawberries. His gaze lowered to her lips. They were berry-pink and just right for the picking. He forgot about their awkward circumstances and the fact that he hadn't shaved or had a haircut in months.

In that moment, all he wanted to do was pull her closer and press his mouth to hers. Her lips were full and shimmered with lip gloss. It had been so very long since he'd been with a woman—

"Now." Her voice cut through his wayward thoughts.

When his gaze rose up to meet her eyes, she stared up at him with determination. Did she know where his thoughts had drifted? He hoped not. Having her know that he was attracted to her would just make this uncomfortable arrangement unbearable. He lowered her feet to the ground.

"Come with me." This time he was the one issuing orders and he wasn't going to take no for an answer.

He led the way into the darkened house. He knew that in its day the house was impressive, but now the blinds were lowered and dust covered most everything. But it didn't matter to him. He never spent time on the first floor. He stuck to his suite of rooms. And that's where he led Gabrielle.

Into the expansive foyer with its white marble floor and large crystal chandelier. He turned toward the sweeping staircase that curved as it led to the second floor.

"Where are we going?" she asked.

"To get you cleaned and bandaged."

"I'll be fine."

She didn't trust him. That was fine. She had no reason to trust him. He wasn't even sure he trusted himself now that he had a faulty memory and tormenting dreams. But this wasn't about her trusting him. This was about her welfare and making sure she didn't have any serious injuries.

"You need someone to help you." He turned to her at the bottom of the stairs. "You can't reach the cuts on your back. And as fate would have it, today is Mrs. Kupps's day off."

He started up the steps, hoping she would see reason and follow him. The very last thing he needed on his conscience was her being injured because of him and then getting an infection. He may have royally messed up the night of the accident and no matter how much he wanted to go back in time, it was impossible. However, right now he could help Gabrielle. If only she would allow him.

At the top of the steps there were three hallways—one to the left, which was where his mother had had her suite of rooms, another hallway to the right, where the people he'd considered friends used to stay, and then the hallway straight back, which led to his suite of rooms and his office that overlooked the ocean.

He stopped outside the last door. He hadn't made his bed. He hadn't straightened up in forever. And it hadn't mattered to him for months. But now, it mattered. Now he was embarrassed for Gabrielle to see his inner sanctuary. Later tonight he would do some cleaning.

"Is something wrong?" she asked. "If you changed your mind, I can go."

"No. Nothing's wrong." And with that he swung open the door. It wasn't like he was trying to impress her. That ship had sailed a long time ago. In fact, he'd lost any chance to impress her before they'd even met.

The room was dark as the heavy drapes were drawn as they always were, but he knew his way around without bothering with a light. However, he realized that Gabrielle would have a problem, and he reluctantly switched on the overhead light.

"Why is it so dark in here?" she asked. "You should open the curtains and let in the sun."

"I like it this way."

"Maybe the sun would give you a cheerier disposition."

Why did she want to go and change him? He didn't want to be changed. This was now his life and he would live it however he chose. "My disposition is fine."

"Really? And you think it's normal to go around scowling at people and barking out warnings for them to go away?"

"I do not bark and I do not growl." He turned on the bathroom light.

"Apparently you don't listen to yourself very often."

"You are—" he paused, thinking of the right word to describe her "—you are pushy and..."

"And right about you."

He sighed. "You don't know everything."

"But I do know that you're going to turn down my offer to help you."

He arched an eyebrow and stared at her, finding that she was beautiful even with her hair all mussed up from the rosebush and cuts crisscrossing her arms. It was then that he recognized just how much trouble he was in. There was something about Gabrielle that got under his skin, that made him feel alive again. And made him want to be worthy of her affection.

And if he wasn't careful, he was going to fall for her—head over heels. And that couldn't happen. She would be crazy to fall for him after the car accident. And he didn't deserve to have love in his life—not that he was falling in love with her. He wouldn't let that happen.

But knowing that it was even a possibility had him worried. The best thing he could do for both of their sakes was to keep her around here for as little time as possible. Maybe he should accept Gabrielle's offer to plan the fundraiser. Not that he relished having more attention cast upon him, but he could shorten her time on the estate without arousing her suspicions. She would never know how she got to him.

"What are you smiling about?" Gabrielle was eyeing him suspiciously.

"Who, me? I don't smile. Remember, I growl."

"Oh, I remember. But I saw a distinct smile on your face, so out with it."

What did he have by holding back? He'd strike the deal, set the timetable and soon his life would return to the way it used to be. Why did the thought of his quiet, lonely life no longer sound appealing?

"I accept your offer," he blurted out before he had an opportunity to change his mind.

Her eyes widened. Today, they looked more blue than green. "You do?"

He nodded. "How long do you need?"

"A few months would be ideal."

Months? He was thinking in terms of weeks. "You'll need to do it faster than that."

She thought about it. "How grand do you want to make it?"

"That's up to you."

"Instead of say a grand ball, we could do a garden party."

"That might not be enough of a draw."

"Okay. Give me a little time and I'll come up with some other ideas."

"Just don't take too long. I'd like to do this in the next few weeks."

Her eyes widened. "You don't give a person much room to work, do you?"

"If you're not up to the challenge—"

"I'll do it."

"Good. Now let's get you cleaned up." He led her into the bathroom and set to work cleaning and medicating her injuries.

He felt terrible that she'd been injured because of him. He would work harder in the future not to be so abrasive. He'd obviously been spending too much time alone.

He stood in front of her as she sat on the black granite countertop. He'd just used a cloth to wash the wounds on her arms with soap and water. Now that they were rinsed off, he was gently patting them dry.

As he stood there, he could sense her staring at him. He glanced up to say something, but when his gaze caught hers, he hesitated. And then her gaze lowered. Was she staring at his lips?

CHAPTER SIX

WAS THAT DESIRE reflected in her eyes?

Deacon swallowed hard. Suddenly the walls seemed to close in around them and the temperature was rising... quickly. He should turn away because if she kept staring at him, he was going to start to think that she wanted him—almost as much as he wanted her.

"You shouldn't do that," he said.

"Do what?" Her voice carried a note of innocence.

He inwardly groaned. "You know what."

"If I did, I wouldn't ask."

Surely she couldn't be that naive. Could she? "Look at me like—like you want me to kiss you."

She didn't blush, nor did she look away. "Is that what you think I want? Or is that what you want?"

Why did she have to insist on confusing matters? He was already confused enough for both of them. "Forget I said anything."

"How am I supposed to do that now that I know you're thinking about kissing me?"

"That's not what I said." He huffed in exasperation. "Turn around."

"Why?"

"Do you have to question everything?"

She shrugged. "If I didn't, I wouldn't know that you want to kiss me."

"Would you quit saying that?" Heat rushed up his neck and settled in his face, making him quite uncomfortable. "Turn around so I can tend to the wounds on your back."

For once, she did as he said without any questions. Thank goodness. He wasn't sure how much longer he could have put up with the endless questions. It would have been so much easier to smother her lips with his own. And then he'd know if her berry-red lips were as sweet as they appeared.

But this was better. With her back to him, he could get a hold on his rising desire. They were oh, so wrong for each other. She was pushy and demanding. She was definitely not the type of woman he normally dated. If he hadn't been alone all these months, he wouldn't even be tempted by her. He assured himself that was the truth.

And then she lifted her shirt, stained with thin traces of blood, to reveal the smooth skin of her back. His assurances instantly melted away. All he wanted to do was run his hands over her body and soothe away her discomfort with his lips, fingers and body.

"Is something the matter?" she asked.

His mouth suddenly grew dry. He swallowed and hoped when he spoke that his voice didn't give away his wayward thoughts. "I—I'm just figuring out where to start."

"Is it that bad?"

He wondered if she was referring to his level of distraction or the cuts and punctures on her back. He decided that she'd given up flirting with him and was at last being serious. "It could be worse."

"That's not very positive."

He was beginning to wonder if along with his memory

loss he'd lost his ability to talk to women. He used to be able to flirt with the best of them without even breaking a sweat, but talking to Gabrielle had him on edge, always worrying that he'd say something wrong, which he seemed to do often.

"I didn't mean to worry you." He grabbed a fresh washcloth from the cabinet and soaked it with warm water. He added some soap and worked it into a lather. "Let me know if this hurts."

"It'll be fine."

He wanted to say that the skin on her back was more tender than that on her arms or hands, but he didn't want to argue with her. It was then that he noticed how her skirt rode up her legs, giving a generous view of her thighs. His hand instinctively tightened around the washcloth as his body tensed.

With great reluctance, he glanced away. It took all of his effort to concentrate on the task at hand. And it didn't help that the task involved running his fingers over her bare flesh. Talk about sweet torture.

He pressed the cloth gently to the first wound. When he heard the swift intake of her breath, he pulled away the cloth. "I'm sorry."

"It's okay. Just keep going."

"Are you sure?"

"Keep going. I obviously can't do it myself."

And so he kept working as quickly as he could. When her wounds were cleaned, rinsed and dried, he grabbed the antibiotic cream, which, thankfully, had something for pain relief. A few of the cuts had required bandages. The others had already started the healing process.

He lowered her top. "There. All done."

She turned to him. "Thank you."

"Don't." He waved off her gratitude. "I don't deserve your thanks."

"Yes, you do. You fixed me all up."

"I'm the one who caused your injuries." He just couldn't seem to do anything right these days.

"No, you didn't. I stumbled and fell. End of story."

"You stumbled because I startled you."

Her green-gray eyes studied him for a moment. "You do have a way of growling—"

His voice lowered. "I don't growl."

She laughed. "You just growled at me."

Had he growled? No, of course not. He wasn't some sort of animal. He was human—a damaged human, but human nonetheless. Still, his tone might have been a bit gruff.

She stepped toward him. "I see the doubt in your eyes."

He narrowed his gaze on her. "If I growl so much, why are you still here?"

"Good question. I guess I'm just holding up my side of our agreement."

For a moment there, he'd forgotten that she was there at his insistence. He knew that if she had a chance, she'd be anywhere else. And he couldn't blame her. He definitely wasn't the most hospitable host.

But when he was this close to Gabrielle, he wanted to be someone else. His old self? No. He'd been too selfish—too self-absorbed. Right now, he wanted to be someone better.

"I'm sorry that I startled you earlier." He made sure when he spoke that his voice was soft and gentle. He would not growl at her. "I never meant for you to get hurt."

She stared into his eyes. "You really mean that, don't you?"

"Of course." His voice took on a rough edge again. He swallowed hard. And when he spoke, he made sure to return to a gentle tone. "I'm not used to having anyone out in the gardens."

"The rose garden is beautiful. That's why I was out there. I could see them from my bedroom window and I wanted to get a better look. Unlike the rest of the grounds, they are well-maintained. They must be special to you?"

"They are. I had them planted for my mother." He missed his mother. She had been kind and gentle. She had been the exact opposite of his brutal father. "Roses were her favorite. She used to spend hours out there. It's where she spent her last days."

Gabrielle's eyes filled with sympathy. She reached out to him. Her fingers wrapped around his hand. She gave him a squeeze. "I know that saying I'm sorry isn't enough, but it's all I have."

He continued to stare into her eyes, and he saw something more than sympathy. There was…understanding. He searched his memory and he recalled her mentioning that she'd also lost her mother. "You understand?"

She nodded. "My mother died giving birth to me, so I never knew her."

Instead of offering her the same empty words, he nodded and squeezed her hand back. It was then he realized her hand was still in his. The physical contact sent a bolt of awareness through his body.

He should let her go. He should step away. But he could do neither of those things. It was as though she were a life-sustaining force and without her, he would cease to exist.

His gaze lowered to her lips. Today they were done

up in a striking purple shade. Against her light skin, her lips stood out. They begged for attention and he couldn't turn away.

This wasn't good—not for his common sense. Because right now, all he could think about was her mouth—her very inviting mouth. He wanted to kiss her. He needed to kiss her. He longed to feel those lush purple lips move beneath his. A groan swelled in the back of his throat, but he choked it back down. He didn't need Gabrielle realizing how much power she had over him.

Because there was no way her kiss could be as amazing as he was imagining. Nothing could be that good. Not a chance.

He needed a heavy dose of reality to get her out of his system. And then he'd be able to think clearly. Yes, that would fix things.

Without giving his actions further thought, he dipped his head. He captured her lips with his own. At first, he heard the swift intake of her breath. She pulled back slightly and he thought she was going to turn away.

Then her hand lifted and smoothed over his beard. It must have caught her off guard. He should shave it, but it never seemed like the right time, until now.

And then her lips were touching his again. Tentatively at first. She didn't seem to know what to make of this unlikely situation. That made two of them, because kissing her was the absolute last thing he thought he'd be doing this morning.

As if he were acting in a trance, he drew Gabrielle closer and closer. He expected her to pull away. To slap him. Or at the very least stomp away.

Instead her hands came to rest on his chest. Her lips began moving beneath his. Her hands slid up over his shoulders and wrapped around his neck as her soft curves leaned against him. Mmm…she felt so good. And she tasted sugar-sweet, like the icing on a donut. And he couldn't get enough of her.

Their kiss escalated with wild abandon. It was as if she were the first woman to ever kiss him. No one had stirred him quite the way she did. He never wanted to let her go.

In the background, there was a noise. He couldn't make it out. And then it stopped. Their kiss continued as his body throbbed with need.

And then the sound started again. He wanted it to stop—for them to be left alone to enjoy this very special moment. The next thing he knew, Gabrielle braced her hands against his chest and pulled back.

It was too soon. He wasn't ready to let her go. And yet she moved out of his embrace. She reached for her cell phone, which was resting on the countertop.

"Hello, Dad. Is something wrong?" She turned her back to Deacon.

He ran the back of his hand over his lips. Instead of getting Gabrielle out of his system, he only wanted her more. He was in so much trouble.

Gabrielle turned back to him. She didn't have to tell him how much she loved her father. It was there in her voice when she spoke of him. It was in her eyes. It was in her actions by coming here and working for Deacon. She was a devoted daughter. Deacon just hoped her father deserved such devotion.

When she ended the call, Deacon asked, "Is everything all right with your father?"

She nodded her head. "He's fine."

Deacon noticed how her gaze failed to meet his. "But he's not happy about you being here."

"No. He isn't." She sighed. "My father used to

be such an easygoing guy. But the accident, well, it changed everything—for both of us."

Right then the wall went back up between them. Deacon could feel the warmth slip away. The chill was as distinct and real as the kiss they'd shared—the kiss that would not be followed by another. He would be left with nothing more than the memory.

"I know how death can change people." His mother changed after his father's death. Even though the man didn't deserve her undying love, she'd given it to him anyway. When his father passed away, his mother was cloaked in sadness. She moved on with her life, but it was never the same. She was never the same again.

Gabrielle's gaze briefly met his. "About what happened between us—"

"It was nothing." He was a liar. A bold-faced liar. "We lost our heads for a moment. It won't happen again." At least that part was the truth.

Gabrielle glanced away. "You're right. It was a mistake."

Her sharp words stabbed at him. He didn't know how much more of this he could take. It was best that they parted ways until he got his emotions under control.

He wasn't mad at her. He was angry with himself for losing control—for complicating an already messy situation.

"I should go." She just turned and walked away.

This situation was such a mess. An awful mess. How in such a short time had Gabrielle taken his dark hopeless life and filled it with light? He didn't know how he'd go back to the dark again.

CHAPTER SEVEN

THE SUN WAS sinking into the sky when Gaby called it quits for the day. Deacon had made himself scarce the rest of the day and perhaps that was for the best—for both of them.

Things were confusing enough. That kiss only intensified the conflicting emotions within her. She had no business flirting with him—coaxing him into kissing her. She should keep a respectable distance from this man. He was trouble.

Wait. Was that the answer? Could she be drawn to Deacon because he was so different from the other professional men she'd dated? Did Deacon's dark side act like a magnet?

Whatever it was, she had to get a grip on it. Because her reason for being here had absolutely nothing to do with becoming romantically involved with Deacon Santoro. And she'd do well to remember the circumstances that had led her here.

Gaby sighed as she let herself inside the guesthouse. There was still enough light filtering in from outside that she didn't turn on the lights. Instead she kicked off her heels and moved to the couch.

Her cell phone rang. She didn't recognize the number.

She was about to ignore it when she thought of her father. Something might have happened to him.

Needing to be certain her father was all right, she answered the call. "Hello."

"Gabrielle Dupré?" The male voice was unfamiliar to her.

Concern pumped through her veins. "Yes."

"My name's Paul. I'm with *Gotcha* magazine. Do you have a comment on the photo?"

"Photo?" She had no idea what this man was talking about. Thinking it was probably a scam, her finger hovered over the end button.

"The one of you in Deacon Santoro's arms. Would you like to comment on why you're in the arms of the man that *allegedly* killed your aunt?"

"There is no photo."

"If you don't believe me, go to our website. It's on the home page, front and center. I'll wait," he said smugly.

Gaby pressed the end button. It didn't matter what they had posted on their website, she wasn't giving a comment. But she wanted to see what had prompted the reporter to call her.

Her fingers moved rapidly over the touch screen and then the website popped up. She gasped. It was true. They did have a photo of her and Deacon.

Her face felt as though it was on fire. That man had made the situation sound so scandalous. Deacon had only been helping her after she'd been an utter klutz.

She studied the photo more intently. She didn't recall Deacon looking at her like—like he desired her. Surely they'd done something to alter the photo. She'd heard they do that all the time to make people thinner or prettier.

Thankfully there hadn't been any cameras in Deacon's house. Her face burned with embarrassment when she recalled how she'd flirted with him and then that kiss—oh, that heated kiss had been so good.

And yet, the kiss could not be repeated.

No matter how good it was, it was a one-time thing—a spur-of-the-moment thing. It didn't matter if his touch had been so gentle and so arousing. There could be no future for them. It was impossible. She was the niece of the woman who'd died because of Deacon's actions. There was no way they could get around that.

And she wouldn't do that to her father. She owed everything to her father—a man who'd always stood by her and who'd encouraged her to follow her love of books and sacrificed so that she could go to college.

She needed to talk to Deacon. She needed to tell him about the photo. She headed out the door. She also needed to make sure he'd heard her when she said that she regretted that soul-stirring, toe-curling kiss—because she did, didn't she?

Now that she had full access to the house, she knew her way around. She knew where Deacon would be, where he spent most of his time—in his office. It was like a one-room apartment. From what she could tell, it was where he took his meals, where he slept—when he slept—and where he worked.

Her footsteps were silent over the carpeting. When she reached his office, the door was open and the soft glow of the desk lamp spilled out into the hallway. But there were no sounds inside.

She stepped just inside the door. Her gaze scanned the room, with its long shadows. The desk chair was empty and so was the leather couch. Her gaze continued around the room until she spotted him standing in the open French doors that overlooked the ocean.

He didn't move. He must be lost in thought. She wondered if she was too late. Had he seen the photo?

She softly called out, "Deacon."

He didn't turn to her as she'd expected. Instead he said, "You shouldn't be here."

"We need to talk."

"If it's business, it can wait."

She crossed her arms and leveled her shoulders. "If you're going to talk to me, you could at least have the decency to face me."

He turned to her. His face was devoid of expression. She didn't know how he managed that when she was certain he was anything but calm—not after that spine-tingling kiss. She supposed that was what made him such an accomplished actor. She, on the other hand, wore her emotions on her sleeve. She didn't like it, but she didn't know how to hide her emotions.

"I'm facing you," he said matter-of-factly. "Now, why are you here?"

"I just had a phone call from a reporter. There's a photo of us on the internet."

A muscle in Deacon's jaw twitched. "Let me see it."

Recalling how the photo made it seem like there was something going on between them, she didn't think Deacon would take it well. "I don't think you want to see it."

He approached her and held out his hand.

She pulled up the picture on her phone. The headline read: Evading the Police in the Arms of a New Lover. Maybe bringing it to Deacon's attention wasn't a good idea after all.

She handed him the phone and waited for his reaction.

For a moment, he didn't speak. He scrolled through the article. With a scowl on his handsome face, he returned her phone.

"I don't even know how they got the photo," she said.

"I do. There was a boat not far off the shoreline. I hadn't thought much of it at the time, but there must have been a photographer on board."

"How can they publish this stuff? The headline is a lie."

"Welcome to my world. The tabloids will do anything for headlines. They are vultures."

"But they know it's not true."

"They don't care about the truth. It's whatever makes them money. I'm sorry you got caught up in it." He raked his fingers through his hair. "Until the police report is released, I'll be in the headlines."

They'd both been dancing around the subject of the car accident for far too long now. She needed some answers and she didn't know how to get them other than being direct. "Deacon, tell me about the accident."

"No." He moved to his desk and started moving papers as though he were looking for something.

"Don't dismiss me. I need to know—I need to know if what my father is saying about you is true."

Deacon straightened and his dark gaze met hers. "Why would you doubt him?"

"Because I feel like I'm missing something. And yet I keep thinking if you were innocent, you would have given your statement to the police. You would have cleared up this mess. Instead you remain tight-lipped about the facts, which says you're guilty. Is that it? Are you guilty?"

His jaw tightened. "I know in part you agreed to this arrangement to get information, but I'm not talking about the accident. Not now. Not ever. So if that's what you're after, you can go back to Bakersfield."

"So you can say I broke the arrangement and have

you press charges against my father? No thank you. I'm staying until my time has been served."

"This isn't a prison." His voice rumbled. "You're free to go."

"When our deal is fulfilled and not a minute sooner."

She paused and studied his face. "You might feel better if you talked about it."

"That subject is off-limits," he said with finality.

She sighed. "Okay then. I'll go work on the plans for the fundraiser. I'll let you know how it goes."

"At this hour?"

"It's not like I have much else to do around here. This place is so big and yet so empty."

His eyes grew dark. "It's the way I like it."

She didn't believe him. He didn't live alone in this big house because he wanted to. There was so much more to him closing himself off from the outside world. How would she get him to open up to her?

Gaby moved to the door. She paused in the doorway. She still hadn't told him the other reason she'd sought him out. She worried her lip. With him standing there looking so cold, it wasn't easy to talk to him. He reminded her of the man she'd met that not-so-long-ago day in the library, but tonight he hadn't told her to get out. Nor had he growled at her. Maybe he was changing.

"What?" he prompted.

"I just wanted to make sure that things were straight between us. You know, about the kiss."

He brushed off her concern. "It's already forgotten. I won't be kissing you again if that's what you're worried about."

"Oh." She wasn't sure what she'd wanted him to say, but that wasn't it.

Without a word, he turned his back to her and stared out at the moon-drenched ocean.

She had been dismissed, quickly and without hesitation. And so had their kiss. Was it just her that had been moved when his lips touched hers?

As she walked away, she felt as though she had lost her footing with Deacon. Her fingers traced her lips, recalling the way his mouth had moved passionately over hers, bringing every nerve ending to life. Her lips tingled at the memory.

He may deny it, but he'd felt something, too. And for the life of her, she didn't know what to do about this attraction that was growing between them.

CHAPTER EIGHT

HE COULDN'T STOP thinking about that picture.

The next morning, Deacon set aside his pen and leaned back in his desk chair. Although he didn't like the invasion of privacy, that wasn't what was eating at him. Nor was it the inflammatory headline. It wasn't any of that stuff.

He pulled up the photo on his computer with the larger monitor. The part that he couldn't get past was that she looked good in his arms. In fact, if he didn't know better, he'd swear they were lovers. And he was certain that's what anyone who caught a glimpse of the photo would think.

He scrolled down, finding there were hundreds of comments. He knew he shouldn't read them, but he couldn't help himself. There were, of course, mean, nasty comments, but to his surprise, there were others in support of them. They commented that sometimes love comes at the most unexpected times. Those people were all wrong—very wrong. Others said he was taking advantage of Gabrielle. That, too, was untrue. He was trying to help her, both financially, with an inflated salary, and so that she could gain her independence from her father. And it certainly had nothing whatsoever to do with love.

Deacon shut down the site. He'd read enough. He

checked the time. It was almost time for him to leave
for his appointment.

He moved to his bedroom to change clothes. Still, he
couldn't stop thinking about Gabrielle.

He knew she wanted answers, but he didn't think
she'd buy his amnesia story any more than the police
had bought it. There had been the skeptical looks followed by the prodding questions that went on and on
with the same answers. It was as if they believed that if
they asked the same questions a hundred and one times,
his answers would change from "I don't remember" to
something they could use against him.

In the short amount of time he'd spent with Gabrielle,
he'd come to respect her. And having her upset with him
for not opening up about the deadly accident was better
than the look she would give him upon hearing that he
couldn't remember it. In her shoes, he probably wouldn't
believe him, either. He couldn't bear to have her look at
him as if he were a liar. He was a lot of things in life,
and some of them were not so good, but he wasn't a liar.

Maybe today he would get those elusive answers. His
attorney had said he had news, but he wouldn't say on
the phone whether it was good or bad. Something told
Deacon that it wasn't good news. But he didn't want to
say anything to Gabrielle until after his meeting, when
he'd hopefully have more information.

Once he left the attorney's office, he had a doctor's
appointment, where they'd run some tests to make sure
he was healing properly. The accident had done significant damage to his body. If he were to pass through the
metal detectors at the airport, he'd surely set them off
with his newly acquired hardware.

In the end, he'd spend most of the day in Los Angeles.
He didn't like these outings. They were fraught with the

stress of being hounded by the press and wondering if the attorney and doctors would have more bad news for him.

Refusing to dwell on the unknowns awaiting him, he gathered the screenplay he'd finished reading. He was on the fence about this one. It was a mystery and he recalled Gabrielle mentioning that she enjoyed reading mysteries. He'd like to get her take on this one before he went any further. He did have a few changes he'd like to see incorporated when the screenplay was rewritten, but he'd run those past Gabrielle after he got her initial reaction.

However, when he opened the door to the office, Gabrielle wasn't at her desk. He walked farther into the room and found the outer door slightly ajar. He dropped the stack of papers on her desk and headed out the door. Once outside, he spotted Gabrielle at the end of the walk.

Deacon called out to her, but she must not have heard him as she kept moving. She turned the corner away from the beach and the guest cottage. Where was she going?

As he followed her, the sidewalk soon became surrounded by overgrown bushes, tall grass and weeds. He frowned. To be honest, he never walked toward the front of the house. It was too close to the road for his comfort with the paparazzi lurking about.

Surely she couldn't be enjoying a leisurely stroll through this thick vegetation, could she? He kept walking. His steps were long and quick as he hustled to catch up with her.

He turned a corner and there she was on the opposite side of the house. She stood in the shadows with a legal pad in one hand and a pen in the other. She was so intent on writing something that she didn't appear to notice his presence.

Once he was within a few yards of her, he called out to her.

Her head jerked up.

"Oh. It's you." And then she flashed him a smile that filled his insides with warmth. "Good morning."

"I stopped down to speak with you and didn't find you at your desk."

She turned back to the legal pad and continued writing. "I had an idea and I needed to check it out. Now, I'm not sure how to make it work."

An idea? Suddenly he grew uncomfortable. If he knew anything about Gabrielle, it was that she wasn't afraid to shake things up. And the fact that she was standing in his overgrown yard making notes didn't sit well with him.

She sent him a mischievous grin that lit up her eyes and intensified that fuzzy warm feeling in his chest. He swallowed hard. "Gabrielle, dare I ask what you have in mind?"

She glanced around. "This used to be a golf course, didn't it?"

He glanced over the neglected grounds and a fresh wave of guilt washed over him. "At one point, it was a private course."

"Wow." Her gaze was glued to the lush green grounds. "How many holes?"

"Nine." He used to spend a lot of time out here entertaining friends and associates. They said he had the best private course in the country. "But it doesn't matter anymore."

"Of course it matters. Why don't you golf anymore?"

"After the accident, my injuries made it impossible."

"And now, can you play?"

"I don't know. I haven't tried." He rotated his left shoulder. There was a dull pain, but thanks to lots of therapy, his range of motion was almost one-hundred-percent. "Not that anyone could golf out here."

"It looks like at one point it was beautiful."

"It was." His mind conjured up an image of the golf course in its prime. It had come with the house and it had been gorgeous, with water hazards and sand bunkers. It might have been a short course, but it had been a fun way to while away a lazy summer afternoon with friends. Those carefree days seemed like a lifetime ago now.

"It's a shame to let it go to ruin. Have you ever considered restoring it?"

He shook his head. He just couldn't imagine golfing when he had so much uncertainty and guilt weighing him down. "I stopped by to let you know that I need to go out for a while."

Her eyes widened and her mouth gaped open, but she quickly recovered her composure. "I didn't know you ever left here."

"I don't unless it's necessary."

Unasked questions filled her eyes, but she was smart enough to leave them unspoken. "Is there anything you need from me while you're gone?"

"Yes. I put a screenplay on your desk. I know you enjoy mysteries and I was interested in your thoughts. The sooner, the better."

"Thoughts? As in a pro-con list?"

He hadn't thought of that, but it wasn't a bad idea. "Sure. That works for me." And then he added, "I'd really appreciate it."

"Well, when you put it so nicely, I'd be happy to do it."

So nicely? He didn't think he'd said it in any special manner. Perhaps she meant since he didn't growl at her. Was Gabrielle having that much of an effect on him?

"I'll be gone most of the day." He turned to walk away.

"Do you mind if I ask where you're going?" When he turned back to her, she added, "You know, in case something comes up while you're gone."

"I'll have my cell phone. The number is listed on your computer."

"Oh, okay." She tried to hide it, but he caught the hint of a frown. "But there's something I want to discuss with you."

He checked the time on his phone. "It'll have to wait."

When he turned to walk away, Gabrielle said, "But it won't take long—"

"I can't be late. I'll talk to you when I get back."

Without another word from either of them, he strode away. He could have told her about his meeting with his attorney, but he didn't want to get her hopes up. He felt the pressure every time she looked at him. She wanted the truth as much as he did. If only he could remember.

This was pointless.

Gaby sat behind her desk later that afternoon. Deacon still hadn't returned. The fact that he'd been gone for hours worried her. Perhaps she should have pushed harder to learn his destination, but she doubted there was anything she could say to get him to open up.

She was quickly coming to the conclusion that no matter what she tried, Deacon wasn't going to let his guard down with her. He was a very determined man. But at least he didn't growl at her any longer. That had to mean something, right?

And now that she had him considering the fundraiser, she had to make it extra special. It was her ticket out of here without jeopardizing the deal for her father.

The fundraiser needed to be something different. Something that would attract big names with big money and also attract the press. She told herself that concluding their deal early was the only reason she was so invested in these plans that kept her up at night. Because there was no way she was trying to improve Deacon's image.

Her gaze scanned across the manuscript that Deacon wanted her to read. It could wait until later. Right now, she was wound up about the fundraiser. It could help so many people, not just Deacon.

After making some notes, Gaby looked up the name and number of the printing company she'd used for the library fundraiser. Lucky for her, she could use a lot of the same contacts for this event. It would cut down on her workload because getting this estate ready for the event was going to take a lot of time.

Gaby recalled seeing a list of estate employees on her first day here when she'd been checking out everything. Now where had she seen it? Her gaze scanned her desktop. Nothing there. Then she turned to the bulletin board behind her desk. No names and numbers.

She logged on to her computer. Maybe they were in here. A lot of pertinent information was stored on the network. She clicked on directory after directory. And then she stumbled across a file titled Personnel Listing. Under Grounds Crew, there were six names listed. Was it possible they were still employees? She knew it was a long shot, but hope swelled within her.

She reached for the phone and then hesitated. Should she do this without checking with Deacon?

She worried her bottom lip. He did give her the lead on this fundraiser. And it wasn't like he had much interest in the plans. But if she could show him what she had in mind, she was certain he would agree. She hoped.

Without letting any more doubts creep into her mind, she picked up the phone and dialed the first number on the list.

CHAPTER NINE

IT HAD NOT been a good day.

Not at all.

Deacon stepped out of the dark SUV and sent the door flying shut with a resounding thud. He pulled the baseball cap from his head, scrunched it with his hand and stuffed it in his back pocket. He removed his dark sunglasses and hung them from the collar of his shirt. He was done with disguises for today.

For all of the good it had done him, he might as well have stayed home. His attorney didn't have any good news for him. In fact, it was quite the opposite. The television network he'd been negotiating with had pulled out of the deal. They felt he brought too much bad publicity to the table and it would ruin their chances of having a hit. Apparently they didn't subscribe to the notion that there is no such thing as bad publicity.

Perhaps Gabrielle was right. Maybe he needed an image makeover. But would that work before the police report was released?

People might think that he'd refused to answer the officer's questions, but it was quite the opposite. In fact, at his meeting with his attorney, he told him in no uncertain terms to light a match under the powers that be. If he was innocent, he needed to be cleared ASAP. And if he had caused the tragedy, then he'd deal with the consequences.

When he'd moved on to his doctor's appointment, he grilled his physician about the gaping holes in his memory and the nightmares that plagued him. The doctor said the memories might all come back to him at once, or they might come back in pieces. His dreams were indicative of them coming back to him bit by bit. The doctor did warn him that the dreams might be real memories or they could be figments of his imagination. Or a combination of both.

When Deacon stepped out of the garage, he ran straight in to Gabrielle. He was not in the mood to be social right now. "What are you doing here? Shouldn't you be working?"

Her eyes widened. "I am going up to my rooms. And no, I shouldn't be working as the workday is over."

He pulled out his phone. It was much later than he'd been expecting. His appointments had taken up his entire day and he still didn't know any more than he had when he'd left that morning.

"I—I didn't realize the time." Not wanting to chitchat, he said, "I'll just be going."

"Wait. I wanted to talk to you."

"About?"

"The fundraiser. I've come up with some really good ideas. I was hoping for your input."

Deacon shook his head. He was in no frame of mind to deal with Gabrielle or the fundraiser. "I don't think this evening is a good idea."

"Are you feeling all right?"

"As good as can be expected. I just..." He paused as he grasped for any excuse to make a quick exit. "I'm just hungry."

"Then I have the perfect solution. It's Mrs. Kupps's night off, so I'll cook us up some dinner."

"I don't want you to go to any bother."

"It's no bother. We both have to eat, don't we?"

Her insistence surprised him. Of course, he realized that her interest was purely for business reasons. And she was right, they did have to eat. So what would it hurt to combine food and work?

"Okay. Count me in." He arched an eyebrow at her. "I take it this means you know how to cook."

She nodded. "Does that surprise you?"

"It's just that I don't know much about you."

"What would you like to know?"

A bunch of questions sprang to mind, like was she seeing anyone? If circumstances were different, would she go out with him? He immediately squelched those inquiries. They were none of his business—no matter how much he longed to know the answers.

He swallowed hard. "How well do you cook?"

A smile lifted her pink lips. "Don't you think you should have asked before agreeing to this meal? Now you'll just have to find out for yourself. Come on."

She didn't even wait for his reply before she started up the steps to the guesthouse. He watched the gentle sway of her hips as she mounted each step. No one had a right to look that good. And oh, boy, did she look good.

He hesitated. Right now, he was truly regretting agreeing to this meal. And it had absolutely nothing to do with his bad day or his uncertainty about her cooking skills and everything to do with how appealing he found the cook.

She glanced over her shoulder. "Well, come on."

Not wanting her to notice his discomfort, he did as she said. He started up the steps right behind her. A meal for two. This was a mistake. And yet he kept putting one foot in front of the other.

He'd spent so much time alone that he wasn't even sure he remembered how to make small talk. Just stick to business. It wasn't like she wanted to have this dinner for them to get closer. She was just anxious to get on with this fundraiser—a fundraiser that he was certain would fail if it had his name attached to it.

What had she done?

Gabrielle entered the galley kitchen. It was small and cozy. If Deacon were to be in here with her, they'd be all over each other—as in bumping in to each other. But now that the seed had been planted, she started to think of other things they could cook up together that had absolutely nothing to do with food.

Her imagination conjured up a shirtless Deacon in her kitchen. Oh, yes, things would definitely heat up. And then she'd be there in him arms. Her hands would run over his muscled chest. And there was a can of whipped cream—

Heat rushed to Gaby's face. This was a mistake.

But as she heard Deacon's footsteps behind her, she knew that it was too late to change her mind. She just had to keep her attention focused on the main course and not the dessert.

She moved to the fridge and pulled the door open. There on the top shelf sat the whipped cream. She ignored it. "What are you hungry for?" She was hungry for... The image of licking cream off Deacon came to mind. She gave herself a mental jerk. "Maybe I, ah, should tell you what I have ingredients for and, um, then we can go from there."

"Are you okay?"

"Um, sure." If only she could get the image of having him for dessert out of her mind. "Why?"

"You're acting nervous. If it's dinner, don't worry. We can order in."

"No." Her pride refused to give up. "I've got this."

Deacon took a seat at the kitchen counter. "I'm not a picky eater. So anything is good."

"Let me see what's in here." Mrs. Kupps had kindly offered to fill her fridge for the times when she was off and for the evenings when Gabrielle might get hungry.

"I've found a steak." Gaby opened the produce drawer. "There are some fingerling potatoes. And some tomatoes, onions, Gorgonzola cheese and arugula."

Her gaze skimmed back over that tempting whipped cream, but she absolutely refused to mention dessert. When he didn't respond, she glanced over her shoulder. "What do you think?"

"Sounds good. I'll just look over this information about the fundraiser while you cook the food."

She closed the fridge and turned to him. "I don't think so."

His dark eyebrows drew together as his puzzled gaze met hers. "What?"

"I'm not cooking us dinner. We're both doing it."

He shook his head and waved off her idea. "That is not a good idea. I don't know my way around a kitchen. That's what takeout menus are for."

"It's about time you learned your way around it." She wasn't about to wait on him. She didn't care how much money he had or how famous he was. "Come on. You can wash the potatoes and get them ready to go in the oven while I get out the ingredients for the salad."

And so with a heavy sigh, he got off the bar stool and made his way into the kitchen. She gave him detailed instructions and they set to work. This wasn't as bad as she'd been imagining.

Gabrielle finished rinsing the lettuce and turned to grab a bowl from one of the cabinets over the counter when she ran in to Deacon. To steady herself, she reached out with both hands. They landed on his chest—his very firm chest. The breath caught in her throat.

He reached out, catching her by the waist. His hands seemed to fit perfectly around her. It was though they fit together. But how could that be?

Deacon was the man who was responsible for her aunt's death. At least that's what her father and the papers were saying. But there was a voice deep inside her that said there was so much more to this man. Was she only seeing what she wanted to see?

Neither of them moved as her gaze rose from his chest to his full beard to his straight nose. And then she noticed his hair. It looked like it hadn't been cut in months. It fell just above his eyes. When their gazes at last connected, her heart pounded. Each heartbeat echoed in her ears.

Was it wrong that she wanted him to kiss her again? That kiss they'd shared was stuck in her mind. No man had ever made her feel so alive with just a kiss. And she hadn't gotten enough. Maybe it was the knowledge that it was wrong that made this thing—whatever you wanted to call it—between them that much more enticing. Deacon was the bad boy and she was the good girl.

Her gaze slipped back down to his mouth. It was surrounded by his mustache and beard. Though they were both well kept, she wasn't sure she was a fan of so much facial hair. Still, she wouldn't pass up the chance to kiss him, beard or no beard.

At that moment, Deacon stepped back. He released her. When she glanced at him, he turned away. Did he know what she was thinking? Did he know that she'd almost kissed him again?

"I just need the olive oil," he said, as though nothing had happened between them.

"I think I saw some in the cabinet to the right of the stove."

"Thanks."

And that was it. They were both going to act as though sparks of attraction hadn't just arched between them like some out-of-control science experiment. Well, if he could pretend nothing happened, so could she. After all, it was for the best.

Refusing to let her mind meander down that dangerous road, she focused on preparing a delicious dinner. In no time, Gaby filled their plates with seared steak, roasted potatoes and a fresh salad tossed with a wine-and-cheese dressing. They took a seat at the kitchen bar and ate in silence. In fact, Deacon was so quiet, she couldn't tell if he was enjoying the meal.

"Do you like it?" she asked.

"Yes." His gaze met hers but then he glanced away as though he wanted to say more but wasn't sure if he should. He stabbed a potato with his fork. "It's the best meal I've had in a long time."

"I doubt it. Mrs. Kupps is a marvel in the kitchen. But thank you for the compliment." It'd been a long time since anyone had taken notice of her cooking, including her father.

She was truly happy he was enjoying the meal. This is the point where she should once again probe him about the accident, but she just couldn't bring herself to ruin the moment. The questions had waited this long, surely they could wait a little longer.

They continued to eat in a comfortable silence. Deacon

emptied his plate first. He politely waited for her to finish before he carried both of their plates to the sink. Together they cleaned up the mess they'd made in the kitchen.

After the dishes were placed in the dishwasher, Deacon said, "I should look over those notes for the fundraiser."

Gabrielle spied a beautiful sunset splashing the sky with brilliant pinks and purples. "Or you could go for a walk with me."

He shook his head. "I don't think so."

"Oh, please? It's such a beautiful evening."

He shook his head.

"Do you ever get out of this estate?"

He frowned at her. "Of course I do. I was just in the city today."

"I don't mean for business or whatever drew you away. I mean get out of here and do something relaxing."

"Not since the accident."

"Because of the paparazzi?"

He nodded. "It stirs up interest in me. And it's not my reputation so much as the people closest to me being harassed. When the reporters start their feeding frenzy, Mrs. Kupps can't even go to the grocery store without being harassed in the parking lot. I thought staying out of public sight would help and it did for a while."

"And then my father stirred things up."

Deacon lowered his gaze and nodded.

"I'm sorry." So he wasn't hiding out here for purely selfish reasons. "Is that why you gave your grounds crew time off?"

"Yes. It just got to be too hard on everyone. Although Mrs. Kupps refused to take paid leave. She said she wasn't going to let the reporters bully her."

Gaby glanced away. Guilt settled over her like a wet,

soggy blanket. Here he was telling her how hard the media had made the life of those around him and she was writing daily reports for *QTR*. She was starting to wonder if her idea to publicly out him was the best approach.

"What's the matter?"

Her gaze lifted and she found him studying her. Apparently the guilt was written all over her face. "It's nothing."

"You're upset because I don't want to go for a walk."

It was best to let him think that was the source of her distress. "Oh, come on. There's no one out on the beach. Let's go."

"I thought the fundraiser stuff needed to be dealt with."

"It does. But there's plenty of time for it. Right now, I'd like to see more of this area. I must admit I'm not used to hanging out in Malibu. And the beach here is so nice. Come on." She reached out and grabbed his hand. "Show me around." She started toward the door, hoping that he'd give in to her tug of his arm.

"But there isn't much to show. It's a beach."

"A beautiful beach with a gorgeous sunset."

He followed her to the door and then stopped. "But I have work to do."

"Don't you ever just want to play hooky?"

There was a twinkle in his eyes. "So that's what you do? Play hooky instead of working."

The smile slipped from her face. She couldn't decide if he was being serious or if he was just giving her a hard time. She removed her hand from his. "I promise you that I work all day. I do a lot—more than what you've asked—"

"Slow down. I was just teasing you." He sent her a small smile.

She studied him for a moment, determining if he were serious or not. "Don't do that."

"Do what? Harass you a little?"

"Yes. Because I don't know you well enough to know if you're being serious or not."

"Perhaps I am too serious these days."

"You think so?" The words slipped across her lips before she could stop them.

His eyes widened. "I didn't know I was that bad."

"Let's just say that a bear with a thorn in its paw is more congenial than you."

"Ouch." He clasped his chest. "You really know how to wound a guy."

"Well, if you want to make it up to me, let's go for that walk."

He hesitated. She waited for him to say no, but instead, he said, "Fine. Lead the way."

She didn't say a word, not wanting to give him a chance to change his mind. Instead, she headed down the steps as quickly as her legs would carry her.

CHAPTER TEN

WHY EXACTLY HAD he agreed to this walk?

Deacon pulled the navy blue ball cap from his back pocket and settled it on his head. And even though evening was descending upon them, he put on the sunglasses that had been dangling from the neck of his shirt. These days, he always took precautions.

He shouldn't be out here, in the open for anyone to approach him—especially the press. The thought of being hounded with question after question about one of the most horrific events in his life almost had him turning around. Instead he pulled the brim down a little farther on his forehead. But the lure of stepping outside of his self-imposed confines was almost too tempting for him.

How could he resist walking along the sandy shore with the most beautiful woman he'd ever known by his side? The truth was, she'd cast a spell over him and he'd follow her most anywhere. And so he kept moving—kept in step with Gabrielle—as they made their way down to the beach.

He scanned the beach, looking for any signs of trouble. There was a man jogging along the water's edge. And coming from the other direction was an older woman walking her dog. Other than that, the beach was quiet.

Before his life had crashed in on him, he would jog on

the beach each morning. And sometimes in the evening, if he had time. He'd come out here to clear his head. It was funny to think that he'd ever taken those simple liberties for granted—

"Don't you think?" Gabrielle's voice cut through his thoughts.

He had no idea what she'd been saying. "What was that?"

"I said the sunset is exceptional tonight. I wish I'd have grabbed my phone from the kitchen counter so I could take a picture of it."

Deacon stopped. This was one small thing that he could do for her. "I've got mine."

He pulled out his phone and snapped a picture. And then he handed it over so Gabrielle could forward it to her phone. When she was done, she returned the phone and that's when their fingers touched. How could such a small gesture get to him? And yet, a zing of nervous energy rushed up his arm and settled in his chest, making his heart beat faster.

"Thank you." When she smiled at him, it was like having the sun's ray on his face.

"You...you're welcome." It'd been a long time since he'd used his manners, but it made him feel more human—she made him feel like a man again. He didn't want this evening to end. "What are you waiting for? Surely you don't want to turn around already."

Her eyes lit up with surprise. "Certainly not."

They set off again at a leisurely pace. Every now and then they passed someone else with the same intention of enjoying such a perfect evening. Deacon couldn't recall the last time he was able to let go of the guilt, the remnants of the nightmares and the worry of what tomorrow would bring long enough to enjoy the here and now.

"I can see why you live here," Gabrielle said. "If I had the opportunity, I'd get a little place along here and wild horses couldn't drag me away."

"Actually I've been considering moving. It's time for a change. Maybe I could move someplace where they don't recognize me."

"I don't think that place exists."

He shrugged. "Perhaps."

"You aren't returning to the movies?"

Was she just being polite? Or had she not really looked at him? He stopped walking and held out his hand in front of them. "With scars like these, no one would want to hire me."

"These are from the accident?"

"Yes."

She reached out and ran her fingertip ever so gently over his skin. "It's not so bad. Maybe some makeup could hide what's there from the camera if you're self-conscious about it."

But makeup could not hide the scars in his mind. They were there—they kept him up at night, walking the halls in the dark. "It's not going to happen."

"Why not try?"

"Because…" Because he didn't deserve to be in front of those cameras any longer. She of all people should understand that. "Why are you being so nice to me?"

She shrugged and then started to walk again. "How am I supposed to act around you?"

"Like you hate me."

"Should I hate you?"

He inwardly groaned. Why did she have to keep turning things around on him? "It's not for me to say how you should feel. It's just that if circumstances were reversed, I'd probably act more like your father."

"And what has that accomplished? He has broken the law and has his daughter bailing him out."

Deacon really wanted to understand her. "So you think by taking the high road that you'll accomplish more?"

"Such as you telling me what happened the night my aunt died?"

"There it is." He stopped next to an outcropping of rocks. "I knew that's why you dragged me out here. You wanted to get me someplace where you could interrogate me."

"That's not true. I didn't drag you out here—"

"But you can't deny that you didn't think about questioning me. You were hoping to wear me down into a confession."

Her gaze searched his. "Do you have something you need to confess?"

He should turn and leave. That's what he'd do if he were thinking clearly. That's what his attorney would advise him to do.

But his feet wouldn't cooperate. He stood there staring into Gabrielle's eyes and could only imagine the pain that she'd been through. And the not knowing, well, he knew all about that. Much too well.

He swallowed hard. "If I told you, you wouldn't believe me."

"Try me."

He wanted to trust her. He wanted to believe that whatever he said would stay between the two of them. But he hardly knew her. And right now, he could count on one hand how many people he trusted.

Instead he turned and climbed up on the rocks. He made his way to a large boulder on the water's edge. He sat down, letting the sea breeze fan his face, and hoped the lulling sound of the ocean would ease the storm raging inside him.

He sat there for the longest time, trying to get his thoughts in order. By then the sun had sunk below the horizon. It was an overcast night with the moon peeking out here and there. Deacon found comfort in the long, dark shadows. He glanced around and found that Gabrielle hadn't left. Instead, she was sitting just a few feet away. She was too far away in the dark to make out her face. As she sat there with her knees drawn up to her chest, he couldn't help but wonder what she was thinking. He hated the thought that he continued to cause her pain. But nothing he could say would fix things.

"If you're waiting for a confession, you're wasting your time." He turned back to the ocean.

Gabrielle moved to settle on the rock next to him. "Is that because you didn't cause the accident?"

Why was he holding back? So what if she didn't believe him. Once he said it, it would be out there. Perhaps she'd believe him. Perhaps she wouldn't. But it was time he told the truth.

"I don't remember." Somehow it was easier having this conversation under the shelter of darkness.

"What don't you remember?"

"The accident." He could feel her intense stare.

"What part don't you remember?"

"All of it. They called it retrograde amnesia or some such thing."

"That's pretty convenient." She said it as a fact.

He turned to her and now that she was closer, he could make out the disbelief written on her face. "Actually, it isn't. I want to remember the accident as bad as you need me to remember. I need to know what I've done." His voice cracked. "I—I need to know if I'm responsible."

For a moment, Gabrielle didn't say anything. "So you're not holding out and trying to bury the events?"

His jaw tightened. He knew that she wouldn't believe him. But then again, why should she?

"No. I'm not lying." He shook his head. "I knew you wouldn't believe me."

"And the delay with the police report?"

"I've had my attorney pressing for its release, but without camera footage or an eyewitness account, it complicates matters. Once the police have finalized the report, it must go up the chain of command, ending with the DA's office. When my attorney checked yesterday, he was told the report should be released soon." When Gabrielle didn't say anything, he glanced over at her. "I'm sorry. I know that's not what you want to hear."

Her gaze met his and she placed a slight smile on her lips. "It's the truth and that's what matters."

"You believe me?" If she did, she'd be the first person to do so.

"Are you saying I shouldn't?"

"I'm just surprised is all."

Gaby paused. "So tell me more about yourself."

"You don't really want to hear about me?"

She nodded. "I do."

"Where do I start?"

"How about at the beginning."

"Well, I was born on Valentine's Day. My father died when I was thirteen. My mother finished raising me on her own. I split my time between the fishing boat and watching movies."

"Fishing and movies. Those are two diverse interests."

"The fishing wasn't a hobby. It was my job. I started when I was thirteen, getting paid under the table, in order to help my mother pay the bills." It hadn't been an easy life and his schooling had paid the price, but he'd graduated by the sheer willpower of his mother. "The movies were my passion. I drove my mother crazy telling her that one day I would be a movie star. And do you know what she told me?"

Gabrielle shook her head.

"She used to say, 'Deacon, you're a smart boy. You can be anything you want to be as long as you work hard and don't give up.'"

"She sounded like a smart lady."

"I thought so, too. And then she met my stepfather. In the beginning, he wasn't so bad. And then they got married. That was when I decided to move to California. I just couldn't stick around and watch those two argue. I tried to talk my mother in to coming with me, but she insisted that her place was with her husband."

"I'm sorry. That must have been tough on you."

"And what's even worse is that when she first found a lump in her breast, that—that man told her it was her imagination. By the time I talked her in to going to the doctor, the cancer was advanced. I brought her here to California. Oh, they tried to help her, but by then the cancer had spread."

Gabrielle reached out, taking his hand in hers. She gave a firm squeeze. It shouldn't, but it meant a lot to him. And it even meant more because she wasn't supposed to be here giving him support. She was supposed to hate him—hate his very existence. The fact that she didn't confused him, yet also intrigued him. There was definitely something different about Gabrielle.

CHAPTER ELEVEN

SHE DIDN'T MOVE.

Gabrielle left her hand securely within Deacon's hold. His hands were large and his fingers long. And his hand fit perfectly around hers. It was as though they were made for one another. Not that she was letting her heart get ahead of her mind. She knew that nothing could ever come of their relationship, whether he'd caused the accident or not.

Because in her father's mind, Deacon would always be responsible for her aunt's death. And she highly doubted that anything would change her father's mind. He was a very stubborn man. She'd inherited his stubborn streak. Or at least that's what her aunt had told her.

However, Deacon was far from the spoiled movie star that her father and Newton had accused Deacon of being. There was a lot more to this man than anyone would guess. He was like an onion, with layer upon layer, and she had an overwhelming desire to keep peeling back the layers until she reached his heart.

"Maybe we should head back." Deacon released her hand and got to his feet.

"So soon?"

He laughed. "We've been out here a long time. It's getting late."

"But we have the whole beach to ourselves." And then she dropped her voice. "We can do whatever we want and there's no one around to see."

"Be careful. Or I just might take you up on the invitation."

A shiver of excitement raced through her. She knew she shouldn't be flirting with him, but she couldn't stop herself. There was something about Deacon that she couldn't resist.

"Maybe I *want* you to take me up on the invitation."

Deacon stood there in the shadows. She wished she could make out his eyes. He was so quiet. Was he considering taking advantage of her suggestion? Her heart thudded against her ribs.

"Gabrielle, don't make offers you aren't ready to fulfill. Let's head back before something happens that we'll both come to regret. I don't want to hurt you."

He held out his hand to her and helped her to her feet. For a moment, they stood there face-to-face. Her pulse raced and her heart pounded. With darkness all around them, a few moonbeams silhouetted Deacon's face. She wanted to tell him that she wasn't fragile. But her tongue refused to cooperate.

Instead of turning and heading back to the estate, Deacon continued staring at her. Was he considering kissing her again? Was it wrong that she wanted him to pull her against his chest and lower his head to hers?

And then he turned away and started climbing down off the rocks. When he was standing on the sand, he turned back to her and held out his hands in order to catch her. Even though she could make it down on her own, she didn't resist his offer of assistance.

He placed his hands on her waist and lowered her ever so slowly. Her body slid down over his. It was tantalizing and oh, so arousing. She was so caught up in the crazy sensation zinging through her body that she never noticed when her feet touched the ground.

Beard or no beard. Scars or no scars. Long hair or short. There was something magnetic about this man. She knew that it wasn't rational. And right now, she didn't care.

Her heart pounded so loud that it drowned out rational thought. She was going to live in the moment and damn the consequences. She tilted up her chin and lifted up on her tiptoes. Her mouth pressed to his.

His lips were warm and smooth. And the kiss, it was full of emotion, of need, of desire. Her hands slid up over his broad shoulders and slipped around his neck. She could get used to this.

Except for the beard. It tickled her. And when he moved to trail kisses down her neck, it tickled so much that she pulled away. A smile lifted her lips as she struggled not to laugh. He sent her a concerned look as though wondering if he had done something wrong.

"It's not you." But when he went to press his lips to her neck again, she placed her hands on his shoulders and held him back.

"What?"

She wasn't sure if he would take offense or not. And so she stood there not saying a word.

He frowned. "Just tell me."

"It…it's your beard. It tickles."

His eyes twinkled with mischief. "It does?" He leaned toward her. "How much?"

Before he could tickle her again, she yanked away from him. "Catch me if you can."

And with that taunt, she ran up the beach. A big smile was plastered across her face. For once, she wasn't the dutiful daughter working two jobs to keep the bills paid and she wasn't answering her father's numerous phone calls to check up on her. She was just Gabrielle Dupré, a woman with a dangerously handsome man chasing her. She could hear Deacon calling out to her, but she didn't stop until she was out of breath.

When she turned around, she fully expected Deacon to be standing there, but he wasn't. She squinted into the shadows. He was quite a way down the beach. What in the world? Hadn't he wanted to catch her?

Disappointment socked her in the gut. They'd been having so much fun. Where had it gone wrong?

Her wounded pride urged her to keep going. But another part of her wanted to wait and find out what was up. The curiosity in her won out. She started to walk back to him.

When she was within a few feet of Deacon, he said. "Sorry. I couldn't keep up. My leg is getting better, but it's not that good yet."

And suddenly she felt foolish. She was worried about him being upset with her when in fact he had an injury. It never even dawned on her that the injuries he'd sustained to his face, arms and hands had extended further.

"I'm sorry. I didn't think."

"It's not your problem. And how would you know?"

They started to walk side by side. She felt awful. She'd just assumed that he was fine. "Are you okay to walk back?"

"Yes. I'm just not up for running. Maybe one day, if I keep going to therapy and doing the exercises."

"You go to physical therapy?" She hadn't noticed him leaving on a regular basis, but then again, she hadn't been here that long.

"Not anymore."

"Why not?" She knew from her father's accident how important physical therapy could be to making a full recovery. "It's really important."

"I'm fine." His dismissive manner bothered her.

"If you were fine, you would have kept up with me or surpassed me. You are not fine. Your therapy is important. You can't just dismiss it because you don't want to do the work."

He arched an eyebrow. "And since when does my welfare matter to you?"

"It—it doesn't." Did it? She glanced away from him, not wanting him to read anything in her eyes. "But that doesn't mean it shouldn't be important to you."

"I don't think it's going to matter. All I do is haunt that place." He gestured toward the mansion in the distance.

"If you refuse to leave home, I can help you with the exercises."

"I don't need help." His voice rumbled with agitation, letting her know that she'd pushed as far as he was going to let her go.

And so they walked in silence. She wasn't sure what to say now. He'd made it clear he didn't want her help and he refused to go anywhere to get help. She couldn't believe this, but she'd met someone who was as stubborn or perhaps more stubborn than her father. They at least had that in common.

The thought of who could be more stubborn made her smile and the more she thought about it, a giggle started to form. And before she knew it, she was laughing. Maybe it was her nervousness or maybe it was the stress, but it felt good to laugh. Talk about a cathartic moment.

Beneath one of the estate security lights, Deacon stepped in front of her. "What's so funny?"

The frown on his face just made her laugh some more. It was almost like an out-of-body experience. She couldn't help herself. And it just felt so darn good.

"Stop it. Right now." His eyebrows were drawn into a firm line.

"I—I can't." She laughed some more.

She could see that the more she laughed the angrier he was getting. She really had to pull herself together. She had no idea what had come over her, but she needed to get a grip.

With a frustrated groan, Deacon turned and started to walk away. That was definitely not a good sign, at all. The elation in her started to ebb.

"Wait." She rushed to catch up with him, all the while trying to catch her breath.

"I don't care to be laughed at."

"I wasn't laughing at you. Not really." And then she thought about it a little more. "Well, maybe some. But it really wasn't that bad."

"I don't want to be laughed at."

Totally sober now, she said, "I just started thinking about you and my father and what you two have in common."

Deacon came to a stop and she almost ran in to him. "You were comparing me to your father?"

"Yes, in a way."

"What way?"

"You are both so stubborn. I was trying to figure out which one of you is the worst, but I couldn't decide."

"And that made you laugh."

"Yes, I guess it did."

He shook his head. "I don't understand you."

"That's okay. I don't really understand myself, either." It was the truth. She understood the parts of her that were like her father, but the other parts, the silly parts, sometimes surprised her. "I honestly don't know why I laughed. But once I did, it felt good. It's been a very long time since I laughed like that. You should try it some time."

He looked at her like she'd just grown an extra head. "You want me to laugh for no reason at all."

She shrugged. "Don't put it down until you've tried it."

He shook his head again. "It must be a woman thing."

Before they went their separate ways, Deacon asked for the fundraising plans. She ran upstairs and retrieved the papers. She was kind of hoping he'd follow her upstairs. His kisses were more addictive than the squares of chocolate with caramel centers that she enjoyed each night while reading.

She hurried back down the steps. "This is everything I have so far."

When she handed over the papers, their fingers touched. To her surprise, he didn't rush to pull away. Neither did she. Their gazes met and her heart careened into her throat.

Her gaze lowered to his mouth. She'd never been so tempted by anything in her life. What was it about this man that muddled her thoughts? It was as though he had some sort of magnetic force and anytime she was near him, she was drawn in.

And then he stepped back. "Thanks for these. I'll look them over tonight."

She choked down her disappointment. "Good. The sooner I jump on these plans, the better."

"Then how about a breakfast meeting?" When she didn't immediately respond, he asked, "You do eat breakfast, don't you?"

At last, she found her voice. "Yes, I do."

"Good. We'll discuss this in the morning." He gestured toward the papers. "Good night."

She stood there for a moment watching him retreat to the main house. What was wrong with her? She knew better than to fall for him. It was the ocean breeze and his deep voice that caused her to lose focus for just a few moments. She was fine now. Realizing that she shouldn't be standing around staring at Deacon like some besotted schoolgirl, she turned and headed up the steps.

Before it got much later, she needed to file her daily report with *QTR*. She carried her personal laptop to a chair on her private balcony and sat in one of the comfy chairs.

She opened the laptop and typed in her password. Once she had her email open, the words came pouring out of her.

Tonight we walked on the beach. It was like a scene right out of a movie, with the lull of the water in the background and the gentle breeze. It was amazing.

Beneath the moonlight, we kissed. I don't think my feet were touching the ground. His touch—it was amazing. I know that I shouldn't feel anything for him because of the accident, but the harder I fight it, the more attracted to him I become.

His kiss awakened a part of me that I'd forgotten about. There was a rush of emotions unlike anything I've ever experienced before. It's all so confusing. Maybe I'm just lonely. It has been over a year since I dated anyone. Work and caring for my father has consumed my life. When I leave here perhaps I need to revisit the dating scene and update my online profile. Because there's no way what I'm starting to feel for Deacon is real. It can't be!

She read back over what she'd written. What was she thinking? She could never tell anyone her most intimate thoughts—most especially a tell-all magazine. Talk about creating sensational headlines.

With a shake of her head, she highlighted it all. Then she pressed the delete key. But she still had to find something to write in her report.

And after what she'd learned today, she was beginning to suspect there was no story here. But she had promised that she would document the details relating to the accident. And she liked to keep her word. So she started to write out in as much detail as she could what little Deacon had told her about the night of the accident.

But with every word she typed, guilt weighed on her. How could she betray Deacon's trust? Even if now it was to help *clear* his name?

Her emotions warred within her. She knew how Deacon felt about the paparazzi and tabloids. He would consider what she was doing as an utter betrayal. Could she blame him?

She hadn't taken any of this into consideration when she'd agreed to this plan. Getting close to Deacon, gaining his trust, was changing everything. And now she was utterly confused. More than anything, she wanted to leave. Each day that passed, her confusion over where she stood with Deacon grew.

Gaby saved her report to the drafts folder. She wanted more time to consider her actions. In the meantime, she jotted a brief email stating that there was nothing new to report.

She closed her laptop and leaned back in her chair. Her presence on the estate had nothing to do with the accident and everything to do with protecting her father from prosecution. And so she would keep her word to

Deacon and stay until the fundraiser. And once it was a huge success, she could return to her life. A life without a brooding movie star with the ability to make her laugh and feel lighter than she had in years. Suddenly, returning to her prior life didn't sound so appealing. But life here on this Malibu estate wasn't reality. It was some sort of dream and soon she'd wake up—probably about the time the police report was released. And she worried about the steep fall back to earth.

CHAPTER TWELVE

MAYBE THIS HAD been a mistake.

Deacon sat across the table from Gabrielle. The table was done up with a light blue linen tablecloth. Fine china was laid out. The yellow napkins were folded into the shape of bow ties. A vase of yellow roses had been placed in the center. This was Mrs. Kupps's doing. The last time the table had been so fancy had been before the accident. These days, he ate at his desk with a tray of food. No flowers. No company.

What had he been thinking to invite Gabrielle to breakfast? Perhaps it was the fact that when she smiled, the whole world was that much brighter. And when they talked, she didn't hold back. She was filled with optimism. He gave himself a mental jerk. That line of thought could get him into trouble—big trouble. It was best to focus on the business at hand.

But that would be easier said than done with the table all decked out to impress Gabrielle. When he'd mentioned all the needless fuss to Mrs. Kupps, she'd clucked her tongue at him. She told him he needed to do everything he could not to run off Gabrielle, as she was the sunshine in his otherwise gloomy world. It was as if she was worried that he'd grow old alone. He was not some beggar, desperate for anyone's attention.

Is that what Gabrielle thought of him, too? Did she think that he was pathetic and deserving of her sympathy? He would show her. He did not need anyone's pity. He was not some charity case.

"You know this isn't going to work." His words came out terser than he'd intended.

Gabrielle glanced up from where she unfolded the yellow napkin and placed it on her lap. "Which part doesn't work?"

"All of it. Every single last piece of it." That wasn't exactly true, but he was in no mood to be generous. If they were adversaries, then perhaps she wouldn't feel obligated to be nice to him—to let him kiss her.

He watched her closely. He was waiting for her to leave. However, the only visible sign of her discomfort was in her eyes. They widened, but she didn't move. He knew a lot of people would have turned tail and fled by now. But not Gabrielle. She was made of sterner stuff. But he should have figured that when she'd volunteered to take her father's punishment.

She adjusted her napkin and at the same time avoided his gaze. When she glanced back up at him, she said, "I'm assuming you are referring to the fundraiser plans and not the meal."

"Of course."

She nodded. Then she set about removing the lid from the dish of scrambled eggs. She was going to eat? He was setting up for an argument and she was acting as though everything was perfectly fine. Everything wasn't fine.

He couldn't take her lack of reaction any longer. "Are you just going to sit there and ignore me?"

"I'm not ignoring you, but Mrs. Kupps went to a lot of work to prepare this meal and I think it'd be a shame to let it go to waste."

"You're hungry?"

She smiled at him. "Of course I am. I'm sure you'll feel better after you eat."

He wanted to disagree, but his gaze moved to her plate. The food did look good. "But what about the problems with the fundraiser?"

"They aren't going anywhere. We can deal with those later." She scooped up some bacon and added it to her plate. When he didn't move, she said, "Do you want some bacon?" When he didn't respond fast enough, she added, "If you don't hurry, there might not be any left. I love bacon."

He did, too. He held out his hand for her to pass the serving plate. She hesitated as though she weren't so sure she wanted to share, but in the end, she passed it to him.

It was really hard staying upset with her. She was either a very good actress, good enough to be in the movies with him, or she tried not to let things ruffle her. Either way, he was going to have to figure out a different way to deal with her. Because all his huffing and puffing didn't appear to deter her.

Gabrielle continued to fill her plate. "I can't believe Mrs. Kupps made us all of this food."

"She was more than happy to do it. For so long now, she's been begging me for things to do and I've been putting her off."

"I take it you don't have breakfast like this very often."

"No. Not at all. Not since, well, you know." He didn't want to bring up the accident. Not this morning. But since Gabrielle had entered his life, his appetite was back.

Gabrielle buttered her toast. "Well, I will make sure to tell Mrs. Kupps just how good this is."

"I'm sure she would love to hear it. I must admit that I've been lacking on the compliments lately."

"I'm sure she understands that you've been going through a lot."

When they'd finished their meal, which took much longer than he was accustomed to taking to eat, he found himself in a better frame of mind. He assured himself that it had nothing to do with what Gabrielle had said about him needing to eat, and more to do with the fact that he was right about this fundraiser and he would prove it to her.

Mrs. Kupps brought more coffee and then cleared the empty dishes. Both of them complimented Mrs. Kupps on the delicious food. The woman's cheeks grew rosy as she thanked them.

After Mrs. Kupps departed, Gabrielle turned to him. "Now, what were you saying about the fundraiser?"

"I don't think people are going to attend."

"Why would you think that? Are my plans that bad?"

He shook his head. "It isn't anything you've done." Surely he didn't have to spell this out for her. "I'm the problem."

"Oh." Her good mood seemed to have diminished a bit. She sat there and stared off at the shimmering ocean for a moment. When she turned to him again, she had a glint in her eye. "Actually, I think all of your notoriety will work to our advantage."

He had a feeling he wouldn't like where she was going with this line of thought. But it was too late, he'd already been drawn down the rabbit hole. "How's that?"

"You forget that in addition to the car accident, you also have a movie being released next month."

"What about it?"

"I couldn't sleep last night, so I turned on the television. And guess what I saw?"

He sighed. "I don't know, but I'm sure you're going to tell me."

"I saw the promo for your movie. Your name and face were all over the ad. Your movie sponsors aren't backing down from using your brand and you shouldn't, either."

If only people still thought he was that man. Now they all questioned him and his actions—including himself. "I'm not that man anymore."

"Which makes people all the more curious about you—"

"I'm not going to be some sort of freak show for them to come here and stare at."

"Relax." She reached across the table and placed her hand on his. "I promise you, it won't be like that. I believe that people will come out for the event. They will want to get behind a great cause because so many lives have been touched in one way or another by breast cancer."

When she put it that way, he felt guilty for making such a big deal about his circumstances. Some people had it much worse. "So you'll make sure to keep the emphasis of the event on the reason for it and not on the sponsor?"

"Um, yes." Worry clouded her eyes. "Does that mean you don't want to be mentioned at all?"

"That is what I'd hoped."

She worried her bottom lip but didn't respond.

"Go ahead and say it."

"It's just that without your name, I don't know how to make the event stand out."

He reminded himself that raising funds would help save other families from having to go through the pain, the uncertainty and, for some, the loss of a loved one, like he'd experienced. And when it came down to it, if using his name would help raise awareness of the event, didn't he owe that to his mother's memory?

"Okay. You can use my name, if you think it will help."

"I do." Gabrielle pulled out a legal pad from a colorful bag she had on the ground next to her chair. There were handwritten notes on the top sheet. It was a long list. It appeared they were going to be here a while. She sent him a sideways glance. "You aren't going to change your mind after we get this all started, are you?"

He knew once news of the fundraiser was out there that his world would get a lot smaller, with paparazzi hanging from trees and sneaking onto the property. It would be chaos and he'd want to back out. "No. I'll manage."

"Good." A smile eased the worry lines bracketing her beautiful face. "And I think they are really going to have a great time."

He filled his coffee cup, then added a dash of sugar. He'd forgotten how much he enjoyed sitting outside in the morning with the bright sunshine and the cool breeze. He could feel Gabrielle's gaze on him. She was anxious to hear his thoughts, but he didn't think that she'd like what he was about to say.

As he stirred the coffee, his gaze skimmed down over the printout that Gabrielle had given him the night before. She had certainly paid attention to details and made certain that there was plenty of entertainment.

He took a drink of the dark brew and then returned the cup to the saucer. "You do realize that you have so many events listed that it dilutes the entire event."

Gabrielle's eyebrows drew together. "But people need something to do."

"True. But not this many things. This is more like an amusement park than a fundraiser." Before she could argue with him, he intended to prove his point. "You have golfing, amusement rides, clowns, artists, dancing and games. That's a lot. A whole lot."

"But with each of those things, we can raise money."

"How much money are we talking? Really?"

She sighed and gazed down over the list of events. "What are you proposing?"

"That you narrow the list down to two or three things."

She frowned at him. Then she shook her head and looked away.

"What?"

Her gaze met his as she worried her bottom lip.

"Gabrielle, just spit it out." He wasn't good at guessing, especially where women were concerned.

"I was just wondering if it is the money. You know, if sponsoring the event is too much for you."

Oh, that was all. This was something he could deal with.

"It isn't the money." Though this fundraiser would cost a small fortune to pull together, he could handle it. He'd had a number of blockbuster movies and he'd carefully invested the money. When her gaze told him that she still wasn't reassured, he said, "I promise. I'm good financially."

His main concern was for Gabrielle. She had invested herself completely in making this fundraiser a huge success. She had her hopes so high that when it all fell apart, she would have a long way to tumble.

In the short time he'd gotten to know her, he'd learned that she had a big heart—big enough to even care about his welfare, which was more than he'd ever expected. He didn't want her to get hurt because of him and his now tarnished reputation.

"That's good to hear." There was a catch in her voice

as though there were something more she wanted to say, but she decided to refrain.

"You know it's not too late to pull out—"

"No. I really want to do this."

He knew what she meant. She was anxious to get away from him. And he couldn't blame her. She blamed him for what had happened to her aunt. And as much as he wanted to deny it, he couldn't. He didn't know. And his nightmares only confused him even more.

He thought about just calling off the deal. But he knew Gabrielle would take it personally. She had a lot of pride and would think he didn't believe in her ability to pull it all together. He didn't want to do anything else to hurt her. So he would do what he could to help Gabrielle— even at the expense of his privacy.

Deacon cleared his throat. "The events should either be big draws in order to up the ticket price or garner large donations once the guests are in attendance." And he had another observation. "Perhaps keep this an adults-only event. Without children around, people will relax and perhaps they'll be willing to spend more freely."

"That's the exact opposite of how I ran my fundraisers for the library. I did a lot of activities to draw in the kids and by extension their parents." She frowned. "I suppose you're going to want to remove all of the fun events."

He really did hate to disappoint her, but he'd been around these affairs many times in the past. And he knew a lot of the big fish she was hoping to hook would appreciate something more low-key.

"Trust me." He knew that was a poor choice of words where she was concerned, but they were already out there and he couldn't undo them. So he kept going with the point he wanted to make. "I do know what I'm talking about."

"But it'll be boring."

He had to admit some of the charity events he'd attended were boring, but he didn't want to tell her that. He knew Gabrielle would use any excuse to keep her current lengthy list of events.

"Ah… I see. I'm right." Her face lit up.

"What are you talking about?"

"The look you just made when I said that it would be boring. You couldn't deny it."

"I was thinking is all."

"Uh-huh. What if we compromise?"

Oh, no. He had a bad feeling about this. His experience of compromising with a female in his private life consisted of him giving up on what he wanted, so the woman wouldn't be mad at him any longer.

With great trepidation, he asked, "What sort of compromise?"

And so they started with the first activity on the list—dart toss. They discussed it and the type of atmosphere they'd like to present to the people. In the end, it was cut in an effort to make the fundraiser more sophisticated.

After they made it through a quarter of the list and had nixed all but one item, Gabrielle said, "Okay. So we should stick to just a handful of entertainments."

"Or even less. For the most part, the affluent people you'll be inviting will want to be seen." He explained a little more of his understanding of the elite of Hollywood.

Gabrielle nodded. "Okay. I can work with this."

"Now, what were you considering for the main focus of the event?"

She took a moment, as though considering everything he'd told her. "I think we should make it a golfing event. Lots of people golf, both men and women. And you do have an amazing golf course."

"How would you know? It's a mess."

"Mrs. Kupps showed me some pictures. The course needs some TLC, but I talked to your head groundskeeper. He said that with the help of the entire grounds crew, they could pull it together. They might have to bring in some turf, but it is possible to have it together in time."

He arched an eyebrow at her. "You really have worked hard on this."

"I saw an opportunity and I took it. This fundraiser will be great—if you'll agree to it."

His gut told him not to do it. But he saw the gleam of hope in Gabrielle's eyes. He just didn't have it in him to turn her down. What would it hurt to get this place cleaned up? He wasn't even sure if he wanted to live here any longer. It would have to be restored if he were to put it up for sale. So he would let Gabrielle move ahead with her plans and when no one bought the tickets, he would still abide by their agreement. Once the planning was over, he would let her go back to her life.

He told her to take what they'd discussed and refine her list. Include a few more details and they'd go over it tomorrow. And then he would give her his decision about whether they should move forward with it or not.

He had a gut feeling that he'd dug himself a hole. Gabrielle had a determined look in her eye that said she would never give up on the fundraiser. And he was going to have to find a way to be okay with all those people being here on his estate.

Unless…no one bought a ticket or showed up. But then Gabrielle would be crushed and he would be to blame. Either way he would be in trouble.

CHAPTER THIRTEEN

THE PLANS WERE coming together.

Later that afternoon, Gaby straightened her desk. It had been a very productive day. She recalled her breakfast with Deacon. He hadn't been very congenial at first, but once he realized she wasn't going to give up, he became helpful.

And though she hated to admit it, he was right. This event needed a different vibe than the events she'd planned at the library. This was his world and he knew these people, so she'd follow his lead.

It may not be the type of event she was used to planning, but she would work to make it perfect. People would come. They would enjoy themselves, and they would donate to a worthy cause.

By five o'clock she'd also finished reading the screenplay Deacon had given her. She'd made a list of pros and cons and sent it to him in an email. With her tasks done for the day, she shut down the computer and then made her way to the guesthouse.

She brought the fundraising plans with her. She was too excited to stop now. The plans were coming together really well and instead of this event being her get-out-of-jail-free card, it was turning into an event she believed in and wanted to see succeed.

Mrs. Kupps had placed some dinner in the fridge with a note for reheating it. Gaby smiled. The woman was the absolute sweetest. She wondered if Deacon knew how lucky he was to have someone so kind and thoughtful in his life.

Gaby settled at the table with her laptop, a legal pad and all the notes she'd taken during her talk with Deacon. She didn't know how much time had passed when there was a knock at the door.

She couldn't imagine who it might be. Mrs. Kupps had left long ago. And no one could get access to the private estate.

Gaby ran a hand over her hair and a finger around her mouth, making sure there weren't any crumbs from the chocolate chip cookies that Mrs. Kupps had left her. And she rushed to the door. Gaby peered through the peephole and was shocked to find Deacon.

What was he doing here?

Her heart started beating faster. She glanced down at her white shorts and old Support Your Library tank top. Not exactly the most attractive outfit, but it'd have to do.

She swung the door open. "Hi."

Deacon looked uncomfortable as he shifted his weight from one foot to the other. "Never mind. I shouldn't have bothered you."

"It's fine. Do you want to come in?"

He shook his head. "I saw your light on and figured you couldn't sleep, either."

Either? As in he didn't sleep at night? Interesting. "I was going over more plans for the fundraiser."

"At this hour?"

"You gave me until tomorrow to come up with a revised plan."

"I did, didn't I?" When she nodded, he frowned. "If you need more time, it's not a problem."

"Actually, I'm just about finished. Tomorrow works fine to go over the agenda." She was certain that wasn't why he stopped over. "What did you need?"

He glanced down. There was a book in his hand. When his gaze rose and met hers, there was uncertainty in his eyes. "It was nothing."

"Obviously it was something or you wouldn't be here. Are you sure you don't want to come inside?"

He shook his head. "I—I just finished reading this new book and thought you might enjoy it."

The fact he'd thought of her and wanted to share something personal filled her chest with a warm sensation. A smile lifted her lips.

She held out her hand. "What type of book is it?"

He handed it over. "It's a suspense book. But I'm sure you have other books you're already reading."

"Actually, I just finished one last night. So you have perfect timing."

"I do?"

She couldn't help but smile at his awkwardness. When it came to business, he was very sure of himself. But here, with it just being the two of them, he was nervous. And that bit of knowledge chipped away at the wall she'd erected to keep him out of her heart.

He shifted his weight from one foot to the other. "Usually I can figure out what's going to happen in the end, but this book kept me guessing until the last page."

She turned over the book and quickly read the blurb. "It sounds intriguing. I can't wait to read it. Thank you."

"I, uh, should be going." And with that he walked away.

As Gaby closed the door, she was struck by the gesture. It was so small and yet, it said so much about the man. The fact that he liked to read checked off a big box for Gaby—not that she was looking at him as a prospective boyfriend. But the fact that he used his mind for more than just work meant a lot.

And what meant even more was that he was thoughtful. The more she got to know him, the less he seemed like the monster that others had made him out to be after the accident. It was getting harder and harder to view him as the enemy.

"Okay. You have yourself a fundraiser," Deacon said the next day after going over her revised plans for the event in his office.

"I do?" Gabrielle smiled.

He tried to ignore the way her smile warmed his insides. *Focus on the fundraiser.* He cleared his throat. "Do you have a name for it?"

"Actually, I've given this a lot of thought. And you can change it, but how about the Diana Pink-Rose Tournament?"

The title that Gabrielle had chosen couldn't have been more perfect. His mother's name. She would have loved it. He was touched that Gabrielle had included her name in it. A lump of emotion swelled in his throat and for a moment he didn't trust himself to speak.

Misinterpreting his silence, Gabrielle said, "If you don't like it, I could work on some other titles."

He shook his head and swallowed hard. He wasn't the type to let himself get emotional, but Gabrielle was the first person to do something so kind and thoughtful in honor of his mother. She probably didn't even know how much it meant to him and perhaps it was better that way.

It's too bad the fundraiser would never become a reality. He thought it would definitely have been a great event.

His gaze met hers. "It's perfect. Thank you. What made you choose the pink rose for the title?"

She shrugged. "I guess because pink is the color of breast-cancer campaigns."

"Do you know what else pink rose means?"

She shook her head.

"Then come with me." He led her down to the rose garden, where he'd purposely planted a rosebush in every color that he could track down. As they made their way down the steps in the back of the house, he said, "My mother loved roses. And so I made a point of buying as many colors as I could find. I loved watching her face light up with every color that was added to the garden."

"That was very sweet of you. She was lucky to have you."

"No. I was the lucky one." And he meant every word of it. His mother had loved him even when he hadn't made the wisest choices. And she cheered him on when he reached for the stars. "I couldn't have asked for a better mother."

When they stood in the rose garden, Gabrielle's eyes searched his. "What are we doing here?"

"Did you know that each rose has a meaning?"

"I know that red roses mean love. But that's all."

"Ah, but not any love—true love. I'm sure you must get them all of the time."

"I must admit that I've never received any."

The fact that no man had given her roses really surprised him. Gabrielle was so beautiful. Her beauty started on the inside and radiated outward. He'd like to be the first to present her with one. "You should have roses and daily."

Color filled her cheeks. How was it possible that she grew more beautiful each time he saw her? His heart picked up its pace. He couldn't help but stare. He never got enough of looking at her. Was it possible for her to look even more radiant?

It was with great effort that he turned away. He walked down the brick path and stopped next to a white rose. "This one is the traditional rose of weddings. And it represents purity and virtue."

"How do you know all of this?"

"Each time I ordered a new rose, I would do my research. Roses are quite intertwined in history. I would distract my mother from her discomforts with stories that included the various roses."

Gabrielle gazed at him but didn't say anything. Yet there was a look on her face and he couldn't read it.

"What?"

"It's just that you continually surprise me."

"You mean you thought I was nothing but a conceited partygoer."

"Um, no. I don't know why you think that. It's just that I don't know any men who know so much about flowers."

His body tensed. It was even worse than he'd thought. "You think I'm a wimp—"

"No. Not at all. I think what you do here is wonderful." There was sincerity in her voice. She continued down the walk and stopped in front of a pink rosebush. "And how about these? What do they mean?"

"The dark pink petals mean gratitude and appreciation." He moved to a neighboring light pink rose. "And this one means sympathy."

He continued walking through the garden. When he came across his gardening supplies, he grabbed a pair of shears. He moved to some long-stemmed yellow roses. He searched for a perfect bloom and then cut it. He turned and presented it to Gabrielle.

A bright smile lit up her face. "Thank you." She lifted it to her nose and inhaled. "What does it mean?"

"Friendship."

She sniffed the petals again. "Is that what we have here?"

He hadn't tried to define what was going on between them until now. It was more complicated than friendship, but that title was safe and easy, so he went with it. "That's what I'd like to think."

Her eyes reflected her approval. "Me, too."

She'd slept in!

The next morning, Gabrielle awoke with a start. It was Deacon's fault that she'd been awake until the wee hours of the morning. He'd loaned her that book and it was good—no, it was great. She raced through her bedroom, trying to get ready for work as fast as she could. It wasn't that Deacon would be standing there by the office door waiting for her to arrive. It was more a matter of how much she wanted to accomplish that day.

She opened the door of the guesthouse and found a bud vase with a single yellow rose. She glanced around for Deacon, but he was nowhere to be seen. What had happened to the man who used to growl at her? She knew where she stood with his former self, but with this new version of Deacon, she was constantly losing her footing.

Deacon wasn't all good or all bad—he was both, but she was quickly learning that there was a lot more good in him than bad. She picked up the rose and lifted it to her nose. Its perfume was gentle but delightful. She'd never smell another rose without thinking of him.

She loved that each color of rose had a meaning. What

impressed her more was that Deacon had learned the meanings in order to delight his mother.

As she carried the flower into the guesthouse to find just the perfect spot for it, her aunt's words came back to her: *if you find a man that is good to his mother, he will also be good to you.* Gaby had only been a know-it-all teenager when her aunt had given her these sage pieces of advice, but somehow they'd stuck. Someday, some woman was going to be very lucky to have Deacon by her side.

But it wasn't going to be her.

Even if she were drawn to him, the cards were stacked against them. There was just too much baggage between them. Relationships were hard enough under normal circumstances, but theirs was outside the bounds of normal.

As she tried to dismiss the profound meaning of Deacon making this gesture, she recalled what he'd said about yellow roses: *they meant friendship.*

Did that mean he considered her a true friend? The acknowledgment stirred a rush of emotions. She tried to tamp down her reaction, but her heart refused to slow. She once again breathed in the flower's gentle perfume.

The fact that it wasn't her birthday and it wasn't a holiday made this gesture all that much more special. He'd done it just because he could. This was the most thoughtful thing a man had ever done for her.

She knew then and there that she was in trouble. Deacon was working his way through all the barriers she'd built around her heart. Why did it have to be him that got to her? He was the absolute last person she should be interested in and yet, he was the one that kept her awake at night. And when she did fall asleep, he was the one that filled her dreams.

She was still puzzling over what to do about her feelings for Deacon when he materialized in the doorway of the office. He looked quite handsome. The dark circles under his eyes were fading and when he smiled, it eased the worry lines bracketing his eyes.

"I hope you had a good night," he said.

Gaby yawned. She didn't know if there was enough coffee in the world to keep her awake today. "Morning."

His eyebrows gathered. "Don't tell me you were working all night."

"No. I was reading." She recalled the book, so she grabbed it from her purse and handed it to him. "Thank you. It was just as good as you said it would be. It had me guessing right up until the last chapter."

He accepted the book. "I'm glad. But you didn't have to read it so quickly."

"Yes, I did. Once I started reading, I had to keep going. It's the way I am when I get into a book."

When he nodded in understanding, their gazes met and held longer than necessary, and her heart began racing. Her stomach shivered with nerves. She'd never had a problem speaking with anyone until now. When she glanced away from him, her gaze skimmed over the yellow rose. "Thank you for the rose. It's beautiful."

"I'm glad you like it." He stepped back and leaned against the desk opposite hers. "I've been thinking that you have everything pretty much planned out for the event except for the menu."

"I guess I need to do that sooner rather than later so I can give the caterer the menu." She pulled out a pad of paper. "Do you have a preference for the format? Sitdown? Buffet? Finger foods?"

He paused as though giving each option due consideration. "This is going to be more of a garden party than anything else, correct?"

Gaby wouldn't exactly classify the event that way, but for the lack of a better term, she went with it. "Sure." Following his line of thought, she said, "So the finger foods might be best." When Deacon nodded, she added, "And we could have the wait staff mingle with trays."

"Sure, sounds good."

There was one more thing that she'd thought of. She didn't know how Deacon would feel about it since he was in favor of streamlining the event. But she thought that it would add a bit of fun to the event and it could be a big revenue raiser during the afternoon.

"I've been going over the plans and I think there's one more thing we should do."

Deacon's face grew serious. "What would that be?"

"A Chinese auction."

"No."

She frowned at him. "How can you just readily dismiss the idea?"

"Because the basis of the Chinese auction is to ask others to donate items or services. I don't want to ask anyone for anything."

She dropped the pen to the desk and lifted her chin. "Maybe that's your problem."

"What's that supposed to mean?"

"It means that you're trying to get through this difficult part of your life by yourself—by putting a wall up between you and everyone else."

He arched a dark eyebrow. "I let you in."

"No, you didn't. I made my own way past your walls in spite of you."

"This is my life, my choices—not yours."

She glared at him. "And this is my fundraiser and I'm telling you that there will be a Chinese auction."

His voice lowered and rumbled with agitation. "Are you always so stubborn?"

"My father says so, but I don't believe everything he says." She no longer believed what he said about Deacon.

"And you're going ahead with this auction no matter what I say?"

"Yes."

"Then I won't waste any more time trying to talk you out of it." He muttered under his breath as he strode out the door.

Something told Gaby that he regretted giving her that flower. But she wasn't backing down. That was Deacon's problem. When he growled, everyone backed away. He needed to learn that life was about give and take.

CHAPTER FOURTEEN

THERE WAS SOMETHING different about Gabrielle.

Something not quite right.

Deacon had kept his distance from her since their disagreement last week. He didn't know exactly why he'd taken such a strong opposition to her idea of the Chinese auction. It wasn't a terrible idea. He could think of much worse.

He was left with no choice but to admit the truth to himself. He'd created the disagreement on purpose to put some distance between them. And it was all because of that rose and the other ones he continued to leave at her door each morning.

He had mixed emotions about leaving her yellow roses. Part of him said that it was just a friendly gesture, but another part of him wanted them to mean more. And that made him uncomfortable.

Logic said that there was a fifty-fifty chance he was responsible for the car accident. If he were responsible, Gabrielle wouldn't want anything to do with him. But even if he were found innocent, would that really do much to change their circumstances? He was still the other party in a two-party accident.

But when he was outside in the rose garden, he would catch glimpses of Gabrielle. And when she didn't think he was watching, the smile vanished from her face. A glint of worry reflected in her eyes. Was it his fault? Had he upset her that much?

This time he didn't need to hear her aunt's voice in his head to know he needed to somehow fix things. Mrs. Kupps was right about Gabrielle being a ray of sunshine in his otherwise gloomy life. And when her light was dimmed, the darkness and shadows were too much for him.

He approached Gabrielle where she was sitting on the patio. She had pen and paper in hand, but she wasn't looking at either. Instead she was staring out over the ocean with a faraway look in her eyes.

"Mind if I join you?" He stopped next to the table.

She blinked and turned to him. "I don't mind, if you don't."

It wasn't exactly the invitation he'd been hoping for, but he sat down anyway. "Something is bothering you. I'd like you to tell me what it is."

She shook her head. "I'm fine."

"No. You're not. You haven't been happy in a while."

She sighed. "I didn't know that it was that obvious."

"Maybe not to others, but I've gotten to know you pretty well and I know when you have something on your mind. Is it the fundraiser? Are you worried—"

"No. It's not that. Things are going well. In fact, I'm already getting RSVPs to the digital invitations."

Frankly, that was quite a surprise to him. He'd assumed the event would be a failure. Actually, he'd been counting on it. The thought of opening his home to all those people was not something he relished, but it was a problem he'd deal with later. Right now, he was concerned about Gabrielle.

"If it's not the fundraiser, what it is? Maybe I can help."

Her tentative gaze met his. "It's my father."

"Your father? I don't understand. Did something happen?"

"No. At least not that I know of."

He should probably leave it there. It wasn't like he was friends with her father. But the sadness on her face had him searching for the truth. "Then what is it?"

"We've just never been apart for this long. It's always been just the two of us against the world."

Deacon hadn't expected this. "But isn't it nice not to be responsible for caring for him on a daily basis?"

She shrugged. "It never really bothered me. Maybe it should have. I guess I like being needed."

She did? "You mean you don't mind taking care of your father even to the extent of you not having a life of your own?"

"Is that what you think?"

"Well, when was the last time you had a date?"

She glanced away. "It's been a while."

"And when was the last time you did anything with your friends?"

"Lindsay and I went to the movies the other month."

"Other month? That sure doesn't sound like a busy social calendar."

"Why do I need a busy social calendar? So what if I don't have time to hang out. I have two jobs to hold down. And the cleaning and shopping to do." She paused as though she realized that she'd said too much. And then she frowned at him as though he was now the one in trouble.

He drove home his point with one final comment. "Maybe you take on too much."

"I do what I need to do."

There was no talking to her. She obviously couldn't see that she did so much for others that there wasn't any time left for her. He felt bad for her, but his persistence on this subject was only upsetting her more. "I didn't mean to upset you."

She sighed. "It's not you. I'm just frustrated. I'm not sure my father is taking proper care of himself."

This was Deacon's chance to pay her back for all the generous things she'd done for him. And he knew exactly what he must do.

When he looked at Gabrielle, he knew he didn't have any other choice. "Go to your father."

Her head jerked around until her puzzled gaze met his. "But our agreement—"

"I know about our agreement and I don't care. I won't stop you. Go to your father. Make sure he's okay."

"Really?" Immediately her face lit up. "You don't mind?"

"No." He was lying.

He knew that once she passed beyond the estate gates that she would not return. Why should she? She had a life that had nothing to do with him. She had a father that loved her. Friends to do things with. She had a full life.

And what did he have to offer her? He struggled to come up with any reason for her to return. The memory of their kisses passed through his mind. But he knew that had been a fleeting thing—a moment of pity on her part for a man who looked and sounded like some sort of beast.

"Do you mind if I go now?" She looked radiant, like Dorothy about to click her red heels.

He, however, didn't feel like the Wizard. "No. Go."

She ran over to him and hugged him. The moment passed much too quickly and then she pulled back.

He refused to let her see how much her departure bothered him.

Without another word, Gabrielle rushed away. He wasn't even sure that her feet touched the ground, she was so happy to get away from there. How could he take that happiness away from her? He sighed in resignation.

He was happy for her, but he was sad for himself. He just couldn't believe in the short amount of time that they'd been together that she'd come to mean so much to him.

And now he was on his own again.

CHAPTER FIFTEEN

It HAD BEEN a lovely visit.

The weekend had flown by. It had been so good to see her father. The time with him had been exactly what she'd needed. And best of all, Newton had been out of the house. Everything had gone smoothly so long as she stayed away from the subject of Deacon.

She'd tried a couple of times to let her father know that Deacon was treating her really well, but her father hadn't wanted to hear any of it. All he'd wanted to hear regarding Deacon was if she'd gained any information to help move along the legal process. He was still convinced that Deacon had paid off people to bury the accident report. In the end, Gaby had given up because she didn't want to spend the short amount of time she had with her father arguing. Though she didn't believe Deacon was a monster, she couldn't confidently claim his innocence, either. They still didn't know exactly what had happened in the accident. To say she was confused was putting it mildly.

While she was home, she'd cooked for her father. She'd spent quite a bit of time in the kitchen preparing healthy meals. By the time she left, the fridge was full. The freezer was stuffed with meals that just needed reheating. And her father's prescriptions were refilled.

Her father begged her not to return to Deacon's estate, saying that he could take whatever punishment the judge was likely to throw at him. But Gaby told him this was about more than just him. She was doing important work with the fundraiser and she needed to see it through until the end. And that soon she would be back home. With a hug and a kiss, she'd left for the long drive back to Malibu, knowing her father was doing quite well on his own. Perhaps she did fuss over him more than necessary.

Thanks to Deacon, both she and her father were finding that they didn't need each other quite so much. When her time was over at the estate perhaps she could stick her foot back in the dating pool. But as soon as she thought of dating, Deacon's image came to mind.

She tried to imagine him with his hair cut and his face shaved. He'd look like a whole new man and perhaps he'd feel like one, too. Maybe it was time to see how he felt about a makeover.

Monday morning, she opened the door to the guesthouse of Deacon's estate and paused to look around. After waking up for the past week to find a yellow rose at her door, today there was none. It saddened her, but she knew eventually they had to stop. Still, she'd come to look forward to them. And now she tried not to read in too much to their absence.

It wasn't until later that morning, with a check in hand for his signature, that she went in search of him. At that hour of the morning, Deacon was usually tending to the roses. But when she went to the garden, there was no sign of him and it didn't look as though he'd been there that morning. That was odd.

She went to his office, thinking he was working on an important project, but the office was empty and the lights were off. Concern started pumping through her veins.

In the kitchen, she tracked down Mrs. Kupps. "Do you

know where Deacon is?" The woman nodded, but her face said that something was definitely amiss. "You're worrying me. Where is he?"

"He's closed in his rooms."

"His rooms. But why?"

"I don't know. He hasn't said a word to me." Mrs. Kupps shrugged. "He went in there after you left and he hasn't come out. I'm worried about him."

Gaby recalled their last conversation. She thought things had been fine between them, but then she recalled how Deacon had been eager for her to go visit her father. She'd missed her father so much at the time that she hadn't paid much attention to Deacon's reaction, but looking back on things, she should have realized something was off with him.

"Leave it to me. I'm used to dealing with stubborn males."

A weak smile lifted the worry lines on the woman's face. "I knew as soon as I laid eyes on you that you would be the ray of sunshine this house needed. I was just preparing him a late breakfast. You could take it to him, if you like."

"Thank you. I would."

Mrs. Kupps put together a tray of eggs, bacon, toast, fruit and juice. When she handed it over, she said, "Good luck."

"Thank you. I'll need it."

Remembering the day that Deacon had taken her to his room to clean her wounds from falling in the rose garden, Gaby made her way upstairs. The tall double doors were closed, but that wasn't going to stop her.

She leveled her shoulders and then gave a quick knock. Without waiting, she opened the door. She was surprised to find the room so dark. She squinted into the shadows, looking for him.

"Go away!" His deep voice rumbled through the room.

It seemed that he'd regressed. "Your growl isn't going to scare me."

Suddenly he was standing in front of her. Frown lines were deeply etched upon his face. "You're back?" He seemed surprised.

"Of course."

His face quickly returned to its frown. "Well, since you aren't going to leave until you've had your say, get it over with. Quickly."

"I hear that you've been in your room since I left. What's the matter? Are you sick?"

"No."

"Something must be the matter." Now that her eyes had adjusted to the low lighting, she moved to a table and placed the tray. "You have things to do. There's no time for slacking."

"I'm not slacking." Again his voice rumbled. "Now go away. Shouldn't you be with your father?"

So *that's* what was bothering him? She worked to subdue a smile. He had missed her. Who'd have guessed that? In truth, she'd missed him, too. But she wasn't ready to admit it.

She moved past him with sure, steady steps. At the window, she stopped and threw open the heavy drapes, letting the bright morning sun into the room. She turned to find Deacon squinting and trying to block the sun's rays with his hand.

"Close that."

"And let you sit in here in the dark? I don't think so."

He grunted his displeasure. "I'm your boss. You're supposed to do what I say."

"I'm your friend, remember? And I'm doing what's best for you."

"No, you came back because your father probably kicked you out for working here. I bet you don't listen to him any better than you do me."

"When both of you make poor choices, I don't mind calling either of you out on them."

Deacon frowned at her. "I didn't make a poor choice."

"You mean sitting around in the dark is your way of being productive?"

He opened his mouth and just as quickly closed it again. He sighed and glanced away. "If you're going to stay here, shouldn't you be in your office doing some work instead of harassing me?"

"I will just as soon as you start eating that delicious meal Mrs. Kupps prepared for you." He looked at her but he didn't move. She crossed her arms and tapped her foot. "I have all day."

With a look of resignation, he moved to the small table and sat down. "You are certainly something."

"I'll take that as a compliment."

He took a bite of egg. It was followed by a half a slice of toast. Partway through his meal, he stopped and looked at her. "Why do you care?"

"Because you apparently need someone to care about you. You don't seem to do a very good job of it on your own."

"How am I supposed to, when I know what I've done?" The worry and stress lines etched his handsome face.

"I thought you said you didn't remember the accident?"

He let out a heavy breath, causing her heart to lodge in her throat. Did he know more than he'd told her? Had the police report been released? Her mind rapidly searched for the reason for his despair.

"Talk to me," she prompted, needing him to tell her that the worst hadn't happened.

"The nightmares are getting worse. It's hard to tell the truth from the products of my imagination."

"And…" She waved her hands as though trying to pull the information from him.

"And I remember bits and pieces, like the fire burning my skin. I remember your aunt. I remember her saying 'Take care of Gabrielle.'"

"What? She did?" When he nodded, she asked, "Is that why you gave me this job?"

His gaze met hers. "Yes."

Gaby had been right about him. Deacon was a good man—buried beneath a mountain of unnecessary guilt. Her aunt's words were the proof of his innocence that she needed.

"Why are you smiling?" His dark eyes searched hers.

"Don't you understand? You're innocent."

His eyebrows drew together and his forehead wrinkled. "Why would you say that?"

"Because if you were guilty, my aunt never would have asked you to reach out to me and take care of me—not that I need you to." Gaby smiled at him, feeling as though a huge weight had been lifted. When he didn't look convinced, she asked, "What's wrong?"

Deacon rubbed the back of his neck. "Your theory is not proof—not legally."

"It's enough for me. It'll all work out. You'll see." There was one more thing bothering her. "But if you really wanted to fulfill her wishes, instead of having me work here, you could have just offered me money or something, but you didn't. Why?"

Deacon hesitated. "When you went on and on about how you cared for your father after telling me that he could take care of himself, I wanted you to know that you could have a life of your own and you didn't have to sacrifice everything for him."

"It was more than that and you know it."

"Perhaps."

"Perhaps nothing. You wanted to separate me from my father in order to punish him for the pain he caused you."

Deacon's gaze lowered and he nodded. "Yes, I did. I suppose that makes me a bad person."

"No. It just makes you human." She eyed him as he returned to eating. "Speaking of making you more human. What would you say to a haircut and shave?"

"I don't think that's a good idea."

She wasn't going to let him wiggle out of this. He'd been hiding behind all of that hair long enough. "Really? You like having your hair hang in your eyes?"

"No, but it's better than seeing what's beneath it."

So he was worried about the scars. He couldn't hide from them forever. Maybe facing up to them would be his first step back to the life he'd left behind after the accident.

She stepped closer to him. "I'd like to see you. The real you beneath all of that hair."

He looked at her as though gauging her interest. "And what if I'm a scary mess?"

"I'll still think you're handsome." Now where had that come from? She couldn't believe she'd uttered those words, even if it was the truth.

His eyes widened with surprise. "Really? You're not just saying that because you pity me? Which is ridiculous considering I lived and your aunt didn't. Listen to me. I just keep rambling…"

She kneeled down next to him. With her hands, she smoothed his hair back from his face. "There you are. Yes, you're definitely the most handsome man I know."

There she went again, saying the first thing that popped into her mind. But this time, when Deacon reached up and wrapped his hand around her wrist, she didn't regret speaking the truth.

"Okay. I'll do it," he said, "as long as *you* do the haircut and shave."

That wasn't exactly what she'd imagined when she'd proposed the idea. Still, if he was willing to take this big step with her, who was she to deny him?

CHAPTER SIXTEEN

HER HEART POUNDED in her chest.

After gathering the supplies she needed, Gabrielle stood there in Deacon's bathroom holding a razor.

What if she messed up? She wasn't a barber or a hairdresser. Sure she could trim her own bangs when her hairstyle dictated. But there was a big difference between trimming bangs and trimming a man's entire head, on top of giving him a shave.

But with his dominant hand still not working well enough for him to manage a razor, what choice did she have?

Call a professional? The idea was so appealing and yet, she knew that it was an impossibility. Deacon was so certain that beneath all of that hair that he was a monster. And this was her one chance to prove him wrong.

The truth was she didn't know what she'd find beneath his beard. She prayed that in his mind, he'd made the scars much worse than they were in reality. No matter what he looked like, she had to let him know that he wasn't some sort of beast.

The fact that he trusted her enough to allow her to shave and trim him wasn't lost on her. They had come a very long way since she'd started working at the estate. She remembered how awkward it felt working in that office, knowing that he was on the other side of a locked door.

But at the time, she hadn't understood that he had such significant injuries from the accident. That certainly wasn't how the accident was portrayed in the news. In fact, she was beginning to think that nothing in the media was as it seemed.

"Did you change your mind about revealing the real me?"

Deacon's voice jarred her out of her thoughts. "No. Of course not. I'm just trying to decide if I should start with your hair or your beard."

"The hair. That way after you're done shaving me, I can jump in the shower."

"You're sure about this?" She had to hear his answer one more time.

"I am." He studied her for a moment. "If you are."

"I am." She sucked in a calming breath. It didn't work, but she focused on the task at hand instead of her lack of experience.

Trading the razor for a pair of scissors, she set to work. She drew on her memories from her own haircuts and her experience trimming her dad's hair when he was in rehab. Gaby took her time, not wanting to mess up. She knew there was a lot riding on this particular haircut.

Her stomach was a nervous, jittery ball of nerves. Lucky for her, her hands remained steady. A cut here. A cut there. The trimmed locks of hair piled up on the floor. And all the while, Deacon remained quiet.

She walked around his chair, checking for any uneven spots. There was one by his left ear. With great care, she trimmed it.

And in the end, he retained both ears, and no blood

was shed. It wasn't the most stylish haircut, but considering his hair before, it was a large improvement.

Deacon lifted a hand and ran it over the short strands. "Do you want to look in the mirror?"

"I don't have any mirrors. I got rid of them."

"But I have one." She held up a hand mirror.

He turned away and shook his head. "I'll see it when you're all done."

After the trimmings were swept aside, she grabbed a comb and the scissors. Then she set to work trimming his beard as short as she could. She'd never trimmed a man's beard before. Sure, she'd shaved her father when he'd been in the hospital but his stubble was nothing compared to Deacon's full-on beard.

But what got to her more was being this close to him. There was something special about him. It was more than him being a famous movie star. It was an air of strength and power that exuded from him. And she was feeling herself being drawn closer and closer to him.

She'd never experienced such an intense attraction and it scared her. Not the part about her father or the accident. No—it was the fact that she didn't know how she was going to return to a world without Deacon's reluctant grin, or seeing the way his eyes twinkled when he was happy.

As the fundraiser grew closer, her time with Deacon was running out. She wanted this time to count. If all she had left when this was over were the memories, then she wanted them to be earth-shattering, pulse-quickening memories.

Deacon didn't know how much time had passed.

His eyes were closed as he focused on Gabrielle's gentle touch. He didn't know that a haircut and shave could be so tantalizing. Thank goodness she didn't attempt to make small talk because he wasn't sure he'd be able to follow along.

Each time her fingertips brushed over his skin, it short-circuited his thoughts. And each time her body brushed up against him, he longed to reach out and pull her onto his lap. He ached to press his mouth to hers. He smothered a groan.

"Are you okay?" Gabrielle paused.

He opened his eyes to find her staring directly at him. "Um, yes."

"You're sure?"

She'd heard him moan? He smothered a curse. He thought that he'd caught himself. Deciding it was best that he change the subject, he asked, "How's it going?"

"Before I go any further, I need to soften your beard." She turned on the water.

He couldn't see, but he could imagine Gabrielle letting the water get hot and steamy. And the next thing he knew, she was draping a hot towel over his jaw. The heat gave him a bit of a start, but he soon adjusted to it.

All the while, he was tempted to ask for her mirror just to make sure his hair wasn't an utter mess, but then he decided at this point, it didn't matter. If worse came to worse, he'd shave his entire head. At one point in his life, his hair had only been touched by the finest stylist in the movie business, but that felt like a lifetime ago. These days his hair didn't matter to anyone.

Gabrielle moved in front of him. "I have to admit I've only ever shaved my father when he was in the hospital."

"Don't worry. I trust you." It wasn't until the words crossed his lips that he realized what he'd uttered. He would retract the words if he could. But now they were out there. They filled the room with silence as the heavy impact settled in.

Gabrielle immediately turned away so he was unable to read the emotions filtering through her expressive eyes. When she turned back, she removed the hot towel from his jaw.

He didn't know why he'd said such a thing. That wasn't exactly the truth. He knew. He just didn't want to admit it to himself or to anyone else.

He was a man who prided himself on relying on no one. He told himself during all these months of solitude that he was fine on his own because he couldn't trust anyone else in his life. And then Gabrielle burst into his world and little by little she'd chipped away at the crusty shell that he'd armed himself with. And now he was starting to care about her. He didn't know what to do with these feelings.

But it was getting difficult to ignore his body's strong reaction to her with her fussing all about him. And when she stood in front of him to shave him, he had to close his eyes to keep from staring at the most tantalizing view of her firm breasts. But it was too late. The image of her curves straining against the thin cotton top when she leaned toward him was permanently tattooed upon his mind.

Think of something else—anything else.

He didn't want to let Gabrielle know just how much this session of playing barbershop was getting to him. The truth was he was letting himself get too close to Gabrielle. And no matter how he tried to hold her at arm's length, she ended up getting so much closer. But that would all end as soon as Gabrielle revealed his scars.

He told himself that he was ready for her to be repulsed, but he wasn't. One look at him and she wouldn't be able to pack fast enough. The truth was that before Gabrielle, he'd forgotten how to smile—how to laugh. He'd forgotten what it was to sleep at night for more than two hours. She had totally turned his life upside down and made him think of all the things that he could still do.

"Relax." Gabrielle's voice drew him back to the present.

"I am relaxed."

"No, you're not. Your jaw is rigid and so are the muscles in your neck. If you don't trust me—"

"I do trust you. Keep going. I have things to do." The truth was he didn't have any other place that he wanted to be other than right here with her hands moving gently over his skin.

"Look at me when you say those words."

He opened his eyes and found her staring straight at him. "I trust you."

With that admission hanging between them, she continued shaving him. Her motions were slow and deliberate. He banished the worries and drew in a deep, calming breath. The more she worked on him, the more relaxed he became under her skilled hands. He sat there with his eyes closed, enjoying the way her fingers felt on his skin. Her touch was gentle, but it ignited a fire within him.

She ran a towel over his face. "You can open your eyes. I'm done."

When his eyes opened, she was smiling at him. "You're already done?"

"Already? That took close to an hour."

"It did?"

She nodded. "And it was worth every minute. Because just as I predicted, you're amazingly handsome. You'll have all of the women swooning at your feet," she added softly.

"I doubt it." He ran a hand over his smooth jaw. It felt so good to have all that hair removed. The beard had been itchy and too warm.

However, he refused to let himself buy in to Gabrielle's compliment. He'd seen the damage to his face at the hospital. He'd been a mess of angry scrapes and nasty gashes. She was just being nice.

"If you don't believe me, have a look for yourself." She handed him a hand mirror.

He really didn't want to look. He knew that he'd find an angry red map of scars. Still, it couldn't be avoided forever. He might have removed all the mirrors from his home, but he was quickly learning just how many surfaces were reflective.

Not allowing himself an easy out, he lifted the mirror. He blinked. Surely he wasn't seeing clearly. He turned his head to one side and then to the other. Where were all the ugly scars?

"See, I told you." Gabrielle continued to smile at him. "You're as handsome as ever."

"I can't believe it." He ran his fingers over his face. "I know that when they transferred me to another hospital, they mentioned something about bringing in a world-class plastic surgeon, but I didn't think there was any hope of salvaging my face."

"I'd say that surgeon is quite gifted."

The angry red lines had faded. The surgeon had hidden most of the scars. Others were fine white lines, but they didn't make him look like Frankenstein. He'd never be the way he used to be, but at least now he wouldn't scare children.

He turned to Gabrielle to thank her for helping him through this difficult step. But when he faced her, the words caught in the back of his throat. She looked at him differently. Not in a bad way. More like a woman who desired a man. Was that possible? Or was he reading what he wanted in her eyes?

As though in answer to his unspoken question, she bent over and pressed her lips to his. At first, he didn't move. He didn't want to do anything to ruin this moment. And yet she pulled back, ever so slightly.

Need and desire pumped through his veins in equal portions. When she looked at him, he felt like a whole man. Not like a man haunted by his past and worried about his bleak future. She looked at him as if she couldn't imagine him doing anything bad. And he so wanted to believe it, too.

Giving in to the urgent need consuming his body, he slipped his arms around her waist and gently pulled her back to him. Her warm, soft curves pressed against his hard muscles and a moan formed in the back of his throat.

He didn't know why fate had brought them together, and in this moment, it didn't matter. The only thing he cared about was Gabrielle's happiness. He wanted to give her a good memory—something to overshadow some of the pain he'd caused.

In all honesty, the memory they were creating would be something he'd cherish, too. He'd never known anyone as generous of heart, as understanding and as bossy as Gabrielle. And he knew no matter how long he lived, he'd never find anyone else like her.

As their kiss deepened, he longed to have all of her. But he had to be sure she wanted the same thing. He wouldn't rush her.

With every bit of willpower, he pulled back and waited until her gaze met his. "Are you sure about this?"

She nodded.

That wasn't good enough, he had to be absolutely sure

she wanted him as much as he wanted her before he carried her into his bedroom and laid her down on his king-size bed. "Gabrielle, do you want to make love?"

"I thought I made my desires clear just a moment ago."

"I need to be sure. I… I don't want to do anything to upset you."

Her eyes reflected the desire warming his veins. "Then let me make this perfectly clear. I, Gabrielle Dupré, want to make love to you, Deacon Santoro."

That was all he needed to hear. He scooped her up in his arms and carried her to the bedroom. He laid her gently on the bed. Nothing had ever looked so good—so right.

He knew after tonight that nothing would ever be the same for them, but he would deal with the aftermath later. Much, much later…

CHAPTER SEVENTEEN

THE NEXT MORNING Gaby awoke alone.

She reached out, running her hand over Deacon's pillow. It was cold to the touch. Her gaze searched the bedroom. There was no sign of him.

The convergence of disappointment, embarrassment and sadness left her grappling to keep a lid on her emotions. He regretted their night together. A sob caught in the back of her throat.

No. Don't lose it now. You're stronger than this.

As she looked to see the time, her gaze stumbled across a yellow rose on her bedside table. It hadn't been there last night. She was certain of it.

She withdrew the rose from the vase. As she stared at its velvet petals, she wondered what Deacon was trying to tell her. Did he want to go back to being friends? Or was she reading too much in to it? Maybe, in this case, a rose was just a rose.

She glanced at the clock. She realized if she didn't hurry, she'd be late to work. Finding out where her relationship now stood with Deacon would have to wait until later. She was expecting phone calls that morning about the fundraiser. And no matter what happened between her and Deacon, she intended to do her best job.

She scrambled out of bed and rushed to get dressed.

There was something else she needed to do that morning—conclude her arrangement with *QTR*. She may not know the exact circumstances of the accident, but she knew Deacon hadn't been at fault and didn't deserve any further bad press.

When she returned to the guesthouse, she knew she'd made a big mistake. Not the night she'd spent with Deacon. One minute, he'd been so tender and loving. Then in the next moment, he'd been hot and passionate. It was a night of surprises and delights. No, her problem was agreeing to do an exposé about him. Now that she knew about her aunt's request, she was certain he was innocent. Her aunt would never have asked a killer to look after her. And now Gaby had to try to undo some of the damage.

So far *QTR* hadn't printed anything that she'd given them, not that there was anything noteworthy. Hopefully it wasn't too late to call off the arrangement.

Gaby retrieved the number of the editor at *QTR*. The phone rang and rang. She began to worry that no one would answer.

Suddenly there was a male voice. "Hello."

Gaby was startled. This certainly wasn't the perky young female editor that she'd been assigned to. "I'm sorry. I must have rung the wrong number."

"This is Elle McTavish's desk."

Gaby swallowed down her nervousness. "I was hoping to speak with her."

"And who is this?"

"Gaby, um, I mean Gabrielle Dupré. And who is this?"

"Thomas Rousseau."

As in Quentin Thomas Rousseau II. Gaby's stomach clenched. Oh, boy. She'd heard stories about the man. None of it was any good. He was legendary. She wasn't sure what was going on, but she had the feeling that it wasn't going to be good.

She gripped the phone tighter. "Could I leave a message for Ms. McTavish?"

"I've taken over for her."

But he was the owner, not an editor. Gaby clenched the phone tighter. "I see. Then perhaps you are the person I should speak to."

"I'm listening."

"I've changed my mind about doing the story about Deacon Santoro."

"I see." His voice was smooth and patient. "But my understanding was that's what you wanted—for the world to know about Santoro—and how he's evading the law."

At the beginning, that was exactly what she had wanted. But now she knew that her aunt hadn't blamed Deacon and, therefore, neither should she. He was not the beast she'd originally thought. He was just a man—a man who had punished himself needlessly.

"That was before—"

She stopped herself from saying too much. The less she told this man, the better. She had learned firsthand how words and images could be twisted into something they're not.

"Before what?"

"It was an accident. That's all."

"Have the police said this?"

"No, but they will."

"Miss Dupré, what changed your mind about gaining the truth and forcing the police's hand in delivering their findings about the incident?"

She worried her bottom lip. What was she supposed to say now? She didn't want to break Deacon's confidence. She didn't want to share her aunt's last words with the world.

"Miss Dupré?"

"I want to end our arrangement."

"Is that because you're now romantically linked with Mr. Santoro?" The man's voice took on a hard edge. "Yes, I saw that photo of you in his arms. I was not happy to be scooped by another magazine."

"It wasn't the way it looked." At least at *that* moment, everything had been innocent. Now everything was exponentially more complicated.

"Tell me about it." His tone was more congenial. He wanted her to give him a story but she refused to do it.

"You and I don't have a signed agreement. Remember, your magazine wanted to wait until you could ascertain what information I would provide."

"There was a verbal agreement, was there not?"

"Sounds like a case of 'he said, she said.'"

Regretting the deal she'd struck with the magazine, and now this man that she didn't trust in the least, she said, "I am calling off the arrangement. Besides, I never gave you anything you could use."

The line went dead.

She had to admit that had gone a little better than she'd expected. And as she set aside her cell phone, she felt a bit lighter. She didn't care how hard up she was for money, she was never working for a gossip rag again.

Now she had to deal with Deacon. She had no idea what to make of his disappearance that morning. He did say that he didn't sleep much. Maybe he'd just gotten up early.

And to complicate matters, she needed to come clean about her liaison with *QTR*. She felt now that her relationship with Deacon had shifted, she needed to be completely open and honest—even if he didn't like what she was about to say.

How was he supposed to face her after last night?

Deacon moved to the window in his office. She was going to look at him differently. She was going to expect things of him—things he couldn't give her.

And yet he didn't want to lose her. He told himself that it was the fact she was the best assistant he'd ever had. And this fundraiser, if it worked out, might help fund a breakthrough in the fight against breast cancer. There was too much riding on them continuing to work together.

Was it possible to wind back the hands of time? If they didn't talk about it, could they pretend that amazing night of lovemaking had never happened?

"Deacon, we need to talk."

He didn't move as he stared out the window of his office. She'd just said the five words he'd been dreading. It was time he put his plan in action.

Deacon turned to her. "I wanted to talk to you, too. I have another screenplay and I'd like to get your thoughts on it."

"It can wait—"

"No, it can't. If I don't get the rights to it, someone else will. I know it."

"But what I have to say—"

"Can wait." He saw the frustration reflected in her eyes. He owed her more than a quick brush-off. He swallowed hard. "I wasn't expecting last night. It wasn't something I planned."

"Me neither."

That was good to hear. It meant she had to be as confused as him. "Then you'll understand when I say I need time to process this. My life—it's not the best time to start anything serious."

Disappointment dimmed her eyes. "I understand. But I feel I owe you the truth about something."

Revealing secrets and truths were things people did when they were establishing a relationship. When they were building a foundation. He didn't intend to do any of those things with Gabrielle. Because when that police report was released—when he was sure his whole world would come crashing down—he didn't want Gabrielle hurt any more than she already would be.

Whatever she'd done or thought she'd done, it wouldn't compare to his transgressions.

"Now isn't the time for sharing." He averted his gaze. "We can talk another time."

"But—"

"Please." She didn't know how hard she was making this for him.

Because in a different place, at a different time, under different circumstances, he would have welcomed her into his life with both arms. Turning her away was the hardest thing he'd ever done.

As he watched her walk away, he felt the distance grow between them. It was like the sun had been eclipsed from his life. And as much as he wanted to go after her— to pull her into his arms—his feet remained rooted to the floor.

He clung to the fact that she was better off without him.

CHAPTER EIGHTEEN

It was all coming together.

Beneath the blue skies, Gaby stood to the side of the golf course and gazed out over the estate grounds. Deacon's grounds crew were miracle workers. Of course, it helped that they'd enjoyed months of paid leave and were now anxious to get back to work. Gaby couldn't imagine what it would be like to have all that free time. Right now, she didn't have enough hours in the day to do everything that needed done.

And ever since they'd made love, Deacon had held her at arm's length. She didn't understand it. Had she done something wrong? Had he not enjoyed it? Whatever it was, he wasn't talking and she was left with nothing but doubts and worries. Thankfully the fundraiser was only a couple of days away and there were so many last-minute details to attend to that she didn't have time to get lost in her thoughts.

Every last ticket for the event had been sold. Now if only they'd all show up. The food had been ordered. The catering service had been reserved. The rose garden was already in order. Deacon had seen to that. But there was something she was forgetting. She just couldn't put her finger on it.

"You wanted to see me?" Deacon's voice came from behind her.

"I did." She tried to hide her surprise at him actually seeking her out instead of calling her on the phone. "What do you think?"

"About what?"

She subdued a sigh. What was wrong with him? "Look around. The grounds are done. The men have been working on it every day from dawn until dusk."

Deacon remained quiet as he took in his surroundings. His expression was masked behind a look of indifference. How could that be? Didn't he notice what a mess the estate had been? Even she had been out here every day going over the details to make this place spectacular.

"It looks good." He still didn't smile.

"Good? That's it. This place is amazing. Anyone would be amazed by the transformation." There was something more to this. Something that he wasn't telling her. "Deacon, we need to talk about the other night—"

"There's nothing to talk about."

She was tired of being patient—of thinking he just needed time to adjust to the change in their relationship. "I don't believe you."

"What?" He gave her an innocent look.

"Don't go acting like you don't know what I'm talking about. You've been avoiding me at all costs ever since we made love."

"I've been busy." His phone chimed. He withdrew it and held it up as proof of his business. Then he silenced it and slipped it back in his pocket.

"Fine. We'll play it your way."

"I'm not playing. What happened was a mistake. One we shouldn't repeat."

She managed a shrug as she wasn't so sure she trusted

her voice. It took her a second to swallow the lump in the back of her throat. With a blink of her eyes, she mustered up what she hoped was a blank expression. He wasn't the only actor here.

Willing her voice not to waver, she said, "And the golf course? What do you think of that?"

"It's good."

She planted her hands on her hips. "After all this work, *good* is all you have to say?"

His gaze didn't meet hers. "I don't know what you want me to tell you."

"More than that. My lunch was good. Your haircut is good. But the transformation of this estate from an unruly jungle to a work of art is spectacular."

He sighed and then proceeded to rub the back of his neck. "I just can't shake the feeling that something is going to go terribly wrong." He turned to her and apparently her thoughts were reflected on her face because he said, "What happens if the report on the accident comes out between now and then?"

"We deal with it."

"What if it says I'm to blame?"

In all honesty, she wasn't sure how she'd cope if the report really did say that Deacon was responsible for the accident that stole away her aunt, no matter how sure she was that he was innocent. But now Gaby understood why he'd pulled away from her. The accident was like a deep chasm between them, and try as they might, it was hard to cross.

She wanted to believe she would be able to move past the accident—to not hate him if the truth turned out to be different than what she imagined. But she knew that emotions could be tricky. Her father was a prime example—who'd have thought he would be arrested for stalking and harassment? Her father had never been in trouble with the law before in his life.

Not wanting to get caught up in the what-ifs and maybes, she said, "Would you like to give it a go?" She gestured toward the golf clubs that were all spiffed up and standing next to the house in a special shed. "The clubs are just waiting to be used."

He hesitated and she was certain he was going to turn her down. And then he said, "I'll do it, if you do."

She shook her head. "Not me."

"Why not?"

"I—I prefer to watch." She really didn't want to admit that she didn't know a putter from an iron. Those were terms she'd heard the groundskeepers throwing around.

Deacon arched an eyebrow as he stepped closer to her. "Are you afraid I'll beat you?"

He was challenging her? Oh, boy. Maybe it was time for her to fess up. "No. I'm not worried." There was a glint of excitement in his dark eyes. He definitely had the wrong idea and so she said, "I don't know how to golf."

His eyes widened. "But you're the one who suggested making this a golfing event."

"I know I did. You did happen to notice that most of your yard is taken up by a nine-hole golf course?"

"But usually when you host an event, you know how to do the said event."

Now she understood his confusion. "But see, I'm not the host, you are. The fundraiser is in your mother's name. This is your home. And the people are coming here because of you—"

"No. They are coming because they are curious to see the recluse and find out if I'm an ugly, scarred mess like the tabloids have portrayed."

"Whoa! Whoa!" She waved away all his worries.

"That isn't why they're coming here. They're attending the event to support a worthy cause."

"And I think you see only the good in people."

"What's that supposed to mean?"

"Look at you. You're always so positive. Wanting to believe people are truly good. But they aren't."

She didn't know where all of this was coming from. "I'm not some Pollyanna."

"Yes, you are. You're all smiles and sunshine."

She hadn't meant to mislead him. "I'm human just like you. I have my share of doubts and worries. I just try not to dwell on them."

He rolled his eyes.

"Don't do that. Don't make me out to be like someone up on a pedestal."

"Then tell me that you aren't doing everything you can to convince yourself that I'm innocent. Go ahead. Deny it."

"But my aunt—"

"She was probably in shock. She probably hadn't even understood what had happened. The only thing she could think about was her love for you."

She shook her head, refusing to believe his version of events. "Now that I've gotten to know you, I just can't believe you would be reckless with your life and that of others."

"But see, that's the point. I have been in the past. I've bought super cars and I've taken them out on the road to see how fast they could go—to push the envelope. Doesn't that make me reckless?" When she couldn't argue with him, she remained quiet. His gaze implored her to affirm his actions. "Go ahead, say it."

"No." She wasn't going to help convict him when there wasn't any evidence. Because if he were guilty—if he did act recklessly—she would have lost not one but two people that she cared deeply about in that accident.

"Gabrielle, you can't bury your head in the sand and pretend the accident didn't happen. The reality is my nightmares grow stronger every night. You have to accept that—that I'm responsible for what happened. No amount of positivity will be able to overcome the fact that I—I killed your aunt."

Each word he threw at her was a blow at her heart. Tears pricked the back of her eyes. "Why are you doing this?"

Deacon hated hurting her.

But he didn't have a choice. More of his memories were starting to come back to him. He remembered being in the car. He recalled the blinding headlights headed straight for him. The rest was bits and pieces, but he couldn't shake the guilt mounting within him.

And now he was making a mess of things with Gabrielle. He'd only wanted to help her. He should have done it from a distance. Bringing her here to his estate was his first mistake. The second mistake was getting caught up in her greenish-gray eyes and letting himself be drawn in by her pouty lips. Now he had to untangle the ties that bound them together. It was best for Gabrielle.

He cleared his throat. "I never should have let things get this far. You and I need to part now, before either of us gets hurt."

"Are you saying you never cared? That this thing between us is all in my imagination?"

Why did she have to make this harder on herself? He couldn't tell her what she wanted to hear—not if he wanted her to leave, if he wanted to save her from more pain.

"It was fun and nice." He glanced away, unable to

stand the hurt reflected in her eyes. "But it wasn't real. It would never last."

His phone vibrated again. What in the world was going on? His email was busier than ever. Using his phone as an excuse not to face the pain he'd caused Gabrielle, he pretended to check it. In truth, he couldn't care less about business right now—right when he was sending away the woman that he'd come to care about deeply—

The breath caught in his throat as his gaze strayed across a bit of news. There was a distorted picture of him with ugly scars, next to a photo of Gabrielle. The headline read, The Beast Wins Beauty?

"What is it?" Gabrielle asked. When he didn't respond, she asked again, "What's the matter?"

He ignored her as his gaze skimmed down over the slanderous piece of trashy journalism. The fact that Gabrielle was *quoted* in the article stabbed him in the chest. Each breath was painful.

All this time, he'd thought she was so amazing with her ability to see the good in him. At first, he hadn't wanted to believe in her generous heart, but she'd worn him down and snuck past the wall around his own heart. And it'd been a lie. All of it.

"Deacon, I'm getting worried. What's wrong?"

His gaze narrowed in on her. "Why? Are you hoping I'll give you another headline?"

"What?" She reached for his phone. The color drained from her face as she read the article. When she looked up at him, worry lines bracketed her eyes. "I can explain."

"Don't bother." His angry words died in his throat when he realized she'd done what most anyone would have done in her situation. "I probably would have done the same thing in your place."

"But you don't understand. I—I backed out of the deal.

Once I knew you better and you told me what my aunt said to you, I backed out."

He wanted to believe her but he couldn't allow himself. "It looks like you gave them plenty to work with."

"This isn't my stuff. They did a hatchet job on the information I supplied them. Please. You have to believe me."

Anger pulsed through his veins. He was angry at the tabloid for printing outright lies. And he was furious with himself for not listening to his gut. Instead, he'd let down his guard with Gabrielle. He'd let himself fall for her and it'd all been a lie.

"Just go." His voice rumbled.

"But the fundraiser—"

"Is taken care of. You said so yourself. All the arrangements have been made. Now that your end of our deal has been fulfilled, it's time for you to leave."

When she didn't move but rather stood there with tears glistening in her eyes, he said with a low guttural growl that he knew she hated, "Go now. And don't come back."

He turned his back to her because it was killing him to send her away. He would try to forget the happiness that Gabrielle had brought to his life. He would banish the image of her warm smile—a smile that she would get when he walked in the room.

Because none of it had been true. While he'd been falling in love with her, she had been figuring out how best to twist the knife. And she'd succeeded. Worst of all, he deserved it and more after causing the accident.

His last little bit of hope that his name would be cleared was also gone. The future looked bleak. He just hoped the article brought Gabrielle and her father some sort of satisfaction.

CHAPTER NINETEEN

THIS WAS THE absolute last place he wanted to be.

Deacon stood off to the side of his newly manicured lawn. Despite what he'd said to Gabrielle, the estate did look spectacular. She hadn't overlooked a single detail. And his staff had gone above and beyond to make everything perfect for this occasion.

After Gabrielle left, it had been too late to cancel the fundraiser. He knew it was up to him to see it through to the end. Only things weren't turning out quite as he'd imagined.

With not one, not two, but three scandalous headline articles in as many days that featured him in the worst light, he didn't think anyone would attend. Instead, everyone was in attendance. He didn't know if they'd come in spite of the article or to find out if any of the lies were true.

The only person not there was the one person he longed to see—Gabrielle. He knew he should be angry with her, yet when she said that she'd backed out of the arrangement with the magazine, he'd believed her. But it didn't mean they belonged together.

He drew his thoughts up short. Today he had to be a gracious host.

He really couldn't believe all of these people had

shown up. There were fellow actors, directors, pillars of the music industry and people he didn't recognize, but what they all had in common was that they were happy to be here. All were smiling, talking and greeting each other. Food and drink flowed freely. The golf course looked better than it ever had, thanks to Gabrielle's insistence.

He'd already had compliments and slaps on the back that his scars had healed so well. After that doctored photo in *QTR*, where they'd made him to look like some sort of monster, people were pleasantly surprised by his normal appearance. It felt surprisingly good to greet friends and acquaintances. And he had Gabrielle to thank.

A mariachi band played in the background as well-dressed people mingled. Deacon worked his way past the crowd. He was headed for the rose garden, hoping to gain a moment alone. Though people had been accepting of him, it was all a bit overwhelming.

And then Gabrielle appeared in the distance.

Deacon came to a halt. It couldn't be her, could it? Not after the way they'd ended things. He blinked and looked again.

She was gone.

He expelled a disappointed sigh. It must have been someone that resembled Gabrielle. He assured himself it was for the best. She would soon forget him and move on with her life.

And then Gabrielle came back into view. She had on a yellow crocheted dress. The spaghetti straps showed off her slim shoulders. The plunging neckline hinted at her voluptuous breasts. He swallowed hard. A slit ended high up on her thighs, letting the crocheted high-low skirt show off glimpses of her long legs. She really was a looker.

It was then that he noticed a man next to her. The guy was chatting her up. Deacon stood too far away to overhear what was being said, but Gabrielle was smiling. However, it wasn't an easy smile. It looked forced. Yet, the guy acted as though he didn't have a clue she was only putting on a show of being nice to him.

Deacon's body stiffened as this man had the audacity to reach out and put his hand on Gabrielle's upper arm as though they knew each other intimately. If Gabrielle's body gestures were anything to go by, the attention was unwanted. Deacon started forward. Before he reached the two, the guy leaned over and whispered something in Gabrielle's ear. She pulled away. What did the man think he was up to? Couldn't he tell Gabrielle wasn't interested?

Deacon's steps quickened. He would step in. Or should he? He slowed down. Was it his place to step in? After all, he had told Gabrielle to go away. What would he be telling her if he were to step in now?

Yet, this was his estate. He had a right to see that none of his guests were unduly harassed. Determined that he had a right to make sure things were all right, he continued in Gabrielle's direction. He could see that she was no longer smiling and her gaze was darting around as though to find an excuse to slip away from the guy.

Deacon was almost at her side, when someone stepped in his way, blocking his view of Gabrielle. "Excuse me."

"Deacon, old boy. It's so good to see you."

Deacon focused on the man speaking to him. It was his agent. A man he used to speak to at least once a day, but since the accident, his agent hadn't bothered to call. The man had obviously given up on Deacon, figuring his pretty face was gone forever. Now that his face had healed, Deacon wondered if his agent realized he'd given up too soon.

"Harry, it's good to see you." Deacon did his best to smile, even though he didn't feel like it—not for a man who, for all intents and purposes, had told him in the hospital that his future in Hollywood had gone up in flames along with his good looks. Of course, Harry had been smart enough to put it in friendlier terms, but that's what it amounted to.

"You know I've been trying to reach you—"

"I've been busy." Deacon knew whatever Harry wanted would be what was good for Harry and not something that would help Deacon. "Could you excuse me for just a moment—"

"Not so fast. We should talk. This fundraiser was a brilliant idea. It certainly squashes those rumors of you becoming some sort of recluse. I've never seen the estate look better. And you, well, it's remarkable. If I hadn't seen you in the hospital, I'd never believe the extent of your injuries."

"The plastic surgeon did an amazing job," Deacon murmured tightly.

"Indeed. And this event is a great chance to get you back in the swing of things. Everyone seems to be having a great time."

"My assistant gets the credit. This fundraiser was her brainchild." It wasn't until the words were out that he realized Gabrielle was no longer his assistant. She was… well, they no longer had any sort of official relationship, but it sure didn't feel that way to him when he saw that other guy hanging all over her. Where had she disappeared to?

"This assistant, she sounds like a miracle worker,"

Harry said. "Perhaps I should try to steal her away from you."

The forced smile slipped from Deacon's face. "I don't think so."

"Well then, I'll get straight to the point of my calls. I have a part in a movie that I think you'd be perfect for—"

"No."

"No?" The agent's mouth gaped. "But surely you want to get back to work."

"I am working. I'm finding that I like being behind the camera more than I like being in front of it."

"So the rumor is true?"

"Yes. I'm starting to back some movies, and I'll see where things go from there."

The agent nodded as he digested the information. "If you change your mind, give me a call."

"I don't think that will happen." Deacon had to admit it felt good to know what he wanted in life. And what he wanted most was Gabrielle—even though he couldn't have her.

The agent's eyebrows rose with surprise before his face settled into a smile. "I knew you weren't one to hold a grudge. Glad to hear all of the ugliness is in the past." And then as though the man didn't know what else to say, he said, "Well, I should be moving on. I have other people that I need to speak to."

Deacon didn't say a word, not wanting to waylay the man. After the man moved on, Deacon's gaze scanned the area for Gabrielle. He didn't see her. But there were so many people that she could be anywhere.

He started moving through the crowd, but it was slow going with so many people wanting to greet him. He did the obligatory handshakes and pasted a smile on his face.

But he didn't linger. He needed to find her. He needed to—to what? Make sure she was okay? And then what?

He wouldn't know the answer to that until he caught up with her. He stopped and turned in a circle looking for her. She had to be here. And he wouldn't stop until he found her.

CHAPTER TWENTY

She shouldn't be here.

But she couldn't stay away.

To Gaby's surprise, the morning after she'd left the Santoro estate, the complaint against her father had been formally withdrawn. He was free and clear. There was no reason for Gaby to ever see Deacon again—but seeing him was exactly what she had planned.

She owed Deacon an apology. Instead of helping him with this fundraiser, she'd only made things worse for him. *QTR* had issued a series of malicious articles about Deacon. She recalled the morning's headlines on the *QTR* magazine. It was all over the newsstands, grocery stores and internet: Beast Hides from Public & Justice.

It appeared that *QTR* was intent on running a series of damning articles about Deacon. It killed her to read how they'd stolen her words. *QTR* had twisted the facts and made up other things. They'd embarked on an all-out campaign against him. No wonder she hadn't spotted Deacon amongst his guests. The fact that he had even let the fundraiser go forward amazed her.

When he'd banished her from the estate, she'd worried that he would once again hide away in his darkened office and keep everyone outside the tall estate walls. And after those atrocious headlines, she wouldn't blame him if he cut himself off from the outside world.

She didn't care what Deacon said, she knew he had a good heart. She couldn't—she wouldn't—accept that he'd recklessly taken her aunt's life. It had been a horrible accident. End of a very sad story.

She'd been talking frankly with her father—something she should have done before things had gotten out of control. And the fact that her father had agreed to attend the fundraiser with her was the first step on the road to forgiveness, even if her father would vehemently deny it. He said he was only here because Gaby had planned the event. He refused to acknowledge that the event had anything to do with Deacon.

Her gaze scanned the enormous crowd of finely dressed people. Was Deacon really somewhere among them? She had to try and fix things. She at least had to try. She didn't like the way they'd left things.

"Hey—" Newton nudged her "—isn't that the guy that acts in *The Screaming Racers*?"

She hadn't seen the action movie, but she had seen the previews on the television in her father's living room. "Yes, I think it is."

"What do you think he's doing here?"

"Supporting a good cause."

"I don't know. He's a big star. Why would he come here to the beast's lair?"

"Newton, don't start."

"Hey, it's what they called him in the headlines. You know, the story you helped write."

She gave Newton a stern look. "I only agreed to bring you here because you insisted that my father might need help getting around. But we could leave now—"

"Okay. Okay."

He pressed his lips together into a firm line. But his eyes told a different story. If she wasn't careful with him, he would make a scene. She sincerely regretted bringing him. As soon as she placed some tickets in the raffle baskets, she'd gather her father and Newton and they would go.

"Go find my father. You know, the reason you're here?" she said. "I need to go buy some raffle tickets."

"I'm hungry. Maybe we'll get some food." Newton walked away.

With Deacon nowhere in sight, Gabrielle made her way over to the table where they were selling the tickets for the twenty-five elaborate baskets that had been generously donated by area businesses.

Gabrielle couldn't help but smile as she observed all of the people gushing over the beautiful baskets and buying an arm's length of tickets at a time. This event was turning out better than she'd ever imagined. She wished Deacon could find some comfort in knowing that these people were in attendance in spite of the nasty headlines. That had to mean something, right?

With guests still streaming through the gates and the press along the road photographing the event, this was certainly going to give Deacon some positive spin. She pulled her cell phone from her purse. She clicked through to the different social-media sites to find that Deacon's name was trending. And this time, his name was linked with positive news.

Her lips lifted into a broader smile.

She'd done it. She'd kept her word to Deacon. The fundraiser appeared to be a smashing success. But this event wasn't nearly enough to make up to him for the lies that were lining every grocery store checkout and splattered on the internet. If only she could explain properly, maybe he'd believe her.

But where was he? She'd already worked through the crowd of guests and walked the whole way around the estate. And now, she was back where she'd started, in the garden. There had been no sign of Deacon amongst the pink tea roses, the purple climbing roses and the many other varieties of blooms that took root in the impressive garden.

The truth was she shouldn't have left when he'd told her to. She should have...well, she wasn't sure what she should have done. But leaving hadn't been the right answer. Because every minute she was away from him, the gap between them yawned even wider. She hoped it wasn't too wide for her to cross. Because she missed him with every fiber of her body. Life wasn't the same without him in it.

And then she remembered something her aunt had told her way back when she was in elementary school. There had been some trouble between her and another girl. Her aunt's sage advice was that a gentle word or a kind action could be more powerful than the strongest objection or the harshest retaliation. Her aunt had been a gentle soul. And Gabrielle had a feeling that her aunt would understand why she was doing what she was doing with Deacon. Or at least she hoped so.

"Hey, Gaby! Wait!"

It wasn't Deacon.

Her heart sunk a little.

With a forced smile, she turned to find Newton running back over to her again. "I thought you went with my father to find the food."

"Your father found someone to talk to and I decided to bring you a drink."

She realized now that he must have had more than one himself. He lurched toward her, spilling the drink on her bare arm, and then making as if to pat her dry with his free hand, surprising her.

Gaby turned, jerking away from his touch. "Stop. I'm fine…"

It was then that she spotted Deacon. He noticed her at the same time. Newton was still talking, but she was no longer paying attention. Her full focus was on Deacon.

"Excuse me." She moved past Newton and headed straight for Deacon.

Please let him listen to me before he throws me out.

CHAPTER TWENTY-ONE

GABY'S STOMACH SHIVERED with nerves.

As Deacon approached her, she forgot about everyone else around them. In that moment, it was just the two of them. She started moving toward him. Although the closer she got to him, the more she noticed the tenseness of his body and the rigid set of his jaw. She braced herself for a confrontation. She understood how he'd think that she'd turned against him.

They stopped in front of each other. At the same time, they said, "I'm sorry."

Gaby's gaze searched his. "Do you mean it?"

He nodded. "I never should have told you to leave like that."

"And I should have stayed. I need to tell you how sorry I am—"

"You!" Newton wedged himself between her and Deacon. "You killed her aunt. You should be in jail."

A hush fell over the growing crowd.

"Newton! Stop." Gabrielle saw the pain that his words had inflicted on Deacon.

Newton turned on her. "How can you defend him?"

Gabrielle's gaze went from Newton to Deacon. If there were ever a time to be honest with herself and everyone else, it was now. "I'm defending Deacon because I've come to know him. I know that he's a good man with a big heart. He would never intentionally harm a person." She turned to Deacon. She stared deep into his eyes. "I know this because I love him."

"You can't. He's a killer." Newton shouted the accusation.

By then a crowd had formed around them. People were pulling out their cell phones and filming the scene. This mess had gone from bad to worse.

"He's my best friend," she countered.

"Don't," Deacon said. "I can defend myself."

"I'm only speaking the truth," Gaby said, feeling very protective of him.

Before Newton could say another word, Gaby's father rolled his wheelchair between them. He turned to Newton. "That's enough."

"But he is a—"

"Hero," her father said.

"What?" Newton stared at her father like he'd spoken another language.

Her father cleared his voice. "I should have said something earlier. The official accident report was released this afternoon. There is irrefutable proof that Deacon is innocent."

"What evidence?" Deacon approached her father.

"I'll admit my protest in front of your place may have been rash, but it garnered a lot of attention." He held up a hand, staving off Deacon's heated words. "Before you say anything, it was that protest and those interviews that brought forward a reluctant witness. They have a video of the accident. It has cleared you, Deacon. My sister was the one that swerved into your lane."

Gaby reached out and took Deacon's hand in hers. She

smiled through her tears. At last this long, hard journey was over.

She turned to Deacon. "Did you know about this?"

He shook his head. "I haven't touched my mail or listened to my voice mails today. I was busy making sure all of your plans for the fundraiser were carried out."

Gaby's father turned to Deacon. "And I owe you a big apology. Instead of accusing you of horrible things, I should have been thanking you." He held out his hand. Deacon hesitated and then he withdrew his hand from Gaby's grasp in order to shake her father's hand. "Gaby tells me that you don't remember much of the accident, but the witness reported that at great risk, you attempted to save my sister."

Deacon visibly swallowed. "I'm sorry for what you've gone through."

"Thank you." Her father's gaze moved to Gaby and then back to Deacon. "As long as you keep my daughter happy, we'll get along just fine."

Gaby glanced around to find that Newton had disappeared. She scanned the crowd for any sign of him. Thankfully she didn't spot him. She hoped he just kept going. The farther away, the better.

When she finally turned back to Deacon, he presented her with a single, perfect red rose. The simple gesture had a profound effect on her heart and love spilled forth.

Gaby lifted up on her tiptoes and looped her arms around his neck. "There's something else I came here to say."

At the same time, they said, "I love you."

As the crowd of onlookers cheered, Gaby leaned into Deacon's embrace. He claimed her lips with a kiss that promised love and happiness.

EPILOGUE

Six months later...

"I NEED TO talk to you." Gabrielle smiled at her new husband in the back of a black limo.

"Really?" The smile he'd been wearing all day slipped from his face. "I wanted to talk to you, too."

"You did?" Gaby sat up straighter. She couldn't imagine what Deacon had on his mind. "Maybe you should go first."

"Wipe that worried look from your beautiful face. Or else I'll have to put up that privacy divider and give you something to smile about." His eyes twinkled with mischief.

She knew exactly what direction her husband's mind had taken and she shook her head as a smile returned to her face. "That will have to wait." When Deacon made a point of pouting, she added, "There's no time. We're almost to the airport."

He nodded in understanding. "As usual, my wife is right."

"Make sure you remember those words the next time we have a disagreement." The lights of the Los Angeles skyline rushed past the window in a blur as their limo headed for LAX. They were hopping a private plane to Fiji. Their honeymoon was going to be a new adventure for the both of them.

"But if we disagree, we get to have make-up sex."

She couldn't help but laugh at her husband's unabashed eagerness. "Do you ever think of anything besides sex?"

"Not when you're around. You've ruined me." He pulled her closer until she was sitting on his lap. Then he closed the divider. "We should probably save Charles from all of this naughty talk. And this way, I can show you what I was thinking about."

He drew her head down to him and claimed her lips with his own. It didn't matter how many times he kissed her, he still made her heart race. His lips moved hungrily over hers, making her insides pool with desire.

She knew where this kiss was headed and it wouldn't leave time for them to talk before the flight. And there were some things they'd put off discussing for too long. It was best to clear the air now before the honeymoon began.

It took every bit of willpower to place her hands on her husband's muscular chest and push back, ending the kiss. "Deacon, wait."

His eyes blinked open and she could read the confusion in his expression. "What's the matter?"

She moved back to the seat beside him. "You're distracting me."

"But in a good way, right?"

"Of course. But we still need to talk."

The color drained from his face. "What's wrong?"

She couldn't help but laugh at the utter look of panic on his face. "Relax. Nothing is wrong."

"You're sure?"

Gaby nodded. "I know we should have talked about this before now, but I was wondering how you felt about children."

"Children?" His gaze narrowed as he eyed her. "I must say I like them. I happened to be one not so long ago."

"Hah! I've seen your six-bay garage with all those sports cars. You're still a kid at heart."

"Busted. But I do make time for business. Speaking of which, remember how I sued *QTR* for that pack of lies they printed about the car accident?"

She nodded. "How's the lawsuit going?"

"It's over. I got the news yesterday, but with the wedding festivities, I didn't want to ruin anything."

Gaby braced herself for bad news. "Did they get it thrown out of court?"

"It never went to court. *QTR*'s board stepped in and between our combined legal teams we hammered out a reasonable deal. The gist of it is they will be revising their editorial guidelines."

Gaby's mouth gaped as she digested the ramifications of the deal. "You mean no more hatchet jobs?"

"Exactly."

"Deacon, that's wonderful." She rewarded him with a kiss, but before it got too heated, she pulled back.

"Why did you stop again? I have a piece of paper that says we must kiss multiple times a day."

She laughed. "I didn't see that on our marriage certificate."

"It's in the fine print."

"Oh. Okay. I'll have to look closer." She smiled. "And did it say anything about how many kids we're supposed to have?"

"No. How many were you thinking?"

"At least one… Since it's already on the way."

For a moment, her husband didn't speak. He didn't move. She wasn't even sure that he was still breathing.

"Deacon, did you hear me?"

"Say it again." His voice lacked emotion and she was

beginning to wonder if he was having second thoughts about having children.

"We're having a baby."

"That's what I thought you said." He lifted her back onto his lap. Then he placed his large hand over her abdomen. "You're going to be a mom."

"And you're going to be a dad."

A big smile lit up his eyes. "I love you."

"I love you, too."

She reached out, placing her hand behind her husband's head, and drew him toward her. She claimed his lips with her own. No matter how old she got to be, she would never tire of his kisses. And she planned to grow very old with this wonderful man by her side.

* * * * *

THE SHERIFF'S
NINE-MONTH
SURPRISE

BRENDA HARLEN

To #professionalromancefans—avid readers
and tireless ambassadors of the genre.

With sincere appreciation.

Chapter One

Twenty-eight months

Katelyn Gilmore fell back onto the king-size mattress and drew in a long, deep breath as she stared up at the textured ceiling of the Courtland Hotel-Boulder City.

Twenty-eight months devoted exclusively to the establishment of her law practice, working long hours every day, including evenings and weekends, to prove herself to her clients and colleagues. Now, after twenty-eight months, she'd finally allowed herself to venture away from the office for a few days.

Okay, a conference wasn't actually a vacation, but the opportunity to hone her legal skills and enjoy a change of scenery was one that she couldn't refuse. And she was determined to enjoy the weekend—to get out of the hotel when the workshops had ended and breathe in some fresh air. Maybe she'd even take the time to see some sights, have a drink or two at a local bar, maybe flirt with a handsome cowboy—if she remembered how.

She enjoyed the company of men, and her sexual experiences—though limited—had been pleasant enough. Maybe not earth-shattering, but she didn't really believe that earth-shattering sex existed outside of books and movies. The truth was, she felt more anticipation when she was prepping for a trial than thinking about getting naked with a man.

"Which only proves you're getting naked with the wrong men," her sister had told her as she tucked a box of condoms in the suitcase Kate had packed for her trip.

Though Skylar was younger by five years, she had a much better understanding of the way a man's brain worked—and a lot more experience with other parts of the male anatomy.

Kate had removed the box and given it back to her sister. "I'm going to a legal conference at a five-star hotel, not an open house at a brothel."

"Still, you might luck out and meet a guy who is something more than a stuffed shirt," Sky had said, and returned the box to the niche she'd created between Kate's makeup bag and her underwear. "And even if you don't, it's better to be safe than sorry."

Because she agreed with her sister's last point, she'd left the condoms in her suitcase.

She also believed in careful planning and deliberation and wasn't the type of woman to act on impulse. Hooking up with a guy she met at a conference would be exactly that—and a little tawdry, too.

So when she hung up her suits and unpacked her other essentials, she left the condoms in her luggage, certain she'd have no need for them.

Certain…and maybe just a little disappointed.

* * *

Reid Davidson was sitting with his back to the wall and his eyes on the door when she walked into the conference room.

From a young age, he'd learned to be aware of his surroundings and the people around him—it was easier to dodge a backhand if he saw it coming—and the habit had served him well as the Sheriff of Echo Ridge, Texas.

But even if he hadn't seen her arrive, even if his head had momentarily been turned away, Reid would have been aware of her presence. She was the type of woman who snagged a man's full and complete attention and didn't let go.

She had bold blue eyes and sharp cheekbones in a heart-shaped face that was saved from looking prim by a lushly shaped mouth that promised the fulfillment of his wickedest fantasies. Her dark hair, shining with hints of gold and copper, was caught up in some kind of fancy twist that made him want to take out the pins and slide his fingers through it.

After pausing for a brief moment in the doorway, her gaze searching for an empty chair, she moved to the other side of the room with a brisk, confident stride that suggested she was a woman with important places to go and people to see.

Her body—long and lean with curves in all the right places—was buttoned up in a slim-fitting blue suit. The color was both lighter and brighter than navy and brought to mind the fancy glass his grandmother had collected. The skirt hugged her hips, and the matching jacket was fastened below her breasts with a single square button, above which peeked a hint of black silk.

He'd resigned himself to spending the weekend surrounded by lawyers and judges and other legal types. It wouldn't have been his first choice on how to spend three days, but the Echo Ridge town council strongly advocated continuing education for all its employees and, since that council was footing the bill for the weekend, he hadn't balked at the request.

He'd chosen to attend Sentencing Considerations in the Criminal Courts, believing it would be held in Boulder, Colorado, less than a two-hour flight from Echo Ridge. It turned out the conference was in Boulder *City*, which was in Nevada, adding another hour and another time zone to his travel. Although a potentially fortuitous error on his part, as he'd recently decided to move away from Echo Ridge and had, in fact, already applied to fill a vacancy in the Sheriff's Office in Haven, Nevada.

So he'd flown in a day early and made a quick trip to the northern part of the state to meet with the hiring committee before the conference. He'd been advised that a decision would be made before 4:00 p.m. Monday, and he figured the conference would distract him from counting the hours until then. As he watched the stunning brunette settle into her chair, almost directly across from him, he couldn't help but think that she would be an even better distraction.

She unzipped the top of her briefcase and removed a bottle of water, her cell phone and her iPad. If he'd been a betting man, he would have put money on her having been a straight-A student in school—the type who willingly sat at the front of the class to ensure she didn't miss a single word the teacher said.

The good girl had never been his type, and if he really wanted the distraction of a willing female to help get him through the weekend, he'd be better off hitting a club or the hotel bar when five o'clock rolled around. But his gaze lingered on the brunette, because it was a shame that a good girl should have a mouth that suggested it was capable of doing wonderfully bad things.

Now that she was set up, she turned to the balding man in the ill-fitting brown suit who was seated on her left. Making friends with her neighbors, he realized, when she said something, smiled and shook the man's hand. Then she turned to the woman on her other side, a skinny red-head with sharp eyes, and repeated the process.

Having finished with the introductions, she sat back in her chair. As more stragglers found their way to the room and filled the last few seats, she let her gaze move around the table. Then her eyes locked on his, and his stomach clenched as it absorbed the punch of sexual awareness.

He hadn't experienced anything like that in a long while, and he knew then that he wasn't going to walk away from her so quickly when the hour-long session was over.

Most of the seats were taken by the time Kate found the conference room where tables were set up around the perimeter to facilitate discussion. But she found a space between Lyle, a victims' rights advocate from Carson City, and Marcia, a former prosecutor-turned-defense-attorney from Fresno, California.

When she was settled in her chair, she let her gaze scan the room as last-minute arrivals squeezed into vacant seats. Her lazy perusal came to an abrupt halt when she saw him.

He was wearing a light gray micro-check shirt that stretched across mouth-wateringly broad shoulders with a loosely knotted plum-colored tie at his throat. His hair was brown, a few shades lighter than her own, and cut short. His forehead was high, his brows thick, his eyes—green? Brown? She couldn't quite tell from across the distance that separated them, but they were focused and intense. The bronze skin suggested that he spent a lot of time working or playing outdoors. The strong jaw, square and dark with stubble, gave him a slightly dangerous and yet somehow appealing edge.

There was no ring on the third finger of his left hand, resting casually on top of the table, but she knew that wasn't always proof of unmarried status. Then he caught her eye and winked boldly, and she felt heat spread up her neck and across her cheeks as she tore her gaze away. She was embarrassed to have been caught staring. She was also—unexpectedly and undeniably—aware of him on a purely visceral level.

It had been a long time since she'd been attracted to a man and even longer since she'd shared any kind of physical intimacy with one. She didn't know precisely how long, but it had been at least twenty-eight months because she hadn't been away from Haven in that period of time—and she definitely hadn't hooked up with anyone in her hometown. Heck, she couldn't even have coffee with a male colleague during morning recess from court without her sister texting to ask for details before her cup was empty.

So maybe it was the extended duration of her most recent dating hiatus that was responsible for her reaction to him. Or maybe it was his shoulders. Apparently she had a weakness for guys with great shoulders and strong jawlines and—

And somehow her errant gaze had drifted back to him again. Chiding herself for her reaction, she folded back the cover of her tablet and swiped to unlock the screen.

The moderator closed the door, effectively silencing the quiet murmur of conversation and focusing attention in his direction. After a brief introduction, he handed out some case studies for the participants to review and discuss.

As the debate evolved, Kate found herself arguing against the position taken by the broad-shouldered stranger who'd caught her eye. He insisted that adult crimes deserved adult punishment; she maintained that children didn't have experience making decisions or controlling their impulses and shouldn't be held to the same standards as their adult counterparts.

When the moderator finally called time on the session, neither of them had given an inch. And yet Kate found herself invigorated rather than frustrated, because while she didn't agree with her opponent's position, she had to admit that he'd made some good points and he presented his arguments in a rational and respectful manner.

As most of the other attendees funneled toward the door, he moved the other way—toward her. She took her time putting her materials away, pleased to note that her hands were steady despite the pounding of her heart. She uncapped her water bottle and tipped it to her lips to moisten her suddenly dry throat.

He wore jeans with his shirt and tie, and well-worn cowboy boots on his feet. Six feet two inches, she decided when she had to tip her head back to meet his gaze. And his eyes weren't green *or* brown but an intriguing combination of both. Hazel, she decided, though the word failed to describe the magnetism of his gaze. Tiny lines crinkled at the corners of his eyes and bracketed his mouth, and a thin scar slashed through his right eyebrow.

"Reid Davidson," he said.

She took the proffered hand—wide-palmed and strong—and felt a tingle of something dangerously tempting shoot up her arm and arrow toward her center. "Katelyn Gilmore."

"Defense attorney?" he guessed.

She nodded. "Among other things."

"Six months out of law school?"

She narrowed her gaze, not sure if his question was a legitimate guess or a subtle insult. "Four years."

He seemed surprised by that revelation. "Four years and you're not completely disillusioned yet?"

"My determination to fight for justice doesn't blind me to the flaws in our system."

"That's...admirable," he decided.

She slid the strap of her briefcase onto her shoulder. "You're a prosecutor," she guessed.

"No," he said quickly. Vehemently. "I'm not a lawyer."

"So what *do* you do, Not-a-Lawyer Reid Davidson?"

"I'm a sheriff."

She nodded, easily able to picture a shiny badge pinned to that wide chest. "And you throw the book at anyone who doesn't toe the line in your jurisdiction."

He didn't deny it. "It's my job to uphold the law."

"The law doesn't exist in a vacuum," she argued. "It requires context."

"Apparently you have some strong opinions on the subject," he noted. "Why don't we continue this discussion elsewhere, and you can enlighten me?"

She absolutely wanted to continue this discussion—or any discussion—if it meant spending more time with the broad-shouldered sheriff with the mesmerizing eyes and sexy smile.

"What did you have in mind?" she asked, determined to play it cool despite the anticipation racing through her veins.

"I could buy you a drink," he suggested.

She considered herself a smart woman—too smart to hook up with a stranger. But while she didn't know even the first page of Reid's life story, she knew that he set her blood humming in a way that it hadn't done in a very long time. And after more than two years without a man even registering a blip in her pulse, she was too curious to walk away without determining if the attraction she felt was reciprocated.

She wasn't looking for love. She wasn't even looking for sex. But she couldn't deny that she enjoyed looking at Sheriff Reid Davidson.

Sometimes you don't know what you want until it's right in front of you.

With the echo of her sister's voice in her ears, she made her decision. "A drink sounds good."

Reid had never been afraid to admit when he was wrong, and he'd realized—less than halfway through the workshop discussion—that he'd been wrong about her.

Katelyn.

The name struck him as a unique combination of the classic and contemporary, and as intriguing as the woman herself. Because while she might look prim and cool, there was a lot of heat beneath the surface. She argued not just eloquently but passionately, making him suspect that a woman who was so animated in her discussion of a hypothetical situation would be even more interesting up close and personal. Now he was about to find out.

There were two bars in the hotel—the first was an open lounge area that saw a lot of traffic as guests made their way around the hotel; the second, adjacent to the restaurant, was more remote and private. He opted for the second, where patrons could be seated at pub-style tables with high-back leather stools or narrow booths that afforded a degree of intimacy.

He guided her to a vacant booth. When the waitress came to take their drink order, Katelyn requested a Napa Valley cabernet sauvignon and he opted for a locally brewed IPA, signing the check to his room when the drinks were delivered.

After the server had gone, he raised his glass. "To stimulating discourse."

Though she lifted her brows at his deliberately suggestive word choice, she tapped the rim of her glass against the neck of his bottle.

"Where are you from, Sheriff Reid Davidson?" she asked, after sipping her wine.

"Echo Ridge, Texas."

"You're a long way from home," she noted.

"So it would seem," he agreed. "How about you?"

"Northern Nevada, so not quite such a long way."

"Humboldt, Haven or Elko County?"

"You must have aced geography in school," she remarked.

"I didn't ace anything in school," he confessed. "But I recently visited the town of Haven."

"Why were you there?" she asked, then held up a hand before he could respond. "No, don't tell me. I don't want to know."

"Why don't you want to know?"

"Because almost everyone in Haven knows everyone else—or at least knows someone who knows that someone else, and if it turns out that you hooked up with someone I know, this—" she gestured from her own chest to his and back again "—isn't going to happen."

"Is this—" he copied her gesture "—going to happen?"

She sipped her wine. "I'm thinking about it."

"While you're thinking, let me reassure you that I've never hooked up with anyone from Haven." His lips curved as he lifted his bottle. "Yet."

She set her glass on the table, her fingers trailing slowly down the stem. "You're pretty confident, aren't you?"

"Optimistic," he told her. "But I do need to ask you something."

"What's that?"

"Is there anyone waiting for you at home in Haven?"

"Aside from my father, grandparents, sister, two brothers, several aunts, uncles and cousins, you mean?"

"Aside from them," he confirmed.

"No, there's no one waiting for me." She traced the base of her wineglass with a neatly shaped but unpainted fingernail. "What about you, Sheriff Davidson—are you married?"

He shook his head. "Divorced."

"Girlfriend?"

"No," he said again. "Any more questions?"

"Just one," she said.

He held her gaze, waiting, hoping.

"Do you want to take these drinks back to my room?"

Chapter Two

Five weeks later

"I can't believe you're leaving." Trish Stilton pouted as she rubbed a hand over the curve of her hugely pregnant belly. "Especially now, only a few weeks before the baby's due to be born."

Reid dumped the entire contents of his cutlery drawer into a box. Though he didn't dare say it aloud, considering the imminent delivery of his ex-wife's baby, he'd decided that his timing was almost perfect.

"Just last week, I told Jonah that we should ask you to be the godfather, but now that you're moving to Nevada, that's out of the question."

Which further convinced Reid that he'd made the right choice in accepting the offer to take over the sheriff's position in Haven. Though he and Trish had been divorced for more than four years and she'd been remarried for almost three, they'd remained close. Maybe too close.

When she'd walked down the aisle to exchange vows with her current husband, Reid had been the man to give her away. Yeah, it had seemed an odd request to him, but he didn't see how he could refuse. When she'd found out that she was pregnant, she'd stopped at the Sheriff's Office to share the news with Reid even before she'd told her husband. And when she'd cried—tears of joy, because she was going to be a mother, mingled with grief, because her child would never know his grandfather—he'd held her and comforted her.

If she'd asked him to be her baby's godfather—as Jonah Stilton had warned him she intended to do—Reid wouldn't have been able to refuse. How could he refuse any request from the daughter of the man who'd saved his life?

Reid had been an orphaned teenager running with a bad crowd when the local sheriff took him under his wing. He didn't just turn Reid's life around, he saved it, and Reid knew there was no way he could ever repay the man who had been his mentor, father figure and friend. So when Hank realized he wasn't going to beat the cancer that had invaded his body and he'd confided to Reid that he was worried about his daughter, Reid had promised to take care of her. The news of their engagement had been a balm to the older man's battered spirits, and he'd managed to hold on long enough to see Reid and Trish exchange their vows.

"I'm honored that you thought of me," he said to his ex-wife now. "But I'm sure your baby's father would prefer to have his brother fill that role."

"Jonah understands how important you are to me," she said, without denying his claim.

"You're important to me, too, but I think this move is going to be the best thing for all of us."

"But why do you have to go so far away?" she demanded.

"Nevada's not all that far," he said soothingly.

"But Haven?" she pressed. "I looked it up—it might as well be called Nowhere, Nevada, because that's where it is."

"Then I won't expect you to visit," he said mildly.

"Of course, I'll visit," she promised. "Because you don't have any friends or family in that town."

"Actually, I do have a…friend…in Haven."

"A female friend?" she guessed.

He nodded.

"I *knew* there had to be another reason that you suddenly decided to leave Echo Ridge—something more than a temporary job."

"She's not the reason I'm leaving," he said truthfully. "But I am looking forward to seeing her again."

"What's her name?"

Reid shook his head. "None of your business."

Trish smiled. "Afraid I'll track her down and ask about her intentions?"

"Yes," he admitted.

Not that he was really worried. He had no doubt that Katelyn Gilmore could handle his ex-wife. But the attorney had no idea that he was moving to Haven, because they hadn't exchanged any contact information before they went their separate ways after the conference. And with the perspective that came with time and distance, he couldn't help but wonder if he'd made the weekend they'd spent together into more than it really was.

"Well, it would only be fair," Trish said now. "You wouldn't let me go out on a second date with Jonah until you'd done a complete background check on him."

"Because your father asked me to take care of you," he reminded her.

"He wanted us to take care of each other," she said.

And for a while, they'd done just that. But Trish had wanted more than he'd been willing or able to give her—an *irreconcilable difference* that led to the end of their marriage. When that happened, he felt as if he'd let down Hank as much as Trish, but he knew his old friend would be pleased to see his daughter in a committed relationship with a man who could give her everything Reid couldn't.

He was sincerely happy for her, because she was happy. For himself, he'd decided a long time ago that he wasn't cut out to be a dad. A kid who'd been knocked around by his mother's various boyfriends for the first six years of his life, then raised by his widowed grandmother for the next eight before being kicked into and around the system didn't know anything about being a father. He'd lucked out when he'd met Hank. Trish's father had given him an idea of the type of man a dad should be, but Reid suspected it was too little too late, that the scars from his earlier years were too numerous and deep to ever truly heal.

"Now you've got Jonah," he reminded her.

"Yes, I do," Trish said, smiling through the tears that filled her eyes again.

"Jeez, will you stop with the waterworks?" he demanded, passing her a box of tissues.

She plucked one out and dabbed at her eyes. "I can't help it—it's pregnancy hormones."

"Well, let your husband deal with your blubbering—he's the one who knocked you up."

"Yes, he did," she said proudly, rubbing a hand over the enormous swell of her belly. "And those hormones have also led to doing a lot more of what got me into this condition."

He lifted his hands to cover his ears. "Way too much information, Trish."

She laughed through her tears. Then she reached out

a hand to touch his arm. "Can I give you one piece of advice?"

"Can I stop you?" he countered drily.

She ignored his question. "Before you get involved with this woman—before *she* gets involved with you—be honest about what you want and don't want from a relationship."

"I never meant to be dishonest with you," he said quietly.

"I know," she admitted. "The problem was, we rushed into marriage without ever talking about all the things we should have talked about."

He nodded. "But now you have everything you wanted."

"Soon," she amended, rubbing a hand over her baby bump again. Then with her other hand, she grabbed his and drew it to the curve of her belly. "Do you feel that? He's kicking."

He did feel it, little nudges against his palm. He wondered if it hurt her, to have a tiny human being moving around inside of her, but that seemed like too personal a question to ask. Not that his ex-wife seemed to care about boundaries, which was why Reid was moving out of state in an effort to establish some. Instead he asked, "He?"

Trish smiled and nodded. "It's a boy. We're going name him Henry—for my dad."

Reid had to clear the tightness from his own throat before he could respond. "That's a great name."

She watched him tape the flaps of the box shut. "I really wish you weren't going."

He hadn't expected that his ex-wife would make this easy for him, but he hadn't expected that it would be so hard, either. But he didn't—couldn't—waver. He needed to move on with his life, and as long as he was living a stone's throw away from her, he knew that wouldn't happen.

"You're going to be okay, Trish. You don't need me anymore."

She sniffed and knuckled away a tear that spilled onto her cheeks. "But what if you still need me?"

She'd been his family—his only family—for seven years now. But it didn't matter if he still needed her—it was time for him to move on.

Kate thanked the clerk as she slid the judge's signed order into her client's file, tucked the file into her briefcase and turned away from the desk. She exited the courthouse, pausing outside the doors to perch her sunglasses on her nose in defense against the bright afternoon sun, then continued on her way. She'd been told that she moved purposefully, like a woman on a mission, and she usually was.

Today her mission was to get away from the courthouse before she threw up. She crossed the street and ducked into the shade of the trees that lined the perimeter of Shearing Park. The greenspace was usually quiet at this time of day, offering the privacy she needed. She lowered herself onto the wooden slats of a bench and reached into her briefcase for the sleeve of saltine crackers she'd been carrying for the past few days.

She inhaled, taking three long deep breaths. Then she nibbled on a cracker and sipped some water. When she felt a little steadier, she pulled out her cell phone and dialed her office.

"I've got the custody order for Debby Hansen," she said when her assistant answered the phone. "If you want to print up the cover letter and final account so everything's ready to go, that would be great. I'm heading to a settlement conference in Winnemucca this afternoon, but I'll be back in the office in the morning."

She could picture Beth frowning at Kate's schedule on

her computer screen. "I don't have anything about a set-tlement conference."

"I set it up myself—a favor for a friend," she explained. *Lied.*

If she was looking in a mirror, she would see flags of color on her cheeks. Thankfully, Beth wasn't able to see the telltale proof of her deception.

"Okay," the other woman said agreeably. "I'll leave your docket and the files for tomorrow morning on your desk before I lock up."

"Thanks, Beth."

She disconnected the call and nibbled on another cracker. She'd never felt good about lying, but lately she'd been doing a lot of it.

Lying to her assistant, to explain her absences from the office. To her dad, when he said she looked peaked. To her sister, when Sky asked what was wrong. To her grand-mother, when she hinted that Kate was working too hard.

To herself, when she suggested that the first home preg-nancy test was faulty and there was no reason to panic.

It was only when a second, and then a third, test showed the same obviously inaccurate result that she'd decided to see an ob-gyn.

She tucked her crackers back into her briefcase, walked to her car and headed toward Battle Mountain. Because she would rather drive thirty-five miles out of town than risk the inevitable speculation that would follow a visit to a local doctor.

"Good afternoon, Ms. Gilmore—I'm Camila Amaro."

Kate accepted the proffered hand of the woman who entered the exam room. "Thank you for squeezing me in."

"You sounded a little panicked on the phone."

"I'm feeling a little panicked," she admitted.

The doctor didn't go behind her desk to sit down but

leaned back against it, facing her patient. "Is this your first pregnancy?"

She managed a weak smile. "So much for thinking the results of three home pregnancy tests might be wrong."

"False results do happen," the doctor acknowledged. "But a false positive is extremely rare, and the test we ran here confirms the presence of hCG—the pregnancy hormone—in your system."

"I'm really pregnant? I'm going to have a baby?"

"You're really pregnant," the doctor confirmed.

She'd dreaded receiving this confirmation. How could she possibly juggle her professional responsibilities with the demands of a baby? And yet, something surprising happened when the doctor said those three words. She felt a loosening of the knots in her stomach and unexpected joy in her heart.

A baby.

And she knew then that it didn't matter that she hadn't planned for this—she would figure out a way to make it work.

"Do you want to set up a sonogram so we can establish how far along you are and discuss the options that are available to you?" Dr. Amaro asked.

"Five weeks and six days," Kate told her.

"You're sure?"

She nodded. "Broken condom."

The doctor opened the folder she carried and made a note in the file. "Are you in an exclusive relationship with the father?"

The question was matter-of-fact and without any hint of censure, but Kate felt her cheeks flush with embarrassment that she'd been so foolish and careless. A weekend fling had seemed like a good idea at the time—some harmless fun to break the monotony of her everyday life. She'd never anticipated that a few unforgettable nights would give her a lasting reminder of those nights with the handsome sheriff from Texas.

"No," she admitted. "In fact…I haven't seen him since the weekend that we were…together."

"Then maybe we should run some other tests?" the doctor suggested gently.

She wouldn't have thought it was possible, but her already burning cheeks flamed even hotter. She'd been so off-kilter about the possibility of a pregnancy that she hadn't given a thought to any other potential consequences of unprotected sex.

Of course, when the condom broke, she and Reid had talked about their respective sexual histories to reassure one another that there was no cause for alarm. But she nodded her assent to the doctor now. "Yes, please. Whatever you need to do—I want to know that my baby's going to be okay."

"Then you do want to have the baby?" Dr. Amaro asked in the same neutral tone.

Kate nodded again. While she appreciated the woman's professional manner and obvious determination not to influence her decision, there had never been any question in Kate's mind. Even when she'd still been firmly in denial about the possibility of a pregnancy, she'd known that—if she was pregnant—there was no other choice for her but to have the baby.

She'd always wanted to have a family…someday. Of course, she'd expected to be more established in her career—and preferably married—before that dream became a reality, but she was going to play the hand that had been dealt and be the best mother she could be to her baby.

She had no intention of making any claims on Sheriff Reid Davidson of Echo Ridge, Texas. She'd gone to bed with him not just willingly but eagerly, and even if the possibility of a pregnancy had never entered her mind, she alone had chosen to have this baby and she alone would be the responsible for that choice.

And while she had no idea how he would respond to the news that he was going to be a father, she knew that she had to tell him.

Soon.

Chapter Three

Reid stared at the modest pile of boxes in the middle of his new kitchen. He suspected that most people, by thirty-four years of age, had acquired more stuff, but when he and Trish had separated, he'd moved into a fully furnished apartment and let her keep the house and almost everything in it.

While looking at the housing options in Haven, he'd found an in-law suite available to rent only a few blocks from the Sheriff's Office—furnishings available—and decided that was again the easy option. Glancing around his new home, he acknowledged that he should have asked for photos.

Whether or not his decision to move to Haven, Nevada, would prove to be the right one had yet to be determined. But he'd needed a fresh start, he'd liked what he'd seen of the town on his first visit and he'd been assured by Jed Traynor, the former sheriff who had been forced into early retirement by some health concerns—and his wife—that Haven was populated by mostly good people.

And then, of course, there was the Katelyn factor.

He wasn't foolish enough to let his career decisions be influenced by a weekend fling, no matter how spectacular and unforgettable the sex had been. But he'd been thinking about her a lot and he was looking forward to the opportunity to see her again.

Seeing her naked again would be even better.

She was a woman of intriguing contrasts. When she'd walked into the conference room, she'd been the picture of cool professionalism, but it hadn't taken long for him to realize how much heat simmered beneath the surface. The passion she'd displayed in advocating her position in the conference room was just as evident in the bedroom.

She'd made the first move—not just when she'd invited him back to her room, but when she'd kissed him. There had been nothing tentative about that first kiss. No questions or doubts about what either of them wanted. Their mouths had come together eagerly, almost desperately.

They'd both been enthusiastic participants in their lovemaking. Tearing at their own clothes while simultaneously trying to undress each other, laughing when limbs got tangled in uncooperative fabric.

When she'd been stripped down to a tiny pair of black bikini panties and a low-cut bra, he'd stopped laughing.

Hell, his heart had almost stopped beating.

She was so incredibly hot.

So wonderfully agile.

So totally willing.

And even six weeks after only two nights together, he hadn't forgotten any of the details of the time he'd spent in her bed. Not the way her eyes went dark when she was aroused or the soft, sexy sounds that emanated from deep in her throat. Not the rosy pink buds of her nipples or the tiny brown mole beside her belly button. Not the way her hair looked fanned out on the soft pillow behind her head, or the erotic brush of those long tresses as her lips leisurely explored his body. Not the way her thighs quivered when he stroked deep inside her or the way her inner muscles clenched around him when she finally succumbed to her climax.

Yeah, he was definitely looking forward to seeing her again.

With that thought in mind, he decided to abandon his unpacking for a while and wander the neighborhood—to get his bearings. At least that would be the justification if anyone asked. The truth was, he'd already located the most important places: Sheriff's Office; courthouse; Diggers', the neighborhood bar and grill; Jo's, a local pizza place; The Trading Post, the general store; and, a few blocks down from the courthouse, The Law Office of Katelyn T. Gilmore.

Her practice was set up in a beautiful old building with a cornerstone that established the date of its erection as 1885. Maybe the old library, he speculated, since Jed had pointed out the new community center, which included a swimming pool, gymnasium, "the new library," several multipurpose rooms and administrative offices.

"Are you in need of legal counsel?"

Reid turned to face a woman who appeared to be in her mid- to late-sixties, about five-four with shoulder-length dark hair liberally streaked with gray, wearing a plaid shirt with faded jeans and well-worn boots.

"No, ma'am," he said. "Just admiring the building."

"The old library," she said, confirming his supposition. "It was built in 1885, as were most of the buildings on this stretch of Main Street, but the doors didn't open until 1887.

It's rumored that sixteen-year-old Elena Sanchez hid out in the basement of this very building for three weeks in the fall of 1904 to avoid being forced to marry."

"Did she succeed?"

The woman nodded. "With the help of the librarian, Edward Jurczyk, who sneaked in blankets and food for her. Two years later, they were married. Nine years after that, Edward was killed fighting in The Great War in Europe."

"Haven has quite an interesting history," he mused, his gaze returning to the wide front window where Katelyn T. Gilmore was painted in bold black letters outlined in gold and Attorney at Law was spelled out below in slightly smaller letters.

"Katie opened her office here almost two-and-a-half years ago," the woman continued. "If you're ever in need of an attorney, you couldn't do better. She sometimes has office hours on weekends, but she's out of town right now."

"You seem to know a lot about Ms. Gilmore's schedule," he noted.

And sharing more information than you should with a stranger, he wanted to caution. Of course, he kept that admonition to himself, as he was eager to hear anything about Katelyn that she was willing to tell him.

"Of course, I do," she replied. "Katie's my granddaughter."

"I'm beginning to believe that everyone in town knows—or is—a Gilmore." He offered his hand. "I'm Reid Davidson, the—"

"The new sheriff," she finished for him, as she gripped his hand in a surprisingly firm shake. "I know who you are. And I'm Evelyn Gilmore, not some dotty old woman who would spill personal information about my family to a stranger on the street."

Then her gaze narrowed speculatively. "So you apparently know that Haven was founded by the Gilmore family," she acknowledged, "but what do you know about the Blakes?"

He forced his expression to remain blank. "Who?"

She laughed. "It might turn out that you're exactly what this town needs, Sheriff Reid Davidson. You plan on staying beyond the completion of your current term?"

"Maybe you should table that question until after I've actually started my job," he suggested.

"Maybe I will," she decided. "Until then, if you've got time for a cup of coffee, I can introduce you to Donna Bradley. She's been working the counter at The Daily Grind for longer than it's been The Daily Grind.

"Cal's Coffee Shop, it used to be called," she continued. "But Cal died nearly a dozen years ago now and when his granddaughter took it over, she gave it a face-lift and a new name. She was smart enough to keep Donna, though, and if there's any news in town, she's usually the first to know it."

"I've always got time for a cup of coffee," Reid said, looking forward to her commentary on the community and its residents—and hopeful that she'd share more information about Katelyn.

Though Kate had been feeling tired for a couple of weeks, having the doctor explain that fatigue was normal in the first trimester, because her body was expending lots of energy helping to grow a baby, seemed to exacerbate the situation. By the end of the following week, she was really dragging.

Thankfully, she didn't have court Friday morning, but she did have an appointment at the community center in the afternoon to talk to a group of seniors about wills and estate planning. After the session was finished, she decided to call it a day.

Her cell phone rang just as she pulled into the parking lot behind the old library, which housed not only her law office but her apartment above it. Shifting her vehicle into Park, she glanced longingly at the second-floor windows. If she ignored the ringing, she could have her shoes off and her feet up in less than three minutes.

She answered the call, anyway.

"Hey, Kate—it's Liam," her brother said, as if she wouldn't recognize his voice or the number on the display.

"What's up?" It was unusual for him to contact her in the middle of the day, so she knew his call had a specific purpose.

"Do you remember my friend, Chase, from school?"

"Of course," she said.

"Well, I just got off the phone with his brother, Gage, who called me because Chase told him that my sister is an attorney."

"Are you getting to a point anytime soon?"

"Yeah," he said. "Gage's son, Aiden, has been arrested."

Now *that* was a surprise.

Aiden wasn't just a good kid, he was unfailingly honest. The type of kid who wouldn't swipe a pack of chewing gum from The Trading Post. In fact, Kate remembered a time when he'd paid a dollar for ten gummy worms but Samantha Allen, who was working behind the counter, miscounted. When Aiden realized he'd been given eleven candies, he tried to give one back.

"What did he allegedly do?"

"I don't know," Liam admitted. "I didn't think to ask, but Gage is panicking because he's still half an hour out of town and he wanted to know if there was anything you could do to help."

"Okay," Kate decided. "Tell him to bring Aiden in to see me tomorrow morning. I have a couple of later appointments but I should be able to squeeze them in around eleven."

"This can't wait until tomorrow. Aiden's being held for a bail hearing—that's why Gage is so frantic."

"He's a juvenile with no prior record," Kate said, thinking aloud.

"Can you find out what's going on?" Liam asked.

"I'm on my way to the Sheriff's Office right now," she promised.

She parked her vehicle then walked the few blocks to the Sheriff's Office. Judy Talon, the administrative assistant, was seated behind the front desk.

"Hey, Katie—are you here about Aiden Hampton?"

She nodded. "But I don't have any of the details," she admitted. "Can you fill me in?"

Judy glanced at the sheriff's closed door but still dropped her voice when she said, "He was arrested with Trent Marshall."

Under normal circumstances, they both knew that Aiden Hampton didn't keep company with kids like Trent Marshall—and he definitely didn't get in trouble with the law. Unfortunately, nothing had been normal for Aiden since his grandmother had died a few weeks earlier.

"What did they do?"

"Found a car with the keys in the ignition and decided to take it for a spin."

"Joyriding," she realized.

"Some would say," Judy agreed. "The new sheriff is saying grand larceny of a motor vehicle."

"You've got to be kidding."

The other woman shook her head. "I wish I was."

"Grand larceny is a felony."

"Which is why he's being held over for a bail hearing," Judy explained.

"Obviously, Jed didn't tell his replacement how things work around here." Kate glanced at her watch. "What time is the hearing?"

"Ten a.m. Monday morning."

"Oh, no." She shook her head. "I'm not letting Aiden spend the weekend in lockup."

"I hope he doesn't have to," the other woman agreed, though her tone was skeptical.

Kate looked toward the office. When Jed had run the department, the door was almost always open. Now it was closed, and she hoped that status wasn't a reflection of the sheriff's mind. "Can you let the new sheriff know that I need a few minutes of his time?"

Judy picked up the phone to connect with the sheriff, but first whispered, "Good luck."

She didn't let the woman's words unnerve her. After giving a perfunctory knock on the door, she turned the knob.

Be confident. Be convincing. Don't back down.

She repeated the refrain inside her head as she stepped into the office.

Be confident. Be convincing. Don't—

The rest of the words slipped from her mind as familiar hazel eyes lifted to meet her gaze.

And she found herself face-to-face with her baby's daddy.

Reid had been looking forward to the day when he would see Katelyn Gilmore again. He didn't anticipate that it would happen as soon as his third day behind the desk in the Sheriff's Office.

He'd been writing a report when she walked in, and he automatically glanced up—and was immediately sucker punched by her presence.

If the sudden widening of her eyes and the sharp intake of her breath were any indication, Katelyn was just as surprised to see him. Maybe even more so, because while he'd known their paths would cross and had eagerly anticipated that eventuality, it appeared that she'd been unaware of the identity of Haven's new sheriff.

"Reid?"

"Hello, Katelyn." He thought he'd remembered how beautiful she was, but seeing her again proved his memories inadequate.

She was wearing another one of those lawyer suits, this one a deep purple color with a pale pink shell under the jacket, which made him wonder what color lace she might be wearing beneath that. Her hair was pinned up as it had been the day of their first meeting, but he knew now how it felt when he slid his fingers through it as he kissed her. And maybe that wasn't a memory he should linger on while he was wearing his official sheriff's uniform, because the mental image was causing his body to stir in a very unprofessional way.

She opened her delectably shaped and incredibly talented mouth, then closed it again without saying another word.

"You're Aiden Hampton's attorney?" he prompted.

She nodded. "And you're the new sheriff."

"I am," he confirmed.

"But...I thought you lived in Texas. I even—" Now she shook her head. "It doesn't matter."

"What doesn't matter?"

She ignored his question to ask her own. "Why are you here?"

"I applied for the job before I met you," he said, wanting to dispel any concern she might have about his motivation. "In fact, I interviewed with the hiring committee the day before the conference in Boulder City."

Her cheeks flushed as she cast a quick glance at his open office door.

He nodded to the phone on his desk, indicating the light that revealed his assistant was occupied with a call.

"When I told you that I was from Haven, why didn't you mention that you'd applied for a job here?"

"Because you didn't want to know," he reminded her.

Her brows drew together as she recalled that earlier conversation and finally admitted, "I guess I did."

"And when I got the call offering me the job, well, I figured our paths would cross soon enough."

"They're going to cross frequently if you insist on locking up juveniles who should be released on their own recognizances."

He leaned back in his chair. Though he was disappointed that she'd so quickly refocused on her client, he could appreciate that she had a job to do. Any personal business could wait until after-hours. "Grand larceny of a motor vehicle is a felony."

"Grand larceny of a motor vehicle is a ridiculously trumped-up charge."

"Tell that to Rebecca Blake—it was her brand-new S-Class Mercedes, worth close to two hundred thousand dollars."

That revelation gave her pause, but just for a second. "Was the vehicle damaged?"

"Thankfully, no," he acknowledged.

She nodded, and he could almost see her switching mental gears from confrontation to persuasion. "He's a good kid, Reid—a straight-A student grieving for his grandmother."

He wouldn't—couldn't—let sympathy for the kid interfere with his responsibilities. "There are lots of kids who lose family members and don't act out by stealing a car."

"Elsie Hampton helped raise Aiden from birth, after his mother walked out of the hospital without her baby, leaving him in the custody of her seventeen-year-old father. But of course, you didn't know that, did you?"

"How could I?" he countered.

"You could have asked someone," she told him. "Everyone in Haven knows his family and his history. In fact, his dad works with Jed's son at Blake Mining."

He gave a short nod. "Point taken."

"So I can take my client home now?"

"No," he said.

"Why not?" she demanded.

"Because I've already gone on the record stating that he's to be held over for a bail hearing."

She sighed. "Then you're going to have to call Judge Calvert and ADA Dustin Perry and tell them you want to have a bail hearing."

"While I appreciate your passionate advocacy, Katelyn, you don't make the rules around here—I do."

"I get that you're new," she said. "Not just new to this office but new in town, and you might think I'm trying to manipulate you for the sake of my client, but I'm not."

"Well, okay, then," he said, making no effort to disguise his sarcasm. "I'm sure the judge and the prosecutor will both be thrilled to be called out to a bail hearing at four thirty on a Friday afternoon."

"I'm sure they won't be," she countered. "But they'd be even less happy to find out, on Monday morning, that you made Aiden Hampton spend the weekend in a cell."

"If I agree to do this, it will look like your client got preferential treatment," he warned.

"No, it will look like the new sheriff finally took his head out of his butt for a few minutes."

Though her blatant disrespect irked him, Reid couldn't help but admire her passion and conviction.

"Your client was processed by the book," he told her.

"Maybe," she allowed. "*If* he'd actually committed grand larceny of a motor vehicle, but the reality is that he went for a joyride—and joyriding is a misdemeanor offense."

"A gross misdemeanor," he clarified.

"Are you going to make those calls or should I, Sheriff?"

"Are you really trying to put my badge between us now, Katelyn?"

"Seems like you were the one who did that," she said. "And it's Kate. Everyone here calls me Kate."

"Or Katie," he noted.

She frowned. "Only my family calls me Katie."

"I like Katelyn better, anyway."

She huffed out a breath. "The judge and ADA?" she prompted.

He picked up the phone.

Thirty minutes later, all parties were assembled at the courthouse. Less than half that time had passed again before Aiden Hampton was released into the care of his grateful and relieved father.

The assistant district attorney didn't stick around any longer than was necessary to sign the papers. The judge didn't even wait that long. After enumerating the usual conditions for release, he gave the new sheriff a brief but pointed speech about the value of the court's time and suggested that he familiarize himself with the way things were done in Haven, because apparently it was different than what he was used to.

Kate didn't let herself feel sorry for Reid. But she did appreciate that he'd called the hearing, albeit reluctantly, and she said so as they walked side by side out of the courthouse. "Thank you."

"The next time I put your client in a cell, he's going to stay there a lot longer," Reid warned.

"There won't be a next time," she said. "Aiden really is a good kid who chose the wrong way to work through some stuff."

"By hanging out with a friend already on probation?"

"I don't know what he was doing with Trent Marshall," she admitted. "They don't usually run in the same circles."

"I'm guessing you represent the Marshall kid, too?"

She nodded. "And I'm curious as to how the kid already on probation walked away with a summons to court and the kid who's never been cited for jaywalking ends up locked in a cell."

"If you really want to know, I'll tell you—over dinner."

Chapter Four

Kate's mind was reeling. Not just because she was once again in close proximity to the sheriff, with whom she'd had the Best. Sex. Ever. a few weeks earlier, but because she now had to accept that the father of her baby wasn't fifteen hundred miles away but living in the same town.

"Dinner?" she echoed, and realized it could be the perfect opportunity to share her big—and growing—news.

"Traditionally the third and biggest meal of the day," he explained, amusement dancing in those hazel eyes.

"I understand the term," she assured him. "I was just… surprised…by your invitation."

"Surprised is okay," he decided. "But are you hungry?"

She realized that she was. The queasiness that left her feeling unsettled through most of the morning usually disappeared by lunch, and lunch had been a long time ago.

"I could eat," she finally responded to his question, determined not to allow the sexy sheriff's nearness stir other appetites.

"Good," he said. "I'd like to buy you dinner, but I'm going to ask you to decide where since I'm still finding my way around town."

"There are only three places in this town where you can get a decent meal," she told him. "The Sunnyside Diner, which does a great all-day breakfast but isn't so great with other menu options, Jo's Pizza, which makes the best thin crust pizza I've ever had—and their wings are pretty good, too—but eating in means nabbing one of only half a dozen tables crammed into a tiny space and no hope of a private conversation, and Diggers'."

"I've been to Diggers'," he told her. "The food was great."

"It is," she confirmed. "But we can't go there."

"Why not?"

"Because Diggers' is second only to The Daily Grind for gossip in Haven."

"You're worried people will talk about us sharing a meal?"

"I don't want to have to answer questions about how I'm acquainted with the new sheriff," she admitted.

"What's wrong with the truth?"

She shook her head. Now more than ever, she didn't want anyone to know that she'd met Reid in Boulder City, because when her pregnancy became apparent and people started counting backward, they'd suspect the baby had been conceived while she was out of town and she'd rather they didn't know that Haven's new sheriff had been there, too.

"Actually, I was referring to the other truth," he said. "That our paths crossed when you came to my office."

Which was a perfectly reasonable explanation. As an attorney, it made sense that she'd want to cultivate a good relationship with the new sheriff. But she also knew that if she was seen in public with him, it would be all the excuse anyone else wanted or needed to interrupt their conversation to wrangle their own introductions.

"Except that it's Friday."

"And?" he prompted, obviously seeking clarification.

"And my sister, Skylar, works at Diggers' on the weekend," she admitted.

"We could pick up pizza and take it back to my place," he suggested as an alternative.

She hesitated. "Look, Sheriff, despite what happened between us in Boulder City, I'm really not that kind of girl."

"You're not the kind of girl who likes pizza?"

She managed a smile. "I'm not the kind of girl who goes back to a guy's place—or invites him back to hers."

"I wasn't expecting to share anything more than pizza," he said, then shrugged. "Hoping, maybe, but not expecting."

The honest response undermined her resolve. "Why don't I make something for dinner instead?" she impulsively offered.

"I'd never say no to a home-cooked meal."

"I'm not promising anything fancy," she warned. "But you'll be able to eat and we'll be able to talk without a thousand interruptions."

"That works for me," he agreed.

She glanced at her watch, then mentally calculated the time she needed to make a quick trip to The Trading Post before she could start cooking. "Seven o'clock?"

"Sure," he agreed.

"Okay, I'll see you then."

He caught her arm as she started to turn away. "Only if you give me your address."

"Do you know where my office is?"

"You live at your office?"

"Above the office. Apartment 2B."

"I'll see you at seven."

Inviting Reid to have dinner at her place seemed like a good idea at the time—or, if not a good idea, at least a necessary compromise. They needed to talk and she didn't want to have the conversation where anyone might overhear it. But now that he was here, Kate realized she'd made a tactical error.

She loved her apartment—the ultramodern kitchen and open-concept living area with tall windows looking down on Main Street, two spacious bedrooms and a luxurious bathroom. Certainly, it had never seemed small—until Reid Davidson stepped inside. He wasn't a man whose presence was in any way, shape or form subtle, and it was as if he filled every square inch of space with his potent masculinity.

Being near him had her hormones clamoring so loudly she could barely hear herself think. And while her mind was desperately trying to focus on certain facts that needed to be discussed, her body was stirring, aching, wanting.

She took the bottle of wine he offered, and as her fingertips brushed against his, she was suddenly reminded of the way those fingers had touched her—the bold confidence of his hands as they stroked over her body, taking her to heights of pleasure she'd never even imagined.

He'd changed out of his sheriff's uniform and into a navy polo shirt that stretched across his broad shoulders. The hem of the shirt was tucked into a pair of softly faded jeans that hugged his lean hips and strong thighs, as her legs had hugged those hips and thighs, their naked limbs tangled and their bodies moving together.

She set the bottle of wine on the counter and turned to

dump the pasta in the pot of boiling water on the stove, hoping the steam would explain the sudden flush in her cheeks.

"Did you want wine or beer or something else?"

"I'd love a beer if you've got one handy," he said.

She stirred the pasta, then moved to the refrigerator to retrieve a bottle of Icky IPA. "Bottle or glass?" she asked as she pried off the cap.

"Bottle's fine."

Instead of taking the bottle she offered, he wrapped his hand around hers.

"What are you doing?" she asked warily.

"Trying to figure out why you invited me to dinner but haven't made eye contact since I walked through the door."

She lifted her gaze to meet his. "I'm just trying to get dinner finished up."

"Tell me what I can do to help," he suggested.

Go back to Echo Ridge.

The response immediately sprang to mind, but of course, she couldn't say the words aloud without then explaining why his sudden and unexpected appearance in Haven complicated her life.

Instead, she only said, "For starters, you could give me back my hand."

He loosened his grip so that she could pull her hand away without dropping the bottle. "What else?"

She gestured to the living area. "Go sit down."

"You don't trust me to help?"

"There's really nothing you can do," she told him.

"Do you want me to open the wine?"

She shook her head. "I'm going to stick with water—I've got work to do tonight." Which was true, if not the whole truth.

He took his beer and moved around to the other side

of the island. But instead of retreating to the living area and relaxing on the sofa, he chose one of the stools at the counter.

"So what do you think of Haven so far?" she asked, resigned to making small talk for eight minutes while the pasta cooked.

"I like it," he said. "It's a little smaller than Echo Ridge, but there's a strong sense of community here."

"There is," she confirmed, lowering the heat on the burner beneath the sauce. "Even when I was away at school, I knew I'd come back here after graduation."

"Summa cum laude from UCLA Law."

She frowned. "How'd you know that?"

"I met your grandmother," he confided.

"How? When?"

"Last weekend. I was walking down Main Street, trying to get a feel for the town, and our paths crossed. We had coffee together."

"You had coffee with my grandmother?"

He nodded. "She introduced me to Donna Bradley at The Daily Grind."

"You had coffee with my grandmother," she said again.

He studied her as he tipped his bottle to his lips, swallowed. "Why does that bother you?"

"It doesn't bother me," she denied. "But it's a little weird."

"Why?"

"Because she's my grandmother and you're…"

"The guy you had lots of naked sweaty sex with?"

"Okay, yes," she allowed.

"I didn't tell her about the naked sweaty sex," he promised.

"Thank you for that," she said drily.

He just grinned.

And that smile did strange things to her pulse...or maybe it was the heat from standing so close to the stove.

"But I haven't stopped thinking about it—or you," he continued. "I applied for the job before I met you, but you were definitely a factor in my decision to accept it."

"We weren't ever supposed to see one another again," she reminded him of the agreement they'd made in Boulder City.

"And yet, you went to Echo Ridge last weekend." The surprise must have shown on her face because he explained, "You left a message with Deputy Ryker."

She nodded. "A friend of mine from law school lives in Texas. Since I was there, I thought I'd stop by to say hi."

"Texas is a pretty big state."

"Chloe lives just outside of Dallas, so a side-trip to Echo Ridge wasn't really out of my way."

"Oh," he said, sounding disappointed. "I was kind of hoping you'd made the trip to see me."

The timer on the stove buzzed, granting her a temporary reprieve from the increasingly awkward conversation.

"Dinner's ready."

There was something on her mind.

Something more than concern about the client who'd brought her into his office a few hours earlier. When Luke Ryker told him that she'd shown up at the Sheriff's Office, he'd hoped it was memories of the nights they'd spent together that inspired Katelyn to track him down. But she certainly wasn't giving the impression of a woman motivated by carnal desires.

And though she kept up her end of the conversation while they ate, her thoughts were obviously elsewhere.

"Is it convenient or tiresome to live above your office?" he asked, attempting to engage her attention.

Katelyn twirled her fork in her pasta. "It's convenient," she said. "Certainly a lot more convenient than driving twenty miles into town from the Circle G Ranch every day."

He'd heard of the Circle G—reputedly the biggest and most prosperous cattle ranch in all of Haven County. It was also, if he remembered the story correctly, half of the property that was the original source of friction between the Gilmore and Blake families when they settled in the area more than one hundred and fifty years before.

According to local folklore, back in the spring of 1855, a developer sold a 100,000-acre parcel of land in Nevada to Everett Gilmore, a struggling farmer from Plattsmouth, Nebraska. The same developer also sold 100,000 acres to Samuel Blake, a down-on-his-luck businessman from Omaha. Both men subsequently packed up their families and their worldly possessions and headed west for a fresh start.

Everett Gilmore arrived first, and it was only when Samuel Blake showed up with his deed in hand that the two men realized they'd been sold the exact same parcel of land. Since both title deeds were stamped with the same date, there was no way of knowing who was the legitimate owner of the land. Distrustful of the local magistrate's ability to resolve the situation to anyone's satisfaction—and not wanting to publicly admit that they'd been duped—the two men agreed to share the property between them, using the natural divide of Eighteen-Mile Creek as the boundary between their lands.

Because the Gilmores had already started to build their home in the valley—on the west side of the creek—the Blakes were relegated to the higher elevation on the east, where the land was mostly comprised of rocky hills and ridges. The Gilmores' cattle immediately benefitted from grazing on more hospitable terrain, while the Blakes struggled for a lot of years to keep their herd viable—until silver and gold were found in the hills on their side of the creek and they gave up ranching in favor of mining.

"Is there any truth to that story about the ancestors of the Gilmore and Blake families coming to Nevada to settle the same piece of land?" he asked her now.

"It's all true," she assured him. "The Gilmores still own the fifty thousand acres on the west side of the creek and the Blakes own the fifty thousand acres, including all the gold and silver, on the east."

She put her fork down and picked up her glass of water. "You were going to tell me why Trent was given a court date and Aiden was locked up," she reminded him.

"Because Trent was a passenger in the car that Aiden was driving."

"Where'd they find the car?" she asked.

"Parked, with the key in the cup holder, in the driveway of the owner's house on Mountainview Road."

Katelyn shook her head. "Anyone who leaves, in plain view, the key to a fancy car deserves to have it stolen."

"I'll pretend I didn't hear you say that."

"How mad was Rebecca Blake when she realized her car had been taken?"

"Beyond mad," he admitted. "And more than a little embarrassed, because she knew that she'd left the key in it."

"She was at Elsie Hampton's funeral—and she's known Aiden since he was in diapers," Katelyn told him. "As mad and embarrassed as she was, I'm a little surprised that she wanted to press charges."

"It wasn't her choice," he said.

"You do know you'll never get a conviction on grand larceny, don't you? It would be a waste of time and resources to even take it to trial."

"That's an argument better saved for your discussions with the prosecutor," he suggested.

"Maybe it's different in Echo Ridge, but here the prosecutor doesn't usually make decisions about the disposition of charges without first consulting the Sheriff's Office."

"I investigated the complaint of a stolen vehicle and made the appropriate arrests," he said. "Now it's up to your pal in the ADA's office to decide what to do with the defendants."

"Dustin Perry's not my pal," she told him.

"I saw the two of you chatting while waiting for the judge. He seemed…favorably inclined toward you."

"You know, for a guy who was quick to point out that he's not a lawyer, you sound an awful lot like one at times."

He frowned. "Are you trying to spoil my appetite?"

She looked at his almost empty plate. "Not much chance of that."

"What can I say? This is great pasta," he said.

And it was. The red sauce had chunks of tomato, pepper and onion and was just a little bit spicy. But while he'd been mopping up sauce with a second slice of crusty bread, he noticed that she'd hardly touched her meal. She had her fork in hand and was pushing the pasta around on her plate, but she'd rarely lifted the utensil to her mouth.

"I didn't make anything for dessert, but I do have ice cream," she told him.

"What kind?"

She pushed her chair away from the table and went to open the freezer drawer below the refrigerator. Her appliances were all top of the line—as was everything else that he could see. Whoever had renovated the building had spared no expense in the dark walnut cupboards, natural granite countertops, marble tile and hardwood floors.

"Chocolate, chocolate 'n' peanut butter or chocolate chip cookie dough," she offered.

"Nothing with chocolate?" he asked drily.

A smile tugged at the corners of her mouth as she shrugged. "Sorry."

"Do you have cones?"

"No, but I have waffle bowls," she told him.

"Even better," he decided.

"What kind do you want?"

"Cookie dough."

She took the container out of the freezer and set it on the counter, then opened the cupboard and stood on her toes. "If they were more easily accessible, I'd indulge all the time," she explained, as she stretched toward the top shelf.

"If you didn't want to indulge, you wouldn't buy them," he commented, easily reaching over her head for the box.

She pulled open a drawer to retrieve an ice-cream scoop. "That's just the kind of logic I'd expect from a man."

He set the box on the corner, then lifted his hand to tuck an errant strand of hair behind her ear, his fingertip slowly tracing the outer shell.

The scoop slipped from her grasp, bounced on the counter.

"I don't remember you being skittish," he said.

She swallowed. "I'm not usually."

"So what has you strung so tight now?" he wondered aloud. "Are you worried that I'm going to make a move?" He stepped closer, so that she was trapped between the counter at her back and him at her front. "Or that I'm not?"

The pulse at the base of her jaw was racing, and her slightly parted lips—so tempting and soft—were mere inches from his own. Her gaze went to his mouth, lingered, as if she wanted his kiss as much as he wanted to kiss her.

Then she turned her head away and shifted to the left, sidestepping both him and his question.

"What's going on, Katelyn?" he pressed, because it was obvious that *something* was.

She nibbled on her bottom lip as she pried the lid off the ice-cream container.

"Katelyn?" he prompted, ignoring the caution lights that were flashing in his head.

Finally, she looked at him, her big blue eyes filled with wariness and worry. "I'm pregnant."

Chapter Five

She hadn't intended to blurt it out like that, but now that the words had been spoken, Kate actually felt relieved. It was no longer this big secret that she was keeping bottled up inside; she'd done the right thing and told Reid about the baby.

Now she just had to deal with his reaction, whatever that might be.

He reached behind him, his hands curling over the edge of the island countertop, as if he needed the support to remain standing. She understood how he felt—she was more than a little unsteady herself.

She moistened her lips with the tip of her tongue, waiting for him to say something, anything.

"You're sure?" he asked, after a long minute had passed.

She nodded. "I took one of those over-the-counter tests. Actually, I took three," she admitted. "And I got official confirmation from the doctor last week."

He went back to the table for his beer, tipped the bottle to his lips. "That's why you were in Echo Ridge," he realized. "Because you think it's mine."

Her cheeks burned with embarrassment, but she couldn't fault him for asking. She'd jumped into bed with him only a few hours after their first meeting—why wouldn't he assume that was normal behavior for her?

"I know it's yours," she told him. "You're the only man I've been with in…a long time. But considering how quickly everything happened between us, I can understand why you'd ask, why you'd want proof."

He fell silent again, and she found herself babbling in an effort to fill the silence.

"We can have a DNA test as soon as the baby's born. It's possible to do paternity testing before birth, through amniocentesis, but it also increases the risk of miscarriage and I'd rather not take the chance when there are no other factors that warrant it."

He nodded, but whether it was in agreement or understanding, she had no idea.

"I'm not asking anything of you," she hastened to reassure him. "I made the decision to have this baby on my own, and I intend to raise the baby on my own."

That, finally, got a response from him.

"You didn't make the baby on your own," he pointed out.

"Well, no," she agreed, her body humming in remembrance of the pleasures she'd experienced in his arms.

"And I don't shirk my responsibilities," he said with grim resolve.

"I appreciate that, Reid, but—"

He shook his head. "No buts, Katelyn."

She didn't know him well enough to have anticipated his response to the news—whether he'd be shocked or angry or disbelieving, but she'd tried to prepare for all those possibilities. So far, he hadn't responded with any recognizable emotion.

"I think we both need to take some time to think about what this means and where we want to go from here," she suggested cautiously.

Finally, he nodded. "That's probably a good idea."

She exhaled a quiet sigh of relief as she followed him to the door.

He paused with his hand on the knob. "If you need anything, give me a call."

"I will."

Then he leaned down and touched his lips to the top of her head. "Thanks for dinner, Katelyn."

The sweet gesture made her throat tighten. She closed her eyes against the sudden sting of tears as she shut the door behind him and flipped the lock.

Only eight days had passed since Dr. Amaro had confirmed her pregnancy, after which her first thought had been to track down Reid and let him know that she was going to have his baby. Traveling all the way to Echo Ridge only to discover that he wasn't there had been another emotional upheaval. She'd been filled with disappointment and frustration and, yes, relief.

It was as if she'd been given a reprieve, an opportunity to figure out what she wanted to do without having to factor her baby's father into the equation. Finding him in the Sheriff's Office in Haven was just one more surprise she hadn't been anticipating.

Working in family law had shown her that co-parenting could make things a lot easier—or a lot harder. She also knew that if Reid wanted to acknowledge paternity and be a father to their child, there was nothing she could do to stop him.

Was it any wonder that she was feeling exhausted and overwhelmed and terrified?

Because if he didn't want to be involved, she'd have to struggle through every step on her own. Not just pregnancy and childbirth, but midnight feedings, diaper rashes and teething woes. Then skinned knees and long division and, in later years, first dates and broken hearts and various other disappointments.

But she was equally terrified that he'd embrace fatherhood and she'd have to interact with him on an almost daily basis for the next eighteen years and beyond. The recent trend toward shared custody meant that he could be entitled to equal time with the baby who was right now nestled in the warm comfort of her womb. He would have an equal say in where their child went to school and what sports or activities he or she participated in.

And maybe they'd be in complete agreement about all those things—but what if they weren't?

She touched a hand to her still-flat stomach, awed and amazed to think that there was a tiny life growing inside her. A tiny life that would someday call her mama, then mommy and mom and eventually mother, accompanied by a preteen eye-roll.

She had no experience of her own to draw on after that. Theresa Gilmore had died when Kate was twelve, forcing her to negotiate the awkward teen years and all major transitions after that without her guidance. There were so many milestones that she'd marked without her mother's presence: graduation from high school, acceptance to law school, the unveiling of her name stenciled on her office window.

There were so many times over the years that she'd missed having her mom around, but never had she missed her support more than she did upon realizing that she was going to be a mother herself. And now, she was going to have to go through all the phases of pregnancy and child-birth without her, too.

Still, Kate knew she was lucky. Though her father wouldn't be happy to learn that his unmarried daughter was going to have a baby, she didn't doubt that he'd be supportive—or that he'd love his grandchild. Her grandparents and sister and brothers would also be there any time she needed anything. And her best friend, Emerson, a recent new mother, would be able to offer advice and insights.

Despite all the support available to her, she was scared to death that she'd somehow screw this up.

And because her baby had been conceived with a man she barely knew, she'd have to work with him to figure out what was best for their child.

Oh, what a mess I've made of my life.

Except that she didn't really regret anything that had happened, because she already loved her baby more than she'd ever thought possible.

Returning to the kitchen to tidy up the dishes, she noticed the forgotten chocolate chip cookie dough on the counter. She dropped the unused scoop back in the cutlery drawer and took out a spoon. Then she sat down on the cold tile floor and dipped her spoon into the tub.

Because melting ice cream was at least one problem she knew how to solve.

Reid left her apartment with no concept of where he was going or what he was going to do.

Katelyn Gilmore was pregnant—with his child—and he was completely unprepared to be a father.

It wasn't just bad timing. He wasn't one of those guys who always thought he'd be a father "someday" but had to accept that the day would come sooner than anticipated. No, years earlier Reid had consciously decided that he wouldn't ever have a child. He'd even considered having surgery to ensure it couldn't happen, except that the prospect of going under the knife was daunting and condoms were readily available.

But fate had apparently decided to kick that conscious decision to the curb. It was as if all the stars had aligned to screw him over with a broken condom.

Not that he'd ever put much stock in fate or the alignment of stars, but when his ex-wife had met her current husband, she told Reid that fate had put Jonah in her path. He'd countered with skepticism, pointing out that the hand of destiny—if there was such a thing—had better things to do than muck around in the computers at 4evermatch.com. Trish would no doubt get a huge kick out of his current predicament, claiming it was karma because he'd disrespected the higher powers of the universe.

Not that he intended to tell Trish—or anyone else. At least not until he and Katelyn had figured out what they were going to do.

For now, he just started walking. He didn't want to go home. He didn't want to be alone, because then he'd have to think about the news Katelyn had dropped in his lap. He'd have to acknowledge that, all conscious decision-making and careful planning aside, he was going to be a father.

He walked with no clear destination in mind, past the shops and businesses that lined Main Street. He lifted his hand in greeting when Reggie Mann—owner and operator of Mann's Movie Theater—called out to him, but he didn't pause. He didn't want to make conversation; he didn't to make friends.

What he wanted, he realized as he approached Diggers' Bar & Grill, was to get so rip-roaring drunk he could no longer hear the words that continued to echo in his head. Of course, he'd never let the residents of Haven see their sheriff in such a state, but he was off duty and out of uniform, so he figured it was okay to have a drink or two.

The double doors opened into an enclosed foyer that housed two entrances. The one on the left was clearly marked Bar and the one on the right designated Grill. Once inside it was easy enough to move from one side to the other, as both were under the same roof with only a partial wall dividing them, but it allowed families to take their kids for a meal without having to walk through a bar to get to a table.

The interior was deliberately rustic, with floors of unpainted, weathered wood slats, scuffed and scarred from the steady traffic of boot heels. Framed newspaper headlines proclaiming the discovery of gold and silver in the nearby hills hung on the walls along with miners' helmets, metal pans, buckets, coils of rope, pickaxes and a few other items that he had no idea what they were but hoped were securely fastened, because some of them had the potential to be lethal weapons otherwise.

Reid's first day on the job, Jed Traynor had taken him through the door on the right to Diggers' Grill for lunch. Tonight, he went through the door on the left.

There were several patrons already seated at the bar—some of them watching the baseball game on the two big screens, a young couple snuggled close together sharing a plate heaped with cheesy nachos, a trio of older men focused on their drinks.

He straddled a vacant stool and surveyed the labels on the taps in front of him. Not that it really mattered which one he chose—after a few, they all tasted pretty much the same. And his only purpose in being here right now was to drink until his brain was fuzzy enough to let him forget he was going to be a dad.

The irony of the situation was not lost on him. His marriage had fallen apart because he didn't want to have a child with his wife. Now he was going to have a child with a woman he barely knew. And while the situation wasn't what he would have chosen, Katelyn's pregnancy took choice out of the equation.

Maybe it's not mine.

The thought sneaked into his mind, seductively tempting.

But over the years, he'd gotten adept at reading people, and nothing Katelyn had said or done had given him reason to suspect she wasn't being honest with him.

I know it's yours. You're the only man I've been with in...a long time.

And if he needed any more evidence that he could plausibly be the father of her baby, there was the broken condom.

That had created a moment of panic for both of them, but they'd managed to convince themselves that the odds of a faulty bit of latex coinciding with her fertile time were negligible. And they'd put the broken condom out of their minds and made love several more times after that, without any further mishaps, unable to get enough of one another. He hadn't been so hot for any female since he was a teenager and the sight of Lana Doucet in skintight jeans and a clingy sweater was enough to give him a hard-on.

But there was something about Katelyn—from the minute she'd walked through the door of that conference room, he'd wanted her. He'd been sure it was his lucky day when she agreed to have a drink with him. When she invited him back to her room, he'd felt like the luckiest man in the world.

Apparently his luck had run out.

One of the bartenders, an attractive blonde with blue eyes and an easy—almost familiar—smile, made her way down the bar. Reid studied her for a minute, wondering if he'd already met her in town. If he had, he couldn't remember when or where.

"What can I get for you?" she asked.

"I'll have a pint of the Sierra Nevada Pale Ale."

She grabbed a glass from the shelf but paused before setting it under the tap. "Are you sure you don't want something stronger?"

"What?"

"You've got the look of a man who needs a shot—or two dozen—of strong whiskey."

He'd never been the type to turn to the bottle, but he'd never been faced with a situation of such magnitude. "Maybe you're right," he acknowledged. "What do you recommend?"

She replaced the glass and selected a bottle, holding it up for his approval.

Reid nodded and she poured a generous two fingers of Maker's Mark into a whiskey glass, then set the drink on a paper coaster in front of him. "Anything you want to talk about?"

He shook his head. He not only wasn't ready to talk about Katelyn's disclosure, he didn't want to think about it. But even if he wanted to talk, he knew better than to say a word to anyone in this town where everyone seemed to know the Gilmore family.

"I've been told that I'm a good listener," the bartender said to him, her smile encouraging.

"By anyone who wasn't drunk?"

She laughed. "As a matter of fact, yes."

"Well, I have a confession… I've never been told that I'm a good talker."

"Maybe this will help," she said, and poured him another drink.

He stared at the amber liquid in his glass, tempted to throw it back. Then another and another. Until he finally managed to drown out the echo of Katelyn's voice in his head.

I'm pregnant. I'm pregnant. I'm pregnant.

"Do you have a name? Or should I just call you Mister-Not-A-Good-Talker?" the bartender asked.

"Reid," he said.

"Are you new in town, Reid, or just passing through?"

"New in town," he said.

"From…Texas?" she guessed.

He nodded.

"Which would make you the new sheriff."

He nodded again.

"Well, you're a definite upgrade from the old sheriff," she remarked. "I mean, Jed's a nice guy and all, but when women sigh over a man in uniform, they aren't sighing over men like Jed. But you, on the other hand—yeah, women would sigh over you."

He looked up from his drink. "Are you flirting with me?"

"Me?" She seemed genuinely surprised by the question. "No." Then, more emphatically. "God, no."

He lifted a brow.

"Sorry," she said. "I didn't mean to sound quite so vehement, I just didn't realize that you would assume… Although now that I'm replaying the words in my mind, of course you assumed I was flirting with you. But the truth is, I was thinking about someone who hasn't sighed over a man in a long time." She shook her head. "Now it sounds like I'm covering up for my own fumbling attempts at flirting with you, and I'm not, and I'm sorry if I've made you uncomfortable."

"You haven't," he assured her.

"But now I have a question that might," she warned. "What's your relationship status?"

"My relationship status?"

She nodded. "Are you married, engaged or otherwise involved?"

"If you're not flirting with me, how is my relationship status at all relevant?" he wondered.

"I'll tell you the relevance if you tell me your status."

"Are you sure you're not flirting with me?"

"You're cute, Sheriff, but you're not my type. You are, however, the type of guy I can imagine my sister totally going for."

"Thank you, I think. As for my relationship status… there might be a wedding in my not-too-distant future."

"That sucks," she said. "Oh—not for you, of course. It's great for you. But it's not easy to meet guys in this town, especially when your last name is Gilmore, and Katie hasn't had a date in… I don't even know how long."

"Wait a minute." Reid held up a hand. "Did you say your last name is Gilmore?"

She nodded.

"And your sister's name is Katie—or Katelyn?"

She nodded again, confirming his suspicion that everyone in town knew the Gilmores—or *was* a Gilmore.

"Then you must be Skylar."

Her gaze narrowed suspiciously. "How would you know that?"

"Because I know your sister."

"You do?"

"In fact—" he lifted his glass of whiskey, as if making a toast "—she's the woman I'm going to marry."

Chapter Six

Kate was already in her pajamas when her cell phone chimed to announce a text message. She wanted to ignore it. She wanted to burrow under the covers and fall into a deep and dreamless sleep to forget—for at least a few hours—that her entire life was about to change.

Of course, she couldn't do that—at least not without checking the message first to ensure it wasn't a family emergency or a client crisis or anything else that required an immediate response. She paused the baseball game on TV and picked up her phone.

She felt a quick spurt of panic when she read the message and keyed a quick response. Then, after exchanging her pajama bottoms for a pair of yoga pants and tugging a hoody over her T-shirt, she headed out.

Eight minutes after leaving her apartment, she was walking into Diggers'.

Haven was only one of three cities in the whole state of

Nevada where gambling was prohibited, which meant that weekends saw a regular exodus of residents who sought more exciting opportunities than those available within city limits. For those who opted to stay, Diggers' was a popular destination.

Tonight, the local watering hole was doing a brisk business, with most of the seats at the bar occupied. Right now, Kate's sister was simultaneously pouring drinks, taking cash and flirting with several customers. A lot of people knew Dave Gilmore's youngest daughter worked weekends as a bartender at Diggers'—only a handful knew that she was a masters candidate who tended bar not just for tips and fun but to observe human behavior.

Kate spotted Reid right away, sitting between Oscar Weston, a local mechanic who was sipping his usual Budweiser straight from the bottle, and a couple of younger guys sipping scotch, neat, and arguing over the validity of the umpire's call in the same baseball game she'd been watching at home. Despite the presence of other patrons around him, it was apparent that Reid was alone and wanted to be that way.

She squeezed herself between the stools and leaned an elbow on the bar. "Hey, Sheriff."

"Katelyn?" He blinked at her, as if he was having trouble focusing. "What are you doing here?"

"I got a text from my sister, asking me why a drunk guy at the bar believed he was going to marry me." She kept her voice low to ensure their conversation wouldn't be overheard.

"Because I am," he asserted. "And I'm not drunk."

She looked at the empty whiskey glass on the coaster in front of him. "How many of those have you had?"

"Three?" He nodded his thanks to Skylar when she set a mug of coffee in front of him. "I was celebrating."

"What were you celebrating?"

"My impending nuptials," he said, the relatively co-
herent pronunciation suggesting that he wasn't as inebri-
ated as she'd feared. On the other hand, his brain had to
be addled by alcohol if he was thinking a wedding was
anywhere in their future. "Not only am I getting married,
but I'm going to be—"

She pressed a hand to his mouth, anticipating and silencing the rest of his words.

"It's a secret?"

She nodded and let her hand drop away.

He lifted the mug to his mouth, watching her over the
rim as he sipped his coffee. "You are so incredibly beautiful. I thought I remembered what you looked like, but when
you walked into my office… Was that today? Yesterday?"

"Today," she confirmed.

"When you walked into my office today, you took my
breath away."

"Are you sure you've only had three whiskeys?"

He swallowed another mouthful of coffee. "Pretty sure,"
he said. "And though I wouldn't attempt to operate a motor
vehicle right now, I promise I haven't had enough alcohol
to impair my vision."

"Finish your coffee," she suggested. "And I'll take you
home."

He dutifully picked up the cup again. "I've been thinking about you for weeks," he confided. "Dreaming about
you."

She shot a quick glance to the left and then the right,
but no one seemed to be paying any attention to their conversation.

"In fact, I haven't stopped thinking about you since you
walked into that conference room in Boulder," he contin-

ued. Then he shook his head. "No, it was Boulder City, wasn't it?"

She rolled her eyes. "And now you're in Haven, and I need to know where you live so I can get you home."

"133 Chicory Drive."

She was familiar with the street and mentally placed the number. "Norm and Beverly Clayton's place?"

He nodded. "I'm renting the basement apartment."

Which Kate knew had been an in-law suite where Beverly's mom had lived for a lot of years. After she broke her hip and needed to go into a long-term care facility, Norm and Beverly had periodically offered the space for rent.

"Let's get you back there and into bed," Kate suggested.

"If you want me in bed, you only need to ask."

She shook her head, but she couldn't hold back the smile that curved her lips. "Even drunk you can't turn off the charm, can you?"

"Am I charming the pants off you?"

"You already did," she reminded him. "That's why you were trying to drink yourself into oblivion."

Reid didn't tell her again that he wasn't drunk. He just paid his tab, adding a generous tip for the bartender, and let Kate lead him away.

She automatically turned south when they stepped out of the bar. "Where'd you park?"

"I didn't drive, I walked."

He stopped in the middle of the sidewalk. "You're not walking me to my apartment, then walking back, alone, to yours."

"Reid, I've lived in Haven my whole life—I have no concerns about being out on my own after dark."

"But you thought I needed an escort home?"

"Sky's message led me to believe that you were more intoxicated than you apparently are."

"Now that you know I'm not, I'll walk you home," he decided, turning in the opposite direction.

"Fine," she agreed, falling into step beside him. "We'll walk back to my apartment and then I'll drive you to yours."

She turned at the corner of Page Street, then again into the parking lot behind her building. She hit the button on her key fob to unlock the doors, then climbed behind the wheel as he went around to the passenger side of the SUV.

"Why'd you come to the bar?" he asked.

"Because if you get stumbling-down drunk, people are going to gossip and speculate, and I'll feel responsible."

"Why would you feel responsible?" he asked.

She started the car and pulled out of her parking space. "Because I turned your world upside down tonight."

"Yeah, you did," he acknowledged. "And I turned yours upside down by launching super swimmers into your fallopian tubes."

She laughed softly as she turned onto Second Street. "I have to admit, I've never heard the fertilization process described in quite that way."

"I'm just trying to point out that we're both responsible for what happened—and the consequences."

"You're right," she said. "But I can't help wondering if you might have made a different decision about coming to Haven if you'd known I was pregnant."

He shook his head. "I wouldn't have made a different decision," he assured her. "I wouldn't—I don't—want to be anywhere else.

"Well, except maybe a different apartment," he acknowledged as she pulled into his driveway.

"What's wrong with the apartment?" she asked.

He just shook his head. "You have to see it to believe it."

Her gaze narrowed suspiciously. "If you're trying to get me into your bedroom…"

He shook his head. "It's the living room—and the kitchen—you have to see."

She turned off the ignition.

He led her to the side of the house, where there was a separate entrance to his apartment, and unlocked the door.

Kate was still wary, but she followed him inside.

"It's very open," she noted. "Lots of space and natural light. And the decor is…interesting."

"I was looking for a place that was furnished," he explained. "And although I'm not actually allergic to flowers, I want to sneeze every time I walk in here."

She nodded. "There are a lot of flowers."

It wasn't just that the sofa and chairs were covered in bold floral fabrics, but the coffee table, end tables, desk, filing cabinet and lamps were all painted with cabbage roses and daisies and tulips.

"I heard that Beverly took a tole painting class a few years back," Katelyn told him. "I didn't realize how much she obviously enjoyed it."

"There are flowers everywhere," he said. "The kitchen table is covered—I thought it was one of those doily things and figured I could fold it up and put it in the linen closet. But it's painted right on."

She went through the living area to the kitchen to examine the table.

"It's really very well done," she noted, tracing a finger along the delicate edge of the "lace."

"I don't know how long I can live like this," he confided.

"Some women like a man who's in touch with his feminine side."

"I'd rather be in touch with a woman's feminine side."

His response was so predictably defensive, she couldn't help but smile. "Why does that not surprise me?"

"You have a really great smile," he told her. "Every time you smile at me…even when you're not smiling, every time I see you… I don't know how to describe what happens inside me, but I look at you, and I want you."

"You're definitely feeling the effects of that whiskey now," she said, unwilling to admit—even to herself—the powerfully seductive effect his words had on her.

"Why are you so determined to deny what's between us?"

"The only thing between us is the baby that resulted from a broken condom."

"Do you really believe that?"

There was something in his tone, just the slightest hint of an edge that should have set off warning bells in her head, but she was so determined to prove her point, she ignored the signs. "It's true, Reid, what happened in—"

That was as far as she got before his mouth came down on hers.

And if he was under the influence of the alcohol he'd drunk, it certainly didn't affect his aim or impact his skill.

The first time they'd kissed, she'd discovered that Reid was a patient and thorough man. Kissing wasn't just fore-play to him but an incredibly sensual experience that turned her on more than she'd ever thought a kiss could do.

The same focus and skill that had seduced her then was seducing her now. The rational part of her brain told her that this shouldn't be happening, but all rationality was drowned out by the clamoring needs of her body.

She hadn't consciously parted her lips, but suddenly his tongue was dancing with hers, leading it in a sensual rhythm that promised more, so much more. Liquid warmth began to spread through her body, pool between her thighs.

His hands slid under her hoody and skimmed up her

sides. She could feel the heat of his touch through the thin fabric of her T-shirt. His palms brushed the sides of her breasts, and paused when he realized she wasn't wearing a bra.

She held her breath, waiting to see what he would do next. She knew what she *should* do—push him away, say good-night and walk out the door. But her brain and her body clearly wanted different things, and it had only taken one kiss to remind her of the pleasures she'd experienced in his arms. Pleasures she wanted to experience again.

Suddenly his hands were stroking boldly over her bare skin, stoking the fire that was already burning inside her. His callused thumbs scraped over her nipples, making her gasp as arrows of pleasure shot to her core.

He tore his mouth from hers only long enough to yank her hoody and T-shirt up and over her head and toss them aside. Then he was kissing and touching her again, and it was all she wanted, but somehow not enough.

Desperate to touch him as he was touching her, she tugged his shirt out of his jeans and let her hands explore the rippling muscles of his stomach, chest and shoulders. There was just something about those shoulders that made her crazy.

His lips eased away from hers to rain kisses along her jawline…down her throat…across her collarbone…over the curve of her breast. Then they fastened around her peaked nipple and drew it into his mouth, and her knees almost buckled. But Reid's arm was around her back, holding her close. Her fingers dug into his broad, strong shoulders so hard her nails had to be scoring his skin. He merely shifted his attention to the other breast.

"Reid."

It was all she said, all she could manage with so many wants and needs battering at her from all directions.

He lifted his head from her breast, but his hands immediately took over where his mouth had left off, teasing and tweaking the hard buds. In the past few weeks, she'd noticed that her breasts were a little more sensitive than usual—a not uncommon effect of early pregnancy. Apparently they were even more sensitive than she'd realized, because Reid's touch had pushed her almost to the point of climax.

"Do you have any idea how much I want you?" he asked.

She could feel the press of his erection against her belly, and the answering heat spread through her veins, making her eyes cross. "I hope it's half as much as I want you."

His eyes, hot and dark, locked on hers.

"If you're going to tell me to stop, you better say it now," he warned.

She could only shake her head. "I don't want you to stop." She slid a hand between their bodies, stroking him through denim. "I want you."

He sucked in a breath. "You're killing me here, Katelyn."

"Don't tell the sheriff." She tugged on his belt. "He'll lock me up."

"That scenario does hold some appeal," he admitted.

She nibbled on his bottom lip. "Let's get you out of these clothes," she suggested, carefully working the straining zipper over the bulge of his erection.

"And you out of yours," he agreed.

Of course, she was just wearing yoga pants, so he had the easier task. He hooked his thumbs in the waistband and slid them over her hips and down her legs.

"You said you didn't want to go near my bedroom," he reminded her.

"And I wouldn't want to be accused of lying," she said, tumbling with him onto the sofa.

There was laughter and frustration as he tried to wriggle out of his clothes with her body draped over his, but eventually they were both naked and panting, desperate for one another.

"Katelyn—"

She didn't know what else he was going to say, but she suspected she didn't want to hear it, so she took a page out of his book and silenced his words with her mouth. She kissed him long and slow and deep, and while she was kissing him, she positioned her knees on either side of his hips, then eased her lips from his and pulled back so that his erection was poised at the juncture of her thighs.

She was hot and wet for him, her insides trembling with the anticipation of taking his hard length deep inside her, but apparently she still had a few working brain cells because she hesitated. "I know there's no point in worrying about birth control but—"

"I haven't been with anyone else since we were together," he told her. "I haven't wanted anyone but you. But I do have condoms in the—"

He stopped talking when she tilted her hips. She took the tip of him inside her...then a little bit more. Deliberately drawing out his pleasure...and her own. Until he was finally...completely...deeply...inside her.

She closed her eyes, relishing the sensations that were zinging through her system like a thousand tiny little balls inside an out-of-control pinball machine.

Reid gave her a minute to adjust to his size and presence, then he lifted his hips, moving inside her. Slowly at first, establishing an even and steady rhythm...then faster...harder. And those erotic sensations continued to build and multiply until...it was too much.

And everything inside her shattered.

Chapter Seven

Reid woke up naked and alone.

He was sprawled on the flowered sofa with his clothes strewn around the floor, proof that his recollection of the previous evening was more than a dream.

If he'd had any doubts that his memories were hotter than the reality of getting naked with Katelyn, last night's sofa sex had laid them to rest.

Unfortunately, waking up and finding her gone suggested that they still had some issues to resolve. Remembering that she was pregnant multiplied those issues and amplified the importance of finding a resolution.

He made his way to the bathroom, cranking up the hot water in the shower in the hope that it would help clear some of the cobwebs from his brain. He braced his forearms on the ceramic tile as the spray pounded against his back, and he acknowledged that nothing could change the simple and basic facts:

Katelyn was pregnant.

And he was the father of her baby.

Since the idea of drinking himself into oblivion hadn't succeeded, he needed a plan B.

Unfortunately, the only possible fix he could see for this impossible situation was marriage. He vaguely recalled mentioning the idea to Katelyn last night—and that she'd responded with little enthusiasm.

He wasn't exactly thrilled by the prospect, either, but he didn't see any other choice. He'd been taught to take responsibility for his actions, even—and especially—when the consequences were uncomfortable. And marrying the mother of his child was the right thing to do.

He was still freaked out about the idea of being a father—a job for which he had no skills and even less experience—but he could see only one path forward. Maybe it was old-fashioned to want his son or daughter to grow up with two parents, but that was what Reid wanted for his child. The very thing he himself had been denied.

Which meant that he had a major task ahead: convincing Katelyn to marry him.

Kate woke up in her own bed and wanting coffee—desperately.

Dr. Amaro had assured her that she didn't need to give up caffeine completely but had suggested that she cut back to twelve ounces a day. Kate honestly didn't know how much she usually drank—she'd never worried about keeping track before. Her first cup was always at home in the morning, to help kick her brain into gear as she got ready for work, and throughout the day, there was usually a cup within arm's reach on her desk. If she was in court, recess meant a quick trip to the courthouse café for a vanilla latte.

But since she'd vowed to reduce her caffeine intake,

she'd been starting her mornings with a cup of herbal tea instead. She had yet to find a flavor that put her in a good mood to start the day. Today's pick—lemon ginger—was supposed to help combat nausea, but it had a distinctly medicinal taste that wasn't at all appealing. She took another sip and made a mental note to pick up some decaf coffee later. She'd never understood why anyone would drink decaf—what was the point of coffee without caffeine?—but under the circumstances, she thought she might give it a try.

In the meantime, she was going to have to sort out the mess she'd made of her life without the boost of caffeine.

Every decision she made from now on had to take into account not only what she wanted but what was best for the baby she was carrying. She had no idea how sex with Reid fit into that equation. Obviously getting naked with him had been a mistake, even if it had felt really good at the time.

Which wasn't something she should be thinking about right now, so when Sky walked in, Kate was so grateful for the distraction that she didn't think to wonder what her sister was doing in town on a Saturday morning.

Completely at home in Kate's apartment, Sky took a mug from the cupboard and set it under the spout of the coffee maker, then selected a coffee pod and dropped it into the machine. "Is he here?" she asked.

"Is who here?" Kate wondered.

Her sister grinned. "Sheriff Hottie."

She shook her head. "No. Of course he's not here."

"I don't know if I'm relieved or disappointed," her sister admitted.

"Relieved," Kate decided for her.

"There are times when I wish I could be more like you—every aspect of my life ordered and compartmentalized," Sky said. "But there are other times that I worry because your life is so ordered and compartmentalized."

Maybe that had been true before, but her impulsive actions in Boulder City had changed everything. "It's too early in the morning for deep philosophical musings," she protested.

"You need a guy who will shake up your life."

Reid Davidson had undeniably done that, but she still felt compelled to take issue with her sister's phraseology. "I don't need a guy at all."

"You're right." Sky nodded in acknowledgment even as her lips curved. "But you want him."

Since her sister would see right through any effort to deny it, she didn't even try. "Only because I always want what isn't good for me—like Sweet Caroline's caramel fudge brownie cheesecake."

"Mmm," Sky agreed, stirring sugar into her mug. "And why isn't that good for you?"

Kate breathed in deeply, as if the scent of her sister's coffee might be enough to jolt her sluggish brain. "Because one little slice has about a gazillion calories."

"Calories you could burn off with Sheriff Hottie," Sky suggested, taking a seat at the island.

Kate just shook her head. "Not going to happen."

Not again.

Of course, she hadn't intended for it to happen last night, either, but something happened whenever Reid touched her. A hormonal surge that short-circuited her brain, making her body spark like a live wire, humming and crackling with the electricity zipping through it.

She reached into the bread bag, retrieved two slices and slid them into the toaster, focusing intently on the task so she didn't have to look at her sister. Because just the memory of Reid's touch caused her blood to heat and pulse in her veins, and she could feel the warmth spread into her cheeks. "Do you want toast?"

"No, thanks, I ate at home. Martina made huevos rancheros this morning," she said, referring to the Circle G's longtime housekeeper.

"Lucky you." Though just the thought of eggs and chorizo sausage smothered in spicy salsa was enough to make Kate's stomach pitch.

"So," Sky said, when she realized her sister was watching her bread crisp, "are you going to explain to me what that whole 'I'm going to marry your sister' thing was about?"

Kate reached into the cupboard for a plate as the toast popped up. "It was clearly the rambling of a drunk man."

Sky seemed to consider the explanation as she sipped her coffee. "I can believe that alcohol was a factor in causing him to blurt out the declaration, but I suspect he had a reason to be hearing wedding bells. Which leads me to believe that either the new sheriff doesn't always live in the land of sane people or he's the guy you got naked with at that conference in Boulder City."

One of the best things about having a sister was that she could tell her anything. One of the worst things about having a sister was that she told her—and her best friend, Emerson—everything. And they forgot nothing.

"He's the guy I got naked with in Boulder City," she admitted, nibbling on the edge of a piece of toast.

And last night.

But there was no way she was going to share *that* information. It was one thing to confide that she'd had earth-moving sex with a guy her sister didn't know and was never expected to meet, and something entirely different to admit she'd done the deed with the man who was the new sheriff in town.

"And he immediately fell so head over heels in love with you that he decided to apply for Jed Traynor's job so that he could convince you to marry him?" Sky suggested dubiously.

"No. He applied for the position before we met. And I didn't know he was the new sheriff until I went to his office yesterday to discuss a case."

"How's Aiden doing?" Sky asked, proving that Kate's efforts to honor her client's confidentiality were for naught in a town where everyone knew everyone else's business.

"You know I can't talk to you about a client—or even confirm the identity of a client."

"You don't need to confirm it—his dad was overheard talking to Glenn Davis at the hardware store, and he said that you're the reason his son isn't stuck in a jail cell this weekend."

She sighed. "How am I supposed to maintain solicitor-client privilege if my clients—or clients' parents—don't keep their own mouths shut?"

"Okay, I won't ask any more questions about Aiden," Sky promised. "Which brings us back to the new sheriff, his proposal and your baby."

Kate sucked in a breath, then sputtered and coughed on the toast crumbs lodged in her throat.

Sky started to rise, but Kate held up a hand—holding her sister off—and swallowed a mouthful of lukewarm tea.

"Are you okay?" Sky asked.

She cleared her throat and nodded. "Yeah, you just… Where did that that idea about a baby come from?"

"It comes from knowing you, Kate. You're not drinking coffee, you're nibbling on dry toast—and you look like you're having trouble even keeping that down. Not to mention that most guys don't propose after a single weekend with a woman, so I figured Sheriff Hottie had to have a pretty good reason for doing so."

"Okay, you're right," she finally acknowledged. "I'm pregnant."

"You're going to be a mom," Sky said quietly, almost reverently. Then she grinned. "And I'm going to be an auntie." She hopped off her seat and embraced her sister. "I'm going to be the best auntie in the world—I promise."

"You can start by not telling anyone else about my pregnancy," Kate told her.

"I won't tell anyone," Sky assured her. "But how long do you think you can keep it a secret?"

"I don't know, but I just found out myself last week," she admitted.

"And told the sheriff last night—before he wandered into Diggers'," her sister guessed.

She nodded.

"Are you going to say yes?"

"He didn't actually ask me to marry him, Sky."

"But he will."

"How can you possibly know something like that?" Kate challenged.

"I study human behavior," Sky reminded her. "And the new sheriff is the type of man who truly believes it's his duty to serve and protect, and that sense of responsibility extends not just to the residents of his town but even more so to the people he cares about. He's honorable, upstanding and just traditional enough to believe that marrying the mother of his child is the right thing to do."

"No one rushes to the altar because of an unplanned pregnancy in this day and age," Kate reasoned.

"I'm going to offer you a piece of advice, anyway."

"What's that?" she asked warily.

"If you decide to marry him, let Dad walk you down

the aisle—don't run off to Vegas like Caleb and Brielle did," Sky cautioned.

Their brother's impulsive and short-lived marriage was rarely discussed—and never within earshot of their father.

"Dad wasn't mad that they went to Vegas to get married— he was furious that his son had knocked up a Blake." Although technically Brielle was a Channing, her mother was a Blake, which meant, for all intents and purposes, she was a Blake, too—and, therefore, an enemy of the Gilmores.

"But I promise that I won't run off to Vegas to get married," Kate said to her sister now. "Because I have no intention of getting married."

"Maybe you don't," Sky acknowledged. "But I wouldn't bet against Sheriff Hottie on anything."

Reid wanted to respect Katelyn's request for space, but considering that she'd asked for time before he'd left her apartment Friday night—and before they'd gotten naked together again—he figured that action wiped the slate clean.

Recalling her grandmother's mention of Saturday appointments, he tried her office first.

He walked in just as Katelyn was escorting a client to the door. There was no one else waiting in the reception area and the desk that he assumed belonged to a secretary or assistant was vacant.

Still, she didn't acknowledge him until her client had gone. "Did we have a meeting scheduled, Sheriff Davidson?"

"Nothing definite, Lawyer Gilmore."

She smiled at that, just a little.

He held up the manila envelope in his hand. "I have the discovery documents in the Johansen case for you."

She frowned as she took the envelope and lifted the flap.

"The Johansen case?" She pulled out the sheaf of blank papers, then looked at him.

He shrugged. "I figured I should have a pretext to justify my presence at your office."

"Very clever," she said.

"Was that your last appointment?" he asked.

"It was," she confirmed.

"Do you want to grab some lunch?"

"I appreciate the invitation," she said. "But I thought you were going to take some time to think about the situation."

"I've done nothing else since you told me that you're having my baby," he said.

"Why are you suddenly so willing to believe the baby's yours?"

"I wasn't disbelieving so much as stunned," he told her. "When you invited me to your place for dinner, the last thing I expected was for you to say that you were pregnant. And we weren't careless. I've *never* been careless."

"Neither have I," she said.

"I guess it's true that condoms are only ninety-eight percent effective."

"I could have lived a happy and fulfilling life without ever being proof of that statistic."

"And yet, here we are," he said.

"Here we are," she agreed. "And while I appreciate your willingness to charge full speed ahead, I'm not sure the revelation of my pregnancy has fully registered. I only told you about the baby—" she glanced at the watch on her wrist, did a quick mental calculation "—eighteen hours ago, and you were drunk for several of those."

His lips curved in a slow smile as his gaze skimmed over her. "We both know I wasn't drunk last night, Katelyn."

She turned away from him and slid the "documents" he'd given her into the paper tray of the printer beside the reception desk.

"But you're right," he acknowledged. "I didn't take the news well at first. On the other hand, it was the first time a woman's ever told me that she was going to have my baby, so I'm sorry I didn't know the right thing to say or do."

"It was the first time I've ever told a man he was the father of my child, so I might not have handled it the best way, either."

"But when I woke up this morning—alone and naked," he said, with another pointed look at her, "I was resolved."

"Resolved?" she echoed warily.

"To do the right thing."

She shook her head. "We can't get married, Reid—we hardly know each other."

"Living together as husband and wife will change that quickly enough," he told her.

She huffed out a breath. "I told you about the baby because I thought you had a right to know, but I don't want anything from you. As far as I'm concerned, no one else ever needs to know you're the father."

"Which proves your point that we don't know each other," he said. "Because if you knew me, you'd know that I'm not going to walk away from my child—or the child's mother."

Kate lowered herself into Beth's chair and pressed her fingers to her temples, as if that might alleviate the pounding inside her head. She hadn't expected that it would be easy to tell Reid about her pregnancy. She'd been prepared for him to question the paternity of her baby, and she'd expected that he'd need some time to accept the truth of what she was saying. She hadn't been prepared for him to jump from questioning to acceptance in the blink of an eye—and she hadn't expected him to jump from acceptance to marriage at all.

She felt his hands come down on her shoulders, and she jumped.

"Relax, Katelyn," he said, and began to massage gently.

It was easy for him to say—not so easy for her to do. He'd called her skittish the night before, and she couldn't disagree. She was certainly excitable whenever he was near.

And when he touched her, as he was touching her now, she melted. Which was precisely why she shouldn't let him touch her.

But she couldn't bring herself to ask him to stop. She didn't want him to stop. She wanted—

She abruptly severed the thought, unwilling to acknowledge her latent erotic desires.

"I know this isn't what either of us planned, but we're in it together now," he said, as he continued to loosen her muscles.

She wanted to believe it was true. Since the doctor confirmed her pregnancy, she'd felt alone and overwhelmed.

But it wasn't just her baby, it was his baby, too. And if he really wanted to be a *we*, there was part of her that couldn't help but think it would be easier than *me*.

But co-parenting suggested a level of relationship she wasn't ready for, and marriage was several levels beyond that.

"Why aren't you running away as far and fast as you can?" she wondered aloud.

"Because I don't shirk my responsibilities."

She turned the chair so that she was facing him, forcing his hands to drop away. "If you were one of my clients, I'd tell you to demand a paternity test."

"Why would I do that when you told me there's zero chance anyone else could be the father?" he asked.

"Because you shouldn't take my word for it," she protested. "I could be manipulating you for financial gain—or attempting to finagle a marriage proposal."

"I do have some savings and investments, which I'd willingly give to support our child, and I've already suggested marriage, but you're resistant to the idea."

She shook her head. "Do you have no sense of self-preservation?"

"Maybe I haven't known you very long," he acknowledged. "And there are undoubtedly a lot of things I don't know about you, but I know you're not lying about the paternity of the baby you're carrying."

"You seem to be handling the news a lot better than I did," she admitted.

"Believe me, I'm in full-scale panic mode on the inside," he told her.

"I'm familiar with panic. Although when I realized I was late, my initial reaction was denial. Because there are a lot of different things that can mess up a woman's cycle, and whatever had messed up mine, it couldn't possibly be a baby.

"But then a few days turned into a week, then two weeks. So when I was in Elko for a custody hearing, I went to a pharmacy to buy a home pregnancy test."

"It was positive?" he guessed.

She nodded. "But I still didn't believe it. I was sure that the test must have been faulty, or I'd somehow done it wrong."

"There's a wrong way to pee on a stick?"

She managed a smile. "It was easier to believe that than trust the result. So I bought a second test, but it was faulty, too."

"I'm sensing a pattern."

"I just couldn't wrap my head around the possibility that there was a tiny life growing inside of me," she admitted. "Maybe I'd always thought I'd be a mother someday, but someday was supposed to be a lot of years down the road."

"Then you bought a third test?"

"From a different pharmacy, because clearly the entire shipment at the first store was defective. When that test gave me the same result, I finally went to see Dr. Amaro."

"Have you told anyone else?"

She shook her head. "My sister knows, but I didn't tell her. In fact, it was your mention of marriage that tipped her off."

"I was thinking out loud," he admitted.

"Believe me, I know what a shock it is to discover that, after a casual hookup, you're going to be a parent."

"I never would have said, 'Hey, let's have unprotected sex and see what happens,'" he acknowledged, "but the reality of a baby changes everything."

She instinctively touched a hand to her belly. "The reality is only about the size of a lentil right now."

"A lentil? Is that like a bean?"

"Close enough," she said.

"That's pretty small."

She nodded. "But he or she will do a lot of growing over the next seven months."

"Still, a little bean would benefit from having both a mom and a dad looking out for him or her, don't you think?"

Chapter Eight

Kate had never understood why expectant parents referred to an unborn child by cute nicknames, but she couldn't deny there was something about the way Reid said *little bean* that was endearing. She also appreciated that he'd used both gender pronouns rather than defaulting to the masculine as so many people—especially men—tended to do.

Except that, despite his warm tone and conciliatory demeanor, he was doing exactly what Sky had warned her he would do—trying to push her toward marriage so that he could feel better about doing "the right thing."

Thankfully, she knew how to push back.

"Reid, I only found out about the baby a few days before you did, and I'm not ready to think about all the ways my life is going to change. I know it's going to change," she acknowledged, "but getting married is definitely not a change that ever crossed my mind."

"Think about it now," he suggested.

She sighed. "Don't you already have one divorce behind you?"

"Yeah," he admitted.

"So why would you want to rush into another marriage, especially one that would be doomed from the start?"

"Why do you think our marriage would be doomed?"

"Because we'd only be getting married for the sake of our baby," she pointed out to him.

"I can't think of a better reason."

"What about love?" she challenged.

"Is that what you're holding out for?"

"I'm not holding out for anything," she denied. "But whenever I thought about getting married, I assumed it would happen because I was in love with the man I was planning to spend my life with."

"I'm sorry this situation is forcing you to deviate from your plan," he said. "But I'm not going to pretend to be in love with you so you can feel better about marrying me."

"I don't want you to pretend anything, and I don't want to marry you," she told him.

Except that she did want to give her baby a real family— the kind that she'd known for the first twelve years of her life. Since the death of her mother, a crucial piece of their family had been missing, and Kate couldn't help but worry that her child might feel the same emptiness growing up without a full-time father.

"But I appreciate your willingness to do the right thing," she said to Reid now. "Even if we're not in agreement as to what that is."

"Your pregnancy is one of those curveballs life likes to throw at us to see how we'll respond," he told her. "I'm ready to step up to the plate and hit that ball out of the park."

She rolled her eyes. "I'm guessing you're a baseball fan."

"My Rangers tickets were the only thing I was sorry to leave in Texas," he admitted.

"Just one more thing I didn't know about you—because I don't know you," she said again.

"Just one of the many things we have yet to discover about one another," he countered, putting a different spin on the point.

"Well, there's something you should know about me," she told him. "I hate the Rangers."

He winced. "Despite that blasphemous statement, I'm willing to trust that your failure to appreciate America's pastime isn't indicative of greater character flaws."

"I don't hate baseball," she said, eager to clarify her previous statement. "I hate the Rangers because I'm an Angels fan."

"Now that might be indicative of greater character flaws," he said, shaking his head sadly.

"You won't find many Rangers fans in Nevada, and in this part of the state, they're mostly Dodgers or Athletics fans with a handful of Angels and Giants supporters in the mix."

"How'd you end up cheering for the Angels?"

"Three years at UCLA," she reminded him.

"Okay, let's put aside our differences with respect to baseball for the moment and focus on what's best for our baby."

Our baby.

The words spilled out of his mouth easily, as if they didn't twist his stomach into painful knots. And maybe they didn't. Maybe he'd accepted the reality of their situation a lot more easily than Kate had done, because as much as she loved her unborn child already, there were moments when her doubts and fears seemed stronger than anything else.

Her biggest concerns were based on not knowing how she would manage to juggle her career and the demands of a child. And, of course, long before the baby was born, she was going to have to tell her father about her pregnancy.

He'd be supportive, but he'd also be disappointed to learn she would be a mother before she was a wife. And he'd probably wonder if the death of her own mother so many years earlier had somehow caused her to fall into bed with a man she barely knew.

A ring on her finger would reassure her father that, although she'd made a mistake, she'd be taken care of. Because while David Gilmore was open-minded enough to encourage his daughters to be anything they wanted to be, he was also old-fashioned enough to believe a woman needed a man to take care of her.

Yes, as difficult as it would be to tell him she was pregnant, she knew he'd accept the news more easily if it was followed by *and I'm going to marry the father of my baby*.

But she wasn't going to take what looked like the easy path now, because it would only be that much harder later on when the relationship fell apart and their child was caught in the middle of a messy divorce.

"Can we please just take some time before making any life-altering decisions?" she asked him now.

"How much time do you think you need?"

"Eight months?" she suggested, aware that their baby would be born before that period of time had passed.

He folded his arms over his chest and looked at her as if she was a recalcitrant child. Maybe he was practicing his stern father facade and, if so, he was doing a good job—which made her want to both laugh and cry, because her emotions were a complete mess.

"More than a day," she told him.

"Okay," he relented.

"And, in the meantime, can we keep this...news...between us?"

"I'm already an outsider—and not in any hurry to face the judgment that will follow when people find out I got Katelyn Gilmore pregnant."

"I'm willing to keep the paternity of my baby a secret," she reminded him.

But Reid shook his head stubbornly. "I'm not."

He gave her a week.

And every day that passed during that week, he waited for his phone to ring or for Katelyn to show up at his office. But it never happened, and Reid was beginning to suspect that it never would.

So he took the initiative—and a pizza—and crossed his fingers that she wouldn't toss the box back in his face when he showed up at her door.

After buzzing him in, she eyed him with suspicion—and the pizza box with interest. "What are you doing here, Reid?"

"Well, you made dinner for me last week, so I figured it was my turn," he explained. "But I'm not much of a cook, so this seemed like a safer option."

"What's on the pizza?"

"Pepperoni, black olives and hot peppers."

"Since it would be too much of a coincidence to discover that those are your favorite toppings, I'm guessing you asked my sister what I like."

"Guilty."

With a sigh of resignation, she stepped away from the door so he could enter.

He could tell she was wary, so he deliberately kept the

conversation focused on neutral topics while they ate, and they chatted about local news, current events and baseball scores of their rival teams. They didn't discuss Aiden Hampton, although Reid knew that she'd talked to the ADA about a local diversion program that would allow Aiden to take responsibility for his actions and perform community service in exchange for a withdrawal of the charges.

"Let's go to a movie," he suggested, when the pizza box was empty.

"Why?"

"Because it's Friday night and there's nothing good on TV."

"I have a brief to research and write."

"Come on, Katelyn—it's Friday night. Play hooky with me."

She bent down to scoop up a napkin that had fallen onto the floor. "There are only two screens at the local theater—it's quite possible there's nothing good at the movies, either."

"You can choose between the latest Marvel movie and some artsy-sounding film that I've never heard of," he told her, making it clear what his choice would be.

She grinned. "Who doesn't love superheroes in spandex?"

They found seats inside the theater, then Reid went to get snacks while Katelyn thumbed through the messages on her phone, just so that she had something to focus her eyes on while her mind wandered. She wished she'd had the opportunity to get to know Reid better without the specter of her pregnancy hanging over them. But, of course, the tiny life growing inside her changed everything. Even if no one else knew about the baby right now, there would be speculation about the relationship—and more so when her condition became evident.

Reid came back carrying a tray with two soft drinks, a big bag of popcorn, a package of licorice and box of Milk Duds.

"If I didn't know otherwise, I'd think you'd skipped dinner," she commented.

"Those aren't for me." He put the drinks in their respective cup holders, then set the tray of snacks in her lap. "They're for you."

"For me?"

"I didn't know what you liked."

"I like everything," she admitted, keeping her voice quiet to ensure that no one seated around them would overhear their conversation. "But I'm not actually eating for two, you know."

"Then you could share with me," he suggested.

"Hmm…that was your plan all along, wasn't it?"

He winked as he settled into the seat beside her. "Maybe."

It was almost like a real date, and it made Kate wonder how things might have played out if a condom hadn't failed. How would she have responded to discovering that he was the new sheriff of Haven?

She would have been pleased to see him. Because even before she'd begun to suspect that there were consequences of her trip to Boulder City, she hadn't stopped thinking about those two blissful nights. But she also would have been wary of any kind of personal relationship, because he was now wearing a badge in the town where she was building her law practice. It wasn't a direct conflict of interest, but Kate would have wanted to steer clear of the slightest appearance of impropriety.

Of course, being pregnant with the new sheriff's baby

took away that option. And even if no one else knew the truth about their relationship, being seen with him at the local movie theater would generate a fair amount of talk. And maybe, since Reid was prepared to acknowledge paternity of the baby, she was subconsciously hoping that people wouldn't later count the number of weeks between his arrival in town and the arrival of her baby and realize she was pregnant before he showed up in Haven.

The lights in the theater dimmed, and she settled deeper into her seat to focus on the coming attractions. But if she'd hoped the movie might provide a distraction from thinking about her pregnancy, she hadn't anticipated that sitting beside Reid in the dark theater distracted her from everything else. Everything but her awareness of the man.

An awareness that intensified with every brush of his leg and every bump of his arm. And when he leaned close to whisper in her ear, the scent of him—clean, simple and masculine—tempted her more than the buttery popcorn.

Determined to ignore the hunger stirring in her veins, she tore open the box of Milk Duds and popped a chocolate-coated caramel into her mouth, letting it sit on her tongue until it began to melt. And she continued to pop candy into her mouth, one at a time, until the box was empty.

"Licorice?" Reid offered the bag to her.

She shook her head. "No, thanks."

Because she'd already consumed an overload of sugar and it had done nothing to curb her appetite for what she really wanted but couldn't have.

He set the licorice and the half-empty bag of popcorn aside and reached for her hand, linking their fingers together. At first, she felt self-conscious and wondered if the overture was intended as some kind of statement about their relationship. But the theater was dark, making it unlikely that anyone could see their hands.

So they watched the rest of the movie like that, their fingers entwined in the dark. And when she stopped trying to read any deeper meaning into the gesture, she could admit that it felt surprisingly nice.

But she also suspected this was part of his campaign to convince her to do "the right thing," and she wasn't convinced that marriage was the right thing.

She knew that relationships didn't come with guarantees, but getting married because of an unplanned pregnancy seemed like a guarantee of heartache. And yet, she was tempted to accept his offer, because heartache at some distant time in the future seemed preferable to the doubts and insecurities about being a single mother that plagued her now.

Of course, the characters in the movie were battling much bigger problems, so she put aside her own thoughts and concerns and let herself be drawn into the action on the screen.

When the credits began to roll and spectators started to exit the theater, Reid gave her hand a subtle squeeze and released it, preserving the illusion that they were acquaintances simply enjoying a movie together. It was a perfectly legitimate and believable explanation for them being together, but Kate decided that if people were going to talk, she might as well give them something to talk about.

She led the way out of the theater and, after dropping her empty Milk Duds box and drink cup into the garbage, reached for his hand again.

"Thank you," she said, as they exited onto the sidewalk and the crowd began to disperse in various directions.

"For what?"

"For tonight—the pizza, the movie, the snacks. But especially for helping me forget about everything for a couple of hours."

"It was my pleasure," he told her.

"You might feel differently when you're fielding questions from everyone who saw us together tonight."

"There were questions before we hit the ticket counter," he confided.

"From who?" she asked.

"Jolene Landry," he said, naming the owner of Jo's Pizza. "Apparently the pepperoni, hot peppers and black olives combo is known to be your particular favorite."

"I didn't think about that," she admitted.

"Well, Jolene now believes—at least, I think I managed to convince her—that those are my favorite toppings, too."

"But the pizza combined with being seen together at the movie is going to be grist for the gossip mill."

"There is one way we could nip it in the bud," he said.

"What's that?"

"We could announce our engagement."

She sighed. "I should have known you couldn't let it go for ten minutes."

"I let it go for more than three hours," he countered. "But I'll make you a deal."

"What kind of deal?" she asked warily.

"I'll stop bringing up the subject if you promise to give serious consideration to the idea and let me know when you've made up your mind."

"I have made up my mind," she told him.

"*Serious* consideration," he said again.

"Okay," she relented, withdrawing her keys from her pocket as they approached her building.

"Promise?"

"I promise." She unlocked the door. "Good night, Reid."

He held the door. "I'll see you up."

"It's really not necessary," she protested.

"It is," he insisted. "Unless you want me to kiss you good-night right here, where we're illuminated under the security light for anyone who might be passing by."

"Maybe I don't want you to kiss me good-night." Of course, she did, but kissing Reid tended to lead to other intimacies, and she was determined to ignore the sexual attraction between them. Or at least try.

"I still want to see you safely inside," he told her.

Because she suspected it was true, she let him follow her up the stairs to the second floor, where she unlocked the interior door to her apartment and turned on the lights.

He did a quick visual scan of the open area, as if to be sure that everything was as they'd left it, then moved to the windows, checked that the latches were all fastened, and nodded.

"Do you want to look for monsters under my bed, too?" she asked.

"Lead the way."

She shook her head. "I'm *not* showing you my bedroom."

His lips curved in a slow and blatantly sensual smile. "Well, the sofa worked just fine at my place."

She didn't need the reminder. She remembered, in very clear and vivid detail, every kiss and touch they'd shared that night—and the two nights they'd spent together in Boulder City. And that was why it was a bad idea to let him touch her again.

"We have to be smart about this," she told him. "We have to think not just about what we want but what's best for our baby."

"What's best for our baby is to have two parents who are together."

"That's not always true," she said. Being a family law

attorney, she'd had a front-row seat to the drama that ensued when marriages—and families—fell apart, and she had no desire to add a failed union of her own to the statistics.

"You're right," he admitted. "But I know we could make it work, because we're both too stubborn to accept anything less than success—and because the sizzling chemistry between us would go a long way toward smoothing any bumps in the road."

"Just like a guy to think that sex is the answer to everything."

"Not everything," he denied. "But—"

Whatever else he'd intended to say was cut off by the abrupt ring of his cell phone.

Reid cursed under his breath as he pulled the device out of his pocket and glanced at the screen.

"Aren't you going to answer that?" she asked, when he made no move to do so.

"I'd rather not," he admitted.

"It's almost midnight, and no one calls at midnight unless it's important." She lifted her brows as another thought occurred to her. "Or a booty call."

"It's not a booty call," he assured her.

But he touched the keypad to connect the call, and Kate wandered into the kitchen to give him some privacy.

"Sorry about that," Reid said, after he'd finished with the call and tucked his phone away again.

"Was it something urgent?" she asked.

"Everything's urgent to Trish."

"Trish?" she queried, before she could stop herself.

"My ex-wife," he told her. "She called to tell me that she's in labor."

Chapter Nine

Reid didn't think about how his words might be interpreted until Katelyn's eyes went wide.

"You're going to be a father?"

"What? *No!*" His emphatic response was followed by a short laugh. "Well, yes, but only to your baby."

Her brow furrowed, as if she couldn't make sense of what he was saying. "Your ex-wife is having another man's baby?"

"Yes," he confirmed.

"You don't seem too upset by that," she noted.

"Why would I be? The other man's her husband."

"Her husband?"

"We've been divorced for four years," he explained. "And Trish has been remarried for three of those."

She opened her mouth to speak, then closed it again without saying a word.

"You're wondering why she called to tell me about a baby that isn't mine?" he guessed.

"Maybe. Yeah," she admitted.

"Because my ex-wife has no concept of boundaries."

She considered his response before asking, "How long were you married?"

"Two-and-a-half years. But we were friends for a long time before we got married, and we continued to be friends after our marriage fell apart."

"That's…surprising."

"And possibly a mistake," he acknowledged. "I can't imagine ever completely cutting ties with her, but I recently accepted that those ties were a little too close, which is one of the reasons I decided to move away from Echo Ridge."

"And ended up in Haven—having to deal with another woman who's going to have a baby," she noted.

He nodded.

"You know, it's probably not too late for you to get out," she said. "Isn't there a probationary period during which you can decide that the job isn't working out—or that Haven isn't what you were looking for?"

"Whether or not any of this is what I wanted, it's what we've got," he said.

And though the idea of fatherhood was no less terrifying now than when he'd first learned of her pregnancy, he remained committed to doing the right thing. He just had to convince Katelyn to let him.

"Well, if you're determined to stick around, I have a favor to ask," she said.

"Anything," he immediately replied.

"You might want to wait until you know what I want," she suggested.

"Anything," he said again.

"I'd like you to come with me to the Circle G for a barbecue Sunday afternoon."

"You want me to meet your family?"

"You've already met my grandmother and my sister," she reminded him. "But yes, I'd like to introduce you to everyone else, too, so that when I get around to telling them I'm pregnant, they will have met the baby's father."

He was surprised by the invitation, because he suspected that showing up at the ranch with Katelyn would create a lot more speculation than going to a movie in town. But he only asked, "What time should I pick you up?"

After Kate closed the office door behind her last client Saturday afternoon, she sent a quick text to Emerson Kellner—her best friend since kindergarten. Kate had been the maid of honor when Emerson got married three years earlier, and the godmother of her first child at Keegan's baptism six months ago.

Her message, asking if Emerson was up for some company, received an immediate reply: YES! PLEASE!

Aware of her friend's fondness for white chocolate macadamia nut cookies, Kate stopped at Sweet Caroline's Sweets on the way and picked up a dozen of the treats.

"I'm still carrying eight pounds of baby fat," Emerson protested, eyeing the white bakery box in her friend's hands.

"You look fabulous," Kate told her sincerely. "But it's really my godson I want to see."

She'd first held the baby only a few hours after his birth. He'd had wispy blond hair, a pert little nose, a rosebud mouth and tiny hands curled into tiny fists. And when he'd opened his eyes, she'd fallen head over heels in love. Ten months later, she loved him even more.

"He'll be waking up from his nap soon," Emerson promised, moving toward the back of the house. "In the meantime, I've got a pitcher of lemonade out by the pool, where you can tell me about the sexy new sheriff."

Kate stretched out in the lounger beside her friend. "Why are you asking me about him?"

"Because I heard you had a date with him last night."

"I did not," she denied.

"Really?" Emerson said skeptically. "Because Lacey Bolton heard from Deanna Nardone that Megan Carmichael saw you snuggled up with an—" she made air quotes with her fingers "—'unknown hottie' at the movies last night."

"I hate this town," Kate muttered, tipping her head back and closing her eyes.

"Were you at the movies or not?"

"Yes," she admitted.

"And?" her friend prompted.

"It's definitely worth the price of a ticket. If you and Mark want to see it, I'd be happy to watch Keegan."

"I wasn't asking about the movie," her friend chided. "And don't think I didn't notice your failure to comment, positively or negatively, on my description of the sheriff as sexy, which suggests to me—and remember, I know you better than anyone else—that he's got you all churned up inside."

He did, of course, although not only for the reasons her friend was thinking. "His name is Reid Davidson and yes, he's tall, dark and handsome."

Emerson shook her head. "No skimping on details."

"Approximately six-two, short brown hair, hazel eyes, strong jaw, broad shoulders."

"You've always had a thing for guys with great shoulders," her friend noted.

"Is that description adequate?"

"It's helping me put together a mental picture," Emerson confirmed. "But I need a number."

"Seriously, Em, we're not in high school anymore."

"I know. I'm an old married woman stuck at home with a baby now—I need to get my thrills vicariously."

"You're twenty-eight years old, married to the love of your life and Keegan is the most adorable baby in the world."

"It's all true," she admitted. "But I still want a number."

The number system they'd established in high school for rating the guys they liked was hardly unique. Emerson had never dated anyone who was less than an eight-point-five and Kate had never dated anyone at all.

After watching *Erin Brockovich* with her mother, Kate had announced that she was going to be a lawyer someday. Her mother had been both proud and supportive of her goal, and when Tessa died, Kate had been more determined than ever to follow through with her plan. And while her best friend was dating all the cute boys at their high school, Kate was focused on getting into college and then law school. She had no intention of letting any guy— even a ten-plus—derail her plans.

"Assigning a number is insensitive and objectifying," she protested.

"He's a ten-plus, isn't he?" Emerson guessed.

Kate answered with reluctant honesty. "Yeah, he's a ten-plus."

"And they're in short supply in this town," her friend noted. "You better snap him up before someone else does."

"I'm at the building-my-career phase of my life," she said, conveniently ignoring—at least for the minute—that she was also at the growing-a-life phase way ahead of schedule.

"Things don't always go according to plan," Emerson

warned. "You can't predict when you'll meet the right guy and you shouldn't pretend he isn't the right guy just because the timing is wrong."

"But if it's the wrong time, is he really the right guy?" Kate countered, attempting to divert her friend's focus.

"Would you sleep with him?" Emerson pressed, proving the effort ineffective.

She hesitated, just a fraction of a second, before responding, "Actually…I already did."

"Oh. My. God. I should have realized…when you mentioned the shoulders—he's the sheriff you knocked boots with in Boulder City."

Kate rolled her eyes. "Yes, he's the one."

"You told me the sex was spectacular," her friend recalled. "Off-the-charts spectacular, in fact."

"With the proviso that I'd been celibate for a long time prior to that weekend, so my assessment might have been a little bit skewed."

"And now he's Haven's new sheriff." Emerson picked up her lemonade, sipped. "Was that a coincidence or is he stalking you?"

"Coincidence," Kate assured her. "He actually interviewed for Jed's job before the conference started."

"Maybe fate then," her friend suggested.

"Please don't make this into something that it isn't. And please don't tell anyone—even Mark—that I hooked up with Haven's new sheriff."

"I can't lie to my husband," Emerson protested.

"You won't have to lie because it's not going to come up in conversation if you don't bring it up," she said, lifting her hand to cover a yawn.

"Fine—but it's not like he'd tell anyone else."

"Too many people know already."

"Who else knows besides me, you and the sheriff?"

"My sister," Kate confided.

"You told Sky before you told me?"

Admitting that Reid had told Sky—more or less—would create more questions, so she only said, "I saw Sky before I saw you."

"Still." Emerson pretended to pout. "I'm your best friend. I'm supposed to hear all the important stuff first."

"You were the first person I told when I came back from Boulder City," she said soothingly.

That revelation didn't appease her friend, who was studying her through narrowed eyes. "You're still holding something back."

Thankfully, before Emerson could press her further, a cheery babble sounded through the baby monitor on the table.

Kate immediately pushed herself up off the lounger. "Keegan's awake."

"Awake but not fussing," her friend noted.

"That's my favorite kind of baby," she said, opening the sliding door.

"Wait until you have one of your own," Emerson warned, following her into the house. "Believe me, after the first few months of constant demands, you won't be in such a hurry to pick him up every time he makes a sound."

Which was going to happen a lot sooner than her friend suspected—and a lot sooner than Kate ever would have predicted. But now that she'd had a couple weeks to get used to the idea, she could confidently say that the prospect of impending motherhood filled her with more joy than trepidation. She still had fears and concerns, but the happiness that filled her heart when she thought about holding her baby in her arms was so all encompassing, it managed to hold those fears and concerns at bay.

Or it had until today when a client's child-from-hell had

screamed like a banshee for the whole forty minutes she was in Kate's office.

She followed the familiar path up the stairs and down the hall to the nursery, peeking in to see that Keegan had pulled himself up on the bars and was gnawing on the rail, drool dripping off his chin.

He looked up and grinned when he recognized his god-mother.

"Oh, my goodness," Kate said. "Look at all those teeth."

He smiled again, showing them off.

"Aren't you such a big boy now?"

He released his grip on the rail and lifted his arms toward her, a silent request to be picked up. But without the support of the rail, he lost his balance and immediately fell down onto his bottom. His little brow furrowed.

"Oopsie daisy," she said, and he giggled. She reached into the crib and lifted him out. "Kiss?"

He puckered up and touched his lips to her cheek.

"A little sloppy, Keeg," she said. "Hopefully you'll fix that before adolescence." She patted a hand against his bottom. "And give some consideration to potty training, too."

"Do you want me to change him?" Emerson offered.

"I can handle a wet diaper," Kate assured her.

Emerson settled into the rocking chair in the corner of the room, content to let her friend handle the diaper duties. "Remember—he's a boy."

Kate nodded. The first time she'd ever changed Keegan, she hadn't thought to cover him when she pulled the wet diaper away and he'd sprinkled like a fountain. "I don't think I'll ever forget."

Clean diapers and wipes were within easy reach, and she had everything ready before she unsnapped the fasteners of his romper. He immediately twisted, trying to roll away from her.

"Get over here, Mr. Wiggly Worm," she chastised, splaying her hand across his belly to hold him in position.

"He certainly is that," Emerson agreed. "I remember how thrilled I was when he finally rolled over at five months—now I just wish he would hold still every once in a while."

"My grandmother says that new parents spend the first year of a child's life eager for him to walk and talk—and the next sixteen wishing he'd sit down and shut up."

Emerson laughed. "I'm sure there's some truth in that."

When Keegan tried to roll over again, Kate reached for one of his favorite teething toys. She jingled the plastic keys, immediately snagging his attention. He kicked his chubby legs and stretched his arms out for the toy.

She jingled the keys again, then let him take them from her so she could secure the tabs of his diaper and fasten the snaps of his romper. When that was done, she dropped the dirty diaper into the bin beside the table and picked up the baby, propping him against her hip.

"I've figured it out," Emerson said, when they were once again reclining in the loungers by the pool, Keegan sitting in Kate's lap. "What you've been holding back."

The baby tossed the keys to the ground, and Kate reached to scoop them up—a familiar game between them. "What do you think I've been holding back?"

"You're pregnant."

This time the plastic keys slipped out of *her* hand.

"I'll take that as a yes," Emerson said, retrieving the toy for her son.

It wasn't just the words but the absolute conviction in her friend's voice that warned Kate any effort to deny the truth would be in vain. And maybe she'd come here for this—to talk to somebody who knew her better than anyone else and who knew what it meant to be a mother.

"Am I wearing a sign?" she wondered aloud, a little unnerved that first her sister and now her best friend had so readily uncovered her secret.

Emerson smiled. "There are all kinds of signs if someone knows you—especially if that someone has recent experience with pregnancy."

"What kind of signs?"

"You're pale and fatigued and your boobs are practically spilling out of your bra."

Kate's gaze immediately dropped to her chest. "Apparently you know me even better than I realized," she remarked.

"But does *he* know?" Emerson asked.

She nodded.

"How'd he respond?"

"He thinks we should get married."

Her friend's brows lifted. "What do you think?"

"I don't think a broken condom is the first stop on the road to wedded bliss." Kate rubbed Keegan's back. "If and when I get married, I want it to be because I've fallen in love. Maybe that's selfish under the circumstances, but I want what you and Mark have," she said, imploring Emerson to understand.

"Anyone would have reservations in your situation," her friend acknowledged. "But you wouldn't be pregnant if you and the sheriff didn't have some powerful chemistry."

"And if that was a valid reason for a legal union, the traditional wedding vows would forgo mention of love, honor and cherish in favor of lots of really hot sex."

"The love, honor and cherish stuff is easier to do when there's lots of really hot sex added to the mix," Emerson said.

Which wasn't all that different from the argument Reid had made but still didn't hold much sway for Kate.

"I had a client—a young, single mom—come in today with a six-month-old. She wants an order to compel a DNA test so she can get financial support from the baby's father. She also said she wouldn't mind if Dad wanted to take the baby off her hands some of the time.

"Which seemed an odd comment to me, at first," Kate noted. "Until the baby, suddenly and inexplicably, started screaming. The mom checked her diaper, offered a drink and a snack, but nothing soothed the kid. The baby kept screaming until even the mom was crying, and…I'm terrified that's going to be me in the future."

"I've been there," Emerson confided. "There are times when it seems nothing I do will soothe Keegan, then I start to doubt everything I'm doing and feel like a total failure as a mother.

"I can only imagine how much harder it would be if I didn't have Mark to help out, so if you came here for reassurance, I'm not sure I can give it," her friend said. "Don't get me wrong—I love Keegan with my whole heart and I love being a mom, but there are days I'm so overwhelmed, I don't realize until Mark gets home that it's dinnertime and the breakfast and lunch dishes are still in the sink because I haven't had a chance to empty the dishwasher. And I'm still in my pajamas because I didn't have time to get dressed—or even notice that I wasn't.

"It's even worse when Mark's out of town on business. Last week, he was gone for three days. When he finally got back, as soon as he walked through the front door, I handed him the baby and walked out. I just needed some space, just five minutes by myself, so that I could hear myself think."

"Thanks," Kate said drily. "I feel so much better now."

"I wouldn't be a true friend if I told you it was all smiles and giggles," Emerson said. "Although those smiles and giggles do have a way of making you forget about poopy diapers and projectile vomit—at least in the moment.

"Still, I know how much you've always wanted a real family of your own," her friend continued in a gentler tone. "So before you make any final decisions, you need to consider all your options—including saying 'I do' to the sexy sheriff."

Chapter Ten

Katelyn wanted to be at the Circle G around four o'clock. Reid had mapped the route on his phone and discovered it was about a thirty-minute drive from her apartment, so he was at her door promptly at 3:30.

She was ready when he arrived and immediately came out rather than buzzing him in. She was wearing a sleeveless white V-neck top printed with tiny blue flowers over a pair of slim-fitting navy capri pants with white leather slip-on sandals. Her hair tumbled in loose waves over her shoulders, the ends dancing in the light summer breeze.

She looked cool and casual and far too sexy for his peace of mind. Certainly no one looking at her would ever suspect that she was pregnant.

"Boy or girl?" Katelyn asked, fastening her seat belt.

"Huh?" he said.

She smiled as she slid a pair of dark sunglasses over her eyes. "I assume your ex-wife had the baby by now—I was wondering if it was a boy or a girl."

"Oh. Yes, she did. A boy," he told her. "Henry."

"Are you hoping our baby is a boy or a girl?" she asked.

He pulled out of the parking lot and turned onto Page Street. "I can't honestly say that I've given the matter any thought."

"Think about it now," she suggested.

Thinking about her pregnancy was scary enough without imagining the baby that would come at the end. Reid didn't have a lot of experience with kids, but he knew infants were completely dependent on their parents for everything—food, clothing, shelter, attention and affection.

"Or is it too soon to be thinking about the sex?" she wondered.

"I'm always ready to think about sex," he told her.

A smile tugged at her lips as she shook her head. "I meant the sex of our baby."

"Oh. Yeah, it's too soon to be thinking about that," he agreed.

Definitely too soon.

He wasn't ready to be a father, and he didn't imagine himself being any more ready in seven months.

Maybe seven years.

Yes, that might work.

Or, better yet—never.

Unfortunately, that wasn't really an option.

"I've thought about it," she admitted. "I don't have a preference, but it's fun to imagine what our son or daughter will look like."

He considered for a moment, then shook his head. "I don't want to imagine what our daughter would look like."

"Why not?"

"Because now I'm picturing her with dark hair and

blue eyes like her mom, so breathtakingly beautiful that my badge and gun will be my only hope of keeping the boys at a distance."

"And then she'll sneak off for a weekend, somewhere away from the watchful eye of her overprotective father, and get knocked up," Katelyn warned.

He slid her a look. "Not *my* daughter."

"I'm sure that's what my father would have said, too," she agreed. "If anyone had suggested the possibility to him."

His fingers tightened on the steering wheel. "He's going to want to kill me, isn't he?"

"Wanting and doing are completely different things," she said, as if to reassure him. "And I'm not planning to tell him today."

"What are you going to tell him?" Reid wondered. "Will you be introducing me as the new sheriff or your boyfriend?"

The way she nibbled on her bottom lip before responding suggested that she hadn't considered any of the details. "I guess it wouldn't hurt to give them the impression that we're dating," she admitted. "It would certainly make it easier to explain a baby later on—but no PDAs."

"What about sneaking up to the hayloft?" he asked, only half teasing.

"That would be another no," she said firmly.

He wasn't surprised by her response, but he was disappointed. "Anything else I should know before I meet your family?"

"Just don't mention the name Blake and everything should be fine."

"Are the Gilmores and the Blakes still feuding?"

"The Hatfields and McCoys of Nevada," she told him.

"I'll have to remember not to get on your bad side," he mused. "Apparently Gilmores know how to hold a grudge."

"Only as well as Blakes," she retorted.

"And all because one guy got the prime land and the other ended up with some precious metals."

"Wars have been fought over less," she remarked. "And then there was the ill-fated love affair between Everett Gilmore's daughter, Maggie, and Samuel Blake's youngest son, James."

"I haven't heard that part of the story," he admitted.

"It's not unlike so many other forbidden love stories. Boy meets girl, their families disapprove, they run away together. Then the families come together, at least temporarily, to track down their missing offspring and drag them home again."

"Something must have happened to widen the rift again after that," Reid guessed.

She nodded. "Eight months later, Maggie died pushing her stillborn son into the world and James, overwhelmed by grief and guilt, set off on horseback and was never seen again. That story has been retold to each successive generation of Gilmores—and probably Blakes, too—as a warning of the kind of tragedy that results whenever the families forget that they're enemies."

"Just don't tell it to the little bean as a bedtime story," Reid suggested. "It's kind of dark."

"It is," she agreed. "And yet, my brother Caleb managed to forget the ending for a while."

"He fell in love with the daughter of your father's arch-enemy?" he guessed.

"I don't know if he loved her," she said. "But for a few weeks, he was married to her."

"Now that sounds like an interesting story."

"It's not even a unique one. They were young, they

screwed around, Brielle got pregnant and Caleb took her to Las Vegas for a quickie wedding. She lost the baby, they got a quickie divorce—end of story."

"Really?" he said dubiously. "That's it?"

"That's it," she confirmed. "After that, Brielle went away to school in New York City, and I don't think she's been back more than once or twice since."

"Maybe she's still in love with your brother," he suggested.

"Or maybe she's happy in New York," she countered.

"What about your brother—is he happy?"

"He's never given any indication that he's not," she said. "Liam, on the other hand, makes no secret of the fact that he has ambitions other than waking up at the Circle G every morning for the rest of his life."

"What does he want to do?"

"Renovate the old Stagecoach Inn and reopen it as a boutique hotel and spa."

"That doesn't sound like a bad idea," he said. "Aside from the Dusty Boots Motel out by the highway, Haven doesn't have a hotel."

"I don't disagree that a hotel is a good idea—if somebody else wanted to tackle the project, but 'Gilmores are ranchers,'" she said, deepening her voice in what was clearly intended as an imitation of her father.

"Did he object when you decided to go to law school?"

She shook her head. "My dad might have strong opinions about—well, he has strong opinions about everything," she acknowledged. "But he appreciates that everyone, even ranchers, need lawyers."

Reid turned where she indicated, passing through the open gates under an arched metalwork sign announcing Circle G Ranch.

The paved highway gave way to a gravel road and

stones kicked up under his tires, pinging against the undercarriage. He trusted that she knew how to get to the ranch, but the road he was on seemed to go nowhere. Every direction he looked, there was nothing but open fields dotted with cattle and, in the distance, the Silver Ridge Mountains speared into the cloudless blue sky. It was a full three minutes after he'd pulled off the highway before the house—two impressive stories of timber frame and cut stone—came into view.

He parked his truck, noting that there were five pickups, three SUVs and two ATVs ahead of his vehicle in the driveway.

"Good," Katelyn said, already reaching for the handle of her door. "It looks like everyone's here."

"You told me that you had a sister and two brothers," he reminded her, as he unhooked his belt.

"That's right," she confirmed, exiting the truck.

He followed suit, albeit less eagerly. "So who do all these vehicles belong to?"

She laughed at the obvious trepidation in his tone. "The gray truck is my dad's, the red one belongs to my grandparents, the pimped-up Jeep is Caleb's, Liam usually drives the green truck and Sky the blue SUV. The others belong to my uncle and cousins and the ranch foreman."

"This is a usual family dinner?"

"Pretty much," she confirmed, then nudged him with her shoulder. "Come on—I'll introduce you."

She did so, and though she'd given Reid a brief heads-up with respect to everyone else in attendance, it was apparent that Katelyn's family had received no advance warning that she'd be bringing a date.

"Trust me," she said later, when they moved toward the paddock to check out the foal born a few days earlier. "It's better that they didn't know you were coming, because they didn't have a chance to prepare an interrogation."

"Thank you, I think." Then, as he looked around the property, he had to admit, "This place is impressive."

"Six generations of Gilmores have worked to make it a success."

"It must have been quite an experience to grow up here, surrounded by all of this."

"It was," she agreed.

"And a big adjustment—moving from one of the biggest ranches in Haven to an apartment in town."

"It was," she said again.

"You don't miss this?"

She shook her head. "I miss my family sometimes, although it seems as if someone always has an excuse to make a trip into town to check up on me, but I don't miss the ranch."

There was something in her voice, a hint of defiance that he suspected was a deliberate cover of a deeper pain.

"You didn't grow up wanting to be a cowgirl?"

"No," she said. "Not since I was twelve, anyway."

"What happened when you were twelve?"

She was quiet for a moment. "My mom died."

He winced. "I'm sorry, Katelyn."

She just nodded and continued walking. After a few minutes, she stopped beneath a Jeffrey pine, her gaze fixed somewhere in the distance. "My mom loved everything about the ranch," she told him. "And she worked as hard as any of the hands. But sometimes, early in the mornings, she would saddle up her favorite horse and just ride. And sometimes she'd let me go with her. I loved those early morning rides when it was just the two of us."

Reid could see where the story was going now and regretted that he'd asked.

"We were out by the eastern border near the creek that morning. I saw something moving on the ground, but before I could say anything, Honey spotted it, too, and instinctively reared up. My mom was a good rider—skilled and experienced—but she'd been pointing to something in the distance and was unprepared for the abrupt movement.

"She was thrown off the back of the horse," she continued, her voice flat now and all the more heartbreaking for the lack of emotion in it. "And broke her neck when she fell.

"I didn't know what to do," Kate admitted. "She probably had a cell phone, but I didn't think about that at the time. Instead, I raced back to the house, to get help. My dad called 911, then he went after her. By the time he got to her, it was too late."

"I'm so sorry," Reid said.

"I didn't ride for a long time after that," she confided, as they made their way back to the paddock. "I hated Honey, I hated all the horses and the chores and everything about the ranch.

"I don't hate it anymore, but I don't think I'll ever love it the way I used to."

"Losing someone you love has a way of changing things," he acknowledged, reflecting briefly on his abandonment by his mother, his grandmother's death, and then the loss of Hank, too. Each of those events had played a part in making him the man that he was today—and his determination to be a father to the baby Katelyn was carrying.

"I miss her every single day, but now...now that I'm going to be a mother myself, the wound is somehow fresher and deeper again," she told him.

"I didn't tell anyone, when I first suspected that I might be pregnant, but I would have told her. I'm not saying she would have been overjoyed to hear that her unmarried daughter was having a stranger's baby, but she would have listened without judging…and she would have loved our baby."

He slid an arm across her shoulders and drew her to his side, a silent gesture of support. She let her head fall against his shoulder, for just a minute before she said, "Is this a PDA?"

"Nope—there's no one else around, so it's strictly a DA."

She laughed softly. "You know, under other circumstances, I could really like you, Sheriff."

"Why can't you like me under current circumstances?"

"Because current circumstances are complicated."

"Life is complicated."

"And although we're having a simple meal tonight, I should see if Martina and Grams need a hand in the kitchen."

"Very smooth segue, counselor."

She responded with a sassy smile. "Do you want to come back to the house with me?"

"I'll hang out here for a while," he decided.

Ten minutes later, when he was flanked by her brothers and cousins, he was wishing he'd opted to return to the house with Katelyn.

"Are you on duty or off?" Caleb asked, offering a beer to him.

"Off," he said, nodding his thanks as he accepted the bottle.

"I have to make a trip into town later and I wouldn't want to run afoul of the law," Liam said, explaining the soda can in his hand.

"Heather again?" One of the cousins—Mitchell—asked.

Liam grinned. "Yep."

"This is going on what—three weeks now?" the other

cousin—Michael—asked. "That's a long-term relationship for you."

"As much as I enjoy roasting my brother," Caleb interjected. "We're getting sidetracked from the real issue here."

And they all turned, as if on cue, to look at Reid.

He tipped the bottle to his lips, sipped. "Am I an issue?"

"That's what we're trying to figure out," Caleb told him.

"Katie doesn't usually bring a date to family events," Liam commented.

"Katie doesn't *ever* bring a date to family events," Mitchell clarified.

"Then I'm doubly honored to have been invited," Reid said.

"Of course, as a defense attorney, she'd understand the importance of establishing a positive relationship with local law enforcement," Liam noted.

"Which might be why she included you," Caleb suggested.

"I know better than to question a woman's motives," Reid told them.

"We want to know if the two of you are dating," Michael said, cutting to the chase.

"I'm enjoying spending time with her," he said, since he wasn't sure that one date actually qualified as dating.

"You can't have spent much time with her yet," Liam said. "You've only been in town a few weeks."

"Actually, I knew Katelyn before I moved to Haven."

The brothers and cousins exchanged a look, clearly not pleased by this revelation.

"From where and for how long?" Caleb asked.

"From 'none of your business' and as long as 'none of your business,'" Katelyn responded from behind them.

The five men turned to face her.

"You're our sister," Liam reminded her.

"And our cousin," Mitchell piped in.

"That makes it our business," Caleb finished.

"While I acknowledge and appreciate that the name carries a certain weight and status in this town, being born a Gilmore doesn't automatically imply the forfeiture of any expectation of privacy."

Michael slanted a look at Caleb. "Now you've done it."

"When she's really annoyed, she starts with the lawyer-speak," Liam explained to Reid. "And since I've got horses to feed before dinner, I'm going to go do that before she really gets on a roll."

"We'll help you," Michael said.

They all moved away from the paddock together.

Kate folded her arms and leaned them on the rail, her gaze fixed on the foal that was prancing on spindly legs beside its mother.

"I'm sorry," she said. "I knew my family would have questions when we showed up together, but I thought they'd exercise some discretion."

"They're just looking out for you," he noted.

"Maybe," she allowed. "Although sometimes I think they harass people just for sport."

"They did seem to have a good rhythm going with their interrogation, as if they'd had a lot of practice."

"No doubt they have," she agreed, then hastened to clarify. "Interrogating Skylar's numerous boyfriends in high school, I mean."

"What about your boyfriends?"

She shook her head. "I didn't date in high school."

"Not much or not at all?"

"Not at all," she admitted. "I was more interested in studying than boys."

"So when did you have your first boyfriend?" he asked.

"My first year of college, but even he didn't get an invitation home to meet my family."

"Who was the first guy who did?"

"I, uh…actually, I can't remember."

His gaze narrowed. "You remember—you just don't want to tell me."

"It's really not important," she told him.

"Your refusal to share the name suggests otherwise."

She sighed. "If I tell you, you're going to wish you'd let this go," she warned.

"Maybe," he acknowledged. "But I still want to know."

"You," she said.

He waited for her to finish her thought, but that single word was all she said.

"What about me?" he prompted.

"You, Sheriff Reid Davidson, recent transplant from Echo Ridge, Texas, are the first man I've ever brought home to meet my family."

She had to be joking. There was no way he was the first. Except that the flags of color high on her cheeks gave credence to her claim.

"How old are you?" he blurted out.

She laughed. "Twenty-eight." Then, after a tiny hesitation, she added, "Today."

And the surprises kept coming. "It's your birthday today?"

She nodded.

"Happy Birthday."

"Thanks."

His mind was still reeling over the first revelation—that she'd never introduced a man to her family. She must have had boyfriends—because she wasn't a virgin when they were together. But he was beginning to realize he'd misjudged her experience. "So what happened between us in Boulder City…"

"My first ever one-night stand," she admitted.

"And not technically a one-night stand."

She nodded.

"I turned thirty-four in March," he told her.

"Happy belated birthday?"

He managed a smile. "I just wanted you to know that there's a six-year age gap between us."

"Does that bother you?"

"Are you kidding? Guys always want to be with hot young chicks."

She laughed. "Is that what I am—a hot young chick?"

"Very hot—and younger than I realized," he admitted.

"But we're not really together," she reminded him.

"Are you sure? Because I'd guess your family is thinking that we're not only together but that our relationship is pretty serious, since I'm the first guy you've ever brought home to meet them."

"You know why I wanted them to meet you."

"So it doesn't come as a shock when you tell them we're getting married?" he asked hopefully.

Chapter Eleven

Kate shook her head, exasperated by his unwillingness to give up on the idea—and increasingly tempted to take what he was offering. But for the moment, she held firm. "We're *not* getting married."

"I haven't stopped thinking about you since the weekend we spent together in Boulder City," he told her.

"I'm flattered," she said. "But that's no reason to start planning a wedding."

"You're right," he agreed. "But what about a baby? Do you think having a baby is a good reason?"

"I'd say it depends on the preexisting relationship between the expectant parents," she said. "If there was no preexisting relationship, then I'd have to say no—a baby is not a good reason to get married."

"What if those two people, despite having no preexisting relationship, somehow just click whenever they're together?"

"I'm not sure 'click' is either a valid or relevant factor," she said dubiously.

"It's both," he insisted.

"Sometimes an attraction just confuses the issue," she pointed out.

"I'll admit to being confused about a lot of things, but wanting to marry you isn't one of them."

And when he said it like that, with unwavering conviction, she almost believed it was true. But she knew he didn't really *want* to marry her, he just wanted to do the right thing. And she definitely didn't want to have the same arguments with him again.

"We should get back," she said instead. "Dinner will be ready soon."

It was almost dark by the time they'd said their goodbyes to everyone and drove away from the ranch. Though Reid knew her family still had a lot of questions about his relationship with Katelyn, he considered the afternoon a success. Of course, everything would likely change when they found out she was pregnant, so he was grateful she didn't seem to be in a hurry to share that news.

"Your family sure knows how to put on a barbecue," he commented, fondly recalling the platters of ribs and burgers and sausages, heaping bowls of potato salad, coleslaw and macaroni and cheese, the enormous pot filled with homemade baked beans and baskets with thick slices of corn bread. It had seemed like a mountain of food, but the mountain was soon conquered by the Gilmores and their guests.

"My family doesn't believe in doing anything by half measures," she told him.

"I enjoyed meeting them," he said as he turned onto

the highway to head back into town. "Thank you for inviting me today."

"I'm glad you survived," she said, a smile playing at the corners of her mouth. "I know they can be a little... overwhelming at times."

A little overwhelming was something of an understatement. On the other hand, he'd enjoyed watching Katelyn with her relatives—the teasing and shorthand communications that develop through close relationships. The way one person would start a story only to have someone else pick up the narrative of the shared experience without missing a beat.

"You were lucky to grow up in such a close family."

"I know," she acknowledged. "Even if I didn't always think so at the time."

He'd been on his own for so long, he'd forgotten what it meant to be connected to someone else. Being with Katelyn's family today had given him a glimpse, and he was glad their baby was going to be part of that family.

"I realized something else today," she told him.

"What's that?" he asked.

"That you don't talk about your family."

"There's not much to talk about," he said. "For a long time, it was just me and my grandmother. Then I spent some time in foster care, living with other people's families, until Hank took me in."

"Who's Hank?"

"Hank Mahoney was the Sheriff of Echo Ridge when I was growing up there."

"He's the reason you went into law enforcement?" she guessed. "To follow in the footsteps of a man you admired?"

"Yeah," he admitted. "Although it was a little more complicated than that."

"It's a long drive back to town," she reminded him.

She was right, and even if there were parts of his history that he wasn't proud of, she deserved to know his background.

"I first met Hank when I was seventeen," he told her. "Young and dumb enough to attempt to hot-wire the sheriff's truck."

Her brows lifted. "You can really do that? I thought that was just something that happened in the movies."

"I can really do it, but I'm not very good at it—which is why Hank caught me in the act. I'd just been bumped from yet another foster home and, thankfully, he recognized that I was acting out of anger and frustration more than I was looking for trouble, and he gave me a chance."

"Like you did with Aiden, once you knew the whole story."

He kept his gaze focused on the road. "What makes you think I did anything?"

"Haven't you learned yet that it's next to impossible to keep a secret in Haven?" she chided. "When I went to see the ADA about the charges against Aiden, he said Rebecca Blake had already called to tell him that, after consultation with the new sheriff, she supported Aiden's application for the youth diversion program."

"Not a lot of people know about the program," he said, as if that was his only reason for reaching out to Mrs. Blake. "And Aiden's a good candidate, with a father determined to keep him on the straight and narrow."

"How old were you when you lost your parents?" she asked gently.

"I didn't lose them—they lost me," he told her. "My dad was a drunk who took off before I was born. Apparently he came back again, around my first birthday, but didn't hang around for more than a few months. My mom stuck it out for a few more years, hooking up with the occasional boyfriend who made my dad look like a catch. Then when I was about six, she decided that taking care of a kid was too much responsibility and dumped me at her mother's house.

"I don't know what excuse or explanation she offered, but my grandmother took me in and, for the next eight years, she raised me. Then she died, and I had no one.

"I bounced around in foster care for a while, because teen boys don't tend to settle easily into traditional families, and I spent some time in a group home, where I started to run with a bad crowd and made some poor choices."

"Like hot-wiring the sheriff's truck."

He nodded. "I know it sounds melodramatic, but I really believe he saved my life that day."

"Did Hank have any kids of his own?"

"A daughter, Patricia. She was a year ahead of me in school—the cheerleader who dated the quarterback." He lifted a hand to rub the slight bump on the bridge of his nose. "One night when I was leaving school late, I saw them together. They were in the middle of a pretty heavy makeout session and I wanted to look away, but something about the situation set off warning bells in my head.

"Long story short—she was saying no, he wasn't listening, so I intervened. He punched me in the face, broke my nose, Trish helped me mop up the blood and drove me home."

There was something different in his voice when he said her name, an unexpected warmth that made Kate wish she'd never asked.

She definitely shouldn't ask the next question that sprang to mind, but there was a time delay between her brain and her mouth and the words spilled out before she could stop them. "You fell in love with her?"

"No," he denied. "But I married her."

He'd been upfront about his divorce from the beginning, but he hadn't mentioned that his wife was the daughter of a man who'd been his father figure, mentor and best friend.

And again, though she wasn't sure she wanted all the details, she heard herself ask, "How did that come about?"

"Hank got cancer," he said bluntly. "When he realized he was dying, his biggest concern was his daughter. He didn't want to leave her alone, without anyone to look out for her. I told him that I would and put a ring on her finger to prove it.

"I wasn't in love with her," he said again. "But it wasn't just a quick ceremony to appease her dad, either. When I spoke my vows, I intended to honor them forever."

Kate knew that marriage required a leap of faith, regardless of the reasons for it. She also knew there were all kinds of reasons that marriages—even good marriages—fell apart, and she couldn't deny a certain curiosity about his. "What went wrong?"

"We wanted different things," he said.

"That's rather vague," she noted.

"There were issues that drove us apart and no compelling reason to stay together."

His follow-up response didn't do much to expand on the first, but she decided to let it go. No doubt it was, if not painful, at least uncomfortable to talk about a failed marriage. And now that she knew some of Reid's background, she could understand and appreciate why he was so determined to be there for their baby.

Childhood wounds inevitably left a mark, and although she hadn't been so young when she'd lost her mother, the sense of loss and emptiness was still with Kate every single day. She suspected that Reid's experiences had left even deeper scars and that his determination to be there for his child was a way of ensuring his son or daughter had a better start in life than he'd been given.

Katelyn was quiet for a long while after Reid told her about his upbringing, probably questioning his suitability as a parent. He didn't blame her for having doubts—he had more than a few of his own. But a few days earlier, he'd heard her argue a case that made him believe she'd give him a chance.

Her client was a father seeking to alter a custody order. If Reid remembered the details correctly, the dad had worked long hours in the mines and wasn't much of a hands-on parent for the first few years of the children's lives. Now he was a manager, with a more regular schedule and weekends off, and wanted increased access to his children. The mother balked at the request because she was in a new relationship and the children were settled into routines that she didn't want to disrupt.

Listening to the lawyers, Reid couldn't help but wonder if he and Katelyn would someday end up in front of a judge, arguing about who was entitled to what with respect to their child. He didn't want their son or daughter to become a pawn in a game of one-upmanship, but he would fight to be part of the child's life.

For now, though, he continued to hope that wouldn't be necessary. There was still time to convince Katelyn to marry him and give their baby a real family, but he understood her reservations. She was in court almost every day dealing with the aftermath of marriages that didn't work—contentious divorces, property disputes, custody fights. Even if they'd fallen in love after dating a while, she'd undoubtedly have reservations about making any lifelong promises—and he didn't know how to overcome those reservations.

How could he claim to know anything about making a marriage work when he'd already failed to do exactly that? Of course, the circumstances of his first marriage were completely different. Hank had been dying and Reid would have done anything to ease the man's worry in those final days.

He hadn't been in love with Trish and he hadn't pretended that he was. And even though she'd claimed to love him, he suspected the feelings she professed to have were born of a fear of being alone. She wanted to love and be loved, and when Reid couldn't give her what she wanted, she found someone who could.

It was ironic that one of the reasons his marriage had fallen apart was that his wife wanted a baby and he didn't. Now, by accident rather than design, he was going to be a father, anyway. The role he'd been certain he didn't ever want was suddenly his.

More surprising was the realization that he *wanted* to be a father to the baby Katelyn was carrying. In fact, he was starting to accept that he wanted to be a father *and* a husband—he wanted them to be a family. But first, he had to convince Katelyn that it was what she wanted, too.

"Did the judge make a decision in that custody variation hearing you had last week?"

"You were in the courtroom?"

He nodded.

"Since when does local law enforcement take an interest in a standard family law matter?"

"I only popped in to check out the hot young lawyer at first," he admitted. "But your arguments were compelling and, afterward, I found myself wondering if you believed them."

"You're going to have to be a little more specific," she told him.

"You said the variation wasn't about the dad's right to spend more time with his children but about their right to have a meaningful relationship with both parents."

"Wow, you were paying attention, weren't you?"

"The case struck a chord," he admitted.

"Yes, I believe it," she said. "It's important for a child to be given the opportunity to develop a strong and lasting bond with both parents."

"What does that mean for us?"

Her brow furrowed as she turned to stare out the window. "I would accommodate whatever reasonable visitation you wanted."

"I don't want visitation," he told her. "I want to marry you and raise our child together."

"We don't have to be married to co-parent our child," she assured him.

"I don't want our child to be co-parented," he argued. "I want him—or her—to have a real family. And I think you want that, too, you're just afraid to admit it."

"Of course it's what I'd want if our situation was different—if our baby had been conceived in the course of something that actually resembled a relationship rather than as a consequence of a broken condom during a one-night stand."

"Two nights," he reminded her.

"A second night doesn't miraculously turn a casual hookup into a relationship."

"And an unplanned pregnancy shouldn't be used as a roadblock to the development of a relationship," he argued.

"Especially not when there are so many other obvious roadblocks," she agreed.

He turned onto Station Street. "Why'd you go to Echo Ridge looking for me?"

She gave up the pretense that she'd been in Texas for any other purpose. "Because you're the father of my baby."

He nodded. "Now let's consider for a minute what might have happened if I hadn't already agreed to take over Jed Traynor's job here in Haven."

"You would have been in Echo Ridge," she acknowledged, not sure where this new train of thought was leading.

"Most likely," he agreed, making the turn onto Main. "And you would have tracked me down at the Sheriff's Office and told me about our baby, right?"

She hesitated, but she couldn't deny the truth of what he was saying or see how that truth would trip her up. "Right," she confirmed.

"Even though we'd gone our separate ways and you could have kept the news of your pregnancy to yourself."

"You're the father of my baby," she said again. "And fathers have specific legal rights and responsibilities."

He nodded and turned onto Page, then into the parking lot behind her building. "And when you told me about your pregnancy, you gave me the opportunity to exercise those rights and fulfill the responsibilities."

"Because it was the right thing to do."

"And maybe," he suggested, "because there was a part of you that wanted me to step up, not just to be a father but a husband."

Kate thought about his supposition for a long time after Reid had gone. Her initial instinct had been to deny it, of course, but there was some validity to his argument.

She believed that a child had a right to a relationship with both parents; she didn't believe that a child's mother and father had to be married to parent effectively. Maybe marriage would make some things easier, but that was hardly a reason to get trapped into a legally binding arrangement.

Except that the more time she spent with the sheriff, the less the prospect of marriage seemed like a trap. In fact, the idea of marrying Reid was starting to hold some definite appeal.

Chapter Twelve

Two weeks later, Reid had made little progress in his efforts to convince Katelyn to marry him. For every step he took forward, she took two steps back. Sometimes it was a struggle to even get her to spend time with him. She seemed to have a ready excuse whenever he called to make plans, but she was less inclined to turn him down face-to-face. He took that knowledge with him to her door early Friday night.

"If you keep hanging around my apartment, people are going to start to talk," Katelyn warned, but she stepped away from the door so that he could enter.

"I've got nothing to hide." He followed her into the living room, stopping abruptly when he spotted the playpen in the corner, an assortment of colorful blocks scattered across the area rug and a blond-haired, blue-eyed, chubby-cheeked baby wearing an orange T-shirt and brown overalls with a giraffe embroidered on the front.

The baby was sitting upright and gnawing on a purple block, but he glanced up at Reid and grinned, showing off tiny teeth. "Da!"

"Was I in a coma for—" he looked at the baby, estimated his age and added that to the time remaining in Katelyn's pregnancy "—eighteen months?"

"Ha ha." She scooped the baby up from the floor and propped him on her hip. "That's not Daddy, that's Sheriff Davidson."

"Da!" he said again.

"Don't worry," Katelyn said. "He thinks every man is 'Da.'"

"And who is he?" Reid asked.

"This is Keegan," she told him. "My godson. I'm babysitting for a few hours while Emerson—his mom and my best friend—has an appointment at the spa."

"Haven has a spa?"

"Well, right now Andria has a modest setup in her basement, but she's in negotiations with Liam to move her business to the hotel when it opens."

Keegan stuck his thumb in his mouth and dropped his head to Katelyn's shoulder, snuggling in comfortably. Seeing her with the baby in her arms, Reid felt something move inside him—an unexpected warmth that seemed to start in the vicinity of his chest and spread outward.

He'd spent a lot of time reading up on pregnancy and trying to prepare for the baby that would arrive in another six-and-a-half months, but he really didn't know what it took to be a father. Watching Katelyn with Keegan, he was reassured that their child would at least have one competent parent.

"You're a natural," he noted.

"He's an easy baby," she said.

His brows lifted. "Is there such a thing?"

"Well, most of the time he's an easy baby," she amended, as the little guy twisted in her arms to reach toward the blocks on the floor. "He did give me some trouble a few months back when he was teething, but once those pearly whites broke through, he was a smiling—and drooling—baby again."

"How old is he?"

She set Keegan down again, and he immediately grabbed the purple block. "Ten-and-a-half months."

"So we've got a while to wait before our baby will be teething and crawling?"

"And opening cupboards and trying to stick toy keys in electrical outlets."

He noticed that her outlets were protected with plastic inserts. There were also clear rubber bumpers affixed to the sharp edges of the coffee table. "Do you babysit often?"

"I try to take him for a few hours every couple of weeks, sometimes just to give Emerson a break, sometimes so that she and her husband, Mark, can have some time alone together."

"You're a good friend."

"Thank you," she said. "Emerson claims I borrow her baby to pretend I have a life outside of work."

"I guess you don't get out much."

"You've been in Haven long enough now to know there's really nowhere to go."

"Maybe that's why I always end up at your door."

She smiled at that. "Why are you really here?"

"Because I was thinking about you, and while I was thinking about you, I realized I was hungry, so I decided to see if you wanted to grab a bite and catch a movie."

"Dinner and a movie—that sounds a lot like a date, Sheriff."

"Maybe, if you had to put a label on it," he acknowledged. "Or it could just be a couple of friends-slash-colleagues hanging out."

"I appreciate the invitation," she said. "But Emerson is picking up pizza and wings on her way back."

"Maybe just the movie later, then?" he asked hopefully.

"Mark's out of town this weekend so we're having a girls' night—no boys allowed."

"What about him?" Reid asked, jerking his head toward the baby, who'd traded in the purple block for a green one.

"He gets a pass because his boy parts are in a diaper."

He sighed regretfully. "Okay, I guess I'll head over to Jo's and get my own pizza to take home and eat by myself."

She led him back to the foyer, a clear signal that his attempt to elicit sympathy and procure an invitation had failed.

But when she opened the door, he found himself face-to-face with a slender woman with curly reddish hair and a stack of three flat boxes in her hand.

"Well, hello, there," she said, her green eyes sparking with curiosity. "You must be Reid."

"I am," he confirmed, stepping back so that she could enter.

"And Reid was just leaving," Katelyn said.

"Oh," her friend said, sounding disappointed. "Have you had dinner?"

"I'm going to pick up a pizza on my way home," he said.

"Why would you do that when we've got plenty of pizza—and wings—right here?"

Keegan, having recognized his mother's voice, abandoned his blocks and crawled to the foyer, where he was now attempting to pull himself up on her leg.

"There's my little man," she said, smiling down at the baby.

Katelyn took the boxes. "How much food did you get?"

Emerson lifted the baby, rubbing her nose against his and making him giggle, then propping him on her hip. "They had a special on two pizzas and wings."

"We're never going to eat all that," Katelyn said.

"Then I guess it's a good thing we've got the sheriff here to help," she said, winking at Reid.

"I was just on my way out," he reminded her, showing his willingness to accede to Katelyn's wishes.

"Don't go without having something to eat first," Emerson protested.

He looked at Katelyn, silently questioning.

"Fine—you can stay for a slice of pizza," she relented, handing the boxes to him. "I'll get plates and napkins."

"Can you hold Keegan for a sec while I grab drinks?" Emerson asked when he'd set the food on the table.

Before he could respond—which would have been to suggest that he'd get the drinks—she'd shoved the baby at him, leaving him with no choice in the matter.

He looked down at the little guy who was looking up at him, lower lip quivering. "Oh, crap. You're going to cry, aren't you?"

As if on cue, the baby's big blue eyes filled with tears.

"Hey, this wasn't my idea," he said, talking fast in the hope of distracting the kid long enough for his mom to return. "And I don't blame you for being unhappy with the situation, but your mom will be right back, she just went to help—I assume, since she's your godmother, you call her Aunt Katelyn, or maybe Aunt Katie—get drinks so that we can have dinner."

To his surprise and immense relief, the monologue seemed to do the trick. Though the tears didn't dry up, Keegan's lip was no longer quivering and he looked more curious than scared now.

Reid kept talking. "What do you like to drink with your

pizza? Is your beverage of choice milk or juice? And do you drink from a bottle or a sippy cup?"

Of course, Keegan didn't respond to any of the questions, but the little guy at least seemed to be listening.

So was Kate, who had paused in the doorway between the kitchen and the dining room, plates and napkins in hand.

"I'm running out of things to say now," Reid continued in the same easy tone. "But I'm afraid if I stop talking, you'll start crying and your aunt Katelyn will realize I don't have a clue when it comes to babies and then she'll worry I'm going to be a horrible father.

"And while I'll admit that's entirely possible—and probably understandable considering that I have no memories of my own father and didn't have any positive male role models in my life until I met Hank when I was seventeen—I'm going to do my best to be a good dad and hope like hell—

"Heck!" he quickly amended. "I mean heck. I'm going to hope like heck that I don't screw up too badly. I suspect swearing in front of a baby would probably count as a screwup, so maybe we can just keep that to ourselves?

"And maybe you could actually smile and pretend I'm incredibly amusing and entertaining, and maybe that'll help convince Katelyn to give me a chance—"

Kate felt an elbow in her ribs and glanced at Emerson, who was also observing the sheriff's interaction with her little boy.

"If you had to get knocked up, at least you picked a stand-up guy," Emerson noted in a whisper.

"You're making this assessment after overhearing two minutes of a one-sided conversation with an infant?"

"A conversation in which he demonstrated honesty, vulnerability, self-awareness and determination," Emerson noted. "All that, and those fabulous shoulders, too."

Of course, her friend was right. And the more time Kate spent with Reid, the more irresistible he seemed, which made her question why she was continuing to resist.

She pushed aside those tempting thoughts.

"Come on. Pizza's getting cold."

Keegan sat in his mother's lap, gnawing contentedly on a piece of crust while the adults chatted and ate. When everyone had their fill and Kate got up to wrap the leftovers, Emerson said, "Oh, my goodness—is it almost eight o'clock already? I need to get this little guy changed into his pj's and home to bed."

Then she hurried into the bedroom, where Kate had laid a protective sheet on top of her comforter as a makeshift change table for the baby. Kate, of course, followed.

"What are you talking about?" she demanded. "I thought we were going to hang out tonight."

"Except that I forgot the seventeen loads of dirty laundry waiting at home," her friend said as she stripped away Keegan's overalls and T-shirt.

Kate's eyes narrowed. "Oh, no, you don't."

"But I do," Emerson insisted, pulling a sleeper out of the diaper bag. "Soon enough you'll understand how many onesies and burp cloths a baby goes through in a week."

"I'm sure you do have laundry to wash," she acknowledged. "That's not what I'm referring to."

"What are you referring to?" Her friend expertly slid a clean diaper under Keegan's bottom before unfastening and whisking away the wet one.

Kate folded her arms over her chest. "You're taking off because you think that will push me and Reid to spend more time together."

"If you need to be pushed, you're not nearly as smart as I always thought you were," Emerson chided.

But apparently it wasn't enough to push Kate, because Emerson returned to the living room and said to Reid, "Have you got a ring yet? Because The Goldmine has a sale on diamond jewelry this weekend."

Kate sighed. "Emerson's been my best friend since kindergarten," she told him. "But she's never been subtle."

"I've never understood why anyone would tiptoe around an issue when the direct approach gets you to the same place so much faster," Emerson said.

He nodded in acknowledgment of the point before responding to her question. "I might be new in town, but I've been here long enough to know that buying a diamond at The Goldmine would be as discreet as putting an engagement announcement in the Haven Record."

"Sexy *and* smart," Emerson noted. "Okay, putting aside the question of a ring for the moment—what are your intentions with respect to my best friend?"

"You should be more concerned about my intentions," Kate interrupted. "Because right now, killing you seems to be the only way to shut you up."

Her friend just grinned, unrepentant. "You shouldn't issue death threats in front of the sheriff."

But Reid didn't seem to have any qualms about answering Emerson's original question, because he said, "My intention is to marry Katelyn so we can raise our child together."

"And I still maintain that we don't need to be married to raise our child together," she chimed in.

"Blah blah blah," Emerson said, clearly having heard it all before and not at all concerned about upsetting her friend.

"It's true," Kate insisted.

Emerson directed her next comment to Reid again. "All the time Katie spends in divorce court has made her wary of putting her heart on the line."

"Reid doesn't want my heart," she interjected. "He just wants his ring on my finger to legitimize his claim to our child."

He was stunned by her matter-of-fact tone as much as the words. "Is that what you really think?"

Katelyn shrugged, as if it didn't matter. "We both know you never would have proposed if I wasn't pregnant."

"I can't deny that's true, but I don't just want our baby to carry my name," he said. "I want him or her to have the love and support of both parents, not one or the other depending on where he or she's sleeping on any particular night."

"That's a pretty compelling argument," Emerson noted, as she buckled the sleepy baby into his car seat.

"I thought you were in a hurry to get home," Katelyn said to her.

Emerson hugged her friend. "I'm going," she promised. Then she hugged Reid, too. "Don't give up on her—she'll come around."

"I'm keeping my fingers crossed."

"You might have more luck if you put a diamond on hers instead."

Kate shook her head as she closed the door behind her friend. "I'm sorry about that."

"I'm not," he said. "I like her straightforwardness."

"That's one word for it," she agreed.

"And I'm hoping the direct approach will work for me, too," he said, reaching a hand into his pocket.

Her heart started to beat faster when she recognized what was clearly a jeweler's box, and she took an instinctive step back. "What are you doing?"

"I'm proposing, Katelyn."

"Why?"

"Because while I've frequently mentioned that I want us to be married, I've never actually asked you to be my wife."

"You really bought a ring?"

He flipped open the lid to reveal a stunning princess-cut diamond.

As she stared at the glittering stone, Kate wondered why the prospect of marrying a man she'd known only a few months was somehow less terrifying than the idea of having a baby on her own. That he wanted to marry her and be a father to their child told her a lot about the type of man he was, but even if he was willing to vow to "love, honor and cherish" her, she knew he didn't love her.

And she didn't love him.

The five words hadn't fully come together to form a sentence when her heart bumped against her ribs, as if to contradict her claim.

No, her head insisted. It wasn't possible that she'd fallen in love with Reid.

Was it?

She took a minute to review the evidence. Every time she was going to see him, she felt flutters of anticipation in her belly that she knew—only ten weeks into her pregnancy—couldn't be explained away as movements of the baby inside her. She enjoyed talking to him and even arguing with him, because he challenged her to consider different ideas and opinions. And there was no doubt she was attracted to him. Those little flutters were nothing compared to the way her pulse jolted whenever he gave her one of those lingering looks that said he was remembering her naked. Or the way her pulse would race when he touched her—even just a casual brush of a finger down her arm. And when he kissed her—

Ohmygod.

She *was* in love with him.

But her feelings were only one side of the equation. If and when she ever walked down the aisle, she wanted it to be with butterflies in her tummy and hope in her heart— and looking toward a groom whose eyes were filled with love as he looked back at her.

Reid was looking at her now, but all she could see in his eyes was a steely determination to do the right thing.

"Katelyn Gilmore, will you—"

"Stop!"

"You didn't let me finish the question," he said mildly.

"Because if you don't actually ask, then I don't have to say no and we can pretend this never happened."

He rose to his feet again but continued to hold the box open, the brilliant diamond flashing light. "There is another option, you know—you could say yes."

She shook her head regretfully, her throat tight. "I can't."

Then, because she didn't trust herself to hold back the tears that filled her eyes or the newly acknowledged feelings overflowing from her heart, she turned and walked briskly to her bedroom, closing the door firmly behind her.

Chapter Thirteen

She hadn't actually said no, but Reid knew that if he'd pressed the issue, she would have. Maybe they weren't head over heels in love, but he sincerely liked and respected Katelyn. And then there was the sizzling sexual chemistry between them…chemistry that she'd been determinedly ignoring, causing him to suffer through a lot of cold showers in recent weeks.

If she'd said yes to his proposal, one of the perks would be warm showers with his bride-to-be, sliding soapy hands over the sexy curves of her body. Unfortunately, his erotic fantasies seemed destined to remain just that.

If she was adamantly opposed to marrying him—and rushing away in tears didn't suggest that she was on the fence—he had to respect her choice. Even if he wasn't happy about it.

He didn't want to share custody of their child, with scheduled weekend trade-offs and formal discussions about homework or afterschool activities, but he was determined to be there for his son or daughter as much as possible. To be the full-time father he'd never had as a kid.

Still, he was frustrated with the whole situation, so when he stepped outside Saturday morning and saw Norm Clayton pressing one hand to his back while the other struggled with the cord of the lawn mower, he offered to take over. The old man protested at first—after all, the sheriff was paying rent, he shouldn't have to do chores—but Reid assured him that he didn't mind. So Norm retreated inside to his heating pad and Reid welcomed the roar of the mower drowning out thoughts of his aborted proposal.

The backyard required some maneuvering around the climbing structure and sandbox that Norm and Bev had installed for their grandchildren to enjoy when they visited, which got Reid thinking he was going to need a backyard for his son or daughter to run around in. Because he didn't plan on living in the Claytons' downstairs apartment forever and a child needed space.

And toys to scatter around the yard.

And maybe a dog.

He'd finished the cutting and was pushing the mower back toward the garage when he saw Katelyn on the sidewalk.

She smiled, a little tentatively, as she moved closer. "Moonlighting in yard work, Sheriff?"

"Norm's back was bothering him this morning, so I offered to help."

"Did you sell tickets?"

"What?"

"You have an audience," Katelyn noted, sliding a glance toward the neighbor's porch where Beverly Clayton and Frieda Zimmerman were sipping glasses of lemonade.

"They're not watching me," he denied.

"You don't think so?" She lifted a hand in greeting and both women immediately waved back.

"It's a real scorcher today, isn't it?" Beverly called out.

"It sure is," Reid agreed, wiping the sweat from his brow with his forearm.

"Eighty-seven degrees already," Frieda said. "And supposed to get hotter."

"There's an extra glass here," Beverly told him. "If you want some lemonade to help you cool off."

"Or you could just take off your shirt," Frieda suggested as an alternative.

"Frieda!" Beverly admonished.

"We're not out here to watch the clouds move across the sky," her friend and neighbor said bluntly. "We want to see the sheriff's muscles."

Katelyn bit down on her lip, obviously trying not to laugh.

"Maybe next time, Mrs. Zimmerman," Reid said with a smile.

She let out an exaggerated sigh. "Promises, promises."

He put the mower in the garage, then returned to Katelyn. "Were you just in the neighborhood?" he wondered.

"In the neighborhood...hoping to see you."

Suddenly his day was looking brighter. "Do you want to go inside where we can talk without an audience?"

She hesitated, and he knew she was thinking about Mrs. Clayton and Mrs. Zimmerman and worried what they might think if she was seen going into Reid's apartment.

"It's not even eleven—too early for them to suspect we're going inside for a nooner."

His teasing remark earned a small smile, though she didn't look entirely convinced. Her decision was made easier when Frieda grumbled about preferring to be inside with the air conditioning if there was nothing to see outside and the two old women abandoned their posts.

As Kate followed Reid into his apartment, she could see the perspiration glistening on his skin. She'd never thought she would find a sweaty man appealing, but she couldn't deny that the sight of Reid, his T-shirt stretched over those broad shoulders, a dark V dampening both the front and the back of the fabric, made everything inside her quiver.

"Why do you wear jeans to cut the grass in this heat?" she wondered.

"Because the mower might kick up stones or other debris."

Which made sense but was still disappointing, because his legs could rival his shoulders for Beverly's and Frieda's attention—and even her own.

And then, as if he could hear her thoughts, he lifted the hem of his T-shirt and pulled it over his head, then rubbed the fabric across his chest. Her gaze followed his movements, admiring those incredible shoulders, the sculpted pecs, the rippling abs.

"What are you doing?" she croaked through dry lips.

"I thought you'd probably appreciate it if I took a shower."

"Well, undress in the bathroom," she suggested.

His brows lifted. "I only took off my shirt. And you have seen me naked before."

Yeah, but she couldn't let herself think about "before"— when she'd been naked with him—because she was now dealing with an overload of pregnancy hormones that made her want to do all kinds of wickedly wonderful things to him. And let him do anything he wanted to her in return.

"Of course, it's been a while, hasn't it, Katelyn?" he prompted.

Twenty-two days.

Not that she was counting—not really.

But she was staring—she couldn't seem to help herself.

And the amusement that danced in the depths of those hazel eyes left absolutely no doubt that he was aware of the effect he had on her.

"Do you want to join me in the shower?" he asked. "You're looking a little...flushed."

She swallowed. "I'm fine."

He shrugged, and the casual rise and fall of those amazing shoulders nearly made her whimper.

"Why don't you go relax in the living room then?" he suggested as an alternative.

"I'm fine," she said again, unwilling to go anywhere near the flowered sofa where she'd been naked with him twenty-two days ago.

His quick grin confirmed that he knew what she was thinking. "There are cold drinks in the fridge and ice-cream bars in the freezer. Help yourself to whatever you want."

What she wanted was standing in front of her, but succumbing to that desire—again—would complicate her life exponentially. Instead, she waited to hear the bathroom door close, then went to the freezer to see what kind of ice cream he had.

A few minutes later, Kate heard the water running—a sound that elicited mental images of Reid's naked body. She could picture droplets of water sliding over those perfectly sculpted muscles, caressing his taut skin.

Only when she felt ice cream dripping onto her hand did she shove the images aside and the ice cream into her mouth.

He came out of the bathroom a short while later, wearing a clean T-shirt and a pair of cargo shorts. His hair was still wet from the shower and his jaw was unshaven, and all her girlie parts sighed anew with a combination of pleasure and longing.

He opened the fridge and pulled out a can of cola. "Do you want anything?" he asked her.

Nothing I can have.

But, of course, she just shook her head. "No, thanks."

He popped the tab on the can and lifted it to his mouth to drink. She turned away, wandering toward the living area.

"I thought you were going to get some new furniture."

He shrugged. "It's not a priority right now."

"The last time I was here, you claimed to be allergic to the flowers painted on everything."

He smiled, apparently thinking about the last time she'd been there. "The last time you were here is the reason I've grown quite fond of that sofa—flowers and all."

She felt her cheeks burn.

"Why are you here, Katelyn? Since it's apparently—unfortunately—not for an encore performance."

"I'm here because...I wanted to apologize...for last night."

"Turning down my proposal?"

"Walking away in the middle of our conversation," she clarified. "Apparently pregnancy hormones can cause a woman to become...emotional...and I didn't want to have a breakdown in front of you."

"I can handle a few tears," he assured her. "And I *want* to be there for you—in any way that I can."

"That's the other reason I'm here. I got a call from my doctor's office this morning. Everything's fine," she hastened to assure him. "They were just calling to schedule my first ultrasound."

"Isn't it too soon for an ultrasound? Don't they usually happen between eighteen and twenty weeks?"

"Somebody's been reading up on pregnancy," she mused. "But this is an early scan, to calculate the baby's due date."

"You can't just count the number of weeks from the day the condom broke?"

She shook her head.

"So when are you having this ultrasound?"

"Two o'clock Tuesday at the Battle Mountain Medical Clinic."

"Can I go with you?"

"You can meet me there," she suggested.

"Are you honestly worried that someone might see us together in Battle Mountain?"

"No," she said. "I was actually more concerned that if there was a law enforcement emergency, you might have to take off and leave me stranded."

"I can make it work," he told her.

"Okay, then," she relented. "You can pick me up at one."

Reid was impressed by the modern facility and efficient staff at the Battle Mountain clinic, where they were taken to an exam room only a few minutes after checking in. Katelyn hopped up on the table as instructed, while he was directed to stand on the other side of the table, out of the way but able to see everything that was happening.

A few minutes later, the technician came in and introduced herself to the expectant parents, then briefly outlined the procedure for a transabdominal ultrasound and explained how the measurements she obtained would help accurately pinpoint the baby's estimated date of delivery.

Following her instructions, Katelyn folded back the hem of her top and pushed her yoga pants down to her hips to expose her abdomen. The technician keyed some information into the computer, then squirted warm gel onto the expectant mother's belly. She used what she'd told them was a transducer—a small plastic device that sent out and received sound waves (and, in Reid's opinion, looked a little bit like the upholstery attachment of his vacuum cleaner)—to spread the gel around.

He reached for Katelyn's hand, a silent gesture of support, and she offered a small smile in return.

Then his attention shifted to the monitor as the tech clicked the mouse and keyed in the data she was gathering. But Reid was focused on the grainy black-and-white image on the screen, searching for something that looked like a baby. And then he saw it—although it looked more like a blob than a tiny person. Though on closer inspection, he could see a head distinct from the body with stubby legs and little T-Rex arms. But what really struck him when the technician enlarged the image was that something in the center of the body blob seemed to be pulsing.

Katelyn was watching, too, her grip on his hand tightening. "What…is that…the baby's heart beating?"

"That's what it is," the technician confirmed.

Then she clicked some more keys, and suddenly the baby's heartbeat was displayed across the bottom of the screen, the *woop-woop-woop* surprisingly fast and loud in the small room.

Reid looked at Katelyn, who was trying to focus on the screen through eyes blurred with tears. He had a pretty good idea how she felt, because in the first moment he'd recognized that big-headed alien-looking blob as their child, he'd been filled with emotion. And watching and listening to that little heart beating, he was overwhelmed by the knowledge that he'd played even a minor part in the creation of this tiny person.

Later, as he walked out of the medical center beside Katelyn, she reached for his hand. "Thank you for being here with me today."

"Thank you for letting me be here," he said, truly and deeply touched by what he'd experienced—and grateful that she'd included him.

She smiled. "It was pretty amazing, wasn't it? Actually seeing our baby."

He nodded. "For the past few weeks, I've hardly been able to think about anything else. But still, the baby was something vague and distant. Until today. Looking at the image on the screen, hearing the beat of the heart, it suddenly all became real."

"Morning sickness made it real for me," she said lightly. "But I know what you mean. Even though I've experienced changes in my body, they were just abstract symptoms of pregnancy."

He fished his key fob out of his pocket and unlocked the doors of his truck, but he paused before walking Katelyn around to the passenger side. "I know you have all kinds of reasons for believing that marriage isn't necessary or even desirable, but I want our baby to have a real family. I don't want to miss out on the first tooth or first steps because it's not my turn or my day or my weekend. I want both of us to be there for all the milestones."

"I don't want to miss out on anything, either," she admitted. "And if the best way to be sure that doesn't happen is to get married, then let's do it."

"Really?" he asked, equal parts stunned and hopeful. "You mean it?"

She nodded. "I really mean it."

He opened the maps app on his phone. "If we leave now, we can be in Las Vegas in six hours and twenty-two minutes."

But Katelyn shook her head. "We're not getting married today and we're definitely not getting married in Vegas."

"I'm afraid that if we don't do it right now, you might change your mind," he admitted.

"I'm not going to change my mind," she promised.

"Let's make it official, anyway," he said, and pulled a familiar square box out of his pocket. At her questioning look, he shrugged. "What can I say? I'm an eternal optimist."

Then he dropped to his knee again, right there in the parking lot, and said, "Katelyn Gilmore, will you marry me?"

This time, she didn't back away or cut him off. Instead, she held out her hand. "Yes, Reid Davidson, I will marry you."

He rose to his feet and slid the ring on her finger. Then he kissed her, and Kate closed her eyes and let herself be swept away by the romance of the moment.

He kept his arm around her, holding her close for another minute. "Thank you for giving us a chance," he said.

"You might not feel so grateful in another six months, when you haven't had more than three consecutive hours of sleep because our baby's colicky and screaming," she warned.

"Whatever challenges we face, I know we'll get through them together," he assured her.

"The first challenge will be telling my dad."

He opened the passenger door and helped her climb in. "Do you want to do that today?"

"The sooner the better, so we can pick a date and start planning the wedding."

"This weekend works for me," he told her.

"While I appreciate your enthusiasm, if we're going

to get married, we're going to do this right, and not even
my family could pull everything together in four days."

"Okay, how much time do you need?"

"More like four weeks," she decided, crossing her fingers that she'd be able to find a wedding dress off-the-
rack and the minister would be free and Marcella could
squeeze in making a wedding cake and Naomi could do
her flowers and—

"So what changed your mind?"

His question was a welcome reprieve from the details
spinning through her head—until she realized that he expected an answer.

Because she definitely wasn't ready to tell him the
truth—that the reason she'd changed her mind was that
she'd fallen in love with him. Not only because she knew
he didn't feel the same way but because she suspected it
was a truth he wasn't ready to hear.

Since she'd told him about her pregnancy, he'd been
focused on doing what was best for their baby. He certainly hadn't said or done anything to hint that he wanted
any kind of emotional entanglements. In fact, he'd made
it clear he wasn't interested in falling in love.

But she'd seen the look on his face when he saw their
baby on the ultrasound monitor—and she recognized the
surprise and wonder and love, because they were the same
emotions that filled her heart. And if he could fall in love
with their unborn child, she had to hope and believe that
maybe, someday, he might fall in love with her, too.

Chapter Fourteen

Reid and Katelyn drove straight to the Circle G to share their news with her family. David Gilmore understandably had reservations about the quickness of their engagement—especially when he learned of their plan to marry before the end of the summer.

"Is there any particular reason for the rush?" Katelyn's father asked them.

"I thought you'd want to be a father-in-law before a grandfather," she responded to his question.

"Grandfather?" he echoed, clearly stunned. "You're... pregnant?"

She nodded. "The baby's due in February."

Her father's brow furrowed as he did the math. He looked at Reid, his scowl deepening. "You didn't waste any time making your move, did you?"

"I made the move," Katelyn interjected, attempting to take the heat.

Reid appreciated the effort, but he wasn't going to hide behind his fiancée. "I'd say we moved together," he countered.

She smiled at that. "Maybe we did."

"Well, I guess what matters now is that you're doing the right thing," David said. "Getting married and giving your baby a family."

Reid nodded. "Yes, sir. And it would mean a lot to both of us to have your blessing."

"Well, of course, you've got my blessing," his future father-in-law said. "And my checkbook for the wedding."

"That's a generous offer, sir, but—"

"No buts," David interjected. "I want Katelyn to have the wedding of her dreams—or as close as possible within your time constraints."

She hugged her father. "Thank you."

David smiled at his daughter, his eyes shiny. "Now you better give your grandmother a call—she'll want to know what's going on and help you with the planning."

So Katelyn did, and a short while later her grandparents and siblings showed up to join in the celebration.

It didn't take long after that for the news to make its way through town, and everywhere they went, they were offered congratulations and best wishes. If people were surprised by the August 30 date they'd set for the wedding, they didn't show it to the happy couple.

And they *were* happy.

Reid's only cause for complaint was that he barely saw his bride-to-be in the weeks leading up to the big day. He knew she was busy taking care of all the details that went into a wedding: drafting the guest list and sending out evites, finding a dress, then fittings for the dress, meetings with the baker and the florist, then tracking replies to the invitations and working on a seating plan for the reception—which was being held at the Circle G under the cover of huge tents rented for the occasion.

Reid's responsibilities were limited. He gave his notice to Bev and Norm, since he'd be moving in with Katelyn after the wedding, packed up his meager belongings and went into Elko with Caleb and Liam to be fitted for their tuxes.

Which meant he had a lot of time to focus on his job, which he generally enjoyed. His least favorite part of being sheriff was playing politics. But if he wanted to remain in the position, and of course he did, then he'd need to run for reelection when Jed Traynor's current term expired. And that meant gritting his teeth and making nice with the voters, even when those voters drove him crazy with incessant nuisance calls.

Two days before his wedding, the call was from Ruth Fielding.

"I'll send Deputy Neal to talk to Mr. Petrovsky about his cat digging up your flowers," Reid promised.

"Talking isn't going to grow me new flowers," Ruth protested.

He made a note on the pad on his desk. "Perhaps some form of restitution can be arranged."

"We need a leash law for cats," she said. "I have to put my Harvey on a leash when I take him out. It's not fair that obnoxious feline—"

A movement at the door caught his eye and he looked up, a ready smile on his face for his fiancée, who was meeting him for lunch.

The smile froze on his lips when he saw that it wasn't his soon-to-be wife standing in his doorway, but his ex.

"—gets to run free around the neighborhood and create havoc—"

"You're right, Mrs. Fielding," he interrupted. "And I'll send Deputy Neal over right after lunch."

Then he disconnected the call to focus on his unexpected visitor.

"Trish—what are you doing here?"

She shook her head, a gesture of undisguised exasperation. "Reid, you're getting married in two days—where else would I be?"

"Home in Echo Ridge with your husband and child?" he suggested.

"They came with me," she said. "Because Jonah understands why I needed to be here."

"I'm glad someone does," he said, but he pushed away from the desk and embraced her. "You look good."

"It's the boobs." She smiled proudly as she glanced down at her chest. "Breastfeeding has added a full cup size."

He winced. "Please spare me the details."

"This town needs a decent hotel," Trish said. "We're staying in Battle Mountain because Dusty Boots Motel sounds like a place that rents rooms by the hour and I wasn't sure that you'd have space for us to squeeze in at your place."

His head was spinning. He was grateful that she hadn't made any assumptions about staying with him—which would have been more than a squeeze—but he had to ask, "But why are you here?"

"Did you really think you could send me a text message telling me that you were getting married and not expect some follow-up conversation?"

"I thought you might call," he acknowledged.

"I wanted to read the expression on your face when you explained to me how this happened."

"I met a girl, I asked her to marry me, she said yes."

Trish shook her head. "That's a very concise summary—too concise."

And then he heard a familiar voice in the outer office as Katelyn and Judy exchanged pleasantries.

Reid had no idea how the next few minutes would play out, but he didn't have a good feeling.

"I really wish you'd called before you got on a plane," he muttered.

"If I'd called, you would've told me not to come," Trish acknowledged.

"You're right," he confirmed.

"Which is why I didn't call," she said logically.

"Did it ever occur to you that showing up—unannounced and uninvited—might not go over well with your ex-husband's bride-to-be?"

"No," she admitted. "Why would she care? She's the woman you're head over heels for and I'm already married to someone else."

"I don't know that she will care, but—" he gave up trying to explain as his fiancée walked into his office.

"Sorry, I'm late, I got caught—oh," Katelyn's explanation cut off abruptly when she realized Reid wasn't alone. "I'm sorry. I didn't mean to interrupt."

"You're not interrupting," he assured her.

She looked from him to the other woman in his office and back again.

"Katelyn, this is my ex-wife, Trish."

Whatever she was thinking or feeling, Katelyn kept it hidden behind a neutral expression. But she took a step toward Trish and held out a hand. "It's nice to meet you."

"And you," Trish said, shaking the proffered hand. "I'm really looking forward to getting to know you."

"That's going to have to wait." Katelyn offered a polite if cool smile. "I've got to run to a meeting with a client."

"But we're supposed to have lunch," Reid reminded her.

"I got the call just as I was heading over here—that's why I was late," she said.

And though it was a plausible explanation, he didn't believe it was a complete one.

"We can go after your meeting then," he offered.

Katelyn shook her head. "I really don't know how long I'll be. It's probably better if you two go ahead."

"I could go for lunch," Trish said as Katelyn disappeared out the door. "You pick the place, and I'll pick up the tab."

Reid decided to let her, because he instinctively knew that he'd be paying for this later.

When Kate checked her phone, there were half a dozen missed calls and an equal number of text messages from Reid. She replied to the last one, letting him know that her meeting had gone late but confirming that she was home now.

He immediately responded: I'll bring dinner.

Which dashed any hope of putting him off until the next day.

Ten minutes later, he knocked at the door. Though she'd given him a key because he'd be moving in after the wedding, he wasn't yet in the habit of letting himself in.

She put a smile on her face and opened the door.

Reid walked in carrying a large takeout bag from Diggers', and the scent of spicy buffalo sauce and fried grease teased her nostrils and made her stomach growl.

"I'm guessing you never got around to having lunch today," he said, proof that he'd heard the rumble.

"I guess I didn't," she admitted, only realizing it now herself.

He carried the bag of food to the table.

"Why'd you run out of my office today?"

"I didn't run," she denied, opening the cutlery drawer. "I had a meeting."

He reached in the cupboard beside the sink for plates. "Since when is Emerson a client?"

"Since today," she told him.

Because she was a terrible liar, and because she hated the idea of lying to Reid, she'd made her friend give her a dollar as a retainer so she could legitimately claim solicitor-client privilege and not have to admit that seeing her soon-to-be husband cozied up in his office with his ex-wife had sent her to her best friend's house in tears.

"How'd you know I was with Emerson?"

"Because after I had lunch with Trish—and thanks for setting that up, by the way—"

She bristled at the irritation in his voice as she plucked napkins from the holder on the counter. "No need to thank me," she said. "You're the one who invited your ex-wife to our wedding."

"I didn't invite Trish to our wedding," he told her.

"Then why is she here?"

"Because she has no concept of boundaries."

She set the napkins and cutlery on the table, by the plates he'd already put down.

"I don't know what else to say," he admitted. "I know you're not happy that she's here, but I'm not sure why it bothers you so much."

"Because she's beautiful," Katelyn said glumly.

"Really? That's it?"

She glared at him. "No woman ever wants to meet an ex-girlfriend, lover or wife who looks like she walked off the cover of a magazine."

"It's funny that you'd say that."

"I'm glad you find this amusing."

"Because—" he caught her as she tried to move past him and pulled her into his arms "—Trish told me that no woman, even a happily married new mom, ever wants to discover that she was replaced by a younger and prettier model."

"She really said that?"

"You know I don't understand the workings of a woman's mind well enough to make this stuff up."

"Apparently I'm shallow enough to let that make me feel a little better," she acknowledged. "But I'm still not happy she's here."

"Do you want me to tell her not to come to the wedding?"

"If you do, then she'll know I was the one who didn't want her there, and she came all this way to—"

"Katelyn," he interrupted gently. "This is *our* wedding. What anyone else did or wants doesn't matter if it's not what you want."

She sighed, feeling irrational and unreasonable and generally miserable because nothing about the circumstances of their upcoming marriage were what she would have planned. But of course, none of that was Reid's fault. Or at least none of it aside from getting her pregnant. "What do *you* want?"

"I want you to be happy," he said, and sounded as if he meant it. "And if that means banning my ex-wife and her new husband from our wedding, I'll do it."

Of course, she didn't want her soon-to-be-husband's ex-wife there, but how was she supposed to admit that to him?

"Did you go to her second wedding?" she asked instead.

He nodded. "In the interest of full disclosure, I walked Trish down the aisle when she married Jonah."

"Whose idea was that?"

"Not mine," Reid assured her. "I thought the request

was a little odd but, in the absence of her dad, I didn't see how I could say no."

"What did her new husband think about that?"

"He had no objections. It didn't take him long to realize that me and Trish are more like brother and sister than ex-spouses—and of course he knew the truth about why we got married."

"Because her dad wanted you to take care of her."

He nodded.

"And now you're marrying me because I'm pregnant."

He didn't deny it. If the condom hadn't failed, they might have gone out on a few dates, and maybe those dates might have led to a relationship, but there was no way they'd be planning to marry only two months after he'd moved to Haven.

"Is there a point?" he asked.

"Maybe we shouldn't do this."

"Really? Two days before the wedding, you've suddenly got cold feet?"

"It's not sudden," she said. "You know I've had reservations about this from the beginning."

"But we both agreed that getting married is what's best for the baby."

She nodded. "You're right. But this is the second time you're getting married for the wrong reasons."

"Giving our baby a family isn't a wrong reason."

"You probably didn't think you were marrying Trish for the wrong reason, either, but look how that turned out."

"There are zero similarities between my relationship with Trish and my relationship with you," he told her.

"So why won't you tell me why you split up?"

"I really wish you'd let this go, Katelyn."

"I don't think I can."

He scrubbed his hands over his face. "Trish and I split up because she wanted a baby...and I didn't."

"Oh." Kate now wished she hadn't pushed so hard for an answer to her question.

He lifted his gaze to meet hers again. "Obviously, our situation is completely different."

"How can you say that when you just admitted you didn't want to be a father?" she wondered.

"Because it *is* different," he insisted. "Trish and I were talking about the *possibility* of having a child. The baby you're carrying—*our* baby—is *real*."

"Putting aside that nebulous distinction for now, why didn't you want a child?"

"Because I didn't want to screw up my child the way my parents screwed me up," he confided.

"And now those fears have miraculously disappeared?" she asked dubiously.

"Of course not," he said. "I'm still terrified that I'm going to do something—or a thousand things—wrong. But over the past few weeks, I've started to trust that we can figure it out together."

"I don't want to do this without you," she admitted.

"You don't have to," he promised. "I'm not going into this reluctantly or begrudgingly. I *want* to be your husband and our baby's father. I want to go to sleep beside you at night and wake up next to you in the morning. I want to argue with you about whose turn it is to get up with a screaming baby in the middle of the night. I want to share each and every one of our baby's milestones—the good, the bad and the cranky—with you."

"Even if the cranky part is mine?"

He smiled and touched his lips to hers. "Even if the cranky part is yours."

* * *

One of the difficulties of a midweek ceremony, Kate discovered, was trying to juggle her professional obligations with the final wedding preparations as the days and hours counted down. She was scheduled to meet her attendants—Sky and Emerson—at the spa Tuesday afternoon, but she spent the morning in the office, catching up on some paperwork.

Just before eleven o'clock, Beth poked her head into Kate's office. "Do you have time for a walk-in?"

"Who's the client?"

"A Mrs. Stilton. She didn't say what it was regarding, only that it was important she talk to you today."

"Okay," Kate agreed. She clicked the mouse to save the memorandum she'd been working on, then stood up to greet the client Beth escorted to her office.

The ready smile on her face froze when she recognized Mrs. Stilton as her fiancé's ex-wife.

"Reid didn't tell me your last name."

"I was counting on that to get me in the door," Trish admitted.

"Then you're not here for legal advice?" she guessed.

The other woman shook her head. "No, I wanted to talk to you, woman-to-woman, and this was the only way I could think to make it happen without Reid running interference."

"What did you want to talk about?"

"I wanted to know if you're uncomfortable with the idea of me being at your wedding," Trish said.

"I'm not sure how I feel," Kate admitted.

"I get why it might seem strange to you that we came all the way from Texas for the wedding. And, truthfully, my husband warned me that we might not be welcome."

"I was just…surprised…when I saw you in his office,"

Kate said. "And I did wonder why he didn't tell me you were coming."

"He claims he didn't know," Trish said, confirming what Reid had told Kate. "But he should have known that I'd be on a plane as soon as I heard, because I'm the only family he has.

"And yes, I know that we're not technically family anymore," she continued. "But the connection to my dad created a bond between us. When Reid asked me to marry him, I was under no illusions about his feelings for me. My dad was dying and Reid married me so he wouldn't worry about me being alone.

"Not that I'm not capable of taking care of myself," Trish hastened to clarify. "But my dad was overprotective, and the local sheriff, to boot."

"Believe me, I understand about overprotective parents," Kate said, with a slightly exasperated smile.

"Good, because Reid will probably be even worse when he's a father."

"He told you…about the baby?"

"He didn't need to tell me," the other woman said. "I've known him too long to believe that he'd jump into another marriage without good reason, and in his mind, there's no better reason than to give a baby a family."

Kate nodded, acknowledging the fact.

"And since we're sharing secrets, I'll admit that I had mixed feelings about your pregnancy at first," Trish confided.

"Reid told me why you split up," Kate said.

"So you know I wanted to have a baby and he…had some reservations?"

"He said that he didn't ever want to be a father," Kate clarified.

"He's nothing if not honest," Trish mused. "Sometimes painfully so."

"And yet he's the one who pushed for this wedding."

"Because he's also honorable and loyal—and he wouldn't ever want his child to grow up feeling unwanted."

"Like he did," she realized.

Trish nodded. "When Reid confirmed your pregnancy, I had a moment—it was brief, but still a moment," she confessed, "when I wondered why, if he had to get someone pregnant, it couldn't have been me."

Kate decided that was a reasonable reaction for a woman whose husband hadn't wanted to give her a child.

"But after I had some time to think about it more rationally," the other woman continued, "I realized that Reid and I having a baby together would've been a mistake.

"Maybe we would've stayed together and made our marriage work—he's too loyal and stubborn to believe otherwise—but then I would never have met and fallen in love with Jonah, who really is the love of my life. And Reid would never have met you."

Kate appreciated that Trish didn't pretend to believe her ex-husband had deep feelings for his bride-to-be, but the honesty did sting a little.

"I would like to be there when you exchange your vows," the other woman continued. "But Jonah and I won't show up if our presence is going to make you uncomfortable in any way."

"I'd like you both to be there," Kate decided. "And Henry, too. Reid's made a lot of friends in the short time he's been in Haven, but most of those people knew me— or at least my family—first, so it'll be nice for him to have someone there primarily for him."

"Thank you," Trish said.

"And thank you," Kate said. "For coming here to talk to me, but especially for being here for Reid."

Trish smiled. "I'll see you at the church, soon-to-be Mrs. Reid Davidson."

Chapter Fifteen

Kate and Reid had opted for an evening midweek ceremony to coordinate with the schedule of the minister who'd married Kate's parents and baptized Kate and each of her siblings. Unable to choose between her sister and best friend as her maid or matron of honor, she'd decided to have both. Because Reid was new in town and didn't have any close friends to serve as groomsmen, he'd asked Caleb and Liam to stand up for him.

The bride spent the morning of her wedding day in court. After that, she had lunch with Skylar and Emerson before they all headed over to the Circle G together to get ready for the ceremony.

Her grandmother was waiting at the house when they arrived—to ensure everyone stayed on schedule, she claimed.

"You look just like a fairy-tale princess," Emerson said, when she'd finished tying the corset back of the bride's dress.

Kate turned to look at her reflection in the mirror, pleased with the overall effect. Her dress was an A-line strapless gown with chapel-length train. The side-drape helped disguise the subtle swell of her belly and the pearl-and-crystal beading on the bodice did make her feel a little bit like a princess.

But before she got too caught up in the fantasy, she reminded herself that Reid wasn't her prince—he was just a guy who wanted to do the right thing. And she knew he'd do everything in his power to make their marriage work—for the sake of their baby. She also hoped that, over time, he'd start to care for her as she cared for him.

She couldn't pinpoint an exact moment when her feelings for him had started to grow and change. There was no denying that the initial attraction had been purely physical, and that attraction was still there. His smile never failed to make her knees weak, the most casual of his touches made her heart pound, and those shoulders…just thinking about those shoulders made her sigh.

But he was also smart and kind and funny. Sure, he could be a little rigid at times and more than a little stubborn, but the more time she'd spent with him, the more she'd suspected that he was a man she could fall in love with. Until the day she'd cut off his marriage proposal, because she'd realized that she'd already fallen.

And in just a few more hours now, she was going to be his wife.

After Emerson's assessment, Grams looked the bride up and down, then shook her head. "Something's missing."

"Flowers," Sky said. "Dad went into town to pick them up."

Grams shook her head again. "Earrings."

Kate instinctively reached a hand to her ear, where she'd fastened the simple diamond studs that had been a gift from her father for her eighteenth birthday. "I'm wearing earrings."

"With your hair up, you should have something a little... more," Grams said, as she took a small fabric pouch out of her pocket. "I know you're wearing Emerson's veil as your something borrowed, but these could be your something old—if you want them."

"Grams, they're gorgeous," Kate said, admiring the delicate diamond-and-pearl drops in her grandmother's hand.

"They were a gift to me from your grandfather on our wedding day, fifty-eight years ago, so they're definitely old," she said. "But they were also your mom's something borrowed when she married your dad."

"Oh." She swallowed hard and blinked back the tears that threatened as she unfastened her diamond studs.

Kate had been thinking of her mom throughout the day, missing her as she always did when she celebrated a milestone event. But as she fastened the pretty pearl-and-diamond drops to her ears, the knowledge that her mother had worn the very same earrings on her wedding day made her feel a little less lonely for her.

"Now you're perfect," Grams declared.

"You're going to knock his socks off," Emerson said approvingly.

"Hopefully a lot more than his socks."

"Grams!" Skylar protested.

Her grandmother just grinned as a knock sounded on the door.

"Flower delivery," her father announced.

"Just on time." Grams took the box from him and distributed the bouquets of hand-tied calla lilies before ushering Skylar and Emerson out of the room so Kate could have a few minutes alone with her father before they headed to the church.

"Oh, Katie." It was all he said, but there was a wealth of emotion in those two words.

"Don't you dare make me cry," she warned her father.

He smiled, though his own eyes were suspiciously bright. "You're so beautiful." Then he touched a finger to one of the dangling earrings. "Your mother wore those the day we got married."

She nodded. "They were her something borrowed from Grams—and now they're my something old."

"Your mom would be so proud of you today. Always," he amended. "But especially today."

"I miss her," she said softly. "Always, but especially today."

"It took me a long time to accept that she was gone, and though the grief has lessened over the years, I will never stop loving her."

Kate pulled a tissue from the box on the dressing table and dabbed at her eyes.

"My greatest wish for you and Reid is to be as happy as we were together."

She kissed his cheek. "Thank you."

"Now, we better be on our way to the church if you don't want to keep your groom waiting. But if you do…" He let the sentence trail off, an unspoken question.

She shook her head. "I'm ready to start the rest of my life with the man I love."

Her response seemed to satisfy her father, who nodded brusquely. "Well then, let's go."

Half an hour before the ceremony was scheduled to begin, Caleb and Liam left the groom to perform their duties ushering guests to their seats.

A short while later, when Reid heard the knock on the door of the anteroom where he was getting ready, he assumed it was one of Katelyn's brothers. But when he said, "Come in," it was Trish who poked her head around the door.

"Have you worn out the carpet yet?" she teased.

"I'm not pacing—I'm trying to pin this flower thing on my jacket," he told her.

"It's a boutonniere," she said. "And the flower is a calla lily."

"Can you help me?"

"Sure," she said, taking the flower from his hand and sizing him up. "You clean up pretty good, Sheriff."

"I'm more comfortable wearing my badge than a suit," he confided.

"The suit looks good on you. Or maybe it's the impending nuptials that look good on you." She positioned the flower on his lapel, slid the pin into the stem—and swore when she pushed too far and stabbed herself.

"You're nervous," he realized.

"A little," she admitted.

"Why are *you* nervous?"

"Because I really want this to work for you, Reid."

He lifted a brow. "And you think I'm going to screw it up?"

"I think you sometimes hold too much back," she told him.

"I think you sometimes share too much," he countered drily.

"I know I do," she acknowledged. "But we're not talking about me—we're talking about you."

"You're nagging me." He handed a corsage box to her when she finished with his boutonniere. "And on my wedding day, too."

"What's this?"

"Katelyn asked me to give it to you."

She looked at the flower inside the box, then at him. "Why?"

He shrugged. "I don't remember exactly what she said—something about traditions and honoring family members who aren't in the wedding party."

"Oh." Trish's eyes filled with tears. "Damn, I really do like that girl."

"I like her, too," he said.

"She's probably too good for you," his ex-wife warned.

"Probably," he agreed easily.

"And yet, I think she could be exactly what you need—if you let her in."

"I'm marrying her, Trish. I'm not sure how much more 'in' there is."

She sighed. "Well, hopefully you'll figure it out."

And with those last cryptic words, she kissed his cheek and walked out of the anteroom.

A short while later, Caleb and Liam returned, then the minister summoned them all to take their positions at the front of the church. The pews were filled with invited guests and other well-wishers from the community, and the pianist was playing something Reid vaguely recognized but couldn't have named.

Emerson came down the aisle first, wearing a strapless lavender dress and carrying a bouquet of long-stemmed flowers that matched the one he was wearing. She winked at him as she took her place on the opposite side of the aisle. Sky followed a few steps behind Emerson, wearing the same style of dress in a slightly darker shade of purple and carrying a similar bouquet. She gave him a quick thumbs-up as she took her place beside Emerson.

The music changed—and Reid's heart started to pound harder and faster against his ribs. Then, finally, the bride was there, at the back of the church, and Reid felt as if all the air had been sucked out of his lungs.

He vaguely registered the presence of her father beside her, but his focus was on Katelyn—absolutely, undeniably the most beautiful bride he'd ever seen.

He didn't know enough about fashion to know the fabric or style of her dress, he only knew that the sparkly bodice hugged her breasts and the skirt trailed behind her as she made her way down the aisle toward him. Her hair was pinned up in one of those fancy knots that always made him want to unpin it, but today there were loose strands that framed and softened her face. In her left hand, she held a bouquet of lilies. Her right was tucked into the crook of her father's arm.

When they reached the altar, David lifted the delicate veil away from her face and leaned in to kiss her cheek, whispering something in her ear that made her lips curve in a tremulous smile. Then the bride's father offered his hand to the groom before stepping back and taking his seat in the front pew.

"We are gathered together today to celebrate the relationship of Katelyn Theresa Gilmore and Reid Thomas Davidson by joining them in marriage…"

Reid held Katelyn's hand and her gaze throughout the ceremony.

The vows he made to her weren't new, but he wanted her to know that they were true. Maybe he didn't love her, but he would honor and cherish her for the rest of their days together.

When they'd both recited the requisite lines and exchanged rings, the minister said, "I now pronounce you husband and wife." Then he nodded to Reid before addressing his next words to Katelyn. "You may kiss your groom."

Reid lifted his brows in response to the not-quite-traditional instruction; Katelyn only smiled as she pulled his mouth down to hers.

"I can't believe you managed to put together this wedding in four weeks," Reid said to his bride as they finished distributing pieces of wedding cake to their guests.

"There are some benefits to being a Gilmore in Haven."

"Such as rewriting the minister's lines?"

"It was a minor amendment, and Pastor Richards likes to go off script sometimes, just to make sure the congregation is paying attention."

"But kissing the bride is the part a groom looks forward to," he said. "So I kind of feel like I was ripped off."

"Do you really need to be told when you can kiss your bride?"

"No," he said, drawing her closer to him. "One of the benefits of putting a ring on your finger is that I get to kiss you whenever I want."

"You think so, do you?"

"Yes, I do," he confirmed.

And he kissed her then to prove it.

"I think I'm going to like being married to you," Katelyn said when he finally ended the kiss.

"I hope so, because you're going to be stuck with me for a very long time." He gestured to the dance floor where her grandparents were dancing, cheek to cheek. "That's going to be us in fifty years."

"They've been married fifty-eight years," she told him.

"They're an inspiration, that's for sure."

"My parents were the same," Katelyn said. "After my mom died, there were days I wasn't sure my dad would survive the grief of losing her."

"It couldn't have been easy on any of you."

"It wasn't," she confirmed. "But they were so…connected.

Like two halves of a whole, each one incomplete without the other. They met at The Silver State Stampede and immediately fell in love, and there was never any question in either of their minds or hearts that it was forever."

He knew that she'd wanted the same thing—love at first sight and happily-ever-after. And though he was sorry she'd had to compromise her ideals, he intended to do everything in his power to ensure she wouldn't ever regret it.

"Even if it wasn't love at first sight between us, there was definite lust at first sight," he said, attempting to lighten the mood.

She tipped her head back, a smile tugging at the corners of her mouth. "At first sight?"

"Oh, yeah," he confirmed. "The minute you walked into that conference room, a hint of black silk peeking above the button of that blue jacket, the matching skirt displaying mouthwatering long legs that went all the way down to sexy black shoes with heels that put your mouth almost level with mine."

"That's some detailed recollection," she noted.

"You caught my attention," he assured her. "And then you invited me back to your room."

"There were a couple of steps in between," she noted. "But the minute I saw you, I wanted you, too. In fact, the prospect of sharing a bed with you weighed heavily in the yes column when I was considering your proposal."

He smiled. "And you said 'click' wasn't a factor."

"I've reconsidered my position on the matter. In fact, I'm hopeful that later we'll be sharing a naked and horizontal position."

He lifted a brow. "You've got ambitious plans for tonight."

"It *is* our wedding night," she reminded him. "And I

don't think anyone at our respective offices would be surprised if we were a little late for work tomorrow."

"About that," Reid said, withdrawing an envelope from his jacket pocket.

"What's this?"

"Open it and see," he suggested.

She lifted the flap to peek inside. "A travel itinerary?"

"I know we said we shouldn't take any time away right now," her new husband acknowledged, "but Connor promised that he could handle anything that came up in the Sheriff's Office through the weekend and Beth managed to clear your schedule for a few days so that we can have a honeymoon, albeit an abbreviated one."

She pulled the pages out to scan them more closely. "The flight is at 5:50 in the morning?"

"Yeah, so we won't be sleeping in tomorrow. In fact, we're probably going to want to skip out of the party early tonight."

"Or now," she said, sounding excited and just a little bit panicked. "We need to go home and pack."

"I've already packed my bag, your sister packed one for you and our boarding passes are printed."

"You've thought of everything."

"I know this isn't exactly the wedding day of your dreams," he told her. "But I wanted to do it right, as much as possible under the circumstances, and not having a honeymoon just didn't seem right."

"Why San Francisco?"

"It's relatively simple to get there from here, it's close enough that we won't lose a lot of time traveling, and it's one of your favorite cities."

"How did you know that?"

"I asked Emerson for some help with the planning," he admitted. "And bribed her not to breathe a word about it to you—and since your reaction assures me that she didn't, I'm going to be carting a ton of Ghirardelli chocolate back from San Francisco."

"Make that two tons," she said.

"You can cart your own chocolate," he teased.

"It's not for me," she said. "It's for the baby."

"You're going to milk that for the next five-and-a-half months, aren't you?"

"As much as possible," she promised.

He smiled as he dipped his head and touched his lips to hers. "Let's go say goodbye to our guests and get this honeymoon started."

As eager as Kate had been to get back to her apartment—*their* apartment—and get naked with her new husband, now that they were alone together, she suddenly felt shy.

Reid shrugged out of his jacket and tossed it over the reading chair in the corner of her—*their*—bedroom.

"Are you tired?" he asked, somehow sensing her hesitation.

"Tired but not sleepy," she said. It had been a long day, and her limbs were weary but her blood was humming with nerves and anticipation.

"The sugar from that cake should keep you revved for a while—" he grinned as he unfastened his tie "—I hope."

She watched as his nimble fingers made quick work of the buttons that ran down the front of his shirt. Her mouth went dry when the fabric parted, revealing a strip of beautiful, bronzed skin.

"Do you need a hand with your dress?" he asked.

"Probably," she admitted. "Emerson tied up the corset, so I'm not sure how to get out of it."

"I think getting my wife out of her clothes is going to be one of my favorite husbandly duties," he said.

"You might not think so in a few months." She turned her back to him, so he could see how the dress was done up.

"I will always think so," he promised, starting to work on the corset.

When the lace had been loosened and the bodice began to drop, she caught and held it in place.

He didn't say anything about her impeding his efforts but only dropped his head to press a kiss to her bare shoulder. The brush of his lips on her skin raised goosebumps on her flesh.

Then he kissed her again, midway between her shoulder and her neck. And again, at the base of her throat.

She shivered.

"Your skin is so soft…so sweet."

Her eyes closed as his mouth moved up her throat, skimmed over her jaw.

"I want to taste you—" he teased her lips "—all over."

Heat pulsed in her veins, melting her resistance.

She let go of the bodice and wriggled out of the dress.

He stroked his hands down her sides, his thumbs gently caressing the slight swell between her hipbones.

"There's our little bean," he said, his tone soft, almost reverent.

"Actually, our baby is the size of a lemon now."

He shook his head. "Little bean sounds better than little lemon."

"Is our baby still going to be 'little bean' when he or she is the size of a honeydew melon?"

He eased her back onto the bed. "Are you growing a baby in there or making a fruit salad?"

"A baby," she assured him.

"*Our* baby," he clarified, then pressed his lips to the curve of her belly.

"Some men are…turned off by the changes in a woman's body during pregnancy," she said cautiously.

"Some men are idiots."

His blunt response made her smile, but still, she wasn't convinced he knew what he was in for.

"This is still the early stages," she warned. "When our baby is the size—"

He touched his fingers to her lips. "I know your body is going to change as our baby grows inside you, but getting naked with you is always going to be a huge turn-on for me."

"Really?" she said dubiously.

"Really," he confirmed. "You are beautiful and amazing and the sexiest woman I've ever known, and it's going to give me infinite pleasure to prove it to you throughout the next five-and-a-half months and beyond. Starting—" his hands moved to her breasts, already a little fuller and a lot more sensitive, his thumbs tracing around the areola "—now."

That night, all through the night, Kate learned that her husband was a man of his word.

Chapter Sixteen

Kate had always loved California—Sacramento and San Diego and every stop in between—but San Francisco was one of her all-time favorite cities. From the Golden Gate Bridge and the sparkling waters of the Bay to Lombard Street and the cable cars, Chinatown and Fisherman's Wharf, there was so much to see and do that she never got bored. And because Reid had never been to the city, she was able to see it again for the first time through his eyes.

Of course, the sheriff wanted to go to Alcatraz, and his wife did not. She told him, without regret, that there wouldn't be any last-minute tickets available during tourist season, because it was usually true. But the hotel concierge worked some magic and Reid presented her with two tickets for the ferry to the infamous island prison— cleverly hidden in a basket of Ghirardelli chocolate. It was a blatant bribe, but one she couldn't refuse, so they went to the island, toured the prison and the grounds, the former being much creepier and the latter much prettier than she'd anticipated.

Another day, they walked to Pier 39 to see the sea lions sunning on the docks and enjoy the talents of street performers. Later, they browsed the shops at Fisherman's Wharf, ate fresh shrimp out of plastic cups from a local food truck and sourdough rolls from the Boudin Bakery. They rented bicycles and cycled across the bridge, walked hand in hand through Golden Gate Park and took a cable car to Union Square to browse the upscale shops.

And when they finally went back to their hotel room, they made love, every night.

The morning sickness that had plagued her daily for several weeks had passed long ago, though it continued to make an occasional appearance—including their last morning in San Francisco.

Reid set their packed cases beside the door and did a quick check around the room to ensure they hadn't forgotten anything.

"Looks like we're good to go," he said.

Kate nodded hesitantly as her stomach decided it was unhappy with the brioche French toast and fresh fruit cup that had tasted so good only half an hour earlier.

"Katelyn?" he prompted.

"I'm sorry, but—" That was all she managed before she raced to the bathroom and slammed the door.

Reid knew she'd suffered from morning sickness earlier in her pregnancy, but she'd told him—with her fingers crossed—that the nausea had finally subsided. Listening to her retch through the door, he thought that her crossed fingers might have been a little premature.

"Katelyn?" He jiggled the handle of the door, frowning when it refused to turn. She'd been in a hurry to reach the toilet but she'd still managed to lock him out.

"Just give me a minute."

He heard the toilet flush, then the water turn on.

He rummaged through the suitcase for her toiletry bag, pulled out her toothbrush and toothpaste and had them waiting when she unlocked and opened the door again.

"Thanks," she said, not looking at him as she retreated with the items into the bathroom again.

They'd planned to take the BART to the airport, but Reid called the front desk and asked for a cab instead, which bought them a few extra minutes and gave his wife a little more privacy to feel miserable. He also took the plastic liner for the ice bucket and tucked it into his pocket, just in case.

When she came out of the bathroom, she looked tired and pale—not at all like a woman who'd enjoyed her brief holiday. She tucked her toothbrush and paste away again and zipped up the suitcase.

"Sorry for the delay," she said.

"Why are you apologizing?"

"Because I've put us behind schedule and if we miss the train, we'll be late checking in for our flight and—"

"There's a cab waiting for us downstairs," he said.

"To take us to the train station?"

"To take us to the airport."

"That's going to cost a fortune."

"Only a small one," he said. "And worth it, because we won't feel rushed and you'll be able to close your eyes and relax for a little while."

"You're taking care of me, aren't you?"

"I'm trying to," he admitted. "But you don't make it easy."

She didn't respond to that.

"One of the reasons we got married was so that we

could raise our child together. Until the baby's born, we both need to take care of you."

"I'll never object to you taking care of our vomiting child," she promised. "But I don't want anyone watching me throw up. It's humiliating enough to know that you could hear me yakking my breakfast into the toilet."

"In sickness and in health," he reminded her.

"I'm not sick, I'm pregnant, and I really thought the morning sickness had passed. I was throwing up almost every day for a few weeks, then it was just once every two or three days, and for the past couple of weeks, it's only been once a week. The last time was last Sunday, so I probably should have been prepared for this today."

"Then it wasn't because we overdid it these past few days?"

She shook her head. "No. I'm sure the nausea isn't linked to anything we did or ate, and I sincerely hope the last half hour isn't what you remember when you think about our honeymoon in San Francisco."

"It won't be," he promised. "I loved being here with you and seeing the sights, but my favorite memories took place in this room—most of them in that king-size bed."

"Maybe we should get a bigger bed—if you think one would fit in the apartment," she suggested.

"I don't mind a queen," he said. "It makes us snuggle closer."

"You'll be closer than you want when my huge belly's taking up all the space between us. I already feel like this baby's getting bigger and bigger every day."

He laid his hands on the slight curve of her belly. "Co-incidentally, you get more and more beautiful every day."

"We'll see if you still think so in five months."

"I'll still think so in five months," he promised. "And in five years and in fifty years."

And although he said the words to reassure her, he realized that he meant them.

Yeah, he'd proposed to Katelyn because she was pregnant, and he'd campaigned for her to say yes because he wanted to be more than a part-time father to their child. But sometime over the past few weeks, his motivation had stopped being all about the baby. Over the past few weeks, he'd realized that his life was fuller, richer and happier with Katelyn—so much so that he didn't want to imagine a future without her in it.

Kate was surprised by how easy it was to settle into the routines of married life once they got back to Haven.

Although the legal union between a criminal defense attorney and the local sheriff meant that there were some inherent conflicts between them, they adopted a strict rule about leaving work at the office to ensure that nothing interfered with either of them doing their respective jobs. She was fired by one long-time client who didn't believe she could continue to represent him fairly, but for the most part, her practice continued to grow—and so did the baby.

Aiden Hampton had finished his community service before returning to school for the fall term of his senior year, but he and his father continued to attend the grief counseling sessions that had been recommended by the Diversion Program coordinator. Near the end of September, the teen appeared in court for the final dismissal of the charges against him, after which he thanked the judge, then his attorney and even the sheriff who had locked him up—if only for a few hours.

"Do you have to rush back to the office?" Reid asked Kate when court had been dismissed.

She shook her head. "There's nothing that can't wait until tomorrow."

"Good, then you can take a ride with me."

She hitched her briefcase on her shoulder and walked beside him out of the courthouse. He guided her to his personal truck rather than the official vehicle of the Sheriff's Office and opened the passenger door for her. "Where are we going?"

"It's a surprise," he told her.

"What's a surprise?" she pressed.

He just shook his head. "No one warned me about your impatience before I married you."

"You think I'm impatient? Just wait until there's a child strapped into a car seat in the back asking, 'Are we there yet?' every two minutes," she said.

"I can wait," he said, flicking on his indicator before turning into a distinctly residential area. "Because I'm not impatient."

"Are we there yet?" she asked.

He turned again, onto a dead-end street, then pulled up alongside the curb in front of a two-story brick house with a For Sale sign in the front yard.

"Yes," he said. "We're there."

Kate felt a flutter of excitement in her belly as she looked at the house. She was familiar with the neighborhood, of course. There were newer and fancier homes being built on the south side of town, but this area was established, with bigger lots, plenty of mature trees and within walking distance of both the elementary and secondary schools.

"I know the apartment is really convenient to your office and the courthouse," he said to her. "But it's kind of small—plus it was yours before it was ours, so I thought maybe we could choose another place together. Somewhere with room to grow."

"Hey, I haven't put on that much weight," she protested.

He chuckled softly. "I meant to grow our family. Don't you think little bean should have a brother or sister someday?"

She felt the telltale sting of tears behind her eyes. "You want to have another baby with me?"

"Yeah," he said. "I didn't have any siblings growing up, but watching you with yours, I've learned to appreciate the bond you share, and I want that for our kids."

"Brothers and sisters are great," she agreed. "When they're not a total pain in the a—"

He touched a finger to her lips. "Didn't we agree not to use bad language around the baby?"

"Do you really think our baby is hearing anything yet?"

"The books say that babies start to hear sound at eighteen weeks."

"Even if he—or she—can hear what I'm saying, I doubt he—or she—is comprehending," she said drily.

"I'd rather not take any chances that his—or her—first word might be an inappropriate one."

She linked her arms behind his head. "You're going to be a great dad."

"I'm going to do my best," he promised.

"So…how many kids were you thinking you'd like to have?"

"At least two," he said.

"You might change your mind after the first one's born," she warned. "When you've gone a month with no more than two consecutive hours of sleep and you've changed so many diapers you've lost count."

"Trish called today, didn't she?"

Kate nodded.

"You really need to start screening your calls," he advised.

"I like talking to her," she said. "Usually."

He turned her back toward the house. "What do you think? Do you want to look inside?"

"Don't we have to wait for the real estate agent?"

He shook his head. "I've got the code for the lockbox."

"I guess, since you're the sheriff, she figured you were trustworthy?"

"Good guess," he said, leading her to the front door.

"It needs some work," he warned as he turned the key in the lock. "But mostly cosmetic—fresh paint, maybe new carpet or hardwood, updated appliances—and we could take care of that before we moved in."

As he showed her around the empty house—the owner having already moved to Arizona for a job promotion—she had to agree with his assessment. The decor was a little outdated, but she liked the layout—and she loved the spaciousness of the kitchen and the fireplace in the living room and the master bedroom suite.

"What do you think?" he asked, ending the tour at the backyard, slightly overgrown with grass and weeds.

"It might need more work than you realize, once you scrape off wallpaper and pull up carpets," she warned. "Are you sure you're ready to tackle all of that?"

"I want to tackle all of that," he told her. "I want our kids to have a house with a backyard, the lawn scattered with toys, maybe a swing set or one of those climbing things.

"And a dog," he added impulsively. "We should definitely get a dog."

"Let's see how we manage with a baby first," she suggested.

"But what about the house?" he prompted.

And his expression was so hopeful and his enthusiasm so infectious, she threw caution to the wind. "Let's do it."

Ten days later, they signed the final papers and got the keys. That night, they picked up pizza from Jo's and took it to 418 Sagebrush Lane, where they sat on the floor of the living room and ate their first meal in their new home. But they agreed it would be easier to do the work they wanted done before they moved in, and they'd set an ambitious target date of the end of October.

"Speaking of dates," Kate said, as she wiped pizza sauce off her fingers with a napkin. "It's our one-month anniversary tomorrow."

"Is that something we're supposed to celebrate?"

"Not formally," she said. "But I thought I might actually cook something for dinner—and you could pick up caramel fudge brownie cheesecake from Sweet Caroline's for dessert—and we could have a private celebration."

"I like the sound of that," he agreed.

So Kate talked to Emerson and got a recipe that her friend promised was relatively foolproof. After work, she stopped by The Trading Post to get everything she needed to prepare the meal and then meticulously followed her friend's step-by-step instructions.

Half an hour later, when everything was finally ready, she got a text message from Reid.

Sorry. Got a call. Won't make dinner.

She immediately replied:

Ok. Be safe.

Because as disappointed as she was that their plans for the evening had been ruined—or at least delayed—she understood that being married to the local sheriff inevitably meant there would be times when he didn't make it home for dinner. It was even possible that, his best intentions notwithstanding, he wouldn't be with her when she gave birth.

As if unsettled by that possibility, their baby kicked an angry protest. Well, Kate guessed it was a kick, but all she really felt was a flutter. She was exactly nineteen weeks into her pregnancy now, and Emerson had assured her that what she'd originally described as a feeling of little air bubbles popping inside her belly were actually her baby's first movements.

She couldn't wait until the baby was bigger and those movements were stronger, so Reid could feel them, too. But for now, she put a hand on the curve of her belly, instinctively soothing. "It's okay, little bean. We'll make sure you don't make your grand entrance into the world until Daddy's with us."

Then she went to the kitchen to turn off the stove. And though she wanted to wait to eat with Reid, however late that might be, she scooped some rice into a bowl and added a spoonful of the chicken cacciatore because the baby was hungry now—and desperately craving the cheesecake Reid was supposed to bring home for dessert.

She was putting her empty bowl and fork into the dishwasher when her phone buzzed again.

Anticipating an update from Reid, she immediately snatched it up, only to be disappointed when she saw the message from her answering service.

*Urgent. Client wants to meet asap. 775-555-6728

And Kate figured if Reid was working, she might as well be, too.

She was asleep on the sofa, the baseball game on the television now into extra innings, when Reid got home.

The rich scents of tomato and basil lingered in the air—the remnants of dinner she'd cooked for their one-month anniversary.

His wife.

His brilliant and beautiful, sweet and sexy, amazing and pregnant wife.

Damn, he'd lucked out when he'd signed up for that conference in Boulder City. At the time, he'd considered himself lucky just to get the invitation back to her room. He certainly hadn't been thinking that there might be a wedding and a baby in his future. Truthfully, he probably would have run far and fast if anyone had told him that's where he'd end up, so he was grateful he hadn't known, because now he had everything he never knew he wanted.

He picked up the remote and turned off the TV. Katelyn didn't stir. He lifted her into his arms; she sighed and turned her face into his shoulder. She was almost halfway through her pregnancy now and grumbling about the eight pounds she'd put on. Not that the slight swell of her belly was obvious, but apparently her wardrobe options were shrinking as her waistline expanded.

She was still the sexiest woman he'd ever known. And the changes her body was going through as a result of her pregnancy only made her more appealing.

He loved making love with her. And afterward, he loved to cuddle with his hand on her belly. He loved taking her first cup of coffee—decaf—to her in the morning and exchanging brief text messages with her through the hours they were apart. And he especially loved going home at the end of the day to find her waiting for him.

But did he love her?

He wasn't one to get hung up on words. In his opinion, there was far too much emphasis placed on that one particular phrase and too many people who threw it around frequently and easily.

Truthfully, he didn't know if he loved her, but he would do everything he could to make her happy—though she would claim that she was responsible for her own happiness; to take care of her—though she would insist she didn't need anyone to take care of her; and to protect her—though she would argue that she could protect herself.

Yeah, she could argue the opposite side of any issue, and that was just one more thing he loved about her.

He pulled back the covers and laid her gently on top of the mattress, then quickly stripped out of his clothes and slid into bed beside her.

And fell asleep with her in his arms.

Chapter Seventeen

Katelyn was still sleeping when Reid reluctantly slid out of bed in the morning.

He would have liked to stay with her, but he'd agreed to meet Connor at the Sheriff's Office at eight so they could head to the hospital in Battle Mountain. The young store clerk shot during the robbery at The Trading Post had been in critical condition when he was rushed into surgery the night before. Reid had been in the OR waiting room with the parents when the doctor informed them that the surgery had gone well. An early morning call to the hospital revealed that the victim's condition had been downgraded to "serious but stable" and the sheriff was eager to get his statement.

But first, he brewed Katelyn's decaf coffee, as he did every morning, and carried the mug to the bedroom along with a plate bearing a thick slice of Sweet Caroline's caramel fudge brownie cheesecake.

"Good morning, sleepyhead."

She blinked against the harsh glare of the light when he hit the switch with his elbow, but she pushed herself up in bed and brushed back the hair that was falling into her face.

Her eyes lit up when they zeroed in on his gifts. "You remembered the cheesecake."

He chuckled as he set the mug on the bedside table and relinquished the plate to her eager hands. "Of course, I remembered the cheesecake." Then he leaned over to brush her lips with his. "Happy belated one-month anniversary."

"I'm sorry I didn't stay awake until you got home last night." She picked up the fork and dug into the dessert.

"It's okay," he said. "I'm sorry I was late."

Of course, it wasn't the first time and they both knew it wouldn't be the last.

"You missed really hot anniversary sex," she said around a mouthful of cake.

"I'm even sorrier about that."

"Well, we could have really hot morning-after-the-one-month-anniversary sex…after I finish my cheesecake," she told him.

"Words cannot express how tempted I am," he assured her. "But I'm heading back out with Deputy Neal this morning to do some follow-up to our investigation." He kissed her again. "Rain check?"

"Absolutely," she promised.

Kate didn't complain about Reid having to work, even on a Sunday, because she had plenty to occupy her own time—not the least of which was putting together a defense for her newest client. And though it was just as easy to work on her laptop in the apartment, she generally preferred to work at work.

So after she'd finished her coffee and her cheesecake—and how great was it to be married to a man who indulged her pregnancy cravings?—she showered and dressed and headed to her office.

She only felt a little guilty about representing a suspect in the armed robbery that Reid was investigating. They'd both known before they got married that their careers would occasionally put them on opposite sides of the courtroom, and this was just another one of those times.

She unlocked the office door, punched in the security code to disarm the alarm system, then locked the door again behind her and headed into her office.

Beth always emptied the wastebaskets and put the garbage out before she left the office on Friday afternoons, so when Kate hit the light switch and realized there was something in the basket beside her desk, she was immediately uneasy. Moving closer, she saw what looked like a brown paper lunch bag—certainly nothing that would explain her growing trepidation. But the weight of the basket warned the bag wasn't empty, and she used the tip of a pen to open it so she could peek inside.

Then she put the wastebasket down again, picked up the phone and dialed the sheriff's number.

Reid and Connor were leaving Battle Mountain when Katelyn called, so they stopped at her office before heading to their own. She'd hinted about something that might be relevant to their investigation, and though Reid couldn't imagine what it might be, he knew she wouldn't have interrupted him if it wasn't important.

"I didn't touch it."

They were the first words she spoke when they walked into her office.

"Didn't touch what?" he asked cautiously.

"The gun."

Even without any context, the words gave his heart an unexpected jolt.

"What gun?"

It was Connor who asked the question, as Reid's heart was somewhere in the vicinity of his throat, rendering speech difficult.

She pointed to the trash receptacle beside her desk.

Reid shoved his heart back into his chest, looked into the basket and swore. "How did this get here?"

"I don't know." But her face was pale and there was a slight tremor in her voice. "Beth always takes out the garbage on Fridays, and I didn't have appointments yesterday, but I did, um, meet with a client here last night."

"Who?" Reid demanded.

"You know I can't—"

"Screw solicitor-client privilege," he practically snarled at her. "I want to know who was in *my wife's* office with a weapon."

If he'd been thinking clearly, he would've realized that was the absolute wrong thing to say to her. But he wasn't thinking clearly—he couldn't think past the fact that whoever had callously pulled the trigger to put a bullet in the twenty-three-year-old clerk at The Trading Post had then carried the weapon into Katelyn's office.

Didn't she know that desperate people did desperate things? That the client she was determined to protect could have used the gun on her? Didn't she realize Reid could have left one crime scene and come home to find his wife, not sleeping on the sofa with a baseball game on TV, but bleeding out on the floor in her office?

Just the thought made his whole body break out into a sweat.

But Katelyn only straightened her spine and narrowed

her gaze—a warrior ready for battle. "You do your job, *Sheriff*, and I'll do mine."

He knew her mention of his position was intended to draw a line between them, but it also served to remind him that he was there in his professional capacity—and with his deputy as a witness to their altercation, too.

He drew in a deep breath, battling against the fear and impotence that held him captive, and managed a brisk nod. "I assume you have no objection to us taking this—" he picked up the wastebasket again "—into evidence?"

"Of course not," she said, her tone cool and stiff.

"Why don't I head over to the office to get it logged in and sent to ballistics?" Connor suggested.

"You can both go," Katelyn said, but her gaze never shifted away from Reid's. "I have nothing else to say right now."

"Well, I do." Reid shoved the basket at his deputy.

Connor took his cue—and the evidence—and hurried out the door with only a sympathetic glance in his boss's direction.

"I'm sorry," Reid said, after he heard the exterior door open and close again.

Katelyn sighed and lowered herself into the chair behind her desk. "I know."

"That's it? You're not going to apologize?"

"What am I supposed to apologize for?"

It was a reasonable question, but he still wasn't close to feeling reasonable. "Maybe representing scumbag clients," he suggested. "And, by the way, you are *never* again to meet with any of them here alone at night."

"That's not your call to make," she said, her tone icy.

"If you won't think about your own safety, you should at least think about the baby you're carrying. *Our* baby."

"I would *never* do anything to put our baby at risk."

"Oh, well then, why would I worry?" he said, his voice dripping with sarcasm.

She folded her hands on top of the desk, focusing all her attention on the task of lacing her fingers together. When she spoke again, her voice was carefully neutral. "I think you should probably head back to the Sheriff's Office now."

He decided she was right. They were just going around in circles, he was frustrated by her refusal to acknowledge the recklessness of her behavior, and if he didn't walk away, one of them would say something they'd regret.

Kate blew out a weary breath when Reid finally walked out of her office. She stayed where she was after he'd gone, still shaking—with both fear and fury—and not certain her watery legs would be able to support her if she tried to move.

Thankfully, she'd managed to pull herself together by the time she heard a familiar voice say, "Knock knock," from the outer office.

"I'm back here," she said, hastily wiping at her tears before Emerson came around the corner.

"Hey." Her friend gave her a quick hug. "I had some errands to run in town and saw Reid leaving, so I thought I'd stop by and see how your dinner turned out last night."

"It was a complete bust," Kate admitted.

"He didn't like the chicken?"

"He didn't make it home for dinner."

Emerson frowned. "Why…" And then she put the pieces together. "The shooting at The Trading Post?"

Kate nodded.

"It must be hard, not just having plans ruined but knowing your husband's life could be in danger just because he's doing his job," Emerson said sympathetically.

"Of course I worry about him," she admitted. "But I trust that he'll take all necessary precautions to stay safe and come home at the end of the night. Unfortunately, he doesn't seem to have the same faith in me."

"What do you mean?"

So Kate summarized for her friend the argument they'd had after Reid learned about her meeting with the new client—without revealing any details, of course.

"I know you think he overreacted," Emerson said. "But even I was freaked out listening to the story, and you're not my wife or the mother of my unborn child."

"I'm not unsympathetic to his concerns—I just want him to trust me to do my job the same way I trust him to do his," she said.

"Every marriage has an adjustment period as two people who are used to living their own lives suddenly have to learn to communicate and compromise."

Kate shook her head. "This isn't an adjustment problem."

"What do you think the problem is?"

"He doesn't trust me."

"In all fairness, he doesn't really know you," Emerson said gently. "You've been married for a month, and you dated for only a short time before the wedding."

All of which was true, of course. She sighed. "Maybe I shouldn't have married him."

"Is that really how you feel?" her friend asked.

She considered the question for a moment. Though she and Reid had only been married a few weeks, she already couldn't imagine her life without him in it—she didn't want to imagine her life without him in it. Because despite an overprotective streak that rivaled her father's and a frustrating insistence on doing things for her that she was perfectly capable of doing herself, Reid was the man she loved.

"No," she finally said. "I don't regret marrying him."

"Then you're going to have to be patient—and give yourselves both some time to figure things out."

But it was hard to communicate with a man who was hardly ever around. And after the argument in her office, Reid kept himself busy.

At first Kate thought it was just the ongoing investigation that was monopolizing his time, but when that was complete, he spent every free minute at the new house: stripping wallpaper, tearing out carpets, painting ceilings and baseboards and, after Kate had picked the colors she wanted, walls.

He worked hard—every day. Sometimes he was at the house so late, he would crash on the sofa in the living room when he finally got back to the apartment so as not to disturb Kate's rest. At least that was the excuse he gave, but with every day that passed, she felt the distance between them growing.

She'd stayed away from the renovations, because he was worried the dust from sanding and the smell of paint wouldn't be good for the baby. She decided the distance between them wasn't good for the baby—or their marriage—either.

Ten days after their big argument, and three days before they were scheduled to fly to Texas for Henry's christening, she picked up takeout from Diggers' and took it to the new house.

He looked so sexy in paint-splattered jeans with an old Echo Ridge Sheriff's Office T-shirt stretched across those broad shoulders and a slight hint of stubble darkening his strong jaw—and she missed him like crazy.

"I thought you might want to take a break and have something to eat."

He set the roller in the pan and covered it with the

corner of a plastic drop sheet. "I am hungry," he said. "Thanks."

"Maybe we could sit outside?" she suggested. There wasn't any furniture in the house, but there was a patio set that the former owners had left.

"Sure," he agreed.

"You've been busy out here, too," she noted, as they stepped through the patio doors onto the back deck.

"Norm let me borrow his mower," he said.

"It looks good."

"Better, anyway," he agreed.

She opened the bag of food, handed him a foil-wrapped bacon cheeseburger, a paper sleeve of french fries and a can of cola.

"You're not eating?"

"I had something earlier," she said. Which was true— she just didn't specify that 'earlier' was actually lunch.

"Little bean still craving cheesecake these days?"

She shook her head. "Pineapple mango smoothies."

"A surprisingly healthy choice," he noted.

"Well, it's only been three days," she admitted.

For the next few minutes, he focused on eating, though he nudged the fries toward Kate, silently offering to share.

She selected one and nibbled on the end.

When he'd finished his burger, she ventured to ask, "Are we still going to Echo Ridge on the weekend?"

He picked up the can of soda, sipped. "If you want to."

"Of course I want to."

"Okay then," he said agreeably.

"Do *you* want to?"

"Sure."

He offered her some more fries; she shook her head.

"Are you going to initiate any kind of conversation or just answer my questions as succinctly as possible?"

He popped a couple of fries into his mouth, chewed.

"I heard you talking to Emerson," he finally said. "The day you found the gun, I came back with an evidence receipt, and the two of you were in your office."

"Okay," she said cautiously, trying to remember any part of the conversation that could've caused his withdrawal.

"You said you wished you hadn't married me."

Kate immediately shook her head. "No, I didn't. I don't remember exactly what I said," she admitted. "But I know I wouldn't have said that because it's not true."

"Well, it was something along those lines," he insisted. "And it got me wondering…if you wanted out."

She swallowed, her throat tight. "I don't want out." She folded a paper napkin in half, then again, her heart heavy as she contemplated asking the question she wasn't sure she wanted him to answer. "Do you?"

"No." He answered without hesitation, which loosened the vise around her chest a little. "But I don't want you to be unhappy."

"I'm not unhappy being married to you," she said. Then, remembering what her friend had said about honest communication, she elaborated on her response. "I'm also not happy that my husband of six weeks has apparently moved out of our bedroom."

"I didn't move out of our bedroom," he denied. "But I thought we could both use some space."

"You mean *you* needed some space."

"Maybe I did," he acknowledged.

"Have you almost had enough space?" she asked hesitantly. "Because I'd kind of like my husband back."

"Yeah—" he reached across the table and covered her hand with his "—I've had more than enough space."

The vise loosened a little more. "Since I'm pouring out my heart here, there's something else you should know."

"What's that?" he asked, a little warily.

"I didn't just agree to marry you so our baby would have two parents, but because I wanted a partner to share my life, for the rest of my life. And...because I fell in love with you."

He opened his mouth, then closed it again without saying a word, crushing any tentative hope that he might express similar feelings. And then he withdrew his hand, ostensibly to pick up his soda, but she knew the drink was just a diversion.

She pushed her chair away from the table. "Anyway," she said, pleased that her level tone gave no indication that her heart was breaking. "I just wanted you to know."

Reid let her go.

He sat at the table, the bag of garbage balled up in his fist, and watched her walk away because he was an idiot and a coward.

He should have said something. When a woman told a man she loved him, she expected some kind of response. But he'd said nothing, because he didn't know what to say or what to feel. And yes, because he was afraid—afraid to believe her feelings were real, even more afraid to acknowledge his own.

All the books and articles on pregnancy talked about an expectant mother's heightened emotions. It was possible that the love she felt for the baby growing inside her was being extended to him because he was the baby's father. And if so, her feelings could change when the baby was born.

And maybe, an annoying voice that sounded remarkably like his ex-wife said inside his head, he should give her some credit for knowing her own mind and heart. Katelyn was hardly the type of woman to impulsively express her emotions. If she said she loved him, she obviously believed it was true.

And he wanted to believe it, too.

But even if those feelings were real, would they last?

Trish had told him that she loved him. She'd said the words over and over again, urging him to trust her feelings. But in the end, she'd walked away from their marriage. He understood her reasons—she'd wanted something he wasn't willing to give her. And he certainly didn't blame her for choosing to build a life with someone else. But that experience made him skeptical about his new wife's professed feelings.

He didn't doubt Katelyn believed what she was saying right now, but they'd only known one another a short while. He was committed to her and the family they were building together, but he wasn't quite ready to drop the shields around his heart—not even for the woman he'd married.

Chapter Eighteen

A few months earlier, Kate might have thought she'd feel uncomfortable traveling with her new husband to attend the baptism of his ex-wife's baby with her current spouse. Now that she'd gotten to know the other woman and spent some time with both Reid and Trish together, she understood their relationship a lot better. They truly did act more like siblings than exes, and despite her initial predisposition toward her husband's first wife, she genuinely liked Trish and was looking forward to spending some time with her and Jonah and, of course, little Henry.

Any reservations she had as Reid drove from the airport to the Stiltons' house weren't about her husband's relationship with his ex-wife but his current one. Though they were both making an effort to communicate more clearly, Kate sensed that Reid was still holding back.

They arrived just before dinner and after they'd exchanged basic pleasantries, Trish shooed the men—

including Henry—outside to start the barbecue while she showed Kate the house and the room where she and Reid would be sleeping.

"Wow," Kate said, after the quick tour was finished and they'd returned to the spacious open-concept living area. "And you told me you married for love the second time around."

Her hostess laughed. "I did. I just lucked out and fell in love with a man who has a very well-paying job at Texas Instruments." She sat on the ivory leather sofa and tugged Kate down beside her. "Speaking of married...how are things with you and Reid?"

There were so many ways Kate could have answered the question—fine, great, wonderful—that would have put an end to the topic. Or even "it's an adjustment" or "we're figuring things out," either of which would have been more honest but still not too revealing. Instead, she burst into tears.

"Oh, Katelyn." Trish's arms came around her, offering both comfort and support—and the box of tissues from the antique accent table.

A long while later, when most of Kate's tears had been spent, Trish rubbed her back and demanded to know, "What did that big stupid man do?"

The question made Kate laugh even through her tears. "Why are you assuming he did anything?"

"Because I love him dearly, but I'm not blind to his faults."

So Kate started with the confrontation that took place in her office and concluded with her declaration of love—and Reid's silence.

"The problem isn't you," Trish said. "The problem is that no one in his life has ever stood by him, not when it really counted. No one has ever put him first."

Kate was quiet, considering the other woman's words.

"His father didn't even stick around to see him born," Trish reminded her. "His mother walked out on him a few years later—which might have been the best thing that could have happened because she left him with his grandmother. But then she died, and he was truly and completely alone."

"Until he met your dad."

"Which only happened after he'd spent a few years in foster care. But even his relationship with my dad took time to develop. And then my dad died, too."

"He's lost a lot of people he's cared about," Kate acknowledged.

"I'm not done yet," Trish said. "Because, if I'm being completely honest, I abandoned him, too. I told him I loved him and wanted to have a family with him and, when he wouldn't give me what I wanted, I ignored the vows we exchanged to be with someone else."

"I did love him," she said softly. "But I didn't love him enough to sacrifice what I wanted to make him happy."

"Are you suggesting that I should give up my job? Because—"

"No," Trish interjected quickly, firmly. "You shouldn't change anything that makes you who you are, but you need to work with Reid to figure out a compromise you can both live with. And working with Reid won't be easy."

"I'm already realizing it's an uphill battle."

"Just don't stop battling," the other woman urged. "Don't give up on him."

Kate managed a small smile. "I'm not a quitter."

"Good." Trish reached for the envelope on the table. "I took about a thousand pictures at your wedding," she confided. "And I had prints of some of my favorites made for you. So if your resolve ever falters—" she pulled out one of the photos and passed it to Kate "—just look at this."

She glanced at the photo in her hand and felt a tug at her heart. It was a picture of Reid standing at the front of the church on their wedding day. Trish had zoomed in on his face, and the smile that curved his lips was reflected in the happy light in his eyes.

"Do you know what that is?" Trish asked.

"A picture of Reid," she said, stating the obvious.

But Trish shook her head. "It's a picture of the groom," she clarified. "Taken at the exact moment that he saw his bride appear at the back of the church."

Kate looked at Trish, silently questioning.

"Most guests automatically turn to catch that first glimpse of the bride," she explained. "I was looking at Reid as he was looking at you. And what I saw, what anyone can see in that photo, is a man looking at the woman he wants to share his life with—the woman he loves."

Kate shook her head as fresh tears filled her eyes. "I appreciate the pep talk, but Reid doesn't love me."

"I'm not surprised he hasn't said the words," Trish said. "He's never been good at expressing his emotions. But that doesn't mean the feelings aren't there."

Kate wanted to believe the other woman could be right, but Reid's response—or rather complete lack of response—when she confessed her feelings warned her not to get her hopes up.

The baptism of Henry Jonah Stilton was a formal ceremony at the church where his parents had married followed by a big party in their backyard.

Kate didn't know if it was the change of scenery or being away from the demands of their respective jobs or if her husband had finally got over being mad, but Reid was incredibly sweet and attentive throughout the weekend. As the guest of honor was passed from one willing set of arms to another and they slipped away from the crowd and into the house to get their bags before heading to the airport, she was almost sorry to be leaving Echo Ridge.

"It's not going to be too much longer before we can hold our own baby," Kate said as Reid zipped up his duffel.

"Not that you can tell," he said, touching a hand to the gentle swell of her tummy.

"Wrap-style dresses and print fabrics are very forgiving," she confided.

"And stunning," he told her. "Sometimes I look at you and I'm awed that you're my wife, and—" His eyes went wide and whatever else he'd intended to say was forgotten. "Was that...our baby?"

She smiled and nodded. For a couple weeks now, she'd been aware of subtle nudges that were gradually growing stronger, but this was the first time Reid had witnessed any movement.

His lips curved as he felt another kick. "That's...wow." Then his smile faltered. "Does it hurt?"

"No, it doesn't hurt. It's a little distracting at times," she confided. "I feel the baby move and I get so excited, I forget what I'm doing."

He kept his hand on her belly for another minute, and when he finally lifted his gaze to hers, his eyes were moist.

"I'm sorry, Katelyn."

She looked wary. "Sorry you got me pregnant?"

He shook his head. "No. I'll never be sorry about that," he assured her. "But I am sorry about that day in your office—about my response to the situation, and afterward."

"I'd never do anything to put our baby in danger," she said softly.

"I know. But I wasn't just thinking about the baby—I

was thinking about you, too. And when I understood that you'd been in your office with a suspect in possession of a loaded gun… I've worn a badge for almost a dozen years now and I've seen my fair share of bad stuff, and my mind immediately imagined all things that could've gone wrong.

"The rational part of my brain recognized that the situation was controlled, but my emotions weren't," he admitted. "And the thought—as fleeting as it was—that I could've lost you…it cut me off at the knees."

She touched a hand to his arm. "I'm sorry, Reid. It never occurred to me that you were worried about me."

"That might've been because I was yelling at you," he acknowledged ruefully. "But only because I was shaking inside at the idea of you sitting across from a guy willing to pull the trigger of a Glock 17 for less than three hundred dollars in a cash register."

"I was shaking, too," she admitted. "And more than anything, I wanted you to hold me. I wanted to feel your arms—strong and reassuring—around me. But Deputy Neal was with you, and I didn't want to cross the line we've been so careful to draw between our respective jobs and our personal life."

"Can I hold you now?" he asked.

She moved willingly into his arms.

He held her tight and whispered close to her ear, "I love you, Katelyn."

She was still for a minute, her heart—filled with joy and hope—pounding against her ribs. Then she slowly eased back to look at him, not entirely certain she'd heard the words correctly.

But he looked straight into her eyes and said it again, "I love you."

"How… When… Are you sure?"

He smiled as her muddled brain struggled to put together a cohesive thought.

"Yes, I'm sure," he told her. "I think I'd mostly figured it out the night of our first-month anniversary, when I came home and found you sleeping on the sofa. That might also be part of the reason I overreacted the next day—the feelings were still new and overwhelming and then, suddenly, I was imagining how unbearably empty my life would be without you in it."

"Wow, that's a much more eloquent expression of love than you got from me," she told him.

"All that matters is that you do. If you still do."

She lifted her hands to frame his face. "I absolutely do," she said. "I love you with my whole heart, Reid Davidson—today, tomorrow and for the rest of our lives." Then she touched her lips to his. "Let's go home."

When they got back to Haven, Reid surprised Kate by driving to the new house instead of their apartment. He'd put in a lot of hours and she was eager to see the results of the work he'd done, but she was shocked to discover that the house wasn't just in move-in condition but that their furniture had actually been moved in.

"I gave your sister the keys before we left," he explained. "She rounded up your brothers and cousins and supervised the packing and moving."

"Everything looks fabulous," Kate said.

They hadn't yet picked out furniture for the baby's room, but the walls and trim were freshly painted. Kate had chosen "iceberg"—a pale blue color with just a hint of purple, because although they didn't yet know the sex of their baby, she refused to succumb to gender stereotypes in choosing the decor for the nursery.

She paused in the doorway of the next room, where her

queen-size bed and dressers had been set up. "I thought the master bedroom was the one overlooking the backyard."

"It is." He took her hand and led her down the hall to the master, opening the door to reveal their new bedroom set—including a king-size bed.

Kate laughed. "You are worried that my big belly will push you out of bed, aren't you?"

"Actually, I was thinking a little further into the future," he confided. "A bigger bed means more room for our kids to snuggle in with us on lazy Saturday mornings."

"You really are going to be a great dad," she told him.

"I hope so. In the meantime, we've got a great big bed and hours and hours until morning."

"Did you have an idea about how we might fill those hours?"

"Yeah," he said. "I want to make love with my beautiful wife—the woman I love more and more each day."

"What a coincidence," she said. "Because I want to make love with my handsome husband—the man I love more and more each day."

So that's what they did.

And this time, Kate had no doubts that they were truly making love. With every touch of his hands and his lips and his body, he showed her the truth and depth of his feelings for her.

And she loved him back the same way.

Afterward, when their bodies were finally sated but still entwined, they both felt their little bean kick, as if expressing approval that Mommy and Daddy had finally figured things out.

Epilogue

February 14

As Kate's due date approached, she was more than ready to be done with being pregnant. By early February, she was tired of waddling around with an extra twenty-five pounds in her belly.

Reid tried to be understanding and supportive, and he willingly enabled her most outrageous cravings. He even went to The Trading Post one night to get her a bag of dill pickle–flavored potato chips and a package of gummy bears—from which she ate only the orange ones.

Since the responsibilities of an expectant father were limited, he tried to pick up the slack in other ways. And while Kate appreciated his willingness to sweep the floor and fold laundry, what really helped ease the physical discomfort in the last few weeks of her pregnancy was that he told her he loved her, every single day. And—twenty-five pounds of baby belly notwithstanding—he was still happy to prove it to her.

She left work a little early Wednesday afternoon, because her aching back didn't want to sit behind her desk any longer and because it was Valentine's Day and she figured she should put a little effort into making dinner for her husband. But when she pulled into the driveway, Reid's truck was already there. Apparently he'd decided to cut his day short, too.

She set her keys on the hook inside the closet and kicked off her shoes, then followed the sound of chopping into the kitchen. "What's going on in here?"

"You're not supposed to be home yet," he said, setting aside the knife and green pepper to dry his hands on a towel.

"Do you want me to leave?"

"Of course not. I was just hoping I'd have all of this done before you got home." He drew her close—or as close as her belly would allow—and kissed her. "Happy Valentine's Day."

"Happy Valentine's Day," she echoed.

Then she looked around, saw the vase of roses on the table, the candles in holders waiting to be lit, the bottle of sparkling grape juice chilling in a crystal wine bucket. "This is…wow." Then she sniffed the air. "What are you cooking?"

"Spaghetti with meatballs in a basic red sauce with a mixed field greens salad and chocolate chip cookie dough ice cream for dessert."

"Wow," she said again.

His gaze narrowed on her. "Why are you rubbing your back?"

"Oh." She hadn't realized she was doing so and forced herself to drop her hand. "I've been having some twinges."

He was immediately concerned. "Since when?"

She shrugged. "A few days."

"Can you describe the pain?"

"It's just a backache, Reid."

"Back pain can be an early sign of labor."

"I know, but it's really not that bad and—"

"And the sheen of perspiration on your forehead suggests you're in more pain than you want me to know," he noted.

"I'd say it's discomfort more than pain."

He splayed his palms on her belly. "Are you having any contractions?"

"Just Braxton Hicks," she said.

"How do you know they're Braxton Hicks?"

"Because I'm—" she sucked in a breath as her belly tightened "—still several days from my due date and first babies are almost never early."

"I think we should call Dr. Amaro."

"But you went to the trouble of making dinner, and it's Valentine's Day."

He bent his knees so he was at her eye level, and he could see that hers were filled with tears. "It's okay to be scared."

"Are *you* scared?"

"Terrified."

"You're just saying that to make me feel better."

"I'm saying it because it's true," he said. "This is new territory for both of us. But as scared as I am, I know that we can get through this—and everything that comes after—as long as we're together."

She winced as her belly tightened with another contraction and then, as her muscles went lax again, she felt something warm and wet trickle down the inside of her leg.

"Reid…"

"What can I do?" he asked.

"You can call Dr. Amaro now—my water just broke."

* * *

After that, everything happened really fast.

Or really slow, depending on who was telling the story.

Reid called Dr. Amaro, grabbed Katelyn's bag, then hustled—as much as it was possible to hustle a laboring woman—out to his truck.

Nine hours later, very early in the morning of February fifteenth, Katelyn gave birth to an eight-pound, four-ounce baby girl. They named her Tessa Lorraine Davidson, in honor of Katelyn's mother and Reid's grandmother.

Through most of the next day, Katelyn's hospital room seemed to have a revolving door as her dad, grandparents, siblings and various other relatives and friends popped in to check on the new mom and baby. Reid was content to hover in the background while his girls shone in the spotlight, because Katelyn deserved all the credit for bringing their beautiful, perfect daughter into the world and because Tessa was that beautiful, perfect daughter.

And Reid was the luckiest man in the world, because Katelyn wasn't just his wife and the mother of his child, she was the woman he loved with his whole heart—and he knew she loved him back the same way.

* * * * *

MILLS & BOON

Coming next month

CAPTIVATED BY THE
BROODING BILLIONAIRE
Rebecca Winters

Unable to sit there any longer, she stood up. "Thank you for dinner and the opportunity to see the Salon de Dionysus. I feel very privileged that you would allow me a glimpse inside your *saint des saints.*" She'd tried to pronounce it correctly. "But it's getting late and I'm positive you're tired after our long drive today. I'd better go back to my room."

Lines darkened his striking features. "Now that I've been honest with you, why do I get the feeling you're running away from me already?"

He could see through her with those piercing black eyes. She started to tremble. "Because I'm questioning my own judgment. Since we arrived at the estate, nothing feels right."

"That's because what we felt for each other when we first met was like a clap of thunder out of a blue sky. I was reminded of a line in *The Young Fools*, by Verlaine."

"What line was that?" She'd enjoyed much of the French poet's translated work.

"Suddenly a white nape flashed beneath the branches, and this sight was a delicate feast for a young fool's heart."

"Raoul—" Where had he pulled that from? He never ceased to amaze her.

"The reverberations have been growing stronger with every passing minute, so don't deny it." He got up from the couch and reached for her with his strong hands. Their mouths were only centimeters apart.

"I don't deny it, but I'm not looking for any kind of complication. I never want to go through the pain of betrayal again."

She heard his sharp intake of breath. "I'm positive my father lied to me to get his own way. You think I don't understand betrayal?"

Abby shook her head, not immune to the tortured tone in his voice. "I don't know what to think," she cried.

"Then don't," he said before covering her mouth with a kiss so hungry and full of desire, she moaned. Finding herself immersed in sensations her body had never known before, she slid her hands up the silk covering his chest and wrapped her arms around his neck.

Continue reading
**CAPTIVATED BY THE
BROODING BILLIONAIRE**
Rebecca Winters

Available next month
www.millsandboon.co.uk

LET'S TALK

Romance

For exclusive extracts, competitions
and special offers, find us online:

f facebook.com/millsandboon

⊙ @millsandboonuk

𝕏 @millsandboon

Or get in touch on 0844 844 1351*

For all the latest titles coming soon, visit
millsandboon.co.uk/nextmonth